The A...
Rufus ...ey

'MONTY SAVES THE DAY'

By

Philip Huzzey

MAPLE
PUBLISHERS

The Adventures of Rufus O'Malley

Author: Philip Huzzey

Copyright © Philip Huzzey (2023)

The right of Philip Huzzey to be identified as author of this work has been asserted by the author in accordance with section 77 and 78 of the Copyright, Designs and Patents Act 1988.

First Published in 2023

ISBN 978-1-915492-09-8 (Paperback)
     978-1-915492-10-4 (Hardback)
     978-1-915492-08-1 (Ebook)

Book layout by:

    White Magic Studios
    www.whitemagicstudios.co.uk

Book cover, animal sketches & Rufus' sword:
Designed by Philip Huzzey and drawn by Emma Parker.
Map and other illustrations by:
Philip Huzzey

Published by:

    Maple Publishers
    1 Brunel Way,
    Slough,
    SL1 1FQ, UK
    www.maplepublishers.com

A CIP catalogue record for this title is available from the British Library.

In memory of my great friend Clive Scutt, with whom I had many years of fun, laughter and music making.

He was a unique person who stood out from the crowd, without layers or false facades, what you saw was what you got – a kind hearted, considerate, honourable soul.

Should the two of us meet in the afterlife we will make the heavens rock n roll.......

God Bless You.

Welcome to another adventure of
Rufus O' Malley, an Alaskan malamute
and prince from North of the World, who
possesses extraordinary powers.

If you have not already done so I would
recommend reading my first book
'A Newfound Friend', where among other
things you will find further information about
Rufus O' Malley, the lands of Zanimos and
Unger, and a useful map of the region.

I would like to thank you personally for
your interest in Rufus and his adventures,
and sincerely hope you find this story an
enjoyable read.

Contents

Sasha

Chapter 1
A Lovely Surprise

It was September now, and the nights were drawing in and the days getting cooler. It had been a cloudy day, and although there had been no rain, the darkened sky cast an eerie shadow over the city of Ungerborg. It was on days like this the city took on a mysterious atmosphere which tended to make many a stranger feel unsettled and even imbue some with an ominous feeling; however the spirits of city folk were never fully dampened by this haunting ambiance for they were well acquainted with it. Conversely on a sunny day the granite walls and marble towers would sparkle and glitter in the sunshine, filling the castle with a wonderful brightness that brought optimism and cheer to all; but today was not one of those days. Standing in the doorway of his tea house Sasha the fox was peering up over the tall palace wall towards the dismal sky.

"Oh how awful," he said, wearing a glum looking expression.

He closed the door behind him, entered the tea house and proceeded to pull the curtains along the brass poles of each window to keep the misery of the day outside. As usual he was very smartly dressed, and glancing around the room and studying his customers he gave his red cravat a little tug to ensure it was perfectly aligned. The tea house was busier than ever and his face glowed with pride at what he had achieved, but he was not a conceited animal and fully understood this success had also been due to Bloomsberry, a hard working and conscientious rabbit.

"Oh Hamilton would be pleased." he thought to himself.

He had extremely fond memories of when he visited the teahouse as a customer, and how he was always greeted by the friendly and courteous hamster. A smile crept across his face as he pictured her standing in her floral apron with pencil and notepad at the ready to take his order; and all the while she held the most congenial expression. For a moment he was lost in this happy recollection, but it didn't last for long, as the interruption of creaking hinges drew his attention to the opening front door, where he clapped eyes on a most surly looking badger.

The animal never bothered about his appearance and always wore the same denim trousers and black duffle coat.

He was an animal of few words and the two pistols tucked under his leather belt meant he was not to be messed with.

"Brodney!" called out Sasha. "Nice to see you again, how's things!?"

"Not bad," was the laconic reply.

Sasha was about to continue speaking when Brodney moved aside and gestured someone forward.

"This is Barnaby," uttered the badger with a cheeky grin on his face.

Sasha's back suddenly stiffened as he tilted his head back to look up at the face of the animal the size of which he had never seen. He was in fact so big that he could barely stand up without his head touching the ceiling and he had to bend down as he entered the room to avoid hitting his head against one of the wooden beams. For a moment Sasha stood absolutely still with his eyes wide open trying to take in the enormity of the creature. It had long thick fur, brown eyes to match its coat, a muscular body, and ears that lay flat against its immense head - it was in fact a Newfoundland dog.

Astounded by the size of the dog, and feeling uncertain of its temperament, Sasha remained rather quiet; which is not at all like him, as he is normally such a chatterbox and seldom stops talking; even to himself.

"P-p-pleased to meet you Barnaby," uttered Sasha nervously, thrusting out a paw.

But any misgivings he had about this large animal were soon put to rest as his paw was grasped by one many times larger and yet shaken with such gentleness.

"I'm very pleased to meet you Sasha, very pleased indeed." replied Barnaby with a warm smile, which instantly filled Sasha with assurance that the giant dog was actually quite friendly.

"Come in, come in and take a seat," he began.

"Have to find one big enough first," uttered Brodney with an unusual hint of amusement in his tone.

"A seat umm?" responded the fox scratching his head in thought.

"I don't want to be any trouble you know," said Barnaby.

"No trouble, no trouble at all," replied the fox. Sasha thought for a short while and then his face suddenly lit up.

"I've got it, now just follow me," he said with a smile.

He walked ahead and led Barnaby and Brodney further in to the tea house passing many animals seated around tables enjoying their food and drinks. But any conversations were silenced as the animals looked on in awe at the giant dog, many of them even stopping mid way through eating a cake or sandwich; it was as if they were frozen in time.

Sasha took them to a far corner of the room and beckoned Barnaby to take a seat on a red coloured sofa next to the fireplace. To reach the sofa Barnaby had to move a large rectangular wooden table, which to Sasha's surprise he did so easily due to his great strength. He then removed the large red rucksack from his back, while Brodney sat down in a cushioned wooded chair across the table from him.

"Bloomsberry will be over to take your order in a jiffy, and I'll pop back for a natter with you a little later," uttered the fox walking away. Barnaby stood and watched him walk over to a table situated nearest the door of the tea house where Charlie the collie was seated. The two animals were old friends and enjoyed nothing more than a laugh and joke, and sharing the odd bit of gossip. But Sasha hadn't gone over for his usual chat, he had spotted something on Charlie's table that very much interested him, and he wanted a closer look. Charlie passed the object to Sasha who carefully took it in both paws and turned it around at different angles to examine it in more detail. Barnaby was still looking on but was unable to catch a glimpse of the item as Sasha held it very closely and securely; however he did notice the fox's very excited expression. After slowly and carefully placing the object back on the table, Sasha said a few words to the collie then headed off towards the kitchen, leaving Barnaby an uninterrupted view; but he was rather disappointed by what he saw.

"Is that all it is...a jug?" he thought to himself. With a sigh of disappointment he slowly sat down on the sofa causing it to creak under his weight and after a few moments of fidgeting, a small grin on his face signified he was now comfortable. As the day had been a little chilly for this time of year Sasha had made up a fire, and for a moment Barnaby glanced at the playfully flickering flames, and crackling logs with their warming red glow, which created a wonderfully snug and homely feel.

"What a lovely place this is, so warm and cosy", he began, turning to the badger for a response, but this was not forthcoming as Brodney had slid back in to his chair, and as his snoring testified was fast asleep. It was a well deserved rest as he had left Zanimos early that same morning and journeyed all through the Chameleon Mountains just to spend a day meeting traders in the city.

The snoring amused Barnaby, who watched the sleeping Badger for a moment or two before deciding to look around and take in the sights and sounds of the vibrant tea house.

Red bricks had been used to build the external walls, and throughout the room thick black wooden beams extended from the floor upwards to join narrower beams which ran across the whole width of the uneven cream coloured ceiling. Grey slabs formed the floor as they did in most buildings in the city. They had a rough surface and in many places their joints were raised, occasionally causing animals to trip or stumble. Barnaby was surprised by the great number of wooden tables in the room, some were round and others rectangular, and he was impressed that every one had a white table cloth and vase filled with fragrant fresh flowers.

The seats around the tables were varied; for there were plain old nondescript stools, nice comfy armchairs, benches covered in floral padded cushions, and one solitary sofa in which he was seated. At the far end of the tea house was a curtain separating the seated area from

the kitchen, and occasionally he spotted Sasha
or Bloomsberry peering out to keep an eye on
the customers.

Being from North of the World where the
climate was much harsher, Barnaby was
fascinated by the animals in the tea house
as some would be an uncommon sight to him.
Such as the two overweight boars wearing the
blue uniforms of the king's soldiers, who were
scoffing cream cakes while trying to make
conversation. However, as he looked beyond two
quietly speaking rabbits towards the opposite
corner he spotted a group of animals who were
much more familiar.

There were three of them busily chatting away,
while a forth was yawning and clearly having
difficulty staying awake. They had their heads
close together and were whispering through
their sharp yellow teeth, with only an occasional
"shush" from what appeared to be the leader
when their conversation got too loud.

"Winchow!" whispered Barnaby under his breath
in a disapproving tone.

Winchow was the ancient name for weasels
in North of the World, meaning sly and
untrustworthy, and in most cases this was true
of their species. Winchow had lived in North
of the World for centuries, but after many
years of conforming to the laws of the land

they rebelled. Forming a large army of wolves, mink and mercenary rats from Nordeamia, they were the scourge of the north for many years, driving the other animals into hiding; as no one could stand against them. And it was not until Rufus' great grandfather Thadgrum became king of the north, that war was raged against them, and an army of malamutes, snow leopards, bears, giant black eagles, and unicorns joined forces to drive the winchow out of North of the World. The defeated winchow fled in all directions to escape the wrath of King Thadgrum, but a large number set up home in the forests of Arven just west of Unger. Thadgrum being a just and merciful malamute did allow some winchow to stay in the north, but made them swear an oath of allegiance, and pledge they would live good and honest lives and never make war on any animals in North of the World.

Barnaby didn't bear any grudge against the winchow, and being a kind and thoughtful animal would always pass the time of day with them, but he would never befriend or be drawn in to long conversations with them. And the group in the corner with their dark shifty eyes, sneering expressions, and hissing laughter, only served to confirm the scheming and devious nature for which winchow were well known. One of the weasels had noticed Barnaby watching them and he turned and stared back at the Newfoundland. It was the one that Barnaby thought might be the leader, and by his aggressive expression, chain mail and metal helmet he was definitely someone who liked a fight. The weasel opened his mouth as though he was about to snarl in disapproval at the staring Newfoundland, but realising he would be better off not angering the giant dog, no sound was forthcoming. Barnaby gave the weasel a quick false smile and then looked away.

Almost immediately he caught sight of a female rabbit wearing a blue and white checked apron walking towards him.

"And what can I get you sir?" began the rabbit with a most charming smile.

Barnaby thought to himself for a moment, wondering what in fact he would like.

"We have all manner of beverages, and sandwiches and cakes," she continued rather excitedly.

"Sounds yummy, but what I'd really like is a large mug of hot chocolate, I simply love chocolate...is that possible?" he replied with a hopeful expression.

"One large mug of hot chocolate coming up," she announced.

The rabbit was about to walk away when she stopped in her tracks.

"Anything to eat?" she said turning back to him.

"Umm," he uttered thinking to himself.

"Don't suppose you have any chocolate muffins do you?"

"I'm sorry we don't."

"Oh never mind", replied Barnaby trying to hide his disappointment.

"We do have a strawberry and gooseberry tart, with cream on top!" exclaimed Bloomsberry excitedly.

A wide smile crept across Barnaby's face.

"Sounds simply marvellous, I'd love a slice."

"You've got me to thank for that", interrupted a yawning Brodney.

"Really?" uttered Barnaby.

"Yeah...you see fruit isn't grown here, so Unger relies entirely on what I bring up from Delicious Orchard. And I don't charge anything near what I should," he added with a grumble.

Bloomsberry laughed, "You don't do so badly Brodney,"

"Hmm," replied the badger sounding hard done by.

"Anyway, what about my tea!?" he exclaimed earnestly.

"Now don't you go worrying Brodney, I'll bring your usual okay?"

The badger didn't reply but merely nodded his head.

He was a familiar face in the tea house, and always had a pot of tea, cheese sandwiches, and a cheese scone; cheese was a great favourite of his.

"Oh before you go dear lady", uttered Barnaby looking at the rabbit.

"Bloomsberry, please call me Bloomsberry," came the softly spoken reply.

Barnaby smiled.

"Well as I am quite a big fellow, and quite hungry could you possibly make my slice of tart a large one please."

"I'll make sure it's a giant slice."

"Thank you Bloomsberry," beamed the Newfoundland.

The rabbit smiled and walked away towards the far side of the room and disappeared behind the curtain in to the kitchen.

"I should really love to visit this orchard," began Barnaby turning towards the badger.

"Would you be a good fellow and take me there once we arrive in Zanimos?"

Spose I could, but I thought you were in a hurry to see your malamute friend?" grunted Brodney.

Barnaby had become so excited by the thought of an orchard full of lovely fruit, that for a moment he had forgotten his real reason for travelling to Zanimos.

Peering downwards he focused on his rucksack to which he had secured a weapon too long to fit inside. To hide the opulent construction from prying eyes, and remove temptation from would be thieves Barnaby had wrapped it in a red blanket. But even this veil of secrecy could not subdue a crimson glow of brilliance that momentarily permeated through the blanket, indicating the true power of the sword. Barnaby was quite affected by this, and took it as a beacon reminding him to be single minded in undertaking his important task.

"Aren't I a silly old thing, thinking of my stomach once again," he thought to himself. After a moment's reflection Barnaby drew a heavy sigh and looked over towards his new friend, and began to speak with urgency in his tone.

"You know you're right Brodney, quite right indeed, meeting up with Rufus is very important...very important indeed."

It wasn't long before Bloomsberry had brought their food and drink and they were both tucking into it. Barnaby was quick to polish off his large slice of tart and was now ready for his chocolate drink, while Brodney with a napkin tucked under his chin was slowly eating his cheese scone. The Newfoundland had a little grin to himself as he studied the badger eating his food, for with every bite he took his eyes closed, and his face became filled with a beaming expression of contentment. Barnaby then lifted his mug towards his face and closed his eyes as the vapour of the delicious chocolate filled his nostrils.

"Umm how lovely," he thought to himself.

He was about to take a sip when a cool draft of air followed by a loud bang distracted him, and turning towards the direction of the interruption he could see a new customer had entered the tea house.

It was another boar, slightly larger than the other two already seated in the room, and like them he wore the uniform of the king's guard. But there was something special about him, for on the chest of his blue uniform above the royal crest was a gold crown, and unlike the other two he wore a thick brown belt around his waist that had a sheath and sword; he also had a demeanour of importance about him too.

He was in fact Arcadius Tonga, Captain of the guard, though most animals called him Tonga, or captain. He looked around the room for a moment, and spotting Charlie the collie beckoning him over, proceeded to walk towards him.

Bloomsberry who had been peering out from behind the kitchen curtain spotted the boar and quickly followed him to where Charlie was seated.

"Good afternoon Captain Tonga," she uttered in a cheery voice.

"And a good afternoon to you Bloomsberry," replied the boar.

His tone of voice was deep and serious, yet at the same time there was warmth to it that showed he was genuinely pleased to see her.

"Well my dear, as I see our Zamosian friend is here," began Tonga, looking over towards Brodney. "Could I possibly have a glass of fresh strawberry juice?"

"Yes you can," replied Bloomsberry with a smile.

"Lovely, and how about one of your special butter pecan cookies to go with it?"

'Why of course!" exclaimed the rabbit with great pride, as she jotted the order down on her note pad.

Sasha had only recently agreed she could add her own recipes to the tea house menu, and her cookies were now famous throughout the city; with some animals even ordering them to take away.

Tonga had barely taken his seat before Charlie delicately placed the jug in the centre of the table and then peered at the boar's face, eagerly awaiting his response. The reaction was immediate and the collie was pleased to see the effect was no less than he had imagined, for the boar's face instantly lit up in astonishment and disbelief.

"Oh my goodness, where did you get it?"

"Ah ha," replied Charlie raising his eyebrows.

"Oh come on Charlie, tell me?!"

A wide smile crept across the collie's face.

"From Boo San...you know him?"

"The rabbit, yes I know him. Often see him in here."

"Well he always pops in to see me when he's in town, and yesterday he brought in a sack full of items for me to look at.

He loves to show me what he has, and as expected he gave a most detailed and excitable description of everything he took from his sack. I did take a couple of books off him in exchange for an old compass, but to be honest I was rather disappointed, and thought that was going to be it. But then a broad grin appeared across his face and he pulled out a battered old wooden box and placed it on the table. I said sorry that's not for me, but he just laughed and

pointed at the box telling me to look inside, and of course when I did I was flabbergasted."
After staring in amazement for a while, Tonga very carefully clasped the object in his trotters and began to study it more closely.
It was a rare and beautiful piece of pottery, several generations old, and apart from a very feint line that encircled it just above the base, and some narrow cracks underneath the glazing, it was in surprisingly good condition.
To a collector it was a rare and sort after item worth a considerable amount of money, but to Captain Tonga the jug had very special importance.
Formed in the image of a boar, who was holding a black staff with a golden orb, it had a blue coat extending from just below its neck down to a sturdy black base, and a three sided hat adorned with gold trim; gold also appeared on the collars, and sleeves.
The front of the coat had six gold buttons in two groups of three, and to the rear was a sturdy handle in a deep red hue.
The jug was made to hold a pint of ale and was therefore hollow, but the large amount of dust present inside indicated it had not been drunk from in a long while. The boar's head was deep black and its countenance was often disputed. Some would look at the dark and emotionless

eyes and the large threatening tusks, and
say he was a dangerous animal. Yet others
thought the creases on its cheeks, together
with the small pointed beard, gave him a more
mischievous expression.

Captain Tonga's face swelled up with pride as he
read the words engraved on the base.

"Forever grateful," he uttered under his
breath.

"You should feel honoured, deeply honoured."
began the collie, a tone of solemnity in his voice.

Tonga nodded, "I do."

"Well it's yours if you'd like it?"

"Of course I would, now tell me how much you
want?" asked the boar excitedly.

"Well -" began the collie deep in thought.

"I must have it Charlie, after all there's the
family connection."

Charlie rubbed his chin. "Now don't worry I'm
just thinking of a fair price...would five gold
coins and one silver be okay?"

Tonga was all smiles, "That's fine."

Having paid Charlie, he held up the jug to study
it closely, and becoming almost lost in the great
detail of the naval uniform, began contemplating
what it was like to be a sailor in the old times.

"Weren't those the days eh, when we had a
great navy and ruled the waves?" he uttered
with a smile.

'Yes they were, and if it hadn't been for Admiral Lexius Tonga we'd have lost the battle against the Nordeamians."

"True enough," replied the boar before pausing for thought.

"And now at long last I have a tribute to my great grandfather...a Tonga Jug, a real Tonga jug, thank you so much Charlie."

A contented smile crept across the collie's face. "That's my pleasure."

A moment later Bloomsberry rabbit appeared. She held a tray on which was a large white plate with an equally large pecan cookie, and a glass full to the brim with fresh strawberry juice. She rested the tray on the table, removed its contents and placed them in front of the captain whose eyes lit up with delight.

"Thank you my dear," expressed the boar.

The rabbit smiled, "My pleasure captain."

She was about to leave and had almost turned around when she noticed the Tonga Jug on the table.

"Oh that's lovely," she uttered.

Tonga beamed. "Yes it is, isn't it?"

The rabbit turned and walked back off to the kitchen, but after a short while out of curiosity she glanced back to see if captain Tonga was enjoying her creation. Watching him delicately break off a small piece of cookie and begin

chewing it, she was absolutely delighted to see the expression of pleasure on his face.
Charlie had also been watching his friend.
"Nice?" he uttered.
"Scrumptious!"

There was a scrapping of chairs as the weasels began to leave their table, and three of them made their way towards the exit hissing and cackling. Barnaby studied them as they crossed the room line astern behind their leader Belius. To him this weasel or winchow, had a most disagreeable look about him; one that looked exceptionally evil, and definitely dangerous.
As the weasels passed by the table of Charlie and Tonga, the collie could sense an unpleasant atmosphere between Belius and his friend as the two exchanged cursory glances.
Moving across the room Belius paused for a moment to check all his band were following and as usual he was not surprised to find one particular absentee. Accordingly he glanced back across to where they had been seated and observed a lone weasel; head slumped on the table, fast asleep.
"Gritch get Hubble!" he yelled.
"Will do."
Gritch walked back to the table and grabbing the sleeping weasel firmly began shaking him

quite furiously; but it was to no avail as Hubble was unmoved and sound asleep. Gritch unsure what to do for a moment stood watching the snoring weasel with a quizzical expression, but soon realising there was no other way he struck him hard on the nose, snarling as he did so.

"Oww, oww! cried Hubble, rubbing his nose.

"Come on!" shouted Gritch angrily, as he pulled the weasel off his chair.

"I'm coming, I'm coming," replied Hubble stumbling across the floor.

Gritch was tugging the lazy Hubble across the room in an effort to catch up with Belius and the others, when quite unexpectedly his foot caught the edge of an uneven slab and he began to fall helplessly towards the ground. As a sense of panic took over, Gritch instinctively grabbed hold of his fellow weasel hoping this would prevent him from hitting the floor, but instead he propelled Hubble headlong into the nearby table of Charlie and Captain Tonga.

All that happened next can only be described as absolute chaos. Hubble ploughed straight in to the table causing Charlie to fall backwards on to the floor banging his head as he did so, and Captain Tonga spilt strawberry juice over his face and his uniform. But worst of all, the Tonga jug bounced along the table several times until there was no table left.

Captain Tonga could do nothing, and looked on in horror as it left the safety of the table and fell towards the floor. For a moment it was a thing of beauty, a relic of history, telling a story of the past, but all was lost as it hit the hard stone floor and exploded in to pieces.

"No no!" shouted Tonga, feeling ever so helpless. Holding his trotters to his face he began to breathe deeply, trying the best he could to calm himself; but when he saw the culprit of his misery lying on the floor, he lost all self control and grabbed the weasel by the throat.

"You, you imbecile!" he shouted. "Do you know what you've done?!"

But Hubble choking under the grip of Captain Tonga was unable to speak, and even though he struggled vigorously he could not free himself from the firm grip of the furious Boar.

"Now now Captain...it was an accident!" exclaimed Gritch tugging on the boars arms and trying to loosen his grip.

Meanwhile Charlie rubbed his head and slowly shook it from side to side as he came to his senses, and noticing the broken jug lying on the floor, gathered up as many pieces as possible and placed them on the table, and with the most miserable expression began to examine them. The body had broken cleanly away from the base but surprisingly both parts were relatively undamaged, but the head had broken into at least half a dozen pieces, the handle split in two, and the tricorn hat was still scattered over the floor. Then something caught his eye; it was a piece of paper protruding from the body, and so taking great care not to tear it he gently began to pull it free.

"Here what's this?!" he shouted, immediately catching the attention of captain Tonga. Loosening his grip on Hubble, who promptly twisted free, the boar watched with great interest as Charlie unfolded the paper and smoothed it out on the table.

"Why it's a map!" uttered Charlie excitedly. Sketched on stiff parchment paper that had turned yellow and with worn creases where it had been folded, the aged map had become rather faint, but fortunately it was still just legible enough to follow. Tonga looked at the map and spotted a sketch of an opened chest overflowing with jewels.

"Why it's a treasure map!" he exclaimed.

"You know you could be right," replied the collie enthusiastically.

But Charlie and Tonga weren't the only ones looking at the map as Gritch and Hubble were hovering in the background.

"Looks familiar," said Gritch.

"Really," responded Tonga sarcastically.

"Yes you see-"

"You keep out of this!" replied an angry Tonga.

"Hold on a moment, he may know something, "uttered Charlie in a soothing tone, trying to calm his friend.

Releasing a deep sigh to quell his anger Tonga turned towards Gritch.

"Okay then, what is it?"

"It's this contour here", uttered Gritch dragging a sharp nail over the map."I think it's the coastline of Zanimos."

Charlie and Tonga immediately exchanged a fleeting glance of recognition, as they were very mindful of the significance of this disclosure.

"That may be, but it's easier said than done to get there," added a gravelly toned voice.

"Tonga looked up from the map to be greeted by the smirking face of Belius. He disliked the weasel greatly, for he had a reputation for trickery and treachery and it was believed he was responsible for many a robbery in the forest of Arven.

"And besides, can you translate that old writing?" added Belius nodding towards the ancient scribble at the bottom of map.

The boar glanced at the unusual letters and symbols, and feeling mystified looked towards Charlie hoping he might understand them, but

the collie shook his head. Not wanting the
meddlesome weasels to see any more, Tonga
quickly folded the map to hide it from view.
"You're not wanted here, now get out of my
sight!" he shouted.
"No need to be like that Captain, us weasels
could help you find the treasure." said Belius in
a devious tone.
"Why, we could even be partners," he continued.
"Partners," echoed Gritch smiling with his yellow
teeth.
Tonga glanced at Charlie and then stood up and
laughed sarcastically into the face of Belius.
"Partners with you...you must be joking!"
Belius was not amused and instantly fixed his
eyes intently on the Boar, and all in the tea
house were quiet as they watched the two
warriors reach for the hilt of their swords
ready to strike.
As soon as the tea room became immersed
in silence, Sasha and Bloomsberry who were
busy in the kitchen, instantly stopped what
they were doing and looked at each other
with quizzical expressions. Sensing something
unusual was occurring Sasha peered out from
behind the curtain and felt greatly alarmed as
he caught sight of the cause.

Taking centre stage he could see Tonga and
Belius, holding each other's gaze, while waiting
for the other to make the first move.
In the background he noticed two boars had
grabbed their pikes and were moving a little
closer to support their captain. Gritch was also
ready to fight, as was Ruevic the forth weasel,
and both had their beady eyes on the oncoming
boars.
Hubble still feeling a little sore around his neck
was also hoping for a fight, and was eager to
pay back Tonga for strangling him. Bloomsberry
crept to the side of Sasha and let out a huge
sigh as she beheld the dreadful situation. It
didn't look like anything was going to stop this
fight and the eyes of all the other guests were
looking on helplessly, hoping that no blood would
be shed. But just as there seemed no possibility
of avoiding a bloodthirsty conflict the icy
silence had the most welcoming interruption.
"Come come now, we don't want any trouble, do
we?"
The words were soft yet firm and echoed
down from above, distracting the combative
preparation of Belius and Tonga, who
immediately turned to look up at the giant dog.
Barnaby looked at Belius and nodded towards
the direction of the two boars who stood
poised and ready to strike with their impressive

pikes. Belius turned and glanced at the boars before returning his stare to Barnaby. He had heard about the giant dogs who had driven his ancestors from North of the World but had never set eyes on one. And although he felt that this dog didn't look aggressive enough to be a warrior, he still looked an immensely strong and powerful force to be reckoned with.

For a moment Belius was in a quandary, should he fight or walk away; although walking away was not in his nature, and he was leaning towards the fighting option. As it happened his choice of action was abruptly interrupted by a sudden clicking sound that caught his ears. Turning instantly towards the direction of the noise, he was struck by the unfamiliar feeling of trepidation as he came face to face with a pair of guns, cocked and ready to fire.

Having experienced the pain of being shot before, he didn't relish a repeat of the great discomfort he had endured, but once he realised the guns were being held by his old adversary Brodney, his face contorted into rage.

"You always get in my way badger!" he growled.

A fleeting grin shot across Brodney's face.

"Well there'll come a time, one day when you'll regret it, you mark my words," snarled Belius.

Reluctantly motioning to other weasels to follow, he walked towards the front door, but before exiting the room turned back and fixed his piercing eyes on Brodney; before giving Barnaby and Tonga a hateful stare for good measure. And then holding his head high, a defiant expression upon his face, disappeared out of sight, with his gang following and a yawning Hubble closing the door behind them.

"Hurrah for that," shouted Charlie, and the tea house burst in to a loud cacophony of celebration, as relieved onlookers began to talk noisily and excitedly about what they had just witnessed.

Tonga looked over to the two boars and nodded his thanks, and in return they brought their pikes to their side, and pointed them upwards as a salute to their captain.

"Thank you big fella," uttered Tonga looking up at the Newfoundland.

Barnaby smiled, "Pleased to help...and don't forget Brodney, after all he had the fire power."

"How could I?" replied Tonga, after which he gently placed a trotter on the badger's shoulder.

"Thank you my friend," he stated solemnly.

Brodney smiled fleetingly and subtly nodded his head; he was after all a modest animal, and didn't like too much fuss.

"You can always rely on Brodney," exclaimed Charlie with a cheer.

"And what be your name?" added the collie looking toward the Newfoundland.

"I'm called Barnaby."

"Don't think I've ever seen an animal as big as you," replied Charlie, his eyes wide open in amazement.

"Well you come to North of the World and you'll see bigger." responded Barnaby enthusiastically.

The collie found this hard to believe.

"Really?!" he exclaimed in disbelief.

"Yes we have bears; they are much, much bigger than I am,"

The collie looked a little uneasy. "Ahh, not heard of them," he uttered.

"So you're from North of the World then eh?" asked the boar with a surprised expression.

"Yes that's right."

"Don't often get animals from there," replied Tonga.

"No that's true," echoed Charlie.

"Well I'm on my way to Zanimos, to see my friend Rufus 'O Malley. You may have heard of him?" expressed Barnaby proudly.

Charlie and Tonga looked at one another with blank faces.

"Sorry, never heard of him," replied Tonga.

"Me neither," added Charlie shaking his head.

"Oh never mind," came a disappointed reply from Barnaby.

"Anyway we'd better be making a move...got a long day ahead tomorrow," grunted Brodney.

"You're taking Barnaby to Zanimos then?" asked Charlie,

"That's right," replied the badger.

Charlie looked at Brodney for a moment and then back towards the badger as a marvellous idea suddenly struck him.

"Couldn't you take us too?!" he asked excitedly.

Brodney looked surprised. "Spose so...for some consideration mind you-"

"But I'll have to ask the king's permission Charlie...after all as captain of the guard I just can't go off gallivanting whenever I feel like it!" interrupted Tonga.

The collie scratched his chin for a moment.

"If you promise King Rosfarl a share of the treasure, I'm sure he'll let you go Tonga," replied the collie with a smile.

Tonga raised his shoulders. "I suppose he might."

"Treasure in Zanimos, no that's just an old tale, you'd be wasting your time believe me. But if

you want to go on a fools adventure that's your
choice," laughed the badger.

"Anyway we're leaving tomorrow at six in the
morning and not waiting for anyone, so if you
want to come don't be late."

"From the Rosfarl Inn?" asked Charlie.

"Yep."

"Better be on our way," he continued, looking
towards Barnaby.

"I'll get my rucksack then."

I'll be here," uttered the badger.

After collecting his rucksack Barnaby returned
to where Brodney was waiting and looked down
at the pieces of the Tonga jug laid out on the
table.

"Oh that's such a shame," he said softly.

"It's a tragedy," replied Tonga with a forlorn
expression.

Charlie realised how upset his friend was, and
very much wanted to cheer him up.

"Still if it hadn't had broken we'd never have
found the treasure map now would we?"

The boar gave a little smile and nodded.

"That's true."

"Let's have another look at it Tonga?" asked
Charlie eagerly.

"Alright," replied the boar unfolding it and
placing it on the table.

Charlie ran his paw along the map and after studying it for a moment he then let out a little laugh and lay back into his chair.

"What is it?" quizzed Tonga.

"The weasel was right, it is Zanimos, and the area where the treasure chest is shown, is called Smugglers Cove."

Tonga smiled.

"Smugglers Cove...how apt."

But then his happy expression slowly changed to one of bewilderment, as he pointed to some strange script on the map.

"But what about this old writing, it doesn't mean a thing to me...and it might just be the key to finding the treasure,"

Charlie nodded.

"I think you're probably right. But you know I've seen something like this before...if only I could remember where."

"Come on think Charlie," pleaded Tonga.

Charlie moved his eyes from side to side while taking in the occasional deep breath; he was trying his utmost to remember, but no answer seemed forthcoming.

For Tonga this seemed to go on for ages, but in fact it was barely thirty seconds.

"I've got it," snapped Charlie with excitement.

"Well come on," asked Tonga eagerly.

It was on an old sword...a sword I brought from a sea farer many years ago."

Tonga felt a glimmer of hope. "Have you still got it?"

Charlie shook his head, "No, sold it."

Both of them slowly looked at one another, a shared feeling of hopelessness reflecting on their faces, but undeterred by this minor setback, they returned to study to the map with renewed enthusiasm. Brodney looked on with great amusement at the behaviour of the Ungerians as they jabbered excitedly about the treasure they might find.

"Numbskulls," he thought, quietly sniggering to himself.

Gesturing to Barnaby they should leave, the badger made his way towards the front door. Being more polite Barnaby said his goodbyes, but Charlie and Tonga were too engrossed in the map to reply.

Using his long strides the Newfoundland soon caught up with Brodney, and as the two of them reached the front door an excited Sasha called out to them.

"Wait a minute, please wait a minute!"

Barnaby and Brodney turned around and were greeted by the smiling fox who could not stop singing their praises.

"You were wonderful, simply wonderful," he began.

"I was absolutely terrified that someone was going to get hurt, and if it wasn't for you two... well goodness knows what might have happened. I just can't thank you enough!"

"Think nothing of it," responded the badger nonchalantly.

Sasha felt greatly indebted to them for their intervention, and wondered how he could show his appreciation; then a wide smile crossed his face as the obvious sprang to mind.

"Nevertheless, I think you are both very brave, and the next time you visit my tea house, your food and drink is on me."

"Umm, I look forward to that," responded Barnaby closing his eyes and thinking about a large slice of delicious strawberry and gooseberry tart.

"That'll be nice, but we got to be off now," uttered the badger, a sense of urgency in his tone.

"Okay Brodney, safe trip."

Brodney replied with a cursory nod and walked on through the doorway, closely followed by the Barnaby.

"Bye Barnaby," said Sasha.

"Bye bye Sasha," replied the Newfoundland cheerily.

But just as Barnaby was about to step over the threshold he caught something in the corner of his eye; it was Bloomsberry who was standing by the kitchen curtain and waving with great enthusiasm.

"Bye bye Bloomsberry," he uttered, adding a broad smile and friendly wave; and then he was gone.

The two new friends walked along the cobbled street towards the town square, passing a couple of houses on their left while on the opposite side was the imposing wall of the palace grounds.

They were beginning to strike up conversation when they suddenly stopped in their tracks, and stared into the blackness of the alley way that ran between the houses; for each of them had heard the echoing of whispered voices.

They stood still and prepared in case something should appear, but all remained silent and nothing came out from the darkness, so after a while they proceeded on their journey; but now with a little more vigilance.

Entering the market square they could see everything was closing down for the night. The hustle and bustle of customers and traders was over now, as most shop keepers had locked their doors for the night. But there was still an air of friendly banter as the owners of market stalls chatted and joked while dismantling and removing their stalls from the square, which they did twice weekly to allow the soldiers to use the square for drill practice and battle training. About half way along the square they passed a large archway cut in to the eastern wall, and Barnaby took a quick peek inside where he spotted two guards with very sombre expressions standing perfectly still with pikes at the ready.

"Entrance to the palace that is," uttered Brodney.

"Ahh...ever been inside?"

"Not likely," grunted the badger.

And you're not even curious as to what it's like?"

"Nope."

Barnaby smiled. "You can say one thing for the badger he's always straight to the point," he pondered.

They nodded a goodnight to the guards on duty at the entrance to the high town before descending the cobbled causeway that bridged the river Olgen. The tide had turned and was quickly running out to sea, and captivated by the ferocity of the river, they paused for a few moments to follow its progress as it raced under the bridge and onwards towards the Nordeamian Ocean.

Shortly afterwards they were walking through
the low town with its mixture of brick and
timbered buildings, which exuded far more
charm than the stone walls of the high town.
"It's a nice clear night," uttered Barnaby.
The badger looked up at the sky. "Aye, full
moon tonight."
Brodney looked across at the Newfoundland.
"You know I always like to travel at night,
it's peaceful and I feel more at home. I don't
suppose you'd fancy –"
"Yes I'd love to...I couldn't sleep a wink anyway,
and the sooner I can see Rufus the better!"
The badgers face lit up. "Right then, I'll get my
things from the Rosfarl Inn and we'll be on our
way."
"But hold on Brodney, what about Charlie and
Tonga, shouldn't we wait for them?"
The badger grunted and rolled his eyes,
thinking back to the many tales of Zamosian
folklore he had listened to as a small cub, and
how as he grew older he found there was little
or no truth in some of the stories. Like most
youngsters he had ventured into the caves, an
air of optimism about him certain he would find
treasure only to come out feeling very deflated,
as no loot was to be found. And of course when
he returned to town all the grown ups would

smile at him and say, "I told you so!" - which made him feel even worse.

"Look Barnaby, I can tell ya first hand that there aint no hidden treasure in Zanimos, and if we leave without them we'll be doing them a favour. Why, I don't want to see Tonga and Charlie wasting their time getting all excited over nothing. Besides they'll probably see sense by the morning, and then we'd have waited around for nothing...so I say let's go."

"Okay let's go tonight then!" exclaimed Barnaby, feeling very excited at the prospect of seeing his old friend Rufus even sooner than he thought he would.

King Clanask

Chapter 2
King Clanask

Tonga left the tea house shortly after Barnaby and Brodney, and followed in their footsteps towards the market square. He was feeling rather perplexed; for although he found some solace in the thought of finding treasure, it didn't really make up for the loss of the lovely Tonga jug.

He paused for a moment and let out a sigh of frustration.

Fortunately he had reserves of common sense and self discipline and so began to think more rationally; the jug was gone and that was that. "No use harping on about something you can't change," he whispered to himself.

Unexpectedly his thoughts were interrupted by the sound of echoing footsteps, and looking in the direction of the disturbance he caught a glimpse of two creatures moving out from the shadows. Their silhouettes were simple to make out; they were weasels, and Tonga was sure that Belius was one of them.

Not being an animal to run Tonga stood fast and drew his sword, and within moments his thoughts were confirmed, as Belius followed by the ever faithful Gritch appeared in front of him.

The two weasels glanced at each other, emitted their usual silly cackles, before staring at the boar with the most devious expressions.

"What do you want?!" shouted Tonga.

Belius' smile widened "Ah well you see-"

"We want the map, so hand it over!" spouted Gritch threateningly.

Tonga was filled with disbelief at the weasel's demands.

He was of course well aware of their underhand and villainous behaviour, but to try and rob a captain of the guard; well that was just asking for trouble. However, he was quick to realise that their determined expressions showed they were serious about this endeavour, and he knew his only course of action would be to fight to keep possession of the map.

"You what, if you think I'm handing over the map to you, you're deeply mistaken...you want it, come and get it!" he snarled.

Tonga ran his eyes from one weasel to the other, and with sword at the ready stood poised for any attack. He had been in battle before, and was tough, fearless and also very skilled with the blade.

But strangely the weasels made no move at all, instead they turned to each another and began to snigger, they appeared to have a strange aura of arrogance about them too, which puzzled the boar. Tonga waited patiently for the weasels to make a move, but they did not; they just stared intensively with those evil beady eyes and gaping mouths of yellow teeth. This standoff began to frustrate him as he was ready to fight, but in his thoughts one thing was certain; if he would die, so would the weasels. In watching Belius and Gritch so intensely, he had failed to notice the other two weasels tip toeing up behind him. And when he did it was too late........

Belius and Gritch had had no intention of attacking the boar; they were merely a distraction while Hubble and Ruevic crept up behind him. In fact it was quite a hilarious sight, for they had decided that to knock Tonga unconscious they would need additional height; therefore one weasel would have to stand on the back of the other. It was agreed that Hubble would carry Ruevic, but the yawning weasel kept on losing his footing, leaving poor Ruevic desperately holding on to avoid crashing to the ground. Rocking and swaying wildly, the two weasels erratically advanced closer to Tonga until they were within striking distance. Ruevic made several failed attempts to hit the boar due to losing his balance, but finally managed to bring his wooden truncheon to bear just as the boar turned to face him.

The mist hovered over the river Olgen while the sun began to raise its head over the cumulus clouds that were fading in to the distance. Running through luscious green grass he felt young and alive, and unburdened of responsibilities; there was a remarkable new energy about him. Stopping in his tracks for a moment to enjoy the bouquet of sweet fragrant flowers, he took in the cheerful morning songs of birds on the wing. But his peace was short lived as the snout of a sibling struck him from behind causing him to tumble through the dew soaked grass.

"Got you Arcadius!" shouted his younger brother Mathius, running off and laughing at the top of his voice.

"You wait," replied Arcadius, waving a trotter in the air and starting the chase.

He ran so fast, so very fast that he didn't feel like a boar at all, in fact he felt like he had the

speed of a hare, and using this mystical pace to
the fullest, quickly caught up with his brother.
Arcadius and Mathius were running side by side
now, each trying to outpace the other, but a
firm nudge from Arcadius caused his sibling to
spiral to the ground. Mathius had no time to
think as his older brother took the advantage
and quickly wrestled him in to submission. Once
again he had outwitted his younger brother,
however there was no ill feeling from Mathius,
and as he was helped to his trotters by his big
brother he smiled at him affectionately.
Andanius the youngest of the three brothers
who had just reached the hill above them began
to shout out at the top of his voice.
"You wait there; I'm coming to get you!"
Without further pausing he began running down
the hill as fast as possible; the problem was he
ran so fast his trotters could no longer keep up
with the downhill speed of his body, the result
being that he stumbled, and began to roll head
over trotters.
Arcadius and Mathius soon realised they were
in the direct path of their younger brother, but
they seemed transfixed and unable to move;
and besides the matter was soon out of their
hands. For Andanius rolled straight into them
knocking them over like they were feathers,
and the three brothers trundled on down the

hill entwined in a heap, rolling over and over until they came to a sudden separation in the shallows of the river. Then it was laughter, such marvellous laughter; you know the type where your tummy hurts because you can't stop laughing, and the more you laugh the more it aches.

The three brothers now sopping wet, hugged each other and jumped up and down, each one trying to make the biggest splash. Arcadius realised that this was one of those very special, indeed euphoric feelings that should be treasured, and held on tightly to his brothers as they waded towards the bank.

"Yahoo yahoo!" he exclaimed looking up at the tranquil and friendly blue sky. Glancing at each of his siblings in turn he wished this moment would last forever; for he did love them so very much.

Then without warning, he felt his body enveloped by a strange force, it was dominant and unyielding, and was dragging him away from his dream, this lovely, lovely dream; and try as he may it was useless to resist his elevation towards the sky.

"No no, I don't want to leave!" he shouted, looking down at his two brothers as they rapidly diminished in size.

Within moments he was enclosed by wispy cirrus clouds, and as the relentless force continued to drag him upwards, reality began to take over bringing pain and discomfort.

"Oh my head, my head!" he cried.
"Now now, it's alright Captain, you're okay."
Tonga began to open his eyes, and could see the outline of someone leaning over and holding his shoulder, but all detail was blurred and out of focus.
"Take it easy, slowly now, don't rush."
It was the same soft voice as before, and as he rubbed his eyes the shape began to get clearer; it was Bloomsberry and she was holding a warm cloth to his forehead.
Slowly sitting up he felt a large lump on his head which seemed to be the cause of his discomfort.
"Yuck, what's this?!" he said, feeling a greasy substance on his trotter.
"Butter and salt, it's an old remedy to help with swelling."
"And it works?"
"My mother swore by it."
"Here you are old boy this should perk you up," came the unmistakable voice of Sasha, with which a small glass was thrust in front of him. He took hold of it, smiled at the fox and

began to sip from it. The liquid was warm and invigorating and made him feel so much better; it was in fact the sherry that Hamilton had left behind when she went off to Zanimos.

Looking to his left Tonga saw the welcoming smile of his friend Charlie, but instead of reciprocating, his face took on a puzzled expression.

"How did I get here Charlie?"

"We brought you here, Sasha and me. I found you unconscious in the street when I was going home, and ran back to the tea house for help."

"How long ago was that?" asked the boar rubbing his forehead.

Charlie looked towards the fox.

"What do reckon Sasha?"

The fox looked at his faithful pocket watch.

"Umm, I'd say about four hours."

After savouring the remainder of his drink, Tonga lent forward to place the glass on the nearby table, and went to stand up, but as he did so he felt a little wobbly, and dropped back in to his chair.

"Whoa," he uttered trying to shake off the dizziness.

"Steady now," said Charlie in a concerned tone. "Don't rush things, you've had a nasty blow," added the rabbit.

"And I bet I know who's behind this!" exclaimed Sasha.

"Is he right, was it the weasels?" asked the collie.

A look of anger rose in the boar. "Yes, yes it was, and the more fool me for not being ready!" Bloomsberry shook her head in disgust.

"Oh those vile creatures," she said.

"They'll not be allowed in my tea house again!" added the fox shaking his head.

"So what happened Tonga?" asked the collie, in a soft compassionate tone.

The boar looked across at each animal in turn, an uncharacteristic expression of despondence on his face, before he slowly began to tell his story.

"I'd only gone a short way, hadn't even reached the square when out of the darkness came Belius and Gritch...they were after the treasure map."-

"Surprise surprise," uttered Sasha.

The collie's eyes began to open wide.

"Go on," he said excitedly.

But Tonga paused, he was fuming that the weasels had duped him and didn't enjoy talking about it. Nevertheless after a deep breath he picked up where he'd left off.

"I stood still, ready to use my sword if I had to, and told them if they wanted the map to come and get it, but they just grinned and did nothing. I was curious as to why they wouldn't attack, but before it was too late I realised another two weasels had crept up behind me; and then one of them struck me on the head. And that's the last thing I remember, until I woke up in here."

"And the map?!" exclaimed Bloomsberry.

"I don't know," replied Tonga, immediately searching his pockets, and laying the contents on the table.

First came a set of keys, next a whistle, a small diary, a pencil and finally a brown money pouch that Tonga could feel was empty; but there was no map.

"Blighters, they've stolen my money to boot!" yelled the boar.

"They're callus and ruthless...and utterly heartless," added Bloomsberry.

"The collie let out a huge sigh of disappointment.

"They'll be off to Zanimos then, after the treasure."

"But they won't get over the Chameleon mountains; only a Zamosian can get through them," uttered Sasha.

"They'll find a way, you can be sure of that," said Charlie.

"But how?" enquired Bloomsberry.

"I think I know the answer," began the softly
spoken fox as he looked towards the floor with
an expression of shame on his face.
Tonga, Charlie and Bloomsberry looked at each
other, their eyes roaming from side to side
as they tried to fathom out what the fox was
going to say; but fortunately they were quickly
enlightened.
"My cousin Sileenus, he does a lot of business
with the weasels, and has a ship, it's called Lady
Bamboozler."
Sasha's head was still low, because of the great
embarrassment he felt at being related to a
thief and rogue, whose exploits had been so
infamous that King Rosfarl had banned him from
the land of Unger forever.
"That's it, they'll sail to Zanimos!" exclaimed the
boar.
"Avoiding the Chameleon Mountains," added
Charlie.
Sasha felt a gentle rubbing of his shoulders
and looked up to see the sympathetic face of
Bloomsberry.
"Don't you go feeling your at all to blame for
your cousins exploits," she said with a soothing
tone.
Charlie was also full of sympathy for his friend.
"It's not your fault you've a wrong 'un in your
family, you know."

"That's right Sasha, don't you go blaming yourself for that vagabond's behaviour!" stated the boar in a firm tone.

Having been made to feel much better, Sasha slowly raised his head and smiled gratefully at his good friends, and clearing his throat began to speak.

"Well what are we to do about it?"

"We need to get to Zanimos first and ambush them!" exclaimed Tonga.

"But how?!" came a chorused reply from Sasha and Charlie.

Bloomsberry put a foot to her mouth and thought for a moment.

"I have it, I have it!" she announced.

"Ask Brodney to take you through the mountains tonight, rather than wait for tomorrow morning!" she continued smiling enthusiastically.

"Of course!" exclaimed Sasha.

Wanting to make amends for his cousin's blight on his family, and help his friends triumph over the weasels, Sasha quickly stood up and thrust his chair under the table.

"I'll race down to the Rosfarl Inn this very moment and speak with him!" he exclaimed eagerly.

"Tell the badger he'll be paid," uttered Tonga.

Sasha nodded his head and rushed towards the front door, and in an instant was gone.

Time was ticking away slowly it seemed, as Tonga and Charlie sat quietly but impatiently, waiting for the return of Sasha. The two of them looked at each other and simultaneously let out a deep sigh of frustration. But thankfully their low mood was interrupted by the chinking sound of cups and saucers as they wobbled around on a wooden tray that was laid down in front of them; bringing them a welcomed distraction of scrumptious cream cakes and an intoxicating nutty aroma of freshly brewed coffee.

"Bloomsberry, you're an angel," uttered Tonga, with a broad grin on his face.

"Yes you certainly are," added Charlie, gleefully surveying the goodies.

Bloomsberry sat down next to them, picked up the coffee pot and began pouring out the dark fragrant beverage, after which Charlie and Tonga added milk and sugar, while the rabbit added nothing as she liked it just as it came. Tonga's and Charlie's faces lit up as they savoured the homemade apple and cream turnovers that Bloomsberry had made, and relished every bite they took. Quickly polishing off the cakes they both stared eagerly at the remaining cake, each wondering who should be cheeky enough to pick it up.

"And before you ask, that cake's for Sasha," asserted Bloomsberry.

"Of course, he deserves it," uttered the boar innocently.

Tonga and Charlie gave one another a look that had the feeling of disappointment in it; for either one of them could have eagerly scoffed up the last cake.

They all remained still and quiet for a while, each one of them eagerly awaiting the return of the fox but this period of waiting seemed like an eternity. At last their wait was over, as the front door burst open and quickly slammed to as Sasha entered the room. Slowly trudging towards them he wore the look of hopelessness on his face, and on reaching their table drew out a chair and slumped in to it.

"It's too late I'm afraid, Brodney left for Zanimos several hours ago," said Sasha in a despondent tone.

Tonga in particular was extremely disappointed by the fox's news, as he wanted so much to catch up with weasels and get his own back; and it was with a heavy heart that he began to realise this was now impossible.

"Well I guess that's it, there's no way we can get to Zanimos now," he uttered, releasing an enormous sigh.

"Now don't give up, where there's a will there's a way," insisted Bloomsberry.

"She's right Tonga, there must be a way," added Charlie trying to sound positive. He thought for a moment longer and then an idea sprung to mind.

"If only we had a ship, then we could sail to Zanimos just like the weasels-"

"But we have!" exclaimed Sasha excitedly.

"We have?" queried the boar looking toward the fox.

'Yes...King Clanask!" shouted the fox at the top of his voice.

Finding the suggestion quite ludicrous, Tonga leant forward in his chair and shook his head.

"But that's King Rosfarl's ship...we can't take her!"

"If the king knows there's treasure to be found, I'm sure he'll loan us his ship," said Charlie with a mischievous grin.

"That's a good point...I hear the royal coffers are a bit low at the moment," added a smiling Bloomsberry.

Charlie smiled as he knew this was true.

"And don't forget Tonga, if the king gives his permission, you will be in charge of the vessel and representing the land of Unger," uttered the collie sounding full of enthusiasm.

"Quite so," added Sasha taking a bite of his cream cake.

"I suppose I will," replied the boar, his face swelling up with pride.

Charlie quickly rose from his chair eager to get things going.

"Well it's no use sitting around, we need to set sail today if we've any hope of catching up with the weasels," he uttered in an urgent tone.

"Yes and if the king does loan us his ship, we need to get stores and provisions loaded as quickly as possible," added the boar.

Tonga and Charlie bade farewell to Bloomsberry while she was tidying up the table, and then proceeded to exit the tea house. Reaching the corner of the market square the boar and collie turned and waved back at the fox who was standing in the doorway watching their progress.

"Good luck, good luck!" yelled Sasha, and then they were gone.

He closed the door and locked it for the night, and as he walked around the tea house pushing the odd chair under a table to make the furniture look more organised, and the room more tidy, he began to wish he was going off on the adventure with his friends. He had never been on a ship, never been to Zanimos, in fact he'd never been out of Unger, and it all seemed so very exciting to him; but little did he realise what dangers lay in store for his friends.

A gleaming moon peered down in to the darkness guiding Tonga and Charlie along the cobbled street that led them away from the tea house, and they had not gone far when a most strange mood seemed to come over the collie. It was a feeling of apprehension and excitement, and for a moment he felt as though his heart had skipped a beat. It was of course the thought of going in to the palace that had caused it, for he had only been there once before and that was a long time ago, and the thought of going there again was most thrilling. "My goodness, my goodness, am I really going inside the palace?!" he thought to himself, shaking his head in disbelief.

He turned towards the boar with a beaming smile.

"To the palace then Tonga" he gushed.

The boar smiled. "Don't suppose you've been there since you were a pup, have you?" he replied as they entered the market square.

"Not since my birth blessing from King Vorspar."

Now the birth blessing is given to every new born animal in the land of Unger once they are few months old, when an appointment is made to attend one of the four blessing services held every year. On the occasion of the blessing they are taken into the palace and presented to the king who touches their head, wishes them a long and healthy life and gives them a gold coin.

"Before my time Charlie," chuckled the boar.

"Well I'll tell you this Tonga, Vorspar was a good king, and I'm not saying his son isn't, but King Rosfarl spends nearly all his time in the palace, whereas his father could often be seen walking around the city and speaking with his subjects... and they respected him for it you know."

"Yes I've heard that, and I wish King Rosfarl would do the same, but sadly I believe he lacks the confidence to go out and become involved with the ordinary animals. He has no problem giving instructions to his soldiers, and servant's whatsoever, but underneath I believe he is a little frightened that he might fail to capture the hearts of the people as his father had done."

Charlie glanced towards his friend with a questioning expression.

"I've heard tell his royal courtier has a lot of influence, perhaps too much...is this true?"

Tonga sighed, "The frog...yes he does."

"But nevertheless we all love our king!"
exclaimed Charlie trying to cheer up the
conversation.
"Indeed we do."

Charlie and Tonga soon reached the entrance to
the palace quarters which was situated in the
eastern wall of the market square. The on duty
guards duly saluted their captain and moved
their pikes aside to allow them to walk under
the archway and enter the palace quarters. This
was something very new for Charlie, for even
though he knew all the palace guards by sight,
and even passed a few words with some of them
in the tea house, they would never allow him
entry in to the palace grounds; but as he was
with their captain, his way was not barred.
They continued along a short cobbled path
which led through the palace gardens towards
the side of a small building that protruded from
the southern castle wall. Its walls like most of
the cities' were of dense granite, and like the
rest of the palace buildings its gable roof was
covered with deep orange clay tiles. A solitary
guard stood in front of the solid wooden
entrance doors; each with protruding iron
studs, and a circular black wrought iron handle.

As Tonga approached him the guard duly pulled on one of the handles, and with squeaking hinges the door slowly opened.

Charlie recognised the guard as a regular visitor to the tea house, but as he was on duty he wasn't sure that the boar would acknowledge him. However after giving his captain the most perfect salute, the guard gave Charlie a warm welcoming smile to which the collie immediately reciprocated. Following closely behind the boar, Charlie had barely stepped in to the building when a loud reverberating thud signified the door had been closed behind him.

Ahead of them was a wide staircase that rose steeply upwards before curving sharply to the right, it was made of white marble, and on each side were dark wooden arm rails supported by black painted wrought iron legs shaped like barley sugar twists.

As the two animals began to climb the steps Charlie began to feel more excited, he was in the palace after all, and going to meet the king. He wasn't what you would call a nervous animal, in fact he was very logical and wise, and many others would go to him for advice; but the enormity of actually meeting royalty was beginning to make his tummy flutter a little. Fortunately the appearance of a friendly moon projecting beams of light through a giant

stained glass window adjacent to the stairs was
a welcomed distraction; and studying the ornate
features of the glass brought him a sense of
calmness too. Charlie had little memory of his
birth blessing, let alone what the inside of
the palace looked like, but he was absolutely
mesmerised by the enormity and fine detail on
the window.

Facing north, it extended from a few feet
above the ground to just below the top of
the ceiling; in fact the rectangular window
virtually filled the complete wall of the
building. Adorning the outer fringe of it were
a multitude of scenes in a variety of colours
depicting the history of the Land of Unger.
There were boars with their blue uniforms
holding bright red swords or pikes, poised in
a variety of fighting positions. The brightest
yellow and white glass formed the city of
Ungerborg, and scattered across the window in
various vibrant colours were heads of the past
kings of Unger. No history of the country would
be complete without Admiral Tonga of course,
and blue and yellow glass was used to show him
standing at the front of a large green galleon
waving the navy forward in to battle.

Dominating the window and taking centre stage
was the outline of a boar's head made from
the deepest purple, with a vivid yellow crown

on its head. This was to signify that the Land of Unger was ruled by a boar king, and that this was his palace. Clear glass was used where there was no need for colour, allowing plenty of light into the throne room and on to the staircase during the day.

Sadly aging had taken its toll, and in some areas both lead and glass had fallen out leaving missing sections and incomplete pictures, and occasionally strange and ghostly sounds would be produced when a strong northerly wind blew through these openings.

"Well come on let's get a move on!" ushered Tonga, nudging his friend in an effort to speed him up.

"Righto," replied Charlie quickening his step. As they moved upwards they left the brightness of the moon behind them, and the gradual darkness together with the echo of their steps on the marble stairway produced an eerie atmosphere that caused Charlie to feel uncomfortable.

But gradually and subtly a little laughter began to fill the air, it was deep in tone and somewhat uncontrollable, and the further up the steps they went, the louder it became. Charlie put a paw to his mouth as he wondered what could be making this din, and then it came to him, and so he turned towards Tonga with a little smirk on his face.

"It isn't um? -"

"Yes it is" interrupted Tonga with a chuckle.

"Oh," replied Charlie trying to restrain from laughing.

They gave one another a fleeting smile and continued to follow the staircase as it wound sharply to right and then left before they finally arrived in the throne room.

Stepping from the marble staircase they began to walk along a narrow dark red carpet that lie in the centre of the polished wooden floor and covered the complete length of the room. And as they proceeded further into the room their vision of the candle lit scene at the far end gradually became more apparent. Charlie became more excited now as he could clearly make out the ornate gilded thrones in which King Rosfarl and Queen Rosia were seated.

A little unsure of royal protocol he followed the boar's example, and stood up straight, assumed a solemn countenance, and proceeded in a more orderly fashion. But his eyes were on stalks when he saw a most outlandishly dressed creature who was taking centre stage in front of the royal couple.

It was a frog, and he was skipping and singing, pulling faces and telling jokes; and it was he who was causing the king to break into laughter. He wore yellow and blue striped trousers, a pink shirt with frilly cuffs and a ruffled collar, and a bright purple waist coat. He also had a red floppy hat with a bell at the end which would make the most annoying ringing sound every time he shook his head. But the strangest thing of all was not the clothes he wore but the colour of his head and legs which were the most fluorescent green. Charlie had seen the frog before, as he was regularly out in the city doing errands for the king, and in fact he had even done some business with him; although this was never a pleasant experience due to the frog's air of superiority. However, on those occasions the frog was dressed in a smart suit and wore a bowler hat, and his demeanour had been one of seriousness; how bizarre he thought that he could also play the fool.

But Charlie had no idea of how reliant the king and queen were on the frog for performing so many duties. He was their treasurer, fashion guru, butler, official royal advisor, and would even play the foolish court jester. Acting in this wide variety of roles gave him far more influence than he should have had on the king and queen, and Tonga was well aware of how he would cleverly manipulate them; he didn't like nor trust the frog.

Fosfero's antics had the king in stitches of laughter; so much so that he was holding his tummy tightly, as the constant laughing had made it ache. But the frog failed to amuse Queen Rosia who calmly continued her knitting with no show of emotion; other than occasionally peering over her gold rimmed spectacles and shaking her head in astonishment at her husband's excited reaction to the frog's behaviour. As always Fosfero was completely absorbed in his performance, and was revelling in the attention it brought him, but when much to his amazement the applause and laughter ceased, he immediately stopped in his tracks. Finding this most disconcerting he put his front legs on his hips and looked towards the king with a questioning expression. "Your majesty, your majesty, am I no longer funny?"

But there was no reply from the king who was in fact looking beyond the frog and struggling to see the two approaching figures that had caught his attention. The frog put a leg to his mouth and thought for a moment.

"Ah I know," he began excitedly. "Have you heard the one about the weasel and the hedgehog?!"

"Not now Fosfero we have visitors!" commanded the king.

On hearing her husband's words Queen Rosia
stopped her knitting and peered over her
spectacles.

"It's Captain Tonga!" she exclaimed with an
excited tone and a welcoming smile.

She had always had a soft spot for the captain,
and had often thought that if she hadn't been
a princess she would have chosen someone like
him to marry. To her he was a true boar, strong
and brave; qualities sadly lacking in her husband.

The king too thought highly of his captain and
his pleasure at seeing him was reflected in his
beaming smile. The same could not be said for
Fosfero however who disliked Tonga greatly,
and although he tried not to show it, he was
deeply jealous of any advice that the king would
seek from his captain.

Just before they reached the king and queen,
Tonga gestured to Charlie to stop where he
was, while he proceeded to approach the royal
thrones.

"Captain Tonga, this is a surprise," uttered the
queen excitedly.

"Your majesty," replied the boar bowing his
head.

The king as always gave his captain a warm
welcome.

"Tonga, Tonga, lovely to see you," he said in a
deep and friendly tone of voice.

"Sire," replied the boar bowing to his king.
"And um...who's this with you?" questioned the king pointing towards the collie.
Tonga cleared his throat. "Your majesties may I introduce my old friend Charlie...Charlie Butterworth."
"Step forward, step forward my dear Butterworth," beckoned the king.
The collie gave a nervous swallow, followed by a deep breath before proceeding forward; all the while his heart was beating more rapidly as he did so. His movement was closely watched by the frog, whose large bulging eyes swept between him and Tonga, for he was most intrigued by their arrival at such a late hour. Charlie continued forward until he stood next to Tonga.
"Your majesties!" he exclaimed performing a perfect bow.
"Mr Butterworth," replied the queen with a smile.
"Butterworth, Butterworth?" began the king, placing a trotter to his mouth. "Name rings a bell, but I can't for the life of me think why."
"If it pleases your majesties, everyone calls me Charlie."
"Charlie...I like that," uttered the queen with a smile.
A wide grin spread across the king's face.

"Ha ha ha ha, sounds like the name for a rascal, but you don't look like a rascal, does he my dear?"

"He has a very honest face," replied the queen.

"I can assure of this your majesties, he has been a true and loyal friend for many years... and I would trust him with my life," uttered Tonga in a serious tone.

"Enough said then captain; your friend is most welcome here," replied the king, looking at the collie with a most sincere expression.

"Thank you your majesty," replied Charlie.

Charlie was thrilled to be welcomed by the king and with his nerves beginning to settle down, his face took on the picture of a very happy and contented animal.

All was smiles and silence for a moment, until the queen asked the collie a question.

"Now do tell me Charlie, what is it you do in the city?"

"I have a shop in the market square,-"

"He sells bric a brac," spouted Fosfero with an air of disdain.

Tonga was annoyed by the frog's belittling remark and quickly aired his disapproval.

"That's hardly fair!" he snapped.

Charlie found Fosfero's words very hurtful, as he was devoted to his shop, and was extremely proud of all the wonderful goods he sold; and

was certainly not going to let a jumped up frog
run it down.

"Your description of my shop is most inaccurate
Mr Frog," he began assertively.

"Mr Frog indeed!" retorted Fosfero.

"Shush Fosfero, let him speak!" exclaimed the
queen in a chastising tone.

Charlie and Tonga found the queen's
admonishment of the frog very amusing and
after exchanging looks of raised eyebrows they
quietly chuckled to themselves; but they soon
stood to attention when the king spoke.

"Please do continue Charlie," he requested.

Charlie's face took on the proudest expression
as he began to talk about his shop.

"Why your majesties my shop is a veritable
emporium, offering a wide variety of items
from all around the world. And if I haven't got
what you're looking for...well I can nearly always
obtain it."

Why I even supplied these!" he continued
excitedly, pointing towards each side of the
royal couple.

Everyone immediately turned their attention
to the giant ornate and elaborate silver
candlesticks that stood either side of each
throne.

They had a large diameter solid base with a
single stem that reached five feet in height,

and branching outwards and upwards from this some three feet from the base, were four ornate arms forming an outer circle of holders around the central one. Although they looked very impressive, the dancing light from their five candlesticks illuminated areas of tainted finish, signifying they were in urgent need of a polish.

For a moment all onlookers were quiet, as the flickering orange and yellow coloured flames of the candles had a very relaxing; one might even say hypnotic effect on them.

Then after a pleasant sigh the queen began to speak.

"Did you really supply those Charlie?!" she exclaimed gushing with pleasure. "Why I have always thought they look so wonderful."

"Yes your majesty I did," replied the collie with pride.

Then Fosfero had to have his say.

"I couldn't agree more your majesty, they are indeed a very fine pair of candelabrum," he said, glancing around to the collie with a smirk on his face. Charlie was not a confrontational animal by any means, but he didn't take kindly to any disdainful treatment of his shop and business, and felt more than hurt by the frog's sneering behaviour. So being quick witted he hurriedly thought of other items he had supplied the royal family; as further approval from them was a way to get one up on the arrogant amphibian – and then it came to him.

"I also supplied you with a Tonga jug!" exclaimed Charlie enthusiastically.

"You remember," he continued, looking towards the frog.

But before the frog could reply King Rosfarl quickly sat up from his seat with an excited look on his face.

"My goodness, you mean Fosfero bought that from you Charlie?!"

"He did your majesty," replied the collie his face swelling with pride.

The king beamed. "Well should you have anything else of interest we would be most pleased to see it...wouldn't we my queen?"

Charlie nodded excitedly, feeling thrilled by the royal invitation.

"Thank you your majesties, may I say that I have many interesting and beautiful items in my shop, and would be honoured to welcome you at any time," he gushed."

"That would be nice," replied the queen.

"Yes it would my queen, but you know how better at shopping Fosfero is," replied the king.

An expression of importance crept across the frog's face.

"And moreover it is a privilege," said Fosfero with a grin.

"But it would be nice to get out once in a while," said the queen with a frustrated tone of voice.

The king looked a little flustered, for the thought of venturing out of the palace made him feel a little anxious.

"Perhaps one day," he replied, smiling slightly nervously.

Feeling irritated by this typical response, the queen let out a deep sigh and took consolation in her knitting.

Charlie, now much more relaxed had enjoying this banter, however this apparent time wasting was causing Tonga great concern.

He realised it was essential to set sail as soon as possible if they were to have any hope of catching the weasels; and they hadn't even got a ship yet.

"Your Majesty," he began in earnest.

"Yes Tonga," replied the king.

"Charlie and I have a most urgent request that if acted upon,-"

"Could help to boost the royal coffers!" added the collie.

The king and queen stared at each other for a moment and then with questioning expressions looked upon Charlie.

"Did you say boost our coffers?" uttered the king

"And what makes you think they need boosting," added Fosfero.

"Um w-well," stuttered Charlie.

Feeling embarrassed by his foolish remark he looked to Tonga for inspiration, which he found in his warm and friendly face, and together they simultaneously took a deep breath, before facing the king; each of them wearing a most determined expression.

"Sire, we have a proposition," began Tonga.

"And one we could all profit from," added Charlie excitedly.

"Really," replied the king with an expectant expression.

"Yes, you see we've discovered where there might be some treasure," pronounced Charlie enthusiastically.

"Treasure!" exclaimed King Rosfarl.

"Treasure!" shrieked the queen excitedly, dropping her knitting on her lap.

"Yes treasure," replied Charlie.

"And where exactly is this treasure?" questioned the king.

"Well that's the thing your majesty...it's in Zanimos," replied Charlie.

"But how in the land of Unger are you going to get in to Zanimos!?" replied the king shaking his head in bewilderment.

"Well that's a good question sire...and one which we hope you might solve for us?" asked Tonga earnestly.

"If I can help rest assured I will, now what is it you require?" replied the king obligingly.

Tonga gave a fleeting grin, cleared his throat, and delivered his request.

"Can we borrow your ship...King Clanask?"

Zanimos Town Hall

CHAPTER 3

A DISOBLIGING BANKER

It was a gloomy rainy morning, not really
what you'd expect in the autumn, especially in
Zanimos, and this miserable weather had even
dampened the spirits of the normally cheerful
yellow Labrador who had reached the door of
the Town Hall.

"Oh dear, oh dear, oh dear," said Papachuan to
himself as he studied the warped and twisted
roof of the Town Hall.

"It's only a matter of time, only a matter of
time before it all caves in," he said shaking his
head.

He opened the heavy wooden door and stepped
into the large spacious hall where situated
opposite the entrance at the far side of the
hall was a wooden table and with nine chairs;
five in a line along the length facing the
entrance, and two at each end. The table and
chairs were hundreds of years old and had the

most delicate and beautiful carvings of animals
and beasts that had lived in Zanimos at one
time or another; some were recognisable, but
others were more sinister, ghoulish, and some
might say even hideous.

As Papachuan took a few steps into the hall
he was greeted by the sound of rain falling
through the leaky roof, and into the buckets he
had placed over the floor the previous evening.
Plip plop, plip plop, went the rainwater as it fell
into buckets.

He looked up at the ceiling with its many
holes that were dripping water and frowned in
frustration; some of the holes were even big
enough to show a glimpse of the grey sky above.
Papachuan being a Labrador didn't mind the rain
whatsoever, in fact he would have loved nothing
more than to go and play out in it, but as the
Town Mayor of Zanimos he was expected to
behave in a dignified manner.

'Oh to be a youngster with no responsibilities,"
he thought with a smile. He walked over to his
large oak writing desk in the corner of the
hall and slid in to his dark brown sumptuously
cushioned swivel chair. He looked over at the
right hand side of his desk to a red wooden
tray that held a dozen or so notes and letters
from the animals of Zanimos that needed his
attention. Mostly he could answer and resolve

himself, but on occasion he would approach members of the town council for a group resolution; an example of this was a dispute between a family beavers and otters. The otters were angry that the beavers had built a dam that reduced the flow of the river to the region in which they lived. Papachuan and several council members went to the river and after much discussion it was agreed that the beavers build a new dam further downstream, and the otters moved upstream to have unimpeded swimming and fishing, and all was happy thereafter.

Papachuan picked up the envelope from the top of the pile and looked at it for a moment. It was grubby, creased and coated with flour, which told him it was yet another letter from his sister Hannah, asking for help with repair costs for the sails on her husband's windmill. He held the envelope for a moment, and then as a twinkle appeared in his eyes he dropped it back on to the pile.

"A little fun before the day's work I think," he uttered pushing hard with his hind legs and spinning around and around in his chair. However, it wasn't long before dizziness took its toll causing him to lie back in the chair, and as feelings of comfort and relaxation took control, his eyes closed and he drifted off to sleep.

But his slumber was short lived as rain began seeping through the roof above his head.

"Oh no, no, this really is intolerable!" exclaimed Papachuan, as he felt a large raindrop land on the tip of his nose.

He shook his head and stared up at the ceiling, he watched and stared, and gradually a small globule of water appeared, it grew larger and larger, and then when it was too heavy to hang there any longer it parted company with the ceiling and fell towards him. Papachuan held out his paw and felt the dampness as the droplet dispersed on to the pads of his paw. Jumping up from his chair he moved it away from where the new leak had appeared, and placed another metal bucket in its place to catch the water. He then shuffled his desk around so he could place his chair behind it and away from the leak. He sat back in his chair for a moment and folded his arms, sighing deeply as he did so. His eyes raced from side to side as he thought about how the problem of the leaking roof could be resolved.

'Right!' he exclaimed as he pushed onto the armrests and stood up from the chair. "There's nothing else for it I'll just have to go to the bank.

After closing the heavy oak door of the town hall he pinned a hand written note to it that read 'Gone To Bank'. He then turned around and trotted down the three wide steps that led to a cobbled footpath where he turned left. It was still grey and overcast, and there were only a few animals braving the heavy rain and going about their business in the town square. Thankfully the drainage system was working well and the rainwater was running off the square and into the town pond where the falling rain made thousands of tiny ripples as it hit the water. The bank was adjacent to the town hall and only a short distance away, and in a few moments Papachuan had reached the entrance. He glanced over the red stoned walls, and the black iron bars that stood in the two front windows, and the smaller one situated toward the top of the front door before studying the roof. The grey slate tiles were in tip top condition and the rainwater splashed off them and ran down into the black iron guttering and drainpipe. The window frames and front door were perfectly decorated in white gloss paint, and the Bank of Zanimos sign was beautifully handwritten; gold lettering on a black background. Shaking his head in disbelief at the difference in condition between the bank and the town hall, he pushed open the door to step inside. But to his great surprise the door was obstinate and refused to budge, so putting his shoulder against it he gave it a hearty shove. With his solid frame against it the door capitulated, and as it slowly released under his pressure, there was a loud thump.

'Ah, why can't you look where you're going!" came a shrieking cacophony.

The door moving more freely now Papachuan slowly and carefully opened it to reveal the source of the noisy chastisement.

For lying on her back with a broom across her chest, her wings and webbed feet outstretched was Polly Clutterbuck.

Papachuan was opened mouthed and felt extremely embarrassed. "Oh my dear Mrs Clutterbuck I am so sorry", he began as he helped her to her feet.

For a moment the goose looked as she was about to continue to unleash further admonishments against Papachuan, but on rising to her feet and catching the apologetic face of the Town Mayor her expression of anger transformed into a softer and gentle countenance.

"Oh your worship I do hope you will forgive my outburst but I was caught quite unawares and what with the shock of it all...why one minute I was brushing the floor and the next lying on it".

"I'm the one to be forgiven Polly; after all it was me who knocked you over". He rubbed his head as he thought for a moment and then continued. "You know I am always telling animals to think before they act...and look at me. I should have asked myself what was blocking the door before shoving it open, if I had, the accident wouldn't have happened. Nothing broken I hope?" he added smiling warmly.

"No, I'm a tough old goose your worship", she replied brushing some dust from her green piny. Papachuan raised his eyebrows. "Polly you need only call me your worship in relation to official business, and in this case as it isn't, please call me Papachuan."

"If you say so sir," replied Polly.

"I do," replied the Labrador with a smile.

"Not wishing to be rude your worship, I mean Papachuan, but I must be hurrying off to my next job now."

"Of course my dear."

Polly turned and waddled her way across the floor towards the store room situated in the right corner of the building.

Papachuan shook his head and smiled.

"Marvellous in the water these geese, but they don't half look funny when they walk," he thought to himself.

Walking towards the counter he glanced around
at the strange interior of the bank, for it was
very basic; you might even say austere, as it
contained no vestige of colour or warmth.
The floor and lower half of the walls were
covered in dark oak, and the top half of the
walls together with the ceiling were painted in
a dull orange colour; all of which served to make
the room a most unwelcome place to be. There
were wooden bench seats that were hard and
uncomfortable, and the heavily barred windows
obscured a great deal of light which was badly
needed on a dull day like today. The door to
the bank manager's domain, also served as the
counter, and in keeping with the design of the
room was also made from dark oak. The manager
and customers could converse through a window
of thick steel bars, below which was an opening
for monetary and business transactions.
The Labrador had almost reached the counter
when Polly reappeared from the store room
slamming its door behind her.
"Bye bye", she said in a singing tone of voice as
she made her way toward the main entrance.
"Bye Polly," replied Papachuan.
She opened the front door and was about to
continue on her way when she turned and called
out.

"Bye Mr Frazzelbach, I'll see you next week," but as usual Polly expected no reply and promptly closed the door behind her.

Peering over the counter Papachuan could see the familiar sight of Montagu Frazzelbach sitting at his desk; pen in trotter, muttering to himself as he studied a series of entries in an accounts ledger.

He was as dressed in a blue check waistcoat with matching trousers, and perched over his snout was a pair of small round wire rimmed glasses.

Now Montagu, or Monty as he was known, was of good stock and his family had been the bank managers of Zanimos ever since the bank was established some two hundred years ago. This family legacy instilled him with a great sense of pride and diligence, and he showed these qualities in all his duties as bank manager. However he was not the most engaging and friendly of animals, and much preferring his own company would seldom attend town fetes, parties; or even attend important meetings at the town hall. He also had great illusions of grandeur and thought himself far more important that he actually was, and because of this attitude he had the reputation of being arrogant and aloof. As a result he had no real friends, or acquaintances which didn't seem to bother him one bit. As pigs go he was actually quite small, being little bigger than a badger, and Papachuan towered over him.

"Ahem," began Papachuan clearing his voice, to which Montagu made no response. The Labrador frowned.

"If I could just see you for a moment Monty?" he continued in a louder tone.

The pig turned towards the Labrador and peering over his glasses took a watch from his waistcoat pocket that was attached to the middle button of his jacket by a silver chain.

"Well I am rather busy you know," he uttered in a dismissive tone, returning the watch to his pocket.

The Labrador sighed in annoyance.

"So am I Monty, but there is a matter that needs prompt attention and I really must speak with you now."

The Labrador had adopted a serious expression and the pig realising that Papachuan was insistent, begrudgingly slid out his chair, and walked towards counter.

There then followed a series of clunking, scraping and banging noises as Monty struggled to open the heavy bolts to the counter door. Lastly it was the key that had to be turned to free the door, and its reluctance produced a series of creaking and squeaking noises followed by a loud clunk signifying it was finally unlocked. Fortunately new hinges had recently been fitted which enabled the heavy door to move very easily, and so after only the slightest tug it was fully opened.

"You'd better come in then," uttered Monty standing in the doorway.

Papachuan had been in Monty's office on many occasions and nothing seemed to change. There was a row of metal filing cabinets against the wall to the store room, and close by was a round wooden table with four chairs that looked worse for wear. In the centre of the back wall there stood a red brick fireplace that showed signs of cracking in some places, which together with its blackened hearth were the symptoms of many years of use. In the corner adjacent to the counter door was a large steel safe.

Being familiar with the seating arrangements Papachuan walked past the fireplace and sat himself down in a green cushioned wooden backed chair in front of Monty's desk. The chair was basic and uncomfortable, unlike the luxurious one of Monty's with its deeply padded seat, high back, and arm rests. Even so, the pig still felt the need to wriggle around in it to find his perfect position, which caused the cushioning to creak and groan, and triggered a little chuckling in Papachuan.

"Quite comfortable?" began the Labrador.

"All ears."

"Well I'm sure you know why I'm here don't you?" asked Papachuan in a serious tone.

"The roof?" uttered the pig with a sound of contempt.

Annoyed at the Pig's sarcasm, the Labrador lent forward placing his paws on the desk and continued in a sterner manner.

"Yes the roof, and unlike the one on your bank, the town hall roof is leaking like a sieve. I've placed buckets everywhere and before long I'll have run out of them. And what's more it's only a matter of time before the whole thing collapses, and then where will we be?!"

Monty put his trotters together and looked down at the desk for a moment and then peered over his spectacles.

"Look Papachuan, we've been through this many times, and as I've said on numerous occasions there simply isn't enough money in the pot for renovating your roof."

"But Monty, I came to you several years ago, just as I had spotted some warping of the roof and the first leak had started. I asked for a loan to repair it, and you suggested I should wait until there was sufficient money in the town council funds to have the whole roof replaced."

"I said that," replied Monty pretending to act surprised.

"Yes you did!" exclaimed Papachuan.

The pig paused for moment. "Well it makes no difference what I did or didn't say. You can't afford to have a new roof." He replied shrugging his shoulders.

"Of course I'm certain there's enough for some patchwork.

Might even stop the leaks-"

"But that's no good!" interrupted Papachuan. "It's the rotting structure that's causing the roof to warp and the tiles to crack and dislodge. And no matter how much you patch up the tiles, and fill the holes, it won't stop the roof from collapsing."

The pig frowned. "Well let me just peruse your accounts to see how much you have."

"Sixty gold, forty two silver, and twenty seven bronze coins." was the prompt reply from Papachuan.

"Ah, well you'd know off the top of your head I suppose."

"Yes."

"Look I'm sorry," began Monty. "But you simply cannot afford a new roof, and I'm afraid a loan is out of the question as I can't see any way you'd pay it off." He paused and pompous smile crept across his face.

"At least in our life time."

"What about holding a fete, an evening dance, or even a raffle?" responded Papachuan with an air of optimism?

"You tried that last year, and where did it get you. A couple of gold coins I believe?!" replied the pig looking down his snout.

The response was cutting and quashed poor Papachuan's hope, but it lasted merely a moment, and in fact did nothing but harden the Labrador's resolve. Papachuan sat back in his seat; looked down at the table then back at the pig, once more at the table then gazed intently into the pig's eyes, biting his lip as he did so. All was silent for a moment with the two exchanging frozen glances, then slowly the Labrador's face transformed into the sternest of expressions.

"Well what about the bank's new roof. It was almost as bad as the town hall's and yet you managed to have it repaired. And where did the money come from I ask you eh. You answer me that Mr Bank Manager?!" ejected Papachuan angrily.

Monty was off guard, he was in fact utterly flabbergasted by the Labrador's outburst, and sat open mouthed in disbelieve at the tirade he had experienced.

"T-t-that's...none of your business," replied the pig rather hesitantly.

"Oh yes it is!" was the snappy reply.

"I don't have to tell you," responded the pig shaking his head.

The Labrador momentarily sat motionless and inhaled deeply while looking around the room and collecting his thoughts. He then slid forward on his chair, lifted his head and assumed the very proud and important air, that his position demanded.

"I am the Town Mayor and the head of the town council," he began in earnest. "I have been elected by the animals of Zanimos to make this great country a wonderful place in which to live, and I have every right to know where the money came from...every right! he stated firmly, raising his paw in the air.

The pig sighed, "Very well, if you must know. The bank has its own capital from interests on loans, and mortgages, and investments that we make. And we've been doing rather well of late and that's how I could get the roof repaired. Does that answer your question?" replied Monty with a haughty look on his face.

"Well it doesn't seem right!" was the sharp reply.

"The bank, well it's just a bank," continued Papachuan.

The pig frowned in disagreement.

"But the town hall...the town hall is by far the most important building in the whole of Zanimos," began Papachuan, his face glowing with pride. "Why it was built hundreds of years ago for the wizard Mortuleez and his wife Julianna. It's where ambassadors signed peace treaties, and where visiting kings and queens would party and carouse all night with Zamosians. Oh what times it has seen, what great times."

The pig leant back against his head rest and looked up at the ceiling in total ignorance of the significance of what had been said.

"That was in the good old days, long before our time, but alas no royals or dignitaries visit anymore; the wizard's magic has seen to that." Montagu's response had a silencing effect on the Labrador who knew the pig spoke the truth; for although the wizards spirits afforded Zanimos protection, they also brought it isolation.

All was quiet now and it looked as if the last word had been said on the subject of the roof. The pig sank back in his chair with an arrogant expression on his face, and began tapping his

trotters together as if to exhibit an air of
victory.

"Another waste of time," uttered Papachuan,
rising from his chair with a forlorn expression.
"Yes I'm afraid so."

The pig looked up at the Labrador as he
pushed his chair back under the table, an
unsympathetic smile gradually crept across his
face, and the cruel side of his character was
about deliver a final sneering remark. But on
opening his mouth to speak, his attention was
taken up by something so startling it rendered
him completely motionless and he froze on the
spot.

"Ahh you must be Monty!" remarked a rich
velvety voice.

"Rufus!" exclaimed Papachuan turning around
and seeing his new friend standing in the door
way.

The Malamute smiled. "Seems your friend's a
little stunned," he continued, nodding towards
Monty.

"It's alright Monty, its only Rufus; he's quite
friendly you know," uttered the Labrador trying
to ease the pig's nerves.

But Monty remained still.

"Are you alright?" continued Papachuan.

Slowly the pig began to move his eyes back and
forth between the malamute and the Labrador,
before finally plucking up the courage to speak.
"I'm okay, j-j-just a little surprised by
your size!" stuttered the pig, studying the
malamute's most ample frame.
Papachuan smiled. He's a big chap isn't he?"
"Y-y-yes," stammered Monty.
"Well I am very pleased to meet you", uttered
Rufus with an amiable expression.
The malamute's gentle tone and pleasant
manner, had a most calming effect on the pig,
and as his feeling of fear subsided, he began
to return to the normal unapproachable animal
that he was.
Rufus began to study him closely, and using
his special senses to assess the traits of his
character, two words immediately sprang to
mind; aloofness and ignorance.
"Well aren't you going to say hello Monty?!"
exclaimed Papachuan glaring at the pig.
Monty unhurriedly slid off his chair, before
stepping forward, and shaking Rufus' giant paw
with his trotter. Due to their great difference
in height, the pig had to bend his neck upwards
a great deal to see the smiling face of the
malamute, and as he did an uncomfortable
feeling began to take hold as he caught a
glimpse of those large sharp teeth; in fact

Rufus was exaggerating his smile. Of course he was generally a friendly animal, but he did believe that a little teasing, or even frightening was sometimes required, if animals misbehaved or showed unwelcome behaviour. And having formed the opinion that Monty fitted into the latter, he slowly bent down closer and closer and broadened his smile even further.

"Ah y-yes of course. I have heard about your arrival," began Monty a hint of nervousness in his tone. "But I must admit I really didn't envisage that you would be quite so large, or look so fearful."

The remark struck at the softer side of Rufus, who didn't really wish to frighten the pig any further.

"Now don't you worry, most people think that the first time they meet me," he replied in a soothing tone. "Now let us start again," he smiled.

"My name is Rufus O'Malley, and you I believe are Montagu?"

"Yes, yes that's me. Montagu Frazzelbach at your service sir," replied the pig with a touch of pride in his name.

"But most people call him Monty," laughed the Labrador.

Rufus smiled. "Ah Monty...I like that. And you are the manager of this bank I believe," he continued, glancing around the office.

"Yes I am," was the boastful reply.

"A very important position then," replied Rufus in a serious tone.

"Yes, and I don't take my work lightly."

"Unless it's a loan for the town hall," uttered Papachuan in a slightly sarcastic tone.

Monty didn't appreciate this remark and turned towards the Labrador with a scowl.

"We've already discussed this Papachuan, and you've had my final word on the matter...now you must excuse me I have important work to do." The pig peered up over his glasses and began to motion the other two animals out of the office.

"Therefore I must bid you good day." he continued sharply.

"As you wish," replied Rufus calmly turning around and stepping through the doorway.

But instead of continuing to walk he paused for a moment and gently stroked the edge of the door.

"What a solid door this is, it must make you feel very safe," he said looking at Monty with a mischievous smile.

In response the pig merely gave a fleeting grin, for he was impatient to get rid of them, and couldn't wait to close the door and return to his work. Papachuan stared at the pig with a most disapproving look before promptly following his friend out of the bank.

Monty stood and watched the two of them disappear out of sight, and felt most pleased to be on his own again.

"Thank goodness they've gone," he said with a sigh of relief.

He was after all at his absolute happiest when working alone in the bank with no other company to distract him, but sadly his work had become an obsession, and he had long forgotten that he was there to serve the Zamosian animals and not himself.

Feeling more cheerful now he was alone, he began to hum as he pushed the heavy counter door closed. But a strange thing occurred, for although the door started to move as normal, it suddenly stuck fast and refused to budge.

He pushed and pushed, but the door wouldn't shift.

"Strange, this has never happened before?" he thought to himself. Wondering if there might be an obstruction he peered around the door; but there was none. He knelt down on the floor to look underneath, but could see nothing preventing its movement.

"Right let's have another go," he uttered, pushing against the door once more.

But as soon as he exerted pressure on it, the door reacted by creaking and complaining; and it seemed to Monty that it was protesting against being moved. The eeriness of these sounds gave him the jitters and compelled him to stop, and as he did they immediately ceased. He stood still for a moment with a puzzled look on his face; he couldn't understand why the door wouldn't close; especially as it had been fitted with new hinges.

Then slowly but surely the importance of this predicament dawned on him, for the security of the bank depended on the door being locked, and if that was impossible he wouldn't even be able to go home. With frustration taking over he began to walk up and down, to and fro the fireplace he paced, trying to muster up all his strength and determination to win his battle with the door.

He certainly didn't relish the thought of hearing those sinister ghoulish echoes again, but there was nothing else for it; he had to try again.

After a minute he stopped walking and began to shake his right trotter at the door, staring angrily at it.

"You will do what you are told, do you hear me, you silly obstinate door!" he shouted, behaving as though the door understood.

He then took a deep breath, and contorting his face into the most determined expression, summoned up all his strength before throwing himself at the door.

"Move blast you, move, you stupid door!" he shouted pushing the solid structure with every sinew in his body.

Unsurprisingly the chilling screeching and squealing returned, the door became alive, and just like a wrestler it struggled and strained to stand its ground – but how could this be?

This desperate struggle soon brought about his exhaustion, and with strength faded, and energy depleted, he slid down the door and collapsed in a heap on the floor. Pulling himself up, he feebly beat his trotters against the door in a display of angry frustration, before lowering his head to the ground and beginning to sob.

"And what's all this about Montagu Frazzelbach?" came a soft and friendly voice that broke the silence.

The pig wiped his eyes and looked up to see the amiable face of Rufus O'Malley standing over him, and for a moment was filled with thanks that someone had come to help him.

But feeling uncomfortable in this undignified position, he quickly got to his trotters, straightened his waistcoat and assumed his normal haughty composure.

"Err nothing really, um just a little problem with the door," he uttered, trying to subdue his snivelling.

"Door," replied the malamute in a quizzical tone.

"Yes, that's right the door."

"And what is wrong with the door Monty?"

"Well it refuses to close."

The malamute produced a fleeting smile. "I see."

"Well I don't!" snapped the pig. "It's got new hinges on it, so why should it happen now!"

"Have you upset it in any way," replied the malamute, a hint of amusement in his tone.

"Upset it, upset it...how can you possibly upset a door?!"

"Well everything has feelings Monty."

"But it's just a door, a plain ordinary wooden door!"

"You see, that's just what I mean. You called it a plain ordinary door. After all would you like to be called a plain ordinary pig?"

Monty shook his head in frustration.

"Oh this is the most ridiculous thing I have ever heard!"

"I'm just offering you some advice Monty that's all. Perhaps if you were to talk nicely to the door...it might allow you to close it."

"Oh what nonsense!" jeered the pig.
"Well if you won't take my advice then I
really must leave...good day," uttered Rufus,
sauntering out of the bank.

The pig began to feel helpless, dare I say even
distressed. Someone had offered him advice
and as usual he had ignored it, and what's
more he had treated the advisor with absolute
disdain.
"Oh why do I do this?!" he shouted feeling the
conflict inside.
Beginning to panic he trotted towards the front
door calling out as he did so.
"Rufus, Rufus, I'm sorry please come back?!"
He looked down at the floor and felt so annoyed
at himself, he couldn't understand why he
always treated animals like this; deep down he
wanted to be friendly, yet he always found it
hard to accept the need for other animal's help
and advice.
The sentiment of desperation quickly arrived,
coupled with a light dizziness from his failure
to contemplate a solution to his problem of the
immovable door. It all seemed hopeless until he
was addressed in the most assertive tone.
"I'll give you a second chance and no more."
Looking up at the malamute the pig emitted a
giant sigh of relief as despondency was replaced

with optimism, and a forlorn expression with a smile.

"Now Monty lets go and talk to the door, and nicely okay?"

The pig nodded in agreement.

He was extremely relieved Rufus had returned to help, although he could hardly believe what he was suggesting.

"Talking to a piece of wood, what nonsense?!" he thought to himself.

Rufus reached the door and gently stroked the edge of it, just as he had done when he had left the bank earlier with Papachuan.

And upon his subtle touch the solid wooden structure seemed to bend and twist, just as one might stretch in the morning when waking up after a good nights sleep - and then it was still.

The pig shook his head as if he was seeing things, and Rufus looked down at him with a momentary twinkle in his eyes.

"Right then Monty, just say something like...I'd like you to close please."

"As simple as that?" replied the pig with a large frown.

"As simple as that."

The pig found Rufus' solution unbelievable. How could a huge animal like that believe that doors could have feelings?

"What tommyrot, "he thought.

"Come on Monty give it a go," beckoned Rufus enthusiastically.

The pig was looking down at the floor and kicking it with his trotters, as he was reluctant to do as Rufus asked, as he thought the whole idea of reasoning with a door not only stupid; but more importantly to him, humiliating!

For the moment he was just burying his head in the sand, and thinking that by ignoring Rufus the whole situation might just resolve itself, or maybe even the great dog might even close the door for him; after all he was strong and powerful. But he was only fooling himself if he thought the malamute was going to give up.

"Come on now Monty, there's no harm in trying."

Monty slowly and reluctantly began to look up at the malamute, and much to his surprise he found great encouragement from his smiling face and welcoming eyes.

"Okay," he replied softly.

He closed his eyes and began to inhale deeply, but it was no good.

"It's no use, I can't do it...I just can't do it Rufus!"

"Don't say can't, never say can't Monty."

Monty released a long sigh, "Oh very well."

The pig glanced at Rufus and then back at the door, and slowly shaking his head in disbelief at the situation began to speak; but in his state

of great embarrassed he could only manage a
slight whisper:
"I'd be very grateful –"
"That's good, very good, being grateful is so
very important. But louder, say it louder, after
all the door has to hear you,"
The pig cleared his throat.
"I'd be grateful...very grateful if you would
agree to close...please?"
"Very good, very good." said Rufus smiling.
"Now what?" uttered Monty looking confused?
"Well get behind the door and push!"
"Push?"
"Yes push Monty, push!"
Monty stepped behind the door and began to
push it, and much to his surprise and huge relief
it began to move, slowly at first but then it
got easier and easier, and very shortly it was
completely closed and locked. Rufus peered
through the bars of the counter door and began
to clap his hands.
"Well done, well done old chap!" he exclaimed.
Monty looked out towards Rufus.
"Well I suppose I ought to thank you?" he said
with a rather embarrassed look.
"Only if it's sincere Monty, as sincerity is a
value to proud of."
The pig stood still for a moment, for he was
caught between two traits of thought, one

where he would be gracious and appreciative and the other where he would be plain old Monty the proud pig who owed nothing to anyone.

When the words came they were impassive and fleeting.

"Thank you," he said slamming the door of the counter closed.

The malamute remained still and raised his eyebrows, he felt disappointed by the ungracious reply, but after a moment he turned and started off for 'The Wizards' pubic house, where he was due to meet Papachuan.

Sauntering over an old wooden bridge he wondered what would be required to bring out the best in the pig; he could sense goodness and kindness, but how to unlock it was the question? And although his touch of magic had proved successful in making Monty feel powerless, and helpless, it was clear that something more drastic was required to bring out his true character.

Reaching the door to the pub he paused for a moment and slowly shook his head.

"I fear you need a hard lesson in humility Montagu Frazzelbach, a hard lesson indeed!"

Mona

Chapter 4
The Race Is On

Once Tonga was unconscious and Belius had possession of the treasure map he ushered the other weasels to move as quickly as they could as he wanted to get far away from the city. After all, he had no idea how long it would be before Tonga recovered, and there was the strong possibility that someone might find him before he awoke: and in either case he felt sure the boar would try to catch up with him.

"Come on you two pick your speed up!" he yelled looking back at Hubble and Ruevic who were lagging behind.

The four of them had soon entered the low town, where they crept between the old wooden houses, before slipping quietly out of sight, and as they did so the rowdy sounds emanating from the King Rosfarl Inn gradually faded away.

They travelled for several hours with the bright moon for company, yet it seemed ill timed that dark sinister clouds should obscure

its luminosity just as they left the realm of
King Rosfarl and entered Moorsher; a land
famous for its treacherous bogs.

Belius felt safe in Moorsher, for he was one
of the few animals who really knew his way
through the bogs, and once he was winding
his way around this soulless wetland he felt
confident he could lose any one in pursuit; and
not even Captain Tonga would be foolish enough
to follow him, especially in darkness.

He had led his gang of weasels through
Moorsher many times before, but that was
always in daylight hours when the bogs were
more easily seen, yet even in the black of
night the head weasel seemed to know his way
instinctively.

"He must eat a lot of carrots," muttered Ruevic
under his breath.

Even so it was still loud enough for the yawning
Hubble to hear.

"Who does?" he questioned.

"Oh...um...you weren't meant to hear that,"
babbled Ruevic.

"Well I did, so tell me...who eats lots of
carrots?!"

Ruevic moved his head downwards and looked
embarrassed.

"Go on!" continued Hubble nudging his friend.

"Belius," came the reluctant whispered response.

Hubble shook his head in dismay. "What are you talking about?!"

"It's a well known fact isn't it...that eating carrots helps you see in the dark," responded Ruevic convinced this myth was true.

"Oh what twaddle, he's travelled these parts since he was a youngster, and day or night makes no difference to him."

"Quiet back there!" growled their leader.

"Carrots...why you are a twit," sniggered Hubble.

Their leader took them on a meandering route of twists and turns, constantly changing tack to avoid the dark and unforgiving mires that stretched across this heartless land. He also led them across stretches of marshland which had the most horrible smell, and where their feet would sink into the sticky mud. The first time this happened Hubble moaned and groaned and complained so much about getting wet and slimy that Belius turned on him with a heavy rebuke; he never grumbled again.

After his telling off, Hubble remained quiet and began to feel extremely sorry for himself, wishing he had never taken part in this so called adventure. But at long last the most pleasing words were heard from his leader who turned around towards him as he spoke.

"Welcome to Arven my weasels. From now on the journey gets easier, and we'll soon reach Arnog Haven."

Hubble and Ruevic glanced at one another and simultaneously let out a sigh of relief, as they were both fed up with the unpleasant and lengthy journey. The departure from the bogs of Moorsher brought them a welcome change of landscape, but as they entered the deep and dense forests Belius picked up the pace, and reluctantly they had to do the same.

"No peace for the wicked," complained Hubble turning to Ruevic.

"Shush, he'll hear you," replied his friend.

Now Arven was not only famous for its numerous forests, but also for harbouring dangerous outlaws who sort sanctuary, and was definitely a country to be avoided by law abiding animals.

The forests were made up of a variety of different trees, including oak, beech, yew, maple, birch, and chestnut to name but a few; the one exception was pine which although abundant in the Chameleon Mountains was not found in Arven.

The small company of weasels had just reached the end of a tightly grouped redwood forest, where the last tree had a giant gothic shaped hollow so large they were able to walk through it. The scenery then changed to a small clumpy grassed meadow which they trudged across towards the infamous Black Limbed Woods - an area that portrayed everything wicked and villainous.

For here were the black barked witchery trees, each one rumoured to have once been a wicked witch who practiced dark acts of evil for their own gain. The legend goes that one day the forces of good gathered them up, and one by one they were turned into seeds and planted here. Now whether there was any truth in this is hard to say, but the strange shapes of these trees were unlike any to be seen elsewhere in the world. For the base of every tree would curve outwards and then straighten up rather like a hockey stick does, and after climbing for a five or six feet it's broad trunk would divide in to several branches that twisted and spiralled as they stretched up towards the sky; it was as if they were reaching out and pleading for help or forgiveness.

"This place is so weird," uttered Ruevic with a quiet tone of voice.

Hubble nodded. "Yep, it always gives me the creeps."

"Keep up you two!" bellowed Gritch.

"We're coming, we're coming," yawned Hubble so much that his reply was hardly discernible.
Belius growled under his breath.
"Keep them in line Gritch, we can't lose any time," he uttered commandingly,
"You can count on it," replied his second in command, looking back at the two weasels with an angry threatening expression.
A southern breeze had begun to blow causing the witchery trees to sway and bow, and their twisted branches to creak and squeak producing the most sinister sounds. Hubble and Ruevic found these dreadful sounds to be so unnerving, that they promptly burst into speed to close up on the heels of Gritch and Belius; with whom they felt much safer. Then after a moment something caught their attention, and they began to move their snouts excitedly in all directions sniffing out this familiar and long awaited aroma that brought a welcome smile to them both.
"There's salt in the air Hubble, we're near the sea!" exclaimed Ruevic.
"The sea, the sea, oh how marvellous," replied Hubble taking in deep breaths of briny air.
They left the thickly nested trees of the forest behind and emerged close to a wide pebbled beach where they turned westwards and headed towards some distant flickering lights.

This was the hamlet of Arnog Haven a well known refuge for vagabonds, ruffians and all sorts of criminal types. Being situated on the coast made it an important place for importing, exporting and trading goods; most of which were obtained by dishonest means.

Belius kept up the fast pace taking a narrow sandy path that followed the contours of the shoreline. He was at last feeling relieved to be near journey's end, so much so that he didn't chastise Hubble and Ruevic, as they began to chatter excitedly. Before too long they had entered the outskirts of the hamlet and were soon strolling southwards along the main street with its old timber framed houses on either side. In the distance a light mist hovered above the waves through which they could just make out the outline of a sailing ship moored at the end of a dilapidated wooden pier; it was in fact the schooner Lady Bamboozler.

After a few more yards they came across an old curious looking building with a thatched roof and clay whitewashed walls which were now far greyer than white, and its leaded windows were so filthy that it was impossible to see through them. Over the entrance was some white lettering but it was so faded it was totally unreadable. Belius approached the dark wooden door and lifting the latch turned towards his weasels.

"A welcome sight eh lads!" he uttered in an excited tone.

"Tis to be sure," added Gritch.

Hubble and Ruevic looked at one another with a most joyous expression.

"The Slippery Eel...at last!" expressed Hubble with a sigh of relief.

"Thank goodness," uttered a grinning Ruevic.

As Belius pushed the door open they received the customary noisy greeting of laughter and joking, produced by the boisterous and drunken behaviour of the varied clientele. However, the most significant thing that always struck them as soon as they entered was the misty atmosphere of strong sweet smelling fruit that hung in the air. The cause of this could be seen at the far end of the pub behind the bar, as bubbling and hissing, and leaking out steam and vapours was an old brewery. Clearly lots of work had gone in to keeping the giant kettles and fermenting tank clean and shiny, but their age was beginning to show as an undesirable reddish tarnish was now evident on many areas of the copper. Battling with the leaks was a spotted hyena called Viktor, who was tying rags around the problematic pipes, in an effort to seal the joints.

He and his wife Mona had owned the Slippery Eel for several years now, and although no one was quite certain why they had left the country of Dorr in North of the World, there were rumours that Viktor was to be arrested for stealing, fraud and deception, and so fearing for his life he fled Dorr, taking Mona with him. Satisfied he had achieved some success Viktor wiped the grease from his front feet with a dirty old rag and walked over to stand behind the bar.

With a small gold earring in his right ear, a grimy white tee shirt and heavily worn denim trousers held up by a pair of red elastic braces, he cut a comedic appearance. But his scarred face and arms, chipped front teeth, and dark staring eyes testified he was not an animal to shy away from a fight; and this was supported by the heavy wooden cosh he kept under the bar.

His days were divided between bar work and tending to his beloved brewery in which he took great pride, and his hard work was not in vain for his casks of ale were in great demand from countries near and far.

The weary group of weasels had barely set foot in the pub when the colourful variety of ruffians and cutthroats all stopped what they were doing and stared intently at the newcomers, creating a strangely quiet and unnerving ambience - for in the Slippery Eel if your face doesn't fit you had better leave quickly.....

But the silence was momentary as Belius and his gang were well known in these parts, and the onlookers quickly ignored him and his band of weasels and returned to their riotous behaviour. As Belius led his gang across the room he received acknowledgments of respect from many of the animals to which he duly nodded in reply, the exception being the rival weasel gangs who gave merely a passing glance before returning to the traditional weasel pastime of whispering and chuckling; no doubt formulating secret plans of villainy.

The centre stage however was taken by a huge rectangular oak table around which were a large number of disagreeably looking, and very noisy rats, who were dressed in light armour and were very, very, tipsy. But at least in their drunkenness they could sit back and enjoy themselves, and forget that Emperor Porturios had put a price on their heads for desertion. Mona was kept constantly busy replacing their empty jugs with newly filled ones, after which she would take payment from a pile of coins on the table - the rats' drinking kitty.

With her brightly coloured floral blouse, long pleated turquoise skirt, and red and white polka dot scarf she brought a contrasting sight to the otherwise drably clothed animals and grim interior of the pub. However her smiling face, and occasional hysterical staccato laughter did nothing to alter those dark, inscrutable and emotionless eyes, which just like her husband's portrayed a lack of sincerity. Standing next to the bar were two more of Belius' gang; Ugg who was guzzling beer from an old pewter jug, and Yabek who was talking incessantly to a very smartly dressed fox.

The fox looked a pretty sight indeed, having rich crimson velvet breeches and waistcoat, a three cornered red hat adorned with a white feather, and polished high leather boots. Across his right shoulder he wore a wide black leather belt or baldric as it is known, and hanging from it next to his hip was a gleaming and deadly looking cutlass.

Unlike the beer swilling animals elsewhere in the pub, he held a golden goblet filled with the most exquisite port which he would delicately sip and savour: in fact one could be forgiven for thinking he was quite refined. Now if you were a stranger to these parts who had not been in the Slippery Eel before, but had been to Hamilton's lovely tea house, you might be forgiven for thinking that it was the kindly and friendly Sasha standing at the bar dressed in these fine clothes. But on closer observation it was plain to see that qualities of honesty and humility were sadly lacking in this fox, for he was none other than Sileenus, the pirate and wayward cousin of the tea house owner.

As Belius reached Sileenus, the fox gave him a quick insincere smile before turning to Viktor and slapping some silver coins down on the bar. "Four pints of ale for my good friends!" he uttered loudly as if to make a show of it.
"Well Belius, what brings you to the Slippery Eel?" uttered the fox under his breath.
"Ale first then I'll tell ya," grumbled the weasel.
The fox looked intrigued. "Why of course."
Viktor pulled back the one and only hand pump at the bar and as he did so a frothy substance spurted from the tap, filling the bashed and dented pewter jug he had placed before it.
The four jugs filled, the hyena placed them on the bar in front of the thirsty weasels. Ruevic's eyes lit up as he glanced at the frothy ale and as his thirst got the better of him he began swigging from the jug in earnest, but what tasted initially thirst quenching turned into a mouthful of sediment as he had not waited for the yeast particles of the freshly brewed ale to settle to the bottom of the jug.
"Oh yuck," he exclaimed amidst a multitude of coughs.

"That'll teach you for being greedy," uttered Hubble as he over zealously patted him on the back.

"Alright, alright...stop it will you," snapped Ruevic.

Sileenus rolled his eyes in disbelief at what he considered uncultured behaviour by the silly weasel, while Belius and Gritch afforded themselves a little snigger; but Ugg and Yabek found it so amusing they burst in to uncontrollable laughter.

But no one can out laugh a hyena, and the overbearing high pitched cackling of Vicktor soon took centre of attention.

"Hee - hee - hee - hee - hee - hee – hee!" he tittered.

Being used to the Hyena's outlandish laughter, the weasels and fox knew they couldn't continue to hold a conversation, so they just waited for the uncontrollable repeated verse of high pitched nonsense to abate. Meanwhile Sileenus returned to sip his port, while Belius looked in to his jug and watched patiently as the froth slowly disappeared to reveal the dark ruby ale that Viktor was famed for producing. Now certain the sediment was safely at the bottom, he slowly took a little into his mouth and savoured the strong refreshing flavour.

"Umm, good quality that is Viktor, never fails to hit the spot," he uttered, just as the hyena's laughter had reduced to a hissing snigger.

"Thank you my friend," replied the Hyena dispassionately.

Belius turned to look at the pirate fox, and after holding a deadpan expression for a moment, a cunning smile crept across his face.

"I've got a proposition for you Sileenus," he began in a deep throated tone.

The fox fleetingly grinned, "Which involves my ship no doubt?"

"Just for a little trip that's all," chuckled Belius.

"And the payment?"

"More than you'll ever spend Sileenus," whispered Belius.

The foxes' face lit up,"Really?!"

"Oh yeah...but first I need to speak with im," replied the weasel looking across the bar to where a pair of glowing gold ear rings betrayed a shadowy figure sitting in the darkness next to the fireplace.

"Viktor," called Belius, and the Hyena leant forward.

"I need to see the cat."

"Then you'll want this," replied Viktor producing a large dark and dusty darkened bottle with a cork stuck firmly in its neck.

The weasel slapped a gold coin down on the bar. "Thanks."

"I'll be back in a mo," he continued, giving Sileenus a friendly smile.

"Nomah!" he called, as he reached the dark shape warming itself by the fire.

For an instant nothing moved, and then the silhouette slowly stirred.

"Belius," it hissed.

The weasel stepped closer and placed his bottle on the table, and then slid it towards the cat.

"Ahh mead, my favourite...join me will you," beckoned Nomah.

"Of course," replied Belius sitting down and placing his jug on the table.

"And what does the famous leader of weasels want with the humble Nomah?" whispered the cat under his breath, before pulling the cork from the bottle which made a sharp pop as it came free.

"I have a map."

"You have a map...then I suggest you follow it," laughed the cat as he raised the bottle in preparation to pour.

The air entering the dusty bottle produced a glugging sound as it traded places with the amber liquid, which splashed downwards towards Belius's jug, making sharp metallic rings as it fell against the pewter; yet when the cat filled his glass not a sound was heard.

Nomah raised his glass and savoured the sweet tasting liquid.

"Wonderful stuff mead," he whispered.

Belius wasn't amused by the cat's sarcastic comment about reading the map and gave a false grin, before swigging from his jug; which he quickly emptied.

"It's not just any map...it's a treasure map, and if you want some of it you'll help me," snarled the weasel wiping the excess mead from his lips.

Nomah sank back into the soft cushions of his high backed oak chair, and slowly sipped his drink. He was always on the lookout for ways to prosper, and it didn't matter whether it was by fair means or fowl, and the very mention of treasure intrigued him deeply. Not one to wait on ceremony Belius helped himself to more mead, and as he guzzled down the honey flavoured alcohol his eyes remained firmly fixed on the inscrutable cat.

He didn't trust Nomah; in fact who did, for he was not of this land, and it was rumoured that he knew the dark arts of magic; although no one had witnessed him demonstrate any. His kind originated from lands in the Southern Seas, and were seldom seen in this part of the world; indeed many animals were taken aback at their first sight of what appeared to be a strange looking animal.

His coarse fur was mainly black, with the odd patch of brown, and scars were dotted about his body, and with a patch over his right eye, trousers and waistcoat of black leather, and a large curved scimitar sword at his waist, he didn't look like the sort of animal to be messed with. He was a sturdy looking feline; probably about the same size as the Nordeamian Rats who served Sileenus: but then again these were very large rats.

Belius opened up his map and tossed it across the table towards the cat, who whipped out a paw and snatched it, like a viper striking its prey. Nomah ummed and aahed for a moment, and then slowly looked across the table and stared at Belius with his one green eye, which had a momentary mesmerising effect on the weasel. After a further quick glance at the map he returned to gaze at Belius, where upon a most self satisfied grin crept across his face.

"You need my help with the old language, don't you Belilus?"

"Yes I do," nodded the weasel.

"This I can do, but you realise this belongs to the great cat."

The Weasel chucked. "Your Catsumo is long is dead,"

Nomah purred. "Is she?"

It was just after seven o'clock in the morning and King Clanask was making her way along the east coast of Unger through the slightly unsettled Nordeamian Ocean. The white canvas sails on the three tall masks were doing their job soundly as they caught the strong north easterly wind which propelled the ship along at a respectable twelve knots. While not as fast as Lady Bamboozler, King Clanask was a sturdy man of war that packed twelve cannons on either side, which made it more than a match for Sileenus' sailing ship.

The sea being a little rough caused the ship to rear up on the crests of the tall waves and then drop suddenly as they passed underneath, and all the while Charlie felt he was on some sort of carnival ride. His face was beaming with delight as he enjoyed every moment of it, and even when doused by a shower of cool briny sea his expression never changed. Next to him at the helm, was the old shipwright Rumick (Rummy to his friends) who was absolutely thrilled to put to sea in the only surviving ship of the Ungerian navy; especially as this was the flag ship used by Admiral Tonga to defeat the Nordeamian fleet many years ago.

He had worked tirelessly on the ship for many years, as she had been badly damaged in battle and just left to rot, but all those long days

of strenuous work were at last repaid in full,
for his dream of being at the helm was finally
fulfilled.

On board were a number of boars dressed
in flared blue trousers and blue and white
striped shirts, who climbed the rigging to set
the sails, and did all the other sea duties. Like
Rummy they were descendants of sailors who
had fought the Nordeamian Armada, and like
him they were delighted to be doing service
for their king. As after all setting sail in King
Clanask was representing the land of Unger, and
something they were all proud to do.

Mind you the whole process of making the ship
ready for the voyage had been very hurried, as
King Rosfarl was initially very reluctant to loan
Tonga and Charlie his prized possession. But
thankfully the queen was enthusiastic about
the quest to find the treasure, and due to her
incessant and tireless persuasion he finally
gave in. The greedy Fosfero was of course very
excited by the thought of finding treasure,
and unsurprisingly he helped the queen to sway
her husband. It was then a race against time to
find a crew, muster some soldiers, and load the
ship with stores and provisions. But despite the
uphill struggle all was done before first light,
and at six forty five in the morning the ship
weighed anchor and set off from Port Unger to

make her way towards the estuary of the river
Olgen. On the river bank a few animals caught
sight of the great galleon, and with a look of
awe and disbelief at what they beheld, began
waving and cheering at the top of their voices.
To be fully crewed King Clanask would have
needed around one hundred boars, but due to
the lack of preparation and training, a skeleton
crew had set sail that morning. There were just
twelve sailors, four soldiers, Rummy, Charlie,
and Tonga, making eighteen boars and one
collie on board in total. As a consequence this
meant they could not use anywhere like the
full fire power of the ship - for at most they
could only fire around eight of the cannons.
This was still enough to sink Lady Bamboozler,
but if by chance they ran into an unfriendly
looking galleon, they would probably have to run
for it. Below the main deck in the great cabin
at the stern of the ship captain Tonga was
about to address his four soldiers. There was
his long time friend Sergeant Kolo, a reliable
and tough boar who was devoted to his captain
and although he would shout his orders at the
top of his voice he was kind in heart. Buna and
Wicklop were top line soldiers and excellently
trained fighters and held in high regard by
their captain. Then lastly there was young
Tunashi, who was still learning the ropes really,

but this was just the sort of experience his father Sergeant Kolo would wish for him; and that is why he asked his Captain's permission to bring him.

"Right gather round lads," uttered Tonga in a commanding tone, and the soldiers moved closer.

"Now the weasels have got the lead on us, and if they have a ship which we think they may, they'll get to the treasure afore us."

Tonga paused for a moment and his expression became more positive.

"But if we can reach the cave before they leave with the treasure... then we've got em!" he exclaimed.

"Then there'll be a fight captain?" uttered Buna excitedly.

"Oh yes, I owe that Belius," growled Tonga rubbing the small lump on his head.

"At last a fight!" cried out Wicklop

"Sir?" began a timid Tunashi.

"Go on my boy," his captain replied.

Tunashi then cleared his throat."

"Can we possibly reach the cave in time to stop the weasels...after all sir we have to sail all the way around the south of Zanimos?"

Tonga paused for a moment and looked at each of his soldiers.

PHILIP HUZZEY

"Well the lad has a good point...any ideas?" he asked.

There was an initial flurry of ideas banded about, but that didn't last long, and after a few moments all the focus was on Tonga to provide the answer.

Tonga smiled and studied their expectant faces.

"The answer is simple my lads...we are going to sail into the Old Harbour, moor up and trot across Zanimos as quickly as we can.

"Wicklop and Buna looked at one another with doubtful expressions.

"But won't that take longer captain?" questioned Buna.

"Surely we would make better time on the sea?" added Wicklop.

Tonga took a deep breath.

"Rummy tells me that at this time of year there's a chance of strong currents and choppy waters where Nordeamian Ocean meets the Zamosian Sea...and if this happens we would slow down to only a few knots, which would put us even further behind the weasels."

"But what will happen when the Zamosians see us sail into their harbour?" asked Buna.

"Wont they think we're invading?" uttered Tunashi in a worried tone.

The cabin instantly came alive with a cacophony of questions all put to their captain, who for a moment was so surprised by this onslaught, he was speechless; which is not like Tonga at all. But he was not to be shouted down and so he raised his front trotters in the air and motioned for calm.

"Alright lads you've had your say...now listen to me," he began firmly.

"The objective of this expedition is to get our trotters on the treasure...that is either before the weasels get it, or if not, we take it from em...okay."

The soldiers all nodded in agreement.

"Now we are not at war with the Zamosians and we don't want to be...but the fact is that if we do find treasure we will probably have to give them a little of it as it's on their land."

On hearing this the soldiers looked a little glum as the thought of giving treasure away did not go down well with them, and Tonga could see they weren't too happy with this.

"Suppose we give em nothing" uttered Buna defiantly.

"Yeah, why should we, they aint got no army!" added Wicklop excitedly.

Kolo thought his two soldiers though great fighters were speaking out of turn and not thinking properly, and as he glanced at Tonga his expression said it all. Tonga ran his eyes from Buna to Wicklop several times which

made them feel a little uneasy and after a deep
breath he began to speak.

"You two have got to use your loaf," he began
vigorously, and the two boars sank their heads
in shame.

"They might not have an army like us, but they
could soon get up a militia, and if there are
many more like that feisty Badger Brodney we'll
be in big trouble...do you understand?"

Buna and Wicklop submissively nodded their
heads, while Tunashi not wanting any rebuke
from his Captain stood absolutely still and
silent.

"And anyway we will have a better chance of
taking the treasure from the weasels if we can
get help from the Zamosians," he added, in a
slightly softer tone.

"That's very true captain," uttered Kolo in
support.

Tonga walked towards Buna and Wicklow and
patted them on their shoulders.

"Now then lads let's not fall out, we've known
each other far too long for that," he said with a
warm and friendly voice.

"Aye captain we have that," replied Buna with a
smile.

"You can depend on us sir," uttered Wicklop.

Lady Bamboozler was on her way south eastwards on the opposite side of the Zamosian peninsula to King Clanask; and travelling some four knots faster that the boars' ship. Her journey through the azure coloured waters of Auricious Bay may have been less choppy than that of the King Clanask, but even this gentle rolling motion was too much for Yabek and Hubble, who were leaning over the side of the ship, desperately hoping for the journey to end. Yabek could find no relief from the sickness he felt, and peering into the rolling sea below only seemed to make matters worse. He was feeling quite sorry for himself, and the sea certainly didn't cheer him up, as an occasional wave would crash against the ship and splash his face, leaving him with an unpleasant taste of brine. "Yuck, I've had enough of this!" complained Yabek as he stood up and stared across the sea to the distant white cliffs that lie to the east. As Lady Bamboozler got to a half a mile off the Zamosian coastline where the imposing steep chalk faces cliffs made way for the mouth of an estuary, Sileenus gave the order to turn due south and hold a steady course. Passing by the mouth of the estuary, the line of high white rock gradually reduced in height until there was a transformation in to soft underlating sand dunes.

Yabek was captivated by the beauty of the coastline, for he had never seen anything so lovely. He watched the fluffy grass on the dunes bending under the gentle sea breeze, and followed the crests of effervescent waves as they crashed upon the golden sandy beach, that stretched for mile upon mile. For a fleeting moment this wonderful sight took his mind off his upset tummy, but then all of a sudden his ears were filled with the most annoying and repetitive sound.

"Ha ha ha, ha ha ha, ha ha"!

The screeching noise made him look upwards where he beheld a Herring Gull hovering in the breeze a few yards away from the ship. The bird was mainly white under body; with grey feathers on its back, and its broad black tipped vee shaped wings were perfectly shaped for the most dramatic flying displays. To aid streamlining, its pink legs with their webbed feet were tucked up close to its body. The bird had a slightly hooked bill with a red spot, and as it effortlessly kept pace with the ship it turned and peered down at the weasel. Yabek had seen these gulls in the distance but never so close up, and the fact that the bird was so large made him feel uneasy enough to grasp the hilt of his sword.

"Hubble, Hubble, look at this bird!" he cried, but there was no reponse.

Yabek turned towards his friend and began gently shaking him, and soon realised from his heavy snoring that he was fast asleep.

"You're impossible, only you could fall asleep leaning over the side of a ship!" he exclaimed. He turned his attention back towards the gull that was now banking and gliding, and apparently having a great time playing in the air stream. He watched it swoop down towards the top of the waves almost touching them, before soaring upwards until it was high above the ship, where it would wheel around in circles slowly desending to its original position.

"What a show off," thought Yabek to himself.

"You don't look well!" yelled the bird.

"I'm fine just fine," snapped Yabek.

"Don't look it, don't look it," replied the bird.

And then it started again, that tightening of his tummy just like something was twisting a knot inside him: Yebek had no choice but to squeeze his tummy.

"Ow!" moaned the weasel beginning to writhe in discomfort.

"Told you, told you!" screamed the bird.

"Oh go away!"

But the gull was not laughing at the weasel as
Yabek thought he was; for he was actually a
kind and friendly bird.

He had seen this sort of sea sickness many
times before, and he knew of a few remedies
that might help with the problem.

"Ginger ale, ginger ale that will help," uttered
the bird.

But the thought of anything made of ale made
Yabek feel even worse, for part of the problem
was not only the movement of the ship, but the
fact that he had drank far too many jugs of ale
back in the Slippery Eel.

"Oh no, no more ale," uttered the weasel
sounding quite ill.

The bird thought for a moment.

"Try peppermint oil, peppermint oil will help."

"Peppermint oil?" replied Yabek with a
questioning tone.

"Peppermint oil," replied the bird nodding his
head.

"Peppermint oil, right I'll ask if they have any on
board.

Yabek loosened his grip on his sword as he no
longer felt threatened by the gull, and looked
at him with a smile. For a moment it appeared as
if a bond of friendship may have been formed
between the two animals. Feeling grateful for
the bird's advice he was about to express his

thanks, but he was too late do so. For without
warning the gull banked away from the ship, and
using the breeze to his advantage, promptly
gained height and left the ship behind, soon
becoming a mere dot in the sky that within
moments disappeared over the horizon.

The gull was heading towards his home of
Zanimos, and he felt happy that he would soon
be back there. Albert as he was known was
not a typical gull, for his kind are normally
gregarious creatures; you know they like to fly
around in flocks and play follow the leader, but
he was just as happy flying around on his own.
And besides he had a very special friend who
was just about his age who was such fun to be
with that he really didn't miss the company
of other gulls; and anyway none of them could
quite compare with this friend.

In comparison to King Clanask, Lady Bamboozler
sat shallower in the water, and being lighter
and more streamlined could easily outpace
the galleon. She had far less fire power
however, with only five cannons on either side
which were a much smaller bore than King
Clanask's. However, unlike the boar's ship Lady
Bamboozler did have a full complement of crew
courtesy of the rats who had deserted from

the Nordeamian army. And it was a useful fact that many of the rats had already received training as sailors before they ran away to Arven. Sileenus did not fully trust them, but he realised that as long as he paid them well they would remain loyal and do as they were told. Situated on the the main deck between the two masts of Lady Bamboozler was the captain's cabin where Belius, Gritch, Ruevic, and Ugg were sleeping face down on a hard wooden table, while comfortably tucked up under a warm blanket on his padded sofa was the snoring Sileenus. Lying on the floor underneath an old canvas sheet were the most unfriendly looking rats called Spika and Tufta. Throughout the early part of the journey they had each tugged at the sheet in an attempt to get fully covered, as it was not really big enough for both of them. But as neither had won this contest their brown hind quarters, and long pink tails were left uncovered.

Ever so slowly the fox stirred and after a collection of yawns and stretches sat up, rubbed his eyes, and twisted his neck from side to side a few times.

"Spika!" called out the fox, but there was little movement.

"Spika...Tufta!" he yelled, and the two rats quickly cast off the canvas sheet, rubbed the sleep from their eyes and stood promptly to attention.

"What is it boss?" questioned Spika.

"Would you mind popping on deck and finding out where we are?" asked Sileenus with an engaging smile

"Course not captain, we'll have a look for ya won't we Tufta," replied Spika giving his friend a quick glance.

"That we will Spika".

The two rats quickly exited the cabin and made their way to the stern of the ship, where another three rats were standing in a line holding on to the tiller that turned the rudder of the ship and steered her course. One large animal like Rufus or Barnaby could have done this job alone, but as rats are smaller it took three of them.

"Any idea where we are lads," asked Spika.

"We've just passed that estuary," replied the first rat.

"The one that comes from a lake," added the second.

"That's near to Zanimos Town," continued the third.

"That's good lads, we've not too far then," uttered Tufta.

"No not too far!" replied the three rats in chorus.

In the meantime a groggy Hubble had finally been awakened by Yabek and the two weasels were making their way towards Sileenus' cabin. While Hubble lumbered along the wooden deck bent forward and complaining about his sickness, Yabek walked ahead at a faster pace, for he felt more upbeat about the possibility of finding a cure for his tummy pain. This positive thought took his mind off his discomfort for a moment and encouraged him to break into a little sprint as he neared the cabin, but he had not accounted for the fact that the deck was wet and slippery.....

It was too late before he realised this, and with no time to slow down, his legs had been thrown up from underneath his body and landing on his bottom he began to skid uncontrollably towards the cabin doors. The doors were hinged to open inwards and as he collided with them they did just that, and he continued into the cabin. Seeing he was doomed to collide with a wooden table in the centre of the cabin, Yabek quickly covered his face with his front legs and closed his eyes. Fortunately however, his journey across the cabin floor came to an abrupt end, as the expected thud against the table was impeded by something much softer.

"Ow! Ow! What's going on!" shouted a complaining Belius as he began to shake his head and leave his slumber behind.

The others in the cabin began to wake too, and were soon joining Belius with their moaning and wining comments, even though they didn't know what had caused the disturbance.

"What's the meaning of this!" snapped Belius staring evilly at Yabek.

"Sorry Belius, I didn't mean to bump into you, only I slipped over!" uttered Yabek hoping that he had not angered his leader too much.

"Slipped over!" growled Belius.

"Yes," gulped Yabek.

"Why the rush?" uttered Gritch with a scowl.

"Well," began Yabek hesitantly," I'm after some peppermint oil."

"Peppermint Oil?!" shouted Belius.

For a few moments the only lingering sounds were the sea breeze blowing into the cabin, and the splashing of broken waves against the bow of the ship. And during this relative quiet Belius and Gritch looked at one another with blank expressions, for they had never heard of peppermint oil; but a softly spoken voice had the answer.

"I think this is what you're looking for weasel." All eyes immediately turned toward Sileenus who was holding a round bottle with a long neck, and as he brushed dust off the glass face a green liquid became clearly visible.

Yabek's face lit up."Is that it, is that peppermint oil?"
A wide smile slowly stretched across the fox's face before he nodded in confirmation.

Meanwhile, Hamilton was standing in the doorway of her cottage looking at the dark and gloomy clouds which hung in the Zanimos sky, when she caught sight of someone in the distance strolling along the lane which went past her cottage. Initially she couldn't quite make out who it was, but once the animal got nearer she could see that it was a pig.
It was Montagu; he was wearing red and green tartan trousers, a matching waistcoat and was carrying a large red umbrella to keep off the rain.
"Hello, what brings you out on such a horrible rainy day?" called Hamilton as he reached her gate.
Monty was a little caught out, as he hoped to sneak past her cottage without being seen.
"Ah, w-w-well," he began sounding a little hesitant.
Hamilton smiled at him. Well what?" she asked.
"Well, you see," replied Monty holding up a wicker basket. "I'm going to the pick some apples from the orchard and bake a great big

apple pie." Licking his lips he added, "I simply love apple pies."

"But Monty it's raining, why don't you wait until it's stopped."

"Because dear lady it is my day off, and I had already made plans to bake the pie today, and besides there is no way this silly old rain is going to stop me from doing as I wish."

Although the pig's reply was quite sharp it didn't dull the idea that had suddenly sprung to mind and her face lit up.

"Why don't you bring the apples back to my cottage and we can bake the pie here?"

Monty felt awkward; he didn't really want to share his apple pie with anyone.

"Well that's very nice of you, b-b-but I was thinking of having just a quiet tea on my own."

But Monty, I can ask some friends to come too, and I can make sandwiches, and cakes, and a pot of tea. Oh it will be lovely.

Please say you will?" she asked excitedly.

Hamilton's eager request made the pig more uncomfortable as he wasn't used to mixing with other animals and had become accustomed to his own company. His face was contorted as if in some sort of conflict and then from out of nowhere a voice suddenly entered his head. "Go on boy enjoy yourself, have fun, life is too short to miss out on these little parties."

It was a voice he had not heard for years; it was his father's who had sadly long since passed away.

And then much to Hamilton's surprise he unexpectedly accepted.

"Very well then, I shall," he replied, with just the tiniest of smiles.

Hamilton's clasped her front paws together and her expression was one of utter jubilation.

"That's wonderful, simply wonderful. Now what time shall I expect you?"

"Well it won't take me long to get to the orchard from here, and I've only to pick the apples and get back to your cottage. So about an hour I should think."

Hamilton looked back into her Hall and glanced at her dark oak granddaughter clock.

"Well its now two o'clock, and it will take an about an hour to bake the pie and prepare the rest of the tea. So I will ask the others to be here for... say four o'clock. Would that be alright?

"Yes that should be fine. Tell me Hamilton who are you inviting?"

Well, I shall ask Horace, Papachuan, oh and Rufus O'Malley of course," she announced, feeling proud to know the great dog personally.

"Oh that will be nice," he replied with slightly mixed feelings, for underneath it all he still felt uncertain about attending Hamilton's party.

"See you later then," uttered the smiling hamster.

"Righty – ho," replied Monty, as he turned around and started to walk away.

"And you promise you'll come!?" She called after him.

"Yes, yes I'll come!" he shouted back while waving his empty basket in the air.

Hamilton was thrilled to be holding a party in her cottage, as she did sometimes miss running her tea house in Ungerborg, and having her own tea party was a way of making up for it.

She was in fact so excited that in a rush to put her Wellington boots on, she tried to put one on the wrong foot.

"Oh silly old me," she uttered to herself.

Once she had corrected this error she took hold of her pretty flower patterned umbrella, and set off along the lane to tell her friends about the tea party. Off she went, skipping and jumping, and splashing in every puddle she could find; for she was in a very happy mood indeed. After she had gone about a mile, she came to a fork in the lane, where atop a rather corroded metal pole was a wooden sign indicating three destinations of the various paths. It had weathered badly over the years, and apart from being quite rotten, was gradually being covered by thick green ivy, which was twisting around it like a snake around its victim. However the ivy had been cut back a little and the writing on the sign had recently been repainted in clear white lettering.

Pointing back along the lane towards Hamilton's cottage the sign read 'The Sea', 'Delicious Orchard' and 'Smugglers Cove', and to the left it pointed the way to 'Zanimos Town'. However Hamilton took the right fork and proceeded towards 'Leverets Copse' as this was the way to her friend Horace's home.

After a short while the high dense hedgerows that had bordered the lane came to an end as Hamilton reached the entrance to a large green field, in the centre of which were half a dozen large oak trees. The largest of these was very peculiar in appearance, for instead of branches growing out of the top of it, the tree had a bright red roof in the shape of a church spire. And jutting out of the red tiles on one side of the roof was a peculiar looking chimney made of black metal tube which was bent and twisted, and crowned with an inverted conical cover to keep out the rain. At the base of the tree was a large wooden door also bright red, on which was a large brass knocker in the shape of a hare, and on either side of the door was a leaded window with red and white checked curtains drawn open.

Reaching the door, Hamilton gave three raps with the brass knocker. Thump! Thump! Thump! Moments later there was a clunking sound as the door lock was being undone, and once the squeaky door was opened, Horace appeared in the doorway, wearing a paisley print waistcoat.

"My dear Hamilton do come in" he began, with a beaming smile.

Taking her umbrella, the hare closed the door after her.

"Tea my dear?" he asked.

"Thank you, but I'm afraid I haven't got time now Horace".

"Oh what a shame," he replied sounding quite disappointed.

"Well actually, I've come to invite you to tea at my cottage and to sample some of Monty's apple pie".

Horace looked surprised.

"Apple pie, why that sounds lovely, but tell me um...is Monty really going to eat with us?"

"Well I know it's a first, but he said he would."

"Well I never thought I'd see the day."

"I know Horace, but it's a great shame for someone to spend so much time alone, and I realise he can be difficult, but perhaps once he begins to mix with us he might show a more friendly side?"

The hare frowned, "That's if he turns up of course."

"I do hope he does," replied Hamilton in a pleading tone.

Now hamsters are known to easily get in to a flap over things, and realising how much preparation was required for the tea party, her eyes opened as wide as saucers and she released a deep sigh.

Oh dear, oh dear, Horace," she began in a panicky tone of voice. "I don't wish to seem rude but I simply must get a move on for there's so much to do. I've got to tell Rufus and Papachuan, and then get back to my cottage and prepare the tea, and-"

"Now don't worry old girl," interrupted Horace putting a paw on her shoulder.

"I'll tell you what. I'll whiz around and tell the others, while you pop off home and prepare the tea," he added in a calm and helpful tone.

"Oh you are a dear that would be so helpful. After all it would take me ages with my little legs."

The thought of Hamilton's tiny legs going ninety to the dozen, brought a little smile to Horace, and he felt compelled to cough several times to refrain from laughing.

"I'll be off then Horace," she added, opening the front door.

"And what time would you like us for tea?"
asked the hare handing her the pretty little
umbrella.

"Just after four o'clock would be lovely."

As Hamilton made her way back across the field
Horace called out after her.

"You know you wouldn't think this was
September, it's more like April with these
heavy showers."

Hamilton turned and nodded in agreement.

Tonga left his men in the grand cabin checking
their weapons and walked on to the main deck.
He paused for a moment to take in a deep
breath of sea air and squinted as the rain hit
his eyes.

"See it's turned to rain then!" he shouted, as he
approached Charlie and Rumick.

"I'm told there can be a change in weather
as soon as you pass them mountains," replied
Rumick turning and pointing at the distant
Chameleon Mountains.

"Yeah, so have I," added Charlie.

"How much longer do you think Rummy?"
enquired Tonga.

"I don't really know captain as I've not sailed
this far south before, but from what I've been
told, once the chalk cliffs appear we need look

out for the old harbour entrance, which is tricky to find."

"Well we'd better keep our eyes peeled then," replied Tonga.

A broad grin appeared on the collie. "I've got just the thing that might help there," he uttered, holding out a brass telescope.

Tonga's eyes were on stalks. "A telescope, a telescope, why I've always wanted one!" he exclaimed excitedly.

Taking the telescope, Tonga extended it fully and began to peer through the magnifying glass.

"Wow!" he uttered.

"I can see the beach, and the waves crashing on to the pebbles.

He took it from his eye and smiled at Charlie.

"It's amazing!" he giggled sounding like an excited piglet.

A warm expression came across the collie. "You can keep it if you like; I have several in my shop."

Tonga's face lit up. "Oh that is wonderful, thank you Charlie."

For the next half hour or so Tonga was like a child with a new toy, spending every moment looking through his telescope. He must have viewed every point on the compass, but alas there was no harbour entrance. But after sometime scanning the tall forbidding eastern cliffs of Zanimos for what seemed an age, something caught his eye.....

"It's there, it's there!" he yelled at the top of his voice.

"Turn to your right Rummy," he continued.

"To starboard you mean captain," replied Rumick.

"Yes, yes, over there," he pointed.

Charlie and Rumick looked at each other realising they were near the end of their sea trip and felt a little disappointed as both were enjoying the sea voyage very much; however they knew that time was of the essence if they were to intercept the weasels, and so the quicker they landed the better.

Rumick spun the helm and the King Clanask quickly responded accordingly heading westwards towards the land of Zanimos, and as she did so the north easterly winds drove her more urgently onwards. For a moment Rumick could not see the entrance to the Old Harbour and was purely dependant on Captain Tonga for his guidance. All he could see was a wall of tall cliffs towering above, and as the ruggedness of their white chalk grew nearer an emptiness hit his stomach as he became worried about crashing in to them. Then gradually and greatly to his relief, the giant white cliffs opened out like a gigantic mouth to reveal a narrow channel,

and Rumick's upset tummy disappeared as
quickly as it had come.

"Wont' be long now!" he shouted.

"That's good," added the collie.

"Oh Charlie can you go and get my lads, while I
keep a look out?" asked Tonga.

"Charlie feeling thrilled to be on the adventure
was most happy to obey his friend.

"Of course captain," he said with a smile.

"Tonga gave him a friendly salute and then
returned to studying the layout of the land
through his telescope.

Charlie was still very fit for an elderly collie
and in fact could move quite quickly; so dashing
down the steps from the helm deck he turned
left, opened an ill fitting door and climbed down
more steps until he reached the grand cabin.

As he entered he was initially taken aback by
the untidiness of the cabin which looked like
it had not been cleaned since the Nordeamian
wars. In those days this would have been the
captain's cabin, and during the last great see
battle it was occupied by Admiral Tonga; but
alas it now looked more like a storeroom than an
officer's quarters.

There were several open wooden trunks covered
in spider's webs, old paintings depicting sea
battles hanging at every angle on the walls but
straight, and there were neatly wound coils of

rope lying about the floor. At the back near the grubby looking rear windows was a rather grand looking oval table with gilded edges that was covered in all sorts of old things like sea charts, muskets, jugs, and rum bottles; all of which were heavily covered in dust. But the boar soldiers soon grabbed his attention as Charlie became captivated by the thoroughness in which they prepared their weapons. Sergeant Kolo was carefully and deliberately rubbing a stone along each edge of his slender sword known as a rapier, to ensure they had the sharpest cut. Meanwhile his son Tunashi was running his eyes along the shafts of his arrows to satisfy himself that they were straight. Charlie had seen the youngster mature and was struck by how one could be forgiven for thinking a master bowman could be so tender in years. The collie not being a fighting animal couldn't help but feel contradiction in their behaviour, as he witnessed them lovingly prepare these implements of war which may soon be used to kill.

Short swords were carried by Buna and Wicklop, but these were not their main weapons of choice. Buna favoured the musket and was cleaning the inside of the barrel with a rod covered in cotton, while Wicklop who was standing away from the others practicing thrusts and parries with his trusted glaive; a weapon with a long wooden shaft and a pointed blade and hook at the striking end. Unlike Montagu who was an ordinary pig, the wild boars of Unger had a dangerously sharp tusk protruding from each side of their lower jaw line on either side of their mouth which made them look altogether more war like.

Watching the boars made Charlie feel a little in awe of these professional warriors, for they were trained soldiers, while he was just an ordinary shopkeeper with no military training whatsoever.

"Good job they're on my side," he thought to himself.

"Ahem," he began, clearing his throat to get their attention, which did the trick as the four of them turned towards him.

"Right then lads, we've arrived at Zanimos and your captain wants you topside."

After a quick nod of acknowledgement to Charlie, Kolo shouted his order.

"Right you horrible lot let's get a move on then!" he beckoned, and the four soldiers brushed past Charlie so quickly that he almost toppled backwards.

Meanwhile, Rumick and Tonga were staring up at the tall white cliffs in disbelief at their size.

"I've never seen cliffs like this, they seem to go on forever," said Rumick.

"Must be over a hundred foot high too!" exclaimed Tonga craning his upwards as far as it would go.

Walking over to the side of the deck, he looked down at the calm sea, which due to its clarity gave the impression of being shallow enough for one to reach out and touch the seabed - this worried him a little and he turned to Rumick to express his concern.

"Better watch out Rummy it doesn't look very deep, and we don't want to run aground."

"Can you take the helm captain and I'll have a look."

"Of course!" replied Tonga excitedly, as he had longed to steer the ship ever since they had set sail.

"Keep a straight course between the cliffs, okay?" uttered Rumick, moving aside to allow Tonga to take hold of the thick wooden wheel. Charlie and the other boars were now on deck, and they all shared a common look of concern as they watched Tonga steering the galleon along the straight between the tall cliffs.

Tonga saw their expressions and smiled.

"Don't worry lads, it's a piece of cake, "he uttered, trying to cover up a slight nervousness.

However steering a ship competently can take a lot of time to master, for one must understand the effects of tides, currents and the direction and strength of the wind, and the response of the ship. Captain Tonga had no experience of these forces and found it difficult to adjust the course correctly, and as a result King Clanask began to drift closer and closer to the northern cliffs. Tonga seeing he was dangerously off course began to panic and quickly spin the helm to port, but not being used to the rudiments of steering he overdid it, and the ship suddenly veered off in the opposite direction. Charlie and the four soldiers looked on helplessly as the ship sailed on out of control, and headed towards certain doom, but thankfully Rumick came to the rescue in time. "Let me Captain," he uttered taking the helm and correcting their course; and everybody on board including Tonga gave a huge sigh of relief. After quickly undertaking some slight corrections Rumick soon had the ship back on course safely in the middle of the channel again. "I think I need a few lessons in steering Rummy," uttered Tonga.

"Be glad to do that on the way home captain."

"Look forward to it...oh what about the depth. Do you think we have enough water to enter the harbour?"

"We'll be fine captain," replied Rumick
confidently."
"But it looks so shallow," replied Tonga spotting
a shoal of silver bellied fish swimming out from
underneath the ship.
"That's because it's so clear...you see it's so
calm here that the bottom is not churned up
making the sea cloudy."
"So we have enough depth?"
"Believe me captain we've more than enough."
Then much to the surprise of everyone on
board, the two high cliffs began to draw rapidly
apart and King Clanask entered the broader
waters of the Old Harbour of Zanimos.
"Prepare for action lads!" shouted Tonga and
his men stood ready, each of them casting their
eyes along this foreign coastline in search of
movement.

Turning the ship southwards, Rumick looked
across the harbour towards a wooden quay
stretching the full length of the western cliffs,
where to his astonishment there was no activity
whatsoever.
Unable to resist glancing upwards to the top of
the cliffs, his heart skipped a beat as he spied
half a dozen large cannons pointing towards
them. Their presence petrified him, there was
little he could do to avoid being sunk, and as

time ticked away he could only wait for the
booming fire to begin; but mercifully the guns
remained silent. Releasing a deep sigh of relief
he began soaking up this strange environment,
and remembered how Zanimos and Unger were
great allies during the war with Nordeamia and
how important this harbour was in defeating
their navy.

With its narrow channel and steep cliffs
cocooning the harbour, it was a natural shelter
from the fiercest storms, its deep waters
allowed the mooring of great ships and from the
tall cliffs huge cannons could destroy unwanted
intruders; but sadly this once bustling harbour
was now completely run down and deserted.
Rumick looked upon the half moon shaped
buildings that nestled against the cliffs once
used for storing goods, provisions, tools and
parts for repairing the ships. The walls and
roofs of these structures had been covered
with mortar and painted white, but over time
much of the mortar had peeled off revealing
the bare red brick work underneath; which in
some cases had crumbled away. All buildings
were identical, each having a central arched
doorway with two heavy oak doors that opened
outwards, and a square window on either side
with iron railings across it. Some of the oak
doors were now rotten and just about hanging

on by their buckled hinges, and much of the black paint had peeled off the window railings revealing brown rust. For a moment he was concerned at how quickly King Clanask was approaching these dilapidated structures and began to feel annoyed at himself for forgetting to give the order to lower the sails. But to his relief the sudden reduction in speed signified the sailors had used their inititive and done the job without his command.

Rumick carefully adjusted course to enable a gently approach, and within a short while the galleon gently brushed her starboard side against the wooden structure, whereupon the boar spun the helm hard to port to bring her tightly up against the quay.

"Right lads secure the mooring lines!" he shouted excitedly.

Montagu Frazzelbach

Chapter 5
Missing Guest

As soon as she got back to her cottage Hamilton donned her apron and got to work setting the table and preparing food for her guests. She had created a variety of cakes, and while these were baking in the oven she made sandwiches, and prepared the pastry for the apple pie. On opening her ice box, Hamilton was pleased to see a pot of fresh cream on one of the shelves.

"Oh how lovely, that's just what we need for the apple pie, now what else is there to do?" she uttered, taking the freshly baked cakes from the oven.

Pausing for thought she looked around.

"The table is laid, the sandwiches and cakes are ready, and there are cups and saucers on the table."

A little smile crept across her face as she looked on with pride at her beautifully laid table.

Six mats with beautifully painted floral designs were positioned evenly around the dark oak table, each having its own pretty cotton serviette. Highly polished petite silver cake knives and forks were on each side of the mats, and to the right of each mat was a square floral patterned coaster on which Hamilton had placed her most precious white bone china cups and saucers.

Taking the cakes off the baking tray she put them on a round three tiered display stand close to a large salver of sandwiches in the centre of the table, and then covered everything with muslin cloths to maintain freshness.

Feeling very pleased with herself, she gently clapped her paws together as Hamsters do when they are excited.

"Just perfect, just perfect" she said, congratulating herself.

Wondering what the weather was like she then skipped across the room and peered out of the window.

The sky was full of dark black clouds and rain was still teaming down, and as there was no sign of Monty, and nothing further to do, she made herself a cup of tea, and settled down in her favourite armchair. It had been a very busy day, and she was now starting to feel very tired; so tired in fact that within a few minutes she was sound asleep.

It had been a lengthy trek across the Chameleon Mountains, and an hour had passed since bright yellow rays of sunshine signified the beginning of the day, but at long last Brodney and Barnaby reached the outskirts of Zanimos town.

As the two of them reached a humped backed wooden bridge Barnaby decided to turn about and look at the vast range of yellow Mountains they had left behind. He had barely had time to study the different crests, shapes and contours, let alone trace the path they had taken, when the spirits decided it was time for a change – and so it began......

Commencing from the western edge of the mountains, a yellow peak became suddenly infused with an orange hue which began to glow more strongly moment by moment, until it completely eclipsed the yellow; after which it raced down its slopes to the base completing the transition to orange. Next a flickering streak of orange leapt like a leaping ballet dancer across to the adjacent peak and within moments the second mountain had also changed colour. Due to the ever increasing pace of the energetic orange flame racing from peak to peak, it was only a few moments before the whole mountain range had become orange. Barnaby was completely flabbergasted, and looked on intently following every change, and then assuming the transformation was complete he excitedly turned towards the badger.

"The wizards work?"

Brodney smiled and raised his eyebrows, "Aye tis them alright."

Barnaby was enthralled by the whole process of this amazing transformation, but he was in for more surprises, for barely had the mountains taken on their new colour when the most eastern peak burst into a shining and flickering whiteness so bright that it appeared to cast a beam of light on to Zanimos Town. There followed dazzling white flashes across the whole mountain range, accompanied by subdued rumblings which added a mysterious atmosphere to the proceedings. The complete metamorphosis took the spirits less than thirty seconds and yet when complete there was another surprise; for no longer were the mountains orange, but a brilliant white so pure that one could be forgiven for thinking snow was upon them.

"Wow!" exclaimed Barnaby.

"You'll get used to it," replied a nonchalant Brodney.

"I'm not sure I will," chuckled the Newfoundland.

The two of them crossed the creaky old bridge and soon reached the multi coloured buildings of Zanimos Town, where Barnaby feeling close to his friend suddenly quickened his pace leaving Brodney struggling to keep up. But the badger was not one to complain and hurried along as fast as he could; although he was most grateful when the Newfoundland came to a sudden halt in the town square. Unfortunately Brodney had barely caught his breath before Barnaby set off again towards the town pond and all the while he was sniffing the air in search of a familiar scent. Initially there was nothing, but then out of nowhere came a familiar odour, and one he knew well.

Realising his friend had shared his presence; he began tracing the origin and soon trained his eyes on the opposite side of the pond. Strangely, what looked like a wooden bench was almost completely shrouded by a thick grey mist; and although he could make out a dark shadow on the bench it was completely indiscernible. However, his sense of smell had never let him down before and knowing the end of his journey was nearly complete he increased his speed and ran as fast as his sturdy legs could carry him; there was only one thing on his mind – meeting his friend.

Not bothered about sticking to the footpath, he raced around the edge of the pond, churning up clumps of grass with his claws as they gripped tightly on the turf, and as he neared the bench the sinister mist quickly faded to reveal the most welcome sight.

"Rufus, Rufus!" he yelled.

As the Newfoundland rushed towards his friend, a wide jolly smile crept across Rufus' face and he jumped from the bench and stood waiting for Barnaby to reach him.

Moments later they were together, holding each other's front paws and dancing around in circles, laughing and screaming with joyous excitement. They were so pleased to see one another they shouted out each other's name out at the top of their voices while hugging and laughing.

Brodney feeling a little exhausted had taken his time to reach them, and when he arrived on the scene he began to shake his head in consternation at the hollering, laughing and general excitement of the two giant dogs.

"It's marvellous, simply marvellous to see you Barnaby!" cried out Rufus.

"Oh and you too."

"But why are you here my old friend?" questioned Rufus settling down on his four paws and sounding more serious.

"It's your father's idea really,"

"My father?"

"Yes you see King O-"

"Shush!" uttered Rufus not wishing Brodney to hear that he was a prince.

"Sorry," replied Barnaby looking a little embarrassed.

"Go on, go on," ushered Rufus.

"Well you see your father realised that I was really miserable since you had left and my heart wasn't in my work, and so he gave me leave to come and find you."

"And what else?" asked Rufus knowing that wasn't the only reason his father would let Barnaby come in search of him.

"What else?" replied Barnaby scratching his chin.

"Umm," nodded Rufus. "That's not the only reason you're here is it my friend?"

Barnaby's eyes moved from side to side for a moment while he wondered what his friend meant, and then it came to him and his face lit up.

"No it's not," he giggled.

Feeling excited about the surprise he had in store for his friend Barnaby hastily undid his

back pack and laid it on the ground, but as he
grasped hold of the blanket it was he who had
the surprise. "Oh my goodness!" he exclaimed.
As he stood holding the empty blanket,
a combination of despondency and shame
overwhelmed Barnaby who bowed his head and
slumped his shoulders, desperately trying to
think when he could have lost the sword; he had
it with him when he left Ungerborg therefore
there was only one possibility.

"Oh Rufus, I'm so sorry," he began in a
miserable tone.

"I can't believe it, really I can't. I must have
lost it somewhere along the journey."

"Lost what?" queried Brodney.

"A sword, a very special sword," replied a
melancholy Barnaby.

"Well I got a few swords in my shop. You could
always buy one of them...after all a swords a
sword," replied Brodney.

"No it's not," snapped Barnaby
uncharacteristically.

"Hmm," grunted Brodney.

"On the contrary he's right badger, a sword is
not a sword is not a sword," uttered Rufus.

A perplexing expression crossed the face of
the badger.

"What you on about?"

The malamute smiled.

"Not all swords are the same Brodney. For example a good sword should possess balance, strength, and perhaps even beauty...but a great sword, a really great sword like this, will feel at one with its master."

On hearing his friend's words Barnaby instantly swivelled around and gave a massive sigh of relief as he set eyes on the sword he believed to be lost.

"Thank goodness you've got it!" he uttered at the top of his voice.

"Apologies Barnaby but I simply couldn't help myself."

This was yet another example of the malamute's powers, for being unable to contain his eagerness he used a little magic to get possession of the sword without being seen.

Barnaby smiled, "You never cease to amaze me."

Clasping the wire wrapped grip of silver and gold, Rufus held the sword above his head and studied the long broad double edged blade and golden cross guard. Thrilled at holding this beautiful crafted weapon he was as always captivated by the beauty of the gleaming vibrant red and purplish hues of the ruby set in to its gold pommel. Slowly twisting and rotating the great sword to familiarise himself with its weight, the engraved runic symbols on one side of the blade glistened and sparkled making the sword look alive.

Holding the weapon still for a moment, he stared deeply at the ancient words - *Honour - Truth - Justice - Protector - North of the World* - and became imbued with a great sense of pride and responsibility; for he knew that one day soon the fate of his father's kingdom would be his to determine. Thinking quite deeply about this princely duty he quickly realised the significance behind Barnaby bringing him the sword, his consciousness was ignited with alarm and misgivings.

"I suspect treachery afoot," he pondered solemnly.

Nevertheless he wasn't left to dwell on this for very long as an excited Barnaby grabbed his attention.

"A show, Rufus, a show!?" pleaded his friend clapping frantically.

"A show?" quizzed Brodney.

"Oh yes you watch, you'll love it!" exclaimed Barnaby.

The badger looked indifferent, "Will I?"

Rufus wasn't one to show off, but he was so thrilled to be holding the magical sword once again that he was unable to resist the temptation to grant his friend's wishes.

"Well just a teeny one then," he agreed.

However his raised eyebrows hinted to Barnaby
it would be more than just a little performance,
and the Newfoundland immediately understood
he was in for something special.

Barely had Rufus' eyes left Barnaby before
he began to demonstrate his awesome skill of
sword craft.

He moved at incredible speed guiding the sword
in rapid fluid motions including arcs, strikes,
thrusts, and parries, and all the while he would
perform the most elaborate gymnastic twists,
turns and spinning leaps, that were truly magical
to behold. The display looked like a beautiful
dance; full of graceful flowing progressions,
perfect timing and fluid steps, but hidden
within this impeccably executed spectacle was
a lethal precision that only a warrior of the
greatest training could perform. Not normally
an animal to be easy impressed, Brodney found
himself totally mesmerised by every new action
the malamute made, for he had never seen
anything like it in his life. Even though Barnaby
had watched Rufus display his amazing ability
many times before, he was always surprised by
the new and unusual actions his friend would
incorporate which made every performance
unique.

Having completed his final extraordinary feats
Rufus slowly spiralled down from a great height,

settled back on the ground, bowed his head, and pointed the sword up to the sky.

"It's your sword now Rufus, you realise what that means?" uttered Barnaby reverently.

"Yes my friend I do. But all being well my father should have many a new spring left in him."

"I hope so too, but he wanted you to have the protector's sword, so that if the worst happens no one will oppose you when you return to the north."

Being aware that the sensitive nature of this conversation should not be overheard by the badger, Barnaby stepped closer to his friend.

"After all your uncle Sayden is always waiting for an excuse to take over your father's kingdom," he whispered.

"Yes I know," replied the malamute gravely.

"And should that ever happen, I will return to take it back and banish Sayden from our lands," snarled Rufus under his breath. The idea of his untrustworthy uncle taking over the throne had enraged him, and he wanted to vent his anger, but the probing expression of Brodney made him realise he must say no more, and so subduing this fury he smiled cordially at the badger.

"Thank you Brodney for bringing my best friend to Zanimos and making me so happy."

"My pleasure," stuttered the badger still in disbelief at the Malamutes incredible display.

"And I must thank you too," added Barnaby.

The badger gave a nod to acknowledge the Newfoundland's thanks.

"Well come on Barnaby I'll show you around, or would you rather have a rest?" uttered Rufus.

"Well to be honest I am a little pooped."

"Okay well I'll show you my barn and you can have a rest there."

"Barn?" queried Barnaby.

"Yes I've bought a barn, and I'm going to convert it into the most beautiful house...well when I get the time of course."

"Barnaby felt rather surprised that his friend had bought a barn to live in as he expected something much grander, but nevertheless he wasn't about to spoil his friends enthusiasm.

"Oh, yes that would be nice," he replied trying to sound upbeat.

"Follow me then," beckoned Rufus as he began to walk around the pond.

The other two followed after him, and as they reached the town square Brodney spotted something in the corner of his eye.

"Look there!" he yelled.

Startled by Brodney's call, Rufus and Barnaby turned their heads and beheld an object travelling towards them from the south; it was moving at tremendous speed and as it raced towards them it a trail of dust followed closely behind it. Brodney peered at the object and for a moment couldn't think for the life of him what it was; and then it came to him.

"That's gotta be Horace, no one else can run that fast!" he shouted.

"Wonder what's up?" he continued.

Barnaby looked at Rufus and shrugged his shoulders wondering what it could be, while Rufus with his magical powers and incredible senses examined it more closely.

He looked in front of the dust trail and could make out a windswept brown face with a small nose, highly focused eyes, big ears and large hind legs that were driving it forward and creating the dust.

"You're right Brodney it is Horace," he announced.

Barnaby shrugged his shoulders. "Wish I had your sight."

Brodney scratched his head." You can see him?"

"One only has to look Brodney," replied Rufus.

The badger squinted his eyes in an effort to see more clearly, but it didn't improve things.

"Well I can't, but it must be the hare?!"

In a very short while the guessing was over for Brodney as he could clearly identify Horace quickly approaching, but oddly enough although he was now getting close he didn't appear to be slowing down, and continued rushing towards them. For a few moments it didn't look like he would be able to stop, but they needn't have worried for the hare leant back on his hind feet and came to an abrupt halt just in time; however he had created a plume of dust so large that for a moment he completely disappeared in it.

Becoming visible once again Horace shook himself several times before scratching his face and ears to brush the dust away.

"I'm so glad I've found you!" he exclaimed excitedly.

"Really?" replied the malamute with a quizzical expression.

"Yes, you see you're all invited to tea at Hamilton's cottage."

"Oh how super," replied Rufus.

Horace was a little shocked to see a newcomer in their midst, and more so that the animal was almost as big as Rufus.

"And who might you be," questioned Horace looking up at the large brown dog.

"Why I'm Barnaby, and I'm very pleased to meet you," replied the Newfoundland holding out a huge paw.

Horace was a little nervous and looked towards Rufus for reassurance.

"It's alright Horace, he's my best friend,"
uttered the malamute with a smile.

"Pleased to meet you Horace," said the
Newfoundland and the two animals shook paws
and exchanged friendly expressions.

"And I'm pleased to meet you Barnaby."
Never one to shy away from food and drink
Barnaby looked towards Horace with an
appealing expression.

"I don't suppose I could come too?" he asked.

"Why of course, I'm certain Hamilton would
welcome any friend of Rufus."

The malamute's face lit up as he envisaged the
lovely spread that would await them.

"You will simply love her tea Barnaby. Why she
makes the most perfect sandwiches, and as for
her chocolate cake, well words simply cannot
describe it," said Horace licking his lips in
anticipation.

"Hamilton...didn't she own the tea house in
Ungerborg before selling it to Sasha?" asked
Barnaby.

"That she did, and bought my lovely old cottage
too," explained Brodney.

"Well anyway what time is tea, Horace?"
enquired Rufus eagerly.

"About four o'clock."

"Oh not too long then," responded the malamute
happily.

"No not long. Now if you'll excuse me I must dash." uttered Horace quickly racing away in to the distance leaving a tell tale cloud of dust in his trail.

"Are you coming to tea Brodney," asked Barnaby looking towards the badger.

"Nope, I'd better get back and see the missus."

"Quite right too, I'm sure Mrs Badger will be glad to see you," said Rufus.

"I spose so," grunted the badger, as he turned around and walked across the square towards his shop.

"He's a funny one," tittered Barnaby.

"Yes he's a bit gruff, but I've heard he's brave and dependable."

Barnaby nodded, "That's true enough, he proved that in Ungerborg."

"Really...well come and see my barn, and on the way you can tell me all about it."

Barnaby was delighted to recite the events that took place in Hamilton's tea house, but what made it all the more special was at last being in the company of his great friend Rufus O' Malley.

The wicker basket was full to the brim of perfectly round green cooking apples which Monty had plucked from the trees in Delicious Orchard, many of which still had stalks and leaves attached. But he had now been tempted by a tree full of deep purple plums that were just ripe and ready to be picked, and although he had eaten four of five already he still hadn't had his fill.

Standing on the top rung of a wooden ladder he was stretching out to reach a large plum at the end of a branch, but no matter how much he leant over he couldn't quite reach it. On several occasions he had almost got it, his slight touch causing it to sway a little but it had hung on and not fallen. Feeling rather frustrated now, the pig's desire to reach the plum had outweighed his thoughts of safety, and he began to lean over further than ever before, precariously balancing of one leg. At last he was able to take hold of the elusive fruit and was overcome by a great sense of triumph as he pulled it free from the branch.

"Got you!" he shouted with joy.

He felt safe, secure and pleased with himself as he straightened his body and his two legs rested on the ladder one again.

"Safe and sound," he thought to himself with a deep breath.

But then it started; it felt like an earthquake shaking the ladder back and forwards, back and forwards, moving it away from the tree and then bashing back against it. He held on as tightly as he could and closed his eyes hoping that the quake would stop; but it went on and on, until it became so violent that no matter how he tried he could no longer hold on. And then it was all like a dream; a dream in slow motion, as he left the ladder and fell backwards. Backwards and downwards he went releasing his prize plum as he did so and he could do nothing as it disappeared from sight. For a moment his fall was checked by his waistcoat pocket being caught on a large branch, but his salvation was only momentary for the pocket ripped away from his waistcoat and he plummeted earthward. Downwards through the air he travelled, until a hard thud signalled the end of his journey, as contact was made with the ground; and then all was black.

His eyesight out of focus, he couldn't initially make out the shapes of the faces that looked upon him, but after shaking his head in an effort to clarify his vision, the silhouettes were gradually filled with distinct expressions the like of which he had never seen.
There were five or six of them peering down at him, each one had sharp yellow teeth and beady eyes and their constant cackling made him feel very uneasy. Two of them grabbed him by the waistcoat and pulled him upwards towards their

faces, so close that his snout almost touched their noses. Monty had never ever experienced such fear before, for although he was larger than they were, he was a banker and not a warrior; as these animals clearly looked to be.

"Hello piggy," uttered one of the animals under his breath.

"Ahhhhhhhhhh!" cried out Monty fearing for his life.

To Hamilton it had only seemed like minutes, but in fact it was much later when her slumber was broken by a loud rapping noise. After rubbing her eyes and stretching her arms she got up from her chair and walked across to the front door.

"Who is it?" she called, still half asleep.

"Why its Rufus, and I have Papachuan, Horace and my friend Barnaby with me."

Hamilton immediately recognised the strong and clear deep voice of Rufus O'Malley, and opened her front door to behold the welcoming sight of friendly faces.

"Hello Hamilton!" they all said in chorus.

"Hello everyone, it's lovely to see you, please come in," she replied, putting a paw to her mouth to cover yet another yawn.

As her friends entered the hallway she couldn't help but notice a giant brown dog bringing up the rear and for an instant was quite surprised by the presence of this stranger.

"I hope you don't mind my old friend Barnaby coming to tea?" uttered Rufus.

"Of course not, he's most welcome."

The Newfoundland looked down on her with a warm smile and held out a paw. "Thank you very much my dear."

"My pleasure."

Then the giant dog and the petite hamster shook paws and another friendship was formed.

"I must say I never thought I would see another dog as large as you Rufus?" pronounced Hamilton closing the door.

The malamute smiled.

"He's not really as big, he's just more portly," laughed Rufus tapping his friend's tummy.

Barnaby seeing the funny side of it took in a sharp intake of breath as if pretending to be shocked by the comment.

"Oh the cheek of it, the absolute cheek of it," he spouted.

Rufus looked on with an amusing but questioning countenance.

"You know I'm only joking now don't you?"

"Of course I do slim," replied his friend, and the two of them laughed.

Within moments, the cottage that had been so quiet and peaceful was full of chattering voices.

"I can't wait to tuck into Hamilton's lovely apple pie!" said Rufus.

"I think her cheese and tomato sandwiches are simply superb!" said Papachuan.

"And I'm dying to taste your chocolate cake Hamilton!" added Barnaby excitedly.

"Me too!" added Horace, with expectant wide open eyes.

"Apple pie!" exclaimed Hamilton sounding rather worried.

"Why yes Hamilton, we can't wait, can we?" replied Rufus looking at his friends, and licking his lips.

"Yummy!" said Barnaby rubbing his tummy in anticipation.

"Oh but you're far too early, Monty hasn't come back with the apples yet," uttered Hamilton.

"Early!" replied Papachuan, taking a watch from his waistcoat pocket. "Why Horace told us to be here at four o'clock, and it's after four now," he continued.

"But it can't be gone four o'clock, why I only fell asleep for a moment, and anyway Monty would be here by now...wouldn't he?

"Hamilton I can assure you it is eight minutes past four exactly," replied Papachuan, peering over his round spectacles.

Hamilton began to look extremely worried and dashed out into the hall to look at her granddaughter clock, where much to her dread, it agreed with Papachuan's watch. Stepping back in to the parlour she felt disappointed that Monty had not turned up with the apples as he had promised and her glum expression made it clear she was upset.

"What is it, what's the matter Hamilton?" asked Rufus in a concerned tone.

"It's Monty, I wonder where he's got to?"

"Now don't look so worried old girl, knowing Monty he's probably taken the apples home. After all he's really quite a loner you know." said Horace in gentle tone.

"He's more interested in the running the bank than making friends is our Monty," added Papachuan.

"But he said he would come, and I'm certain he wouldn't let us down!" replied Hamilton sounding rather agitated.

"Then what is to be done?" said Horace.

With the exception of Rufus, all the animals looked at each other with blank expressions, as they were not really sure of the best thing to do. They were all sensitive to Hamilton feelings, for her disappointment was clearly shown on her face. But they all felt in their hearts that as Monty was not a very sociable animal, he had just picked his apples and gone straight home.

"Look Hamilton, I know you are disappointed that Monty hasn't turned up, but the five of us can still have a lovely tea party, can't we?" suggested Papachuan in a caring tone.

"Yes, and you've prepared such a wonderful feast that it would be a shame to let it all go to waste," uttered the ever hungry Barnaby with a smile.

While the other animals were trying to cheer up Hamilton, a strange feeling rather like a sixth sense came over Rufus. And through his perceptive powers felt something unpleasant had befallen Monty; he didn't know what it was, but he could feel he was in danger and knew he must act quickly.

"My dear friends," he began solemnly. "This isn't the time to think about food, for I strongly believe something horrible has befallen Montagu Frazzelbach.

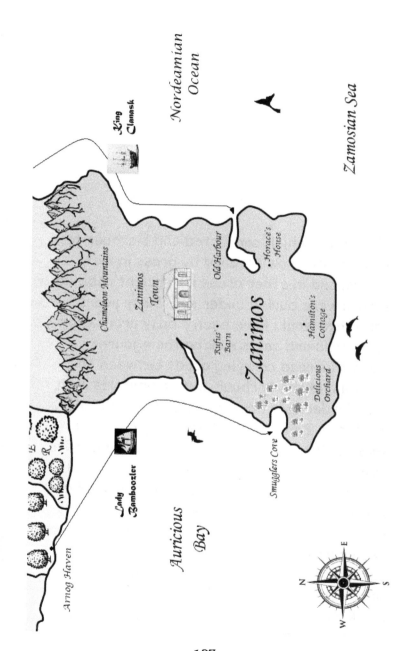

King Clannsk

Nordeamian Ocean

Zamosian Sea

Chameleon Mountains

Zanimos Town

Old Harbour

Horace's House

Rufus' Barn

Hamilton's Cottage

Zanimos

Delicious Orchard

Smugglers Cove

Lady Bamboozler

Auricious Bay

Arnog Haven

N E W S

Chapter 6
Searching Begins

Fleet Road which connected Old Harbour to Zanimos was now covered by grass in most places, and in other areas its ancient cobbled stones were buried under soil. Many years ago there would have been a busy procession of animals and carts making their journey along this road carrying goods between the capital and the harbour. But sea battles with the Nordeamian Empire had put an end to all this as Zanimos had lost every one of its ships, and as it could not afford to rebuild its navy, the harbour had been left unused and derelict. Today only the solitary figure of a yellow Labrador could be seen trotting along the disused road, he was a youngster of about two years old and had a very mischievous, but likeable expression. He reached a point where the road sloped downward through the chalk cliffs to the harbour below, and paused

and lifted his nose toward the easterly wind.
He breathed in the cool fresh air for a few
moments, savouring the odours that blew in
across the headland. Loving the smell of the
salty sea air and the feeling of the wind blowing
in his face he took off and began running over
the gentle rolling slopes of grass that lay on
top of the cliffs. Occasionally he leapt off the
ground hoping against hope that the wind might
just lift him into the air and that he could fly
like a bird; but this was never going to happen
and he quickly fell back to the ground and
continued on his way. He was having wonderful
fun and enjoying every moment but while he
was running and jumping and having a grand old
time playing in the wind, he was not aware that
he was being watched by something circling
high up above. Alas, it was far too late for the
dog to detect the creature as it dived towards
him and began to approach at such a high speed
that it would be upon him in seconds. The dog
continued to race over the rolling banks of
rough grass and leapt from one mound to the
next trying to avoid falling into the ditches
below. He had perfected his timing for bouncing
between these mini hills and was just about
to take his next leap when a series of high
pitched screams and beating wings spoilt his
concentration causing him to lose his footing

and slide down head first into the bottom of a small muddy ditch.

"Ha ha ha, ha ha ha!" cried the bird and the dog looked up to see a Herring Gull circling over head while laughing out loud.

"That's it, that's it!" shouted the dog scraping a piece of mud from the end of his nose.

He then jumped to his feet and racing up the small hill he leapt high in to the air and opened his jaws and snapped at the bird; missing it by only a few inches.

"Ha ha, ha ha, missed me, missed me!" laughed the bird.

"I'll get ya!" barked the dog.

The bird then took off along the top of the cliffs with the dog running after it, barking excitedly as it did so. There was no chance that the four legged animal could catch the speedy bird, and the bird would tease the dog by slowing right down and flying just out of its reach; sometimes hovering motionless in the air. However the dog was fast for his breed and quite acrobatic too, and on several occasions he put on an extra burst of speed and found additional spring in his limbs which enabled him get within just a few inches of the bird, but the result was always the same; a gnashing of teeth and a mouthful of fresh air as the bird flew just out of reach and began taunting him once more.

"Ha ha, ha ha, ha ha!" screamed the gull hovering over the dogs head.

To the dog he looked very cocky, and he felt very frustrated that he could not quite catch him.

"If only I could run faster, and jump higher, I'd show him," he thought. He was certainly not one to give up easily and after catching his breath he resumed his quest of catching the elusive bird. This went on for some time, with the dog feeling forever more confident that he would at last catch the bird; but in truth he never got any closer as the bird always managed to stay safely out of reach. But then much to the dog's surprise it happened; the bird slowed down to torment the dog as he always did, and the dog leapt upwards ever hopeful of catching him, but for some inexplicable reason the bird froze motionless in the air staring out to sea as if hypnotised, and the dog ceased the moment and struck. But what happened next can only be described as panic by both parties, as the gull thinking his end was near began shrieking at the top of his voice, and the dog's initial sensation of triumph changed to horror as his mouth was filled with a salty tasting Herring Gull who was struggling to break free.

As the dog landed back on the grass it hastily began coughing and spluttering until it ejected the gull from its mouth onto the ground in front of him.

"Albert, Albert, are you alright!" shouted the dog, looking extremely worried.

The gull was in a complete state of shock and began to wander around in dizzy circles shaking its head and breathing deeply. It then collapsed on the grass and began to examine its feathers and legs, and to satisfy itself it was unharmed it gave a little flutter of its wings. It then turned to the dog and spoke.

"Okay, Okay, Albert's okay!" it declared, feeling pleased to be unscathed.

The dog let out a sigh of relief, and then looked quizzically at the bird.

"Albert why did you stay still...what happened?" he asked.

Albert stood motionless for a moment, his only movement being his eyes darting back and forth, and then turning towards the dog his mouth burst open and he started to yell excitedly.

"A ship, a ship!"

The Labrador looked puzzled, "A ship?"

"Yes a ship!"

"Where?"

"Follow me, follow me!" squawked the gull, flying off towards the cliff edge.

The Labrador cautiously followed the gull, stopping just short of where the chalk face dropped hundreds of feet to the sea below. His name was Har Vesta, and he and Albert were the very best of friends.

Lying down on the grass with his paws dangling over the edge of the cliffs his eyes opened wide like saucers as he took in a sight he never imagined he would see. It was a galleon, a large galleon, and she was moored in the Old Harbour below. There was some movement on board but what interested Har Vesta were the six creatures that walked along the gangplank on to the quayside.

The black and white border collie was easy to identify as it resembled his old school friends Bella and Toby; but as to the others he had never seen their like before.

There was a slight resemblance to that miserable bank manager Monty Frazzelbach, but in shape only; as apart from this they were very different. Their bodies were larger, and instead of fine pink hair like Monty, they were covered with long dark course fur, and they also had an intimidating tusk on each side of their mouth. All of them carried weapons and wore a leather vest, which Har Vesta thought was probably to protect against minor injuries; and they did indeed look very fierce. Albert and Har Vesta looked at one another for a moment, each wondering who these animals were, and what they wanted, and then the Labrador broke the silence.

"They're invaders!" he shouted.

"Invaders, invaders!" echoed Albert.

"But what shall we do, what shall we do?" continued the bird in a distressed tone.

The dog put a paw to his mouth and thought for a moment, and a few seconds later having found the answer his face lit up.

"Uncle Chuan, we have to tell uncle Chuan. He'll know what to do!" he exclaimed excitedly.

Looking toward the gull he then began his instruction.

"Look Albert, you go and tell uncle Chuan about these invaders, while I wait here okay?"

"Albert do, Albert do!"

"And be quick mind you!" uttered Har Vesta in earnest.

"I be quick, I be quick," responded Albert.

The gull stretched open its wings and leaping off the edge of the cliff caught a strong draft that propelled him out to sea before banking around and heading inland towards Zanimos Town.

Har Vesta watched Albert flying off at great speed for a few moments before returning his gaze to the sight below in the harbour. He felt excited yet at the same time a little nervous, after all who were these creatures that dared enter the harbour and why had they come? He had received training in the art of war as did all the male animals in Zanimos, and had chosed the bow as his favourite weapon, but like most of the others he had no experience of fighting in battles.

The wind was a strong north easterly and Albert had to fly in a north westerly direction and keep adjusting his direction of flight to ensure he was on course for Zanimos Town. As he progressed onwards he flew just north of Fleet Road, and crossed the vast open fields in which crops and vegetables grew. The first field and the largest had a variety of vegetables including carrots, potatoes cauliflowers, lettuce, cucumbers and runner beans to name but a few. In the field was a lot of activity as he observed three rabbits busily collecting vegetables in their trug baskets before tipping them on to an old fragile looking wooden cart. Albert knew the Digger family well. Georgio Digger and his wife Juliet were greengrocers in the town and they very kindly allowed him to pull up the odd carrot if he was unable to find any fish to eat. Carrots were not a typical food that a seagull might eat, but that was Albert for you; a strange bird indeed. He let out a series of cries to catch the rabbits' attention, and Juliet, her son Dimble, and daughter Jess looked up and waved excitedly; Georgio meanwhile was back in town looking after the shop.

Leaving the rabbits behind he glided over a narrow green leafed hedgerow and over flew the recently cut corn, and the adjacent field where the dusty residual signified the wheat had been harvested in the last day or so. Shortly seeing the houses of Zanimos Town he began searching for the home of Papachuan. With his excellent eyesight he quickly spotted the grass triangle where animals would often sit and read a book they had borrowed from the nearby library. Just south of this was a crescent shaped terraced building, and not too far away he spied his objective; the town mayor's house.

Dropping his head forward, he bent his wings backwards and dived downwards at tremendous pace, leaving it until just before he reached the ground before opening his wings to break his speed and settle gently on to the street paving.

For a moment Albert glanced at the familiar red sandstone house before hopping up its three large steps towards the dark green wooden door inset with a shiny brass letter box. Once there he fluttered a few feet off the ground, and taking the knocker in his beak slammed it against the door producing a loud thumping noise. He did this several times but there was no response and when he took off and looked in through the two large front sash windows he was disappointed not to see any movement in the house. Becoming agitated, he wondered what to do next; he realised the great importance of sounding the alert for he had heard stories about armies trying to invade Zanimos in the past. Focusing on the great responsibilities that lie with him, his mind became clearer and less muddled and the cloud of indecision lifted. But even so he had still overlooked the fact that Papachuan spent much of his time in the town hall, and his mind was now set on preparing the town for battle, even if that meant flying up and down the square squawking at the top of his voice, that's exactly what he would do.

"Must get help...must get help!" he exclaimed, taking wing and soaring upwards.

At the end of the street he banked to the right past the greengrocers and entered the square, his head glancing quickly both ways and his eyes searching intently for someone to approach. As usual the square was busy with animals going about their business, and he was just about to burst in to an alarming birdsong when the swaying wooden sign of a badger's head struck him like a beacon of light. Banking over to the right, his wings whirring at great speed he quickly reached the old black door of Brodney's store.

Hovering in front of it he peered through the recently cleaned glass window, and observed Brodney, his wife Glenda, and Polly Clutterbuck engaging in friendly banter.

"Oh Brodney it's simply wonderful!" exclaimed Polly, admiring her new broom that the badger had made for her.

"You can always rely on my Brodney," said Glenda with pride.

"It's wonderful," replied the goose.

"Glad you like it," uttered Brodney.

"And how much did you say it was?" asked Polly opening her purse.

"One gold un," grunted Brodney.

Polly was absolutley astounded by the price and her face froze for a moment; it had been many years since she'd bought a new broom and back then cost only a couple of silver coins.

"Dear me, don't things go up," she muttered while searching in her purse for a gold coin. Glenda was upset at seeing Polly's shocked expression and decided to make a kind gesture. "But as it's you Polly let's make it six silver coins," she uttered gently nudging her husband.

"Oh really, you're too kind!"

Brodney looked towards his wife with a disapproving expression and shook his head, before turning to Polly with a somewhat reluctant smile.

"As it's you Polly," he uttered.

Brodney had barely taken the money from Polly when there was a loud tapping noise on the window of the door; it was a rapid series of taps as if to signify some urgency.

The three of them immediately turned towards the sound of the interruption and beheld a large herring gull vigorously beating his beak against the glass window.

"Why its Albert!" exclaimed Brodney.

"He seems very excited," uttered Polly.

"Better see what he wants," added Glenda.

Polly stepped forward and pulled open the front door of the shop, and Albert immediately flew straight in to the shop and skidded to a halt on top of the counter opposite Brodney. The badger was a little shocked at the bird's urgency and after a quick glance towards his wife, stared at Albert with a quizzical expression.

"Well what's up?!" he snapped loudly.

"Invaders, invaders!" replied the gull excitedly. There were gasps of breath from Mrs Badger and Polly who took it as a serious statement, while Brodney on the other hand finding it rather amusing afforded himself a little smirk.

"What you playing at Albert, Invaders?!" he said, shaking his head.

Now some people might be of the opinion that gulls are stupid creatures; after all they fly around the sky making awfully annoying sounds, and when they speak tend to repeat themselves. But this is in fact not true; and especially so of Albert who was a very bright bird. Albert hopped across the counter until he was inches away from Brodney's face and then he lent so close to him that he almost touched his nose.

"Invaders, invaders!" he bellowed, so loudly that the badger had to put his paws to his ears.

"Okay Albert, now tell me calmly what's this all about?" he asked holding his paws up to signify that he did not want any more of those noisy outbursts.

"There's a ship, a ship in the Old Harbour," replied Albert.

"A ship in the harbour...are you certain?"

"Har Vesta and I have seen it."

"Oh not him!" uttered Brodney.

"Now Brodney you mustn't keep on about that, after all he's Papachuan's nephew, and he's a bright future ahead of him," uttered his wife in a forgiving tone. Brodney was still angry about an incident that occurred over a year ago, when Har Vesta wasn't much more than a puppy.

It was his first time in the shop, and being a normally excited youngster he was sticking his nose into everything, when he accidently knocked a small ball off the counter. It took him sometime to apprehend the elusive bouncing ball as he chased it around the shop, but while doing so he caused absolute chaos by knocking all of Brodney's lovely displays over. It was so bad that it took Brodney and Glenda the best part of a day to tidy the shop up again, and Brodney has never forgotten it.

"Come on Brodney, let's hear what Albert's got to say," began Glenda softly.

Brodney glanced at his wife and smiled, he knew she could always get her own way; especially when she gave him one of her warm and friendly looks.

"So there's a ship in the harbour, Albert?" began Brodney.

"I've told you that, told you that,"

"And what's on the ship?"

"Warriors that's what, warriors!" shouted Albert.

Polly and Glenda turned to each other, and a mutual expression of anxiety appeared on their faces.

"Warriors!" they exclaimed together.

"Big ugly animals with swords and they've come ashore...come ashore!" exclaimed Albert.

Brodney acted quickly, for he knew what must be done. He pulled two pistols from beneath the counter and pushed them under his belt, and from the wall behind he took down a cutlass and belt, put it around his waist and tightened its buckle. A look of dread crossed the face of Glenda as she realised her husband was going to defend the land of Zanimos, but she knew that it was the duty of every male in the country to rise to its defence, and that whatever she said it would fall on deaf ears.

"I have to go," began Brodney hugging his wife and giving her a big kiss on the cheek.

"I know my love, I know," replied Glenda with a tear in her eye.

Brodney walked towards the door and paused as he reached it.

"Look after Mrs Badger, will you Polly?"

A sad looking Polly nodded in agreement.

With the door opened Albert whizzed past Brodney and hovered in the air waiting for his instructions.

"Go to Hamilton's cottage and get help...and fly as fast as you can!"

Albert thinking it strange he would find help at the hamster's home, immediately questioned the badger.

"Hamilton's cottage, Hamilton's cottage?" he cried.

"Yes Albert, you'll find that fella Rufus there, and some more animals, tell em to meet me on the cliffs by the Old Harbour, okay?"

Albert Nodded.

"Now go, go!" shouted Brodney, waving frantically at the bird to leave.

Albert opened his wings, leapt in the air and let the breeze carry him upwards before he rolled over and banked southwards, driving his wings as fast as he could.

Back in Hamilton's cottage the party mood had been well and truly spoilt. The hamster felt very disappointed that Monty had let her down, for she was an animal who put a lot of worth in what others said, and thought it extremely bad manners if an animal promised to do something and then didn't.

Papachuan and Horace were initially not bothered that the pig hadn't turned up, and were selfishly keen to begin eating; especially as there would be more to go around now that Monty wasn't there. But oddly enough from the moment the malamute had exclaimed something had happened to Monty, they both began to feel guilty over their lack of concern.

Papachuan reluctantly looked away from a plate of perfectly cut cheese and tomato sandwiches and turned towards the malamute.

"Are you sure something's happened to him Rufus?" he asked.

"Something is wrong, believe me, I can sense it," replied the malamute solemnly.

Horace and Papachuan looked at each with doubtful expressions, each wondering if the malamute could possibly possess such powers of perception. Barnaby seeing they looked unconvinced felt compelled to speak.

"Now listen to me. I've known Rufus for very many years, and I have learned to trust his feelings, and I would urge you to do the same."

"Alright, supposing you are right and something has happened to Monty, what do we do now?" asked Papachuan.

"Firstly, and to satisfy the pair of you," began Rufus fixing his eyes on Papachuan and Horace, which made them feel a little uncomfortable.

"We need to find out if Monty has actually gone home, or whether for some strange reason he is still in the orchard. And if we can't find him we must mount a full search party...is that agreeable?"

Rufus's look of disappointment at their lack of concern, had instilled them with contrition, and they now felt duty bound to help.

Papachuan nodded. "Yes, that's a good idea."

"A capital suggestion," added Horace.

"Right then, Horace you race off to Crystal Mere to see if he's gone home, and Barnaby, you trot down to the Orchard and see if he's there."

Barnaby and Horace nodded in agreement and immediately set off on their tasks.

Rufus had spoken as though he were in command of an army, and to all the other animals with the exception of Barnaby, he sounded very bossy and self-important. But only the Newfoundland knew his old friend was a prince who was at times used to giving orders.

"And what about me Rufus, what can I do?" asked Papachuan.

"For the time being just wait with me. But if they don't find him I'm sure there will be plenty for all of us to do.

"And you can't stand there just moping
Hamilton, how about making us a nice pot of tea
my dear?" uttered Rufus trying to cheer her up.
"Very well" she replied, trotting off into the
kitchen.
Hamsters love nothing more than keeping busy,
and knowing this fact Rufus thought giving her
a job might take her mind off Monty.
"Come on let's take a seat," beckoned Rufus, and
the two friends sat down at the table together.
"You know Rufus, Monty's such a cold fish that
I'm certain Horace will find him at home, and
probably tucking into his apple pie as well," said
the Labrador looking over his spectacles.
"But don't you trust Rufus's feelings?"
interrupted Hamilton, as she placed the teapot
on the table.
"It's not that at all, it's just that I know Monty
too well."
"Hmm," replied the Malamute raising his
eyebrows.

The three animals settled down with a nice
cup of tea and began chatting about Monty.
They wondered why he wouldn't mix with other
animals, and thought it strange that he spent
so much time in the bank; it was as though
fun and enjoyment were absent from his life.
Papachuan had started to talk about Monty's

great grandfather who had been a very popular mayor many years ago, when a knocking on the front door halted his speech.

"Who is it!" called out Hamilton.

"It's me!"

Immediately recognising Horace's voice, Hamilton threw open the door, whereupon the hare ran straight past her into the parlour, throwing his front feet in the air.

"I've had no luck I'm afraid. I've been to his home, and Zanimos Town, and there's no sign of him!"

"Why that was quick," said Papachuan.

"Oh yes" replied the hare with pride, for he was very proud of how fast he could run.

Hamilton was about to close the door when she caught a glimpse of a large brown figure panting heavily and trotting up the lane.

"Barnaby's here!" she called.

All the animals rushed in to the hallway hoping to hear good news, and eagerly watched as the bulky figure of Barnaby approached the cottage.

"What did you find Barnaby?" asked Rufus.

"No sign of him I'm afraid, but I found this. It was by a ladder that was lying on the ground," he replied, breathing deeply and holding out a paw towards the malamute. Rufus stepped forward and took the piece of cloth from

Barnaby, and began to study it closely. It was red and green tartan patterned material, and had obviously been torn away from some clothing.

As soon as she set eyes on the cloth Hamilton put a paw to her mouth and let out a deep sigh. "Goodness me, Monty was wearing clothes with that same pattern!" she screamed excitedly.

"There, there," began Papachuan, gently putting his paw around her shoulder. "Best if you sit down a while."

The Labrador helped Hamilton to a chair, and as she sat down tears began to well up in her eyes.

"Are you certain this cloth matches Monty's clothes?" asked Rufus, realising this might be a significant find. However, he had to be patient for a response as Hamilton took a handkerchief from her apron pocket, and wiped the tears from her eyes before replying.

"Yes I am, you see Monty was wearing red and green tartan trousers and a matching waistcoat when I saw him earlier."

The malamute placed a giant paw on her slender shoulder and smiled warmly.

"Try not to worry Hamilton, I feel sure he hasn't come to any harm as yet."

"But how do you know, how can you be so certain?" she asked, sounding very distressed.

Barnaby, looking on with his large friendly eyes cleared his throat and spoke softly and reassuringly.

"Rufus wouldn't tell you if he wasn't certain Hamilton. I've known him for a long long time, and somehow he always seems to know if something bad has happened, or even if it is about to."

A small but optimistic smile appeared on the hamster's face.

"Oh I do so hope you're right."

"Barnaby?" began Rufus, an inquisitive tone in his voice.

"Yes."

"Did you see anything else in the orchard?"

Barnaby's eyes lit up with excitement.

"Yes I certainly did...there was a basket of apples, and some of them lying on the ground nearby had bites taken out of them, and all around were a lot of muddy foot prints."

"Could you identify them?"

"Oh yes...they were winchow," uttered Barnaby solemnly.

"Winchow!" exclaimed Rufus clapping his front paws together so powerfully that they made a loud thud.

"Well at least we know who's behind it," he continued.

"What are winchow?" asked Hamilton in a slightly nervous tone.

"You may know them as weasels," replied Rufus. Upon hearing the word weasels poor Hamilton began to feel sick in her tummy as she thought back to those horrible creatures that attacked her and Brodney on the way to Zanimos. Horace also felt a little disturbed, as he remembered Hamilton's vivid story about the incident.

"But there aren't any weasels in Zanimos!" exclaimed Papachuan.

"There are in Unger," replied Barnaby.

"But how did they get here," asked the inquisitive hare.

"Well one thing's for certain they didn't come through the Chameleon Mountains," uttered Papachuan.

All eyes slowly turned towards the malamute for an answer, who was deep in thought trying to fathom it all out; and as usual it didn't take him long to do so.

Lifting up his great head, he peered into the eyes of each expectant animal's face, before quietly and confidently announcing a response.

"They came by boat, that's the only way they could have come."

For a second or two there was disbelief and silence, and so quiet was it that a large house spider could be heard scampering across the floor; but this didn't last long as an explosion of questions immediately followed.

"But who brought them!?" asked Papachuan.

"And why Zanimos, why have they come here?" asked Horace.

"And why have they kidnapped Monty?" asked a concerned Hamilton.

The questions continued to rain down on Rufus and with each animal trying to ensure their question was heard first, their voices rose in volume creating a noisy barrage.

"Alright that's enough!" shouted Rufus in an authoritative tone and the animals obediently ceased their questions.

The malamute raised his front paws as if to gesture that calm was needed and continued to speak.

"The best thing for us to do now is mount a full search party...agreed?"

There followed a quick period of exchanging glances from the others, before they unanimously nodded in agreement.

"Good," replied Rufus.

"Now Hamilton you must wait here in case Monty should turn up, and Horace you should stay here as well," continued the Malamute.

Horace looked disappointed. "Oh must I, and miss all the excitement!"

"Yes you must Horace, after all if Monty turns up at the cottage while we're out searching you can use your great speed to run and tell us."
The malamute smiled and gently touched Horace on the shoulder trying to make him feel better for being left off the search party.
"This is an important task and you are just the animal for the job."
Horace immediately felt better and pricked up his ears.
"But where will you go Rufus?" asked Hamilton.
"To the orchard...we should be able to track Monty and the winchow from there."
"Then we had better not waste any time," uttered Papachuan.
Rufus, Barnaby, and Papachuan quickly bade goodbye to Hamilton and Horace, and made their way out of the cottage.
They were ready to move quickly towards the orchard but something in the distance caught Rufus' eye, and he suddenly stopped by Hamilton's front gate to study it more closely.
It was no surprise to Barnaby that he could see nothing as he knew his friend's sight was far greater than his, but Papachuan was not yet aware of Rufus' special powers and so doubted that anything was there.
"Come on Rufus, we have to get after Monty," uttered the Labrador.

"I would wait just a moment," responded Barnaby.

"But there's nothing there," said Papachuan shaking his head.

"You'll see," replied the Newfoundland.

"What is it my old friend, what do you see?" asked Barnaby excitedly.

"There's a bird, a seabird, and it's coming in our direction."

"Papachuan looked sceptical, but nevertheless he squinted his eyes to try to improve his sight and stared northwards. He was just about to give up looking at the empty sky when a small spec appeared, and soon after it formed a shape he could recognise.

"Why you're right, there is a bird!" yelled the Labrador.

"And I think it's looking for us," replied Rufus in a serious tone.

"But how on earth can you be sure of that?" questioned Papachuan.

"My senses tell me so," responded the malamute solemnly.

Papachuan had only known Rufus a short while, yet his new friend had a confidence and aura of mystique he could feel was very special indeed. Barnaby put a large paw on the Labrador's shoulder.

"One thing you must learn about Rufus, is never doubt him."

Papachuan smiled.

"I think I'm beginning to learn that".

The three animals continued to watch the progress of the gull as it quite quickly approached them. Even though the easterly wind made every effort to throw him off course, the gull's expertise in flying did little to stop him from heading straight on to the waiting malamute and his friends.

While observing the approaching bird, Rufus became conscious of something more than his exceptional senses at play here, for he was overcome with an emotion rarely felt since he had been in the company of his old friend Apolyus; a giant bird and guardian of North of the World. The nearer the bird got the stronger this feeling became, and he soon realised he could bond with it mentally. This sort of connection scarcely happened to him, but when it did occur it was always with birds, not any particular type you understand, but it was evident that some birds had this special telepathic ability; and it appeared the approaching sea gull was one of them. Oddly enough he had perceived this supernatural stimulus more recently in Zanimos, but having no need to create any link had ignored it, but as the gull approached him Rufus felt certain it was this bird's telepathic transmission he had detected before.

Papachuan watched the bird closely as it glided and banked and wheeled around in the sky using the wind currents like a toy to play with, and as it got closer a smile crept across his face.
"Why it's Albert!" he exclaimed waving his paws in the air excitedly.
"Albert, who's he?" asked Barnaby.
"He's a friend of my nephew Har Vesta, but I wonder what he wants?"
Rufus glanced at Papachuan. "I have the strangest feeling it is all to do with Monty," he declared.
And they didn't need to wait much longer to find out, for Albert dived steeply, then flew straight and level for a short while before opening his large wings and coming to a halt on Hamilton's gate post. The gull was breathing heavily and took a little while to get its breath back. He knew the town mayor very well, and Har Vesta had told him all about Rufus - whom he had seen on a few occasions from a distance - but he had never met the other giant dog before. He looked at Rufus and Barnaby and studied them closely for a moment.

"You're just about as big as Rufus," squawked Albert.

"Just a little wider around the middle that's all," replied a grinning Barnaby.

"Rufus chuckled briefly before addressing the gull.

"Look Albert what's your message?" he began in earnest.

"Message message, oh yes message," replied the gull trying to recall what he had to tell them.

"Well go on then!" uttered malamute impatiently.

"Invaders, invaders...landed in Old Harbour they have!" babbled the gull.

"Invaders!" uttered Papachuan and Barnaby in chorus.

"What do they look like?" asked Rufus.

"Quite big, big and fierce. Yes big and fierce!" shouted Albert.

Rufus' thoughts ran wild for a moment, he knew weasels had probably kidnapped Monty, but weasels are not very big animals; so what were these? But whatever they were, he knew quick action was required.

"Right then, off we go to Old Harbour!" he ordered without hesitation.

Starting off at a quick trot with Papachuan and Barnaby following just behind him he led them towards Zanimos Town while Albert flew overhead. Onwards the three friends went and all the time Rufus was slowly increasing the pace, and although the Labrador could run quickly, poor old Barnaby was finding it hard going. But nevertheless, the Newfoundland being aware of the great importance of speed was making every effort to keep up.

They had just passed the sign to Leverets Copse and taken the left fork northwards to Zanimos Town when an important thought struck Papachuan.

"Rufus what about weapons, we can't meet these invaders without them!" he called out after the malamute.

"That's right we need to arm ourselves if we're to fight," added Barnaby sounding concerned.

Rufus didn't reply immediately but kept up his fast pace while contemplating an answer; and then it came.

"We'll get them on the way. You can get your sword from your rucksack in my barn Barnaby, and you can pop in your house to get yours Papachuan!"

It was simple and made sense. They had to pass Rufus' barn to get to Fleet Road anyway, and popping into Papachuan's house in the town would only take them an extra few minutes. Barnaby and Papachuan both felt greatly relieved that they would have some weapons

to take with them and they gave one another a
smile of relief.

"Ah what about Brodney, he's a useful fellow in
a fight," uttered Papachuan.

"I should say he is," reinforced Barnaby,
remembering the incident with the winchow in
the tea house in Ungerborg.

Rufus had only met Brodney a few times but
he could sense that Underneath the gruff
and grumpy exterior he was a good and brave
animal. He was about to agree that they should
ask Brodney to come when he was beaten to it
by Albert.

"No need to ask, no need, he's on his way there!"

"What do you mean?" asked Rufus looking up at
the gull with a quizzical expression.

"He sent me get you, and meet him on the cliffs
above the harbour."

"So he's the one who spotted the invaders?"
asked Rufus.

The gull shook his head, "No, no I did!"

Rufus frowned and looked up at the gull for a
moment, feeling he would really like to get this
straightened out; and so he immediately came
to an abrupt halt. Papachuan's eyes were like
saucers as he was caught out by this sudden
stop and not wanting to bump in to his friend
he dug his hind legs in to the soil and came to a
stop just inches behind him; meanwhile Barnaby

slowly trotted up to them and sat down panting,
as he was grateful of the rest.

The gull had not noticed the three dogs stop
and flew onwards until he heard his name being
called out by Rufus.

Albert...Albert come back!" yelled the
malamute, and the gull banked over and glided
back towards them. Harnessing the strong
easterly wind to gain tremendous speed he
quickly reached the three dogs, initially
choosing the large head of the Newfoundland
for a landing spot. But the moment his
pink webbed feet touched the dogs head,
threatening giant paws were trying to knock him
away.

"Get off, get off me!" shouted Barnaby, and the
bird quickly hovered to a safe range above the
flailing paws.

Rufus frowned in frustration.

"Come here Albert!" he called in a commanding
tone, and the gull settled down on the track
just in front of him.

"Now Albert, let's get this straight. You
spotted the invaders and went to tell Brodney,
and he told you to fetch us, now that's right
isn't it?"

"Yes, yes, and...no," replied Albert.

The malamute felt confused, he thought he
would get a direct answer from Albert; but

questioning a seagull isn't straight forward, as they have a strange way of explaining things.

"So did you or didn't you spot the invaders?" continued Rufus firmly.

"Yes, yes, I saw em, but I wasn't the only one, wasn't the only one!" screamed the gull a little excitedly.

Rufus was normally a cool headed animal but the bird's lack of clarity was beginning to make him feel exasperated.

"Who else saw them!" he yelled.

The gull didn't like Rufus' tone or his serious expression and thought it safe to hop a short distance away from him.

"It was Har Vesta...Har Vesta and me saw them." On hearing his nephew's name Papachuan felt very worried.

"And where is Har Vesta now?!" he shouted.

"He's on the cliffs, on the cliffs, on look out."

"We must get to him Rufus, before these invaders do," pleaded Papachuan, feeling concerned about his nephew's safety.

Rufus had met Papachuan's nephew on several occasions and had grown to enjoy his company. He was young and excitable, and Rufus could feel he was brave; but was he foolhardy enough to take on the invaders by himself?

Hamilton Smythe

CHAPTER 7
A BOND IS FORMED

Wasting no time in summing up the situation, Rufus knew there was only one thing for it, he could run faster than most any other animal and could reach the cliffs far quicker than his two friends; and if he waited for them it might be too late.

"Don't worry Papachuan, I'll go," he said solemnly.

The Labrador breathed a sigh of relief.

"Thank you."

"Now then," began the malamute, "let's get busy,"

"What should we do Rufus?" asked Barnaby, stretching his legs.

"You two go on and get your weapons, and then come to the cliff top as fast as you can. Albert and I will go there directly and meet Har Vesta and Brodney...okay?"

Barnaby and Papachuan gave each other a quick glance before turning towards the malamute and nodding their heads.

In actual fact if one had studied this more closely one might have noticed that Barnaby gave more of a bow than a nod; for only he knew his friend to be of royal blood.

They then parted their ways, the Labrador leading the Newfoundland northwards, while the malamute took off across the open countryside eastwards towards the Old Harbour with Albert flying overhead. Since leaving Brodney in the town the gull had felt like he was on a mission of great importance and to be flying over head this strange and mysterious animal made him feel that he was part of something significant in the annals of Zanimos. For Albert this was quite an unusual feeling, as he was used to living his life as he wished with no responsibilities; and apart from playing chase with his friend Har Vesta, flying freely over the oceans was his greatest joy. He began to think that in the future animals would read about this invasion of Zanimos and that as part of the defending force his name would go down in history; and for a moment he began to feel smug about it.

"Albert famous in history, famous in history," he thought to himself.

And then without warning an uninvited voice
entered his head. It was soft yet, at the same
time firm, and he felt compelled to obey it.
"Albert, fly higher and tell me what you can
see."
It almost sounded hypnotic as though it was
influencing him to follow its command, and yet
there was a kindness and honesty that he could
not ignore; and so he did as it commanded.
Lifting his wings he let the easterly wind
quickly carry him upwards towards the heavens.
The low lying fields and hedges were soon far
below and as he continued to climb he caught
a glimpse of the green tinted Nordeamian
Ocean; his sign to follow the coastline north.
During this time Rufus was racing across fields,
jumping hedges and ditches and anything else
that stood in his path, and his pace and sure
footedness was a vision to behold; and he kept
this up for mile after mile and never faltered.
Albert began to circle high above the Old
Harbour and was extremely relieved to see his
friend Har Vesta lying on the cliff watching the
invaders below, and then that voice came into
his head again.
"What do you see, what do you see?" it asked.
Without questioning Albert responded.
"I see six invaders leaving the harbour, Brodney
walking along Fleet Road and Har Vesta lying on
the cliffs."

His voice then became a little agitated.
"No Har Vesta stay where you are, stay where
you are!" he called out.
"What is it?"asked the voice in earnest.
"It's Har Vesta, he's left the cliffs and is
running down the road towards the invaders!"
"Then come down and follow me!" exclaimed the
voice so loud that for a moment the bird was
deafened.
Albert searched below with his excellent
sight and much to his amazement he spotted
an animal below running at what seemed an
unbelievable speed. As he rolled over and
dived towards the ground he soon recognised
the animal as Rufus O'Malley and in an instant
realised that it was his voice that had spoken
to him. He didn't understand how he could do it,
but the word 'magic' sprang to mind.

It had seemed like hours since Albert had left
him, and Har Vesta was beginning to feel he'd
been forgotten about. He knew that his Uncle
Chuan would know what to do and he was hoping
that would include drumming up a small army;
but why hadn't anyone arrived yet. Har Vesta
always called his uncle, Chuan, and Papachuan
always called his nephew Vesta. Although when
he was a boisterous puppy and misbehaving
Papachuan would adopt a stern tone and call

him Har Vesta to keep in him line; the infamous wrecking of Brodney's store was one such occasion.

Apart from scratching his ears from time to time Har Vesta had been lying still and quiet, while keeping a continued watch on the invaders below.

"Oh if only I had my bow, why I could pick them off one at a time," he uttered, feeling deeply disheartened.

But being without a weapon wasn't the only thing that vexed him; he was fed up waiting for help to arrive, and as he glanced back up the hill there was no sign of anyone. Trying to rationally think things through, he wondered what his clever uncle would do in his situation.

"Perhaps I should run down and attack them, I might even scare them off," he thought.

But he soon realised that was silly, for although he might be able to overpower the black and white dog, he would be no match for five armed soldiers.

Although he was only a youngster he did have a good head on his shoulders and was a very practical thinker.

He recognised the most important thing was preventing the invaders from reaching Zanimos Town, where they would have a free reign to run amuck and slaughter the townsfolk at will.

Therefore it was paramount he hold them off until the alarm was raised and the militia mustered to defend it. Toying with different ideas, his eyes moved rapidly from side to side as he tried to find a solution, he had a multitude of ideas, most of which were none starters, until finally a broad smile slowly crept across his face.

"Delay them, yes that's the answer, delay them," he whispered under his breath.

"Right then, that's it," he added nodding his head.

Not wanting the invaders to spot him too early, he slowly but surely crept on his stomach over the grass until he finally reached Fleet Road. He paused for a short while and took a deep breath in preparation of his charge, and as he had been taught began to concentrate on his objective, blocking out all other thoughts; unfortunately in this intense focus he didn't hear Brodney calling out his name.

"Here we go!" he shouted not caring if he was heard by the invaders, and leaping up like a jack in the box he took off and raced across the cobbled stones downwards towards them. His eyes were bright and focused, his breathing was deep and fast, and any feeling of anxiety was ousted in favour of anger.

"How dare you come into our country without invitation, how dare you!" he screamed at the top of his voice.

Getting closer to the intruders Har Vesta was soon able to make out the fierce expressions of the soldiers, and the strange tusks protruding from their mouths made them even more dangerous. But his plan was not to engage them, just to bark and growl and keep out of their distance, in the hope that help would soon arrive. He hadn't been running very long when he noticed the surprise on their faces indicated he had been spotted, and so determined more than ever to look more fearsome he stretched every sinew in his body to increase momentum; hoping this might drive some panic in to them.

"A large dog captain and it looks like its attacking us!" bellowed Sergeant Kolo.
"Right spread out lads!" ordered Tonga.
Watching the large dog approach Charlie felt worried about any possible conflict with the locals, as he feared this could escalate in to all out war between Unger and Zanimos.
"Tonga, please be careful, we don't want to harm any Zamosians!" he pleaded.
"I know Charlie, but he doesn't look very friendly does he?"

"But he's not armed; he can't possibly be a threat."

"Alright, we won't attack unless he does...okay."
Charlie smiled and gave a sigh of relief. "Thank you."

"Alright lads hold fast and don't –"

"Twang!" went the bow as Tunashi released the string, and a swish indicated an arrow had been released. All heads instantly turned towards the young boar, who looked very pleased with himself until he saw the look of disbelief on their faces and realised he had made a grave mistake.

Now the distance between Har Vesta and Tunashi was around three hundred yards; a distance which an arrow can travel extremely quickly. So please understand that the description of the frenzied events occurring after the release of the arrow, are in fact much longer than its actual flying time.
Hence this is what happened next.......

As soon as Charlie realised what Tunashi had done he put a paw to his mouth; a look of dread appeared on his face.

"No, no!" he shouted sorrowfully fearing for the Labrador's life.

Anger began to well up in Captain Tonga, for he was just about to order his troops not to attack unless necessary and one thing he could not tolerate was disobedience in his soldiers.

"You fool, you fool!" he shouted, and the young boar feeling deeply ashamed looked towards the ground avoiding the face of his harsh looking Captain. His father looked awkwardly embarrassed for he had especially asked if his son could come on this mission, but now he wished he had not.

"What made you do it son?!" yelled the Sergeant.

Tunashi lifted his head showing that his eyes were welling up with tears and looked very upset.

"I thought that was what I should do; shoot an arrow before the enemy could get to us...just like in training."

"I'm sorry," sobbed Tunashi looking towards the captain and his father for sympathy.

"Sorry won't make it right...if you kill that dog we'll be at war with Zanimos, you realise that don't you." His captain's words cut deeply and he felt the lowest he had ever done so in his life. The six of them could only look on as the arrow made its way towards the oncoming and unsuspecting Har Vesta, and it appeared that there was nothing to be done to prevent the Labrador from being hurt or possibly killed; and to think it could was hopeless. But Charlie wasn't about to give up, and hoping he could attract the attention of Har Vesta he began to run up the hill towards him, screaming at the top of his voice as he did so.

"Look out, look out!"

But it was all in vain as Har Vesta kept coming. At that same moment from high above a gull banked over to its left and took a curved descent towards Har Vesta, making shrieking warning sounds as it did so; it was as if it too was trying to warn the dog. Tunashi feeling full of guilt at what was about to happen looked down at a tuft of grass on the road and hoped it would be over soon; but all other eyes were either on the Labrador or the arrow.

Albert continued to warn his friend with his loud cries and began to dive as fast as he could; he even had the crazy idea he might even be able to stop the arrow. Brodney too knew something was wrong and although he was too far away to make out the arrow he could tell from Albert's behaviour that Har Vesta was in danger.

The arrow reached the top of its arc and began to plummet toward the approaching Har Vesta, who feeling braver than ever began to bark at the top of his voice.

"Go home, go home invaders, you're not welcome here!"

The arrow rather like a guided missile was locked on to its target and was within seconds of impact. Sunlight appeared and catching the deadly sharp arrow head made the steel glint and sparkle which caught the attention of Har Vesta who looked upwards towards it. He had been taught to draw a bow by his uncle Chuan and he immediately recognised that the source of light was an arrow. His reaction was to sit on his back legs and bring himself to an abrupt halt, but then all he could do was helplessly look upwards, watching the arrow as it fell towards him.

Continuing to stare upwards and realising that death would soon be upon him, his mind was unexpectedly flooded with thoughts of loved ones. He thought about his father who had expected him to carry on the family tradition of milling, and how he'd argued that he wanted adventure and not to be stuck in a mill. And then of his loving mother who doted on him, and how devastated she would be if he died, and lastly of his sister Emilia whom he loved very much. A tear ran down his cheek as he was resigned to his destiny, and he sat patiently waiting for his end; but then something unexpected occurred.

The pointed head of the arrow began to glow, and the red glow turned into orange flickering flames that danced along the shaft until reaching the feathered flights. A blinding incandescent brightness followed causing all onlookers close their eyes, and when they opened them all that remained was a plume of smoke.

Har Vesta had closed his eyes shortly before he thought the arrow would reach him, and now greatly relieved he was not injured, slowly began to open them. The plume of smoke had been taken away by the sea breeze, and as he had missed the destruction of the arrow he began to pat his body with his paws just to ensure he had sustained no injury.

"I'm alive, I'm alive," he cried excitedly, wagging his tale and running around in circles.

Within moments the black and white dog had reached him and Har Vesta returning to his role of protector of Zanimos curled back his lips to show his sharp teeth.

"Who are you?!" he growled.

The invading dog stood still in his tracks for a moment and studied the aggressive stance of the Labrador, and although he understood the other's actions he was very pleased that he had not been hurt.

"My name is Charlie," replied the collie, "and I am so glad that you are not hurt."

A warm cordial expression that could only be from a genuinely friendly animal immediately put the young Labrador at ease, and soon the two were shaking paws and all smiles.

"Thank you Charlie...I'm Har Vesta by the way."

"Nice to meet you Har Vesta."

The Labrador began to shake his head.

"I don't quite understand it, the arrow was nearly upon me, yet it seems to have disappeared."

"You didn't see what happened then?" asked Charlie.

"No, I had my eyes closed."

"It was unbelievable...it well, sort of burned up, and disappeared.

"Burnt up...disappeared?!" replied Har Vesta in a disbelieving tone.

Charlie opened his paws and raised them towards the sky.

"Believe me that's exactly what happened," he uttered softly, still not able to acknowledge it himself.

"You're joking, you're making this up," laughed Har Vesta.

"No I am not," replied Charlie sternly, but the Labrador was not listening, as he was concentrating on the remainder of the collie's party who had begun to ascend Fleet Road towards him.

As Tonga approached, Har Vesta maintained a wary countenance, as this was not only a stranger, but an animal he'd never seen before; and worse still an invader. However, the boar's look of genuine concern and his kind words soon made the Labrador feel much more comfortable in his presence.

"I don't mind telling you I am so grateful that you were unharmed," said Tonga in a caring tone.

"Thank you," replied the Labrador with a smile.

"And so am I!" shouted a grateful Tunashi as he reached Har Vesta.

The young boar paused for a moment and felt so relieved he had not harmed the dog.

"I'm sorry, I'm really sorry, I didn't really know what I had done when I released the arrow," continued Tunashi in a subdued tone.

The two animals stared at each other for an instance and then shook paw and trotter, they were both young, both inexperienced but a great friendship had begun that day.

Har Vesta looked at Tunash's bow and quiver of arrows and smiled.

"Call yourself an archer...well I wouldn't have missed.

The boar being proud of his archery quickly leapt to defend himself.

"I didn't!" was his simple response.

"Then why am I not dead or wounded?"

"I told you...the arrow burnt up...why don't you believe me?!" uttered Charlie zealously.

"I saw that too," declared Kolo.

"And then it turned to smoke," Uttered Wicklop

"And then just disappeared!" exclaimed Buna excitedly.

"Maybe it was a faulty arrow?" added Tunashi scratching his head.

Tonga had listened to these so called explanations, but having had much battle experience he doubted any of these reasons were true.

"No lads, there's something odd here," he said solemnly.

"Could it be magic?!" questioned Charlie, with a look of excitement.

"Magic?" laughed Kolo.

The sergeant looked towards his captain for some form of support as he too was a seasoned soldier and was not one to believe in magical powers, but he was disappointed to find Tonga's eyes were focused elsewhere.

"What is it Captain?" he began.

"There...look there," replied Tonga pointing to the top of the cliffs.

In spite of the captain's clear direction, everyone was distracted by a sturdy badger coming down the road towards them.

"Why it's Brodney!" uttered Charlie, recognising the gruff face of his old friend.

"No, no, look higher...up on the cliffs, and to the west!" yelled Tonga earnestly.

Everyone trained their eyes accordingly, and apart from the Har Vesta, they all felt slighty alarmed. For standing up straight and tall on the top of cliffs, with an almost regal stance was a very imposing animal; and he was watching them.

Bigger than a boar its size reminded Tonga of the Newfoundland he had met in the tea house.

"What is that?!" exclaimed Buna.

"It's pretty big!" shouted Wicklop.

"Looks like a wolf to me!" exclaimed Kolo feeling a little concerned.

Tonga turned towards the Labrador.

"You don't have wolves here, do you?"

The Labrador smiled." No we don't, and anyway he's not a wolf, he's an Alaskan malamute and his name is Rufus...Rufus O'Malley!" he uttered with pride, as if he was a personal friend.

For some strange reason Charlie remembered the name, he'd heard it before, but where; and then it came to him.

"Isn't he the one Barnaby was looking for?"

"Yes that's right," replied Tonga.

"Well hopefully he's friendly then," replied Charlie.

"Oh yes he's friendly, very friendly...and there's something special about him," uttered the Labrador excitedly.

The captain frowned. "What do mean by special?"

Har Vesta ruminated for a moment before trying to explain further.

"Well it's difficult to say really...but he has this sort of aura around him that makes you feel safe when he's nearby, and you can sense he's good and kind. My uncle Chuan says he's also very clever and wise...and what's more," he continued in a more serious and dramatic tone, "he also told me Rufus came into Zanimos through the Chameleon Mountains, on his own, without a guide. And he's never heard of an outsider getting past the wizard's magic before...so he has to be extraordinary doesn't he?!"

Kolo glanced at his captain.

"I wouldn't go anyway near those mountains, even if I was offered a fortune in gold."

"I don't think anyone in their right mind would," replied Tonga, and the two boars gave one another a fleeting smile.

Charlie found Har Vesta's talk about Rufus very interesting, for there was nothing he enjoyed more than listening to bizarre tales from well travelled traders who visited his shop.

"So there might just be something supernatural about him," gushed the collie excitedly.

"Well let's not get too carried away now...not until we have proof anyway," uttered Tonga, still not entirely convinced that magic had saved Har Vesta's life.

But the captain's words only served to start a free for all, where all sorts of ideas were banded around about what caused the arrow to disappear. Among these were questions as to whether or not the malamute actually did have magical powers; and if so did he possibly destroy the arrow, or was it just a strange phenomenon that had occurred. But they couldn't seem to agree on anything, especially Wicklop, Buna and kolo whose enthusiastic disagreements were beginning to get a little heated. Tonga was about to call for quiet when he was distracted by the approaching Brodney. As he neared the group, the badger could clearly see that the invaders were none other than his old friend Charlie, and Tonga, and some other boars he recognised from Unger.

"Why it's you Charlie, and Tonga too!" uttered Brodney sounding a little disappointed. After all he was ready to fight off a band of invaders and now he felt deflated knowing this wasn't the case. The conversation, or rather disagreement about Rufus came to a welcoming halt, as everyone turned towards the approaching badger.

"Well you're a sight for sore eyes Brodney," uttered Charlie.

And then the collie's face took on a slightly annoyed look.

"By the way why didn't you wait for us, after all you did say you'd guide us through the mountains," continued Charlie in an annoyed tone.

But Brodney being Brodney wasn't about to have his actions questioned and took offence if anyone did.

"I don't wait for no one Charlie, I'm me own animal...besides I prefer to travel at night and that's what me and that Barnaby agreed to do." Realising his curt reply had shocked Charlie, the badger's countenance began to soften a little."

"Now look Charlie, I've told you there's no treasure in Zanimos, and anyway I thought you'd have seen sense and given up on the idea -"

"Well Belius doesn't think so!" interrupted Tonga sharply.

The badger frowned. "Belius?" he queried.

"He stole my map!" snapped Tonga.

"That was careless captain," replied the badger.

"Careless...he and some of his treacherous gang knocked me unconscious," snarled the boar.

"I see, and now you've come to track em down eh?" replied Brodney.

"That's right, it's my map and I have the full support of King Rosfarl in my quest to get the treasure."

To Har Vesta the question of treasure existing in Zanimos brought to mind the stories told to him as a puppy by his Uncle Chuan.

Of the safe times when the wizard Mortuleez and his wife Julianna ruled Zanimos, and no other country dared attack their realm.

And even how upon their death, they pledged to protect the country by enchanting the mountains that border with Unger.

Recalling tales of deeper history brought a sudden chill to his spine as he pictured a giant black cat with dark powers called Catsumo, who had made a secret hide out in the caves of Smugglers Cove.

"Brodney, do you think this treasure has anything to do with Catsumo!" he asked excitedly.

The Badger shook his head." Catsumo, no that's just a rumour," he replied dismissively.

"Well I'll ask Uncle Chuan about it, he knows all about Zamosian history," replied Har Vesta; a slight defiance in his tone.

"You do that," grunted the badger.

The face on the young Labrador suddenly beamed with joy.

"In fact I'll do that immediately!" he shouted and began to run back up the Fleet Road at great speed.

Brodney scratched his head.

"Spose he'll calm down one day," he grumbled.

Tonga's eyes followed Har Vesta and he soon noticed the reason why he had taken off, for two animals had just appeared on the brow of the hill.

"Why isn't that Barnaby on the right!" yelled the boar pointing to the larger of the two animals.

"Yep that's right, and the other's Papachuan, he's our town mayor," replied Brodney.

Ahh...is he like our king then?" asked Tonga.

Brodney laughed. "He'd love to hear to you say that.

No, we don't have a king, we have a council, and a mayor who is sort of in charge, we elect them every two years."

"That sounds a good way of doing things, very fair indeed," said Charlie.

"True, but we'd better not mention this back in Unger, it might give the animals ideas, might even lead to a revolution," responded Tonga in a serious tone.

"Anyway, like to meet our mayor?" asked Brodney.

"Yes I would," replied Tonga enthusiastically.

"Right then lads lets go and meet some more Zamosians!" continued the captain loudly.

As the group made their way up Fleet Road, Tonga let the others walk ahead while he purposefully fell back in line next to Tunashi. The young boar noticed this and began to feel a little worried that his captain was going to unleash another torrent of admonishments. He felt his commander's trotter on his shoulder and cringed in readiness for more harsh words; but they never came. Instead there were only soft words of wisdom and encouragement.

"Learn to think before you act, not just of what you are going to do, but what you are going to cause to happen too. And always remember that with great skill comes great responsibility."

With this Tonga patted him on the shoulder and walked off ahead towards the front of his troops.

In those few words Tonga had revived the young boar and filled him with great pride, and if anything he had raised his self esteem too.

"My captain says I have great skill," he muttered under his breath feeling happy once again.

There were smiles all around as Barnaby greeted Tonga and Charlie, and all three of them were greatly pleased to renew their friendships; and also very relieved that a conflict had been avoided. After watching these old pals meet up, a happy Har Vesta proudly introduced his uncle to Tonga and Charlie. Although initially uncertain as to how they should behave in the town mayor's presence, they soon found from his friendly greeting that he had no heirs or graces and they immediately felt at ease. Introductions were made all around, and in a few moments everyone knew everyone, and noisy and jovial banter ensued. However the main theme soon turned towards Har Vesta and the miracle of the disappearing arrow, which for a moment filled poor old Tunashi with embarrassment. Tonga not wishing to have his soldiers arguing again quickly cleared his throat to catch their attention and then gave them a stern glare.

"Let's not get too carried away this time eh lads?!" he said.

"No captain," they replied in chorus.

A hugely relieved Papachuan took hold of his nephew and gave him a friendly lick on his head.

"Oh Uncle Chuan!" complained an embarrassed Har Vesta, before smiling and nuzzling up

against the side of his uncle's face; for he
dearly loved his mother's brother.

Rufus remained some distance away from this
gathering and stood as still as a rock, closely
observing the behaviour of the new arrivals.
One of his amazing qualities was to be able to
sense an animal's true character, and he did
this by observation, listening and sometimes
by talking; and his heightened senses played an
important part too. Having satisfied himself
that all was well he decided to walk towards the
group and as he did so Albert flew around in
circles overhead. Tonga noticed this large dog
approaching and immediately stopped talking
and began to watch him with interest. He was as
tall as Barnaby, yet more slender and powerful
looking, and his large mouth made him look very
dangerous. His motion looked effortless as he
jumped from the grass covered hill onto the
cobbled road, a move that impressed Tonga
and made him wonder how fast this beast could
actually move if he had too.

In the meantime Albert had caused alarm
among the boars who quickly dispersed when
he dived down towards Har Vesta, and it was
only the soft tone of Papachuan explaining he
was a friend that prevented swords from being
drawn; but at least Tunashi had learnt his
lesson and kept his arrows in his quiver. Once

Albert had fluttered to a halt on the road next to Har Vesta the two friends had a huge hug. "Didn't think you cared," Joked the Labrador." "Albert cares, Albert cares!"

On seeing his friend approaching, Barnaby called out.
"Rufus, come and say hello, these fellows aren't invaders after all. In fact I've met Charlie and Tonga before!"
The malamute went to each stranger in turn and introduced himself. Buna, Wicklop, sergeant Kolo and even captain Tonga were on the face of it friendly enough, but Rufus could sense that these seasoned soldiers were a little guarded as they were not yet really sure of him. But as Har Vesta had mentioned earlier, there was a special aura about him which made one feel at ease, and in a very short time even the boar soldiers felt as though they had known him for years; such was his wonderful charisma.
Although all the newcomers to Zanimos were quite impressed by Rufus, the young Tunashi was exceptionally captivated by this splendid animal, and extremely thrilled to meet him.
"Pleased to make your acquaintance," he uttered enthusiastically.
"And yours," replied Rufus with a warm smile.

Charlie too was friendly and trusting of the malamute, for he had heard tales of these great dogs, and of the noble King Odana who ruled over the five provinces of North of the World; what he didn't know of course was he was shaking paws with his son.

All through his introductions Rufus could hear whispering in the background, and although he didn't let on, he could hear every single word.

"Do you think he's a wizard?" said Buna gently nudging Wicklop.

"I don't know, but he does have a special presence about him."

"I know, I can feel it too...it's just as Har Vesta told us," replied Buna.

Sergeant Kolo who had been listening put his head between the two off them, and took hold of each one by the shoulders.

"Why don't you ask him lads?" he uttered in a hushed tone.

"Ask him?" replied Buna, taken aback by his sergeant's suggestion.

"Yes," replied Kolo nodding his head, "ask him straight out if he can do magic."

"You're not serious sarge?" asked Wicklop.

The sergeant drew a deep breath.

"We've been in many battles lads, but have you ever seen anything like that...because I haven't?"

Kolo walked off towards his captain and left the two boars deep in thought; for they both had to agree that what they had witnessed earlier was quite remarkable.

Rufus knew from experience that whenever magic was witnessed in his presence he would soon be asked if he was a sorcerer or wizard, and he felt certain that was about to happen. He never used his powers to show off, only when he deemed it necessary; and on this occasion it had almost certainly saved a life. Meanwhile he detected Buna and Wicklop arguing about who should actually pop the question and ask him outright if he could do magic. He could hear their hushed bickering and couldn't help but smile to himself, as here were two seasoned warriors, yet they appeared to be in awe of him; mind you he had experienced this many times before. However, in the end they both plucked up enough courage to ask the question.

"Mr Rufus!" they called loudly.

The malamute slowly wheeled around to meet their gaze, while everyone else looked on with quizzical expressions.

"It's just Rufus, and I know what you're going to ask."

He stared at the two of them for a while, and it seemed that they had lost their tongues, for both were silent. They looked towards their sergeant for help but he too was reluctant to speak; for he like them didn't want to make a fool of himself.

Tonga looked puzzled "What's this all about!" he yelled.

Kolo cleared his throat. "Well captain we were just wondering?" but then even his voice froze and he spoke no further.

"Well what is it Kolo?" uttered Tonga with a frustrated expression.

All attention was on Kolo now, and not one for being seen as a coward he stood up straight and readied himself to ask the question; which in his heart he felt a little silly for asking.

"The lads and I," he began slowly, and then he blurted the rest out. "We'd like to know if you can do magic Rufus?"

The malamute lifted his head backwards and laughed, while everyone waited with baited breath for his response; everyone except Barnaby that is, for he already knew the answer.

Rufus walked over to Har Vesta and put his giant paw on the Labrador's shoulder.

"Well I certainly couldn't let any harm come to this crazy young thing could I."

Har Vesta looked up towards Rufus with an initial expression of gratitude, which soon turned to amazement.

"Then you can?!" he exclaimed.

"I can do many things young Har Vesta," was the solemn reply.

There followed a deep intake of breath and look of awe from the ones who had seen the arrow burn up and disappear, and overcome with a sense of wonder and amazement they were imbued with feelings of deep trust and loyalty toward this unique animal.

Realising that Rufus had saved the life of his beloved nephew, emotions began to well up inside Papachuan, and he placed an ever grateful paw on the muscular shoulder of the great malamute.

"Thank you so much Rufus, I'm forever in your debt for saving Har Vesta," he expressed gravely.

Rufus slowly turned to Papachuan and smiled; it was a warm, kind and genuinely contented smile, and then he edged closer.

"Having the gift to do special things is gratitude enough, you owe me no debt my friend," he uttered with deep sincerity.

Then changing his tone in to one of great urgency, he spoke loudly and deliberately.

"The important thing now is to find Monty, don't you think so?"

The Labrador realising the significance of these words nodded in agreement.

"No time to waste then," he uttered in a pressing tone.

"None at all...we must be off to Delicious Orchard immediately!" replied the malamute.

Tonga and Charlie looked at one another with puzzled expressions, they had come to track down the weasels and not some animal whom they had no interest in; after all it was the treasure they wanted.

"I'm really sorry but we haven't got time to go after your friend," began Charlie, a slight tone of sympathy in his voice.

"We're after the weasels," added Tonga resolutely.

Brodney laughed. "And your so called treasure," he chuckled.

The remark stirred annoyance in the boar, and his anger was fuelled further by recollection of the ignominious theft of his map. His pride hurt, he was not only focused on possession of the treasure, but also on repaying Belius for his treachery.

"If you won't come with us, we will go on our own!" he shouted.

Papachuan and Charlie looked at each other
awkwardly as they didn't want the group to
be split up and go on separate missions, and
besides thought Papachuan "Who are they to go
where they want in my country?"
For an instant things looked difficult, and a
darkened atmosphere hung in the air, but as
always Rufus knew the way forward.
"Captain Tonga," he began in a commanding tone,
which made the boar prick up his ears and turn
towards him.
"Yes."
"I believe your quest and ours is but the same."
"It is?" replied Tonga with a quizzical look.
"Yes, you see you are here to track down the
winchow," the malamute grinned, "sorry I mean
weasels...and it is these same creatures that
have kidnapped a Zamosian."
"And it is this Monty that they've taken?" asked
Tonga.
"Yes, so you see if we track down Monty we are
certain to find the weasels."
"Then we must waste no further time," uttered
Tonga excitedly.
"So let us make haste and find these vermin!"
cried Rufus, as he began trotting up the
cobbled stones.
As the others began to follow, Kolo gave his
commander a quick glance.

"Are you happy for him to lead us captain?"
Tonga smiled and nodded. "Yes I am."
"Then so am I."
In fact everyone felt honoured to follow Rufus,
for there was a general feeling that something
momentous was in the making, something
extremely special was occurring, and all were
proud to be a part of it.
After the group had reached the chalk
escarpment and had begun to journey deeper
in to Zanimos, Rufus used this telepathic link
to contact Albert. His instructions were clear;
fly ahead to Delicious Orchard, reconnoitre
the area and report back with any useful
information. Complying immediately, Albert
made use of the strong easterly currents to
make rapid progress towards the western
horizon.

Belius

Chapter 8

Monty's Trek

From the moment he had been grabbed by the two weasels and one of them had uttered "Hello piggy," Monty's carefree day had become a nightmare. He had never seen their like before and they certainly did not have the presence of tolerant or kind animals.

And this was proven when sharp swords were pressed against his neck and body to force him into a nearby ditch, where they all hid from a giant brown dog that had been spotted coming in their direction.

They all watched it sniffing around the area for a few moments before it trotted off back the way it had come. Belius had seen his type before, back in Hamilton's Tea House, siding with his enemy Brodney; but he couldn't be certain it was the same dog.

Once all was clear they moved out of the ditch and grouped together next to a particularly ancient and enormous apple tree.

Belius then stared at the pig intently.

"Bring him ere," he growled, wanting to examine him more closely.

For a moment Monty froze and was reluctant to move but a prod in the side by the hilt of a sword from Yabek soon changed that and he advanced towards the chief weasel.

"Who are you?" asked Belius under his breath.

"Um um, I'm M-montagu, Montagu Frazzelbach," he replied nervously.

"Really, and what do you do-"

"He's just a silly old fruit picker," interrupted Hubble with a chuckle.

The displeased look of Belius said it all, and Hubble was quiet.

Turning his attention back to the pig he continued his questioning.

"Well what do you do?!" he bellowed.

Monty cleared his throat; he was still very much in shock, but thinking about his self important role in the town made him feel a little less frightened.

"I manage the Bank of Zanimos," he uttered slowly, and with air of importance.

A pleasant surprise crept across the face of Belius.

"A bank manager you say, and where exactly is this bank?"

Monty smiled nervously. "It's in Zanimos Town."

"He could be useful Gritch," continued Belius turning to his second in command.

"He could slow us down."

"He won't do that, will you Mr Pig?" growled Belius.

Montagu shook his head. "N-n-no, of course not."

"Couldn't we pop in to his bank and make a large withdrawal," laughed Ruevic.

"What, and risk running into Zamosians, don't be silly!" snapped Belius.

"It was just a thought," replied Ruevic submissively.

"A stupid one," said Hubble.

"Yeah stupid," added Ugg giggling.

"Quiet you lot!" yelled Belius.

"We can't leave him ere, so we take him with us alright", commanded the leader.

Yabek looked closely at the pig and scowled. He then drew his sword and pointed it towards the pig's throat. Monty took one look at the ferocious weasel and his deadly sharp sword and began to shake nervously.

"We could do him in, save us a lot of trouble if we did," uttered Yabek.

"Yeah do him in," added an excitable Ugg.

Fear building and tummy churning, Monty desperately blurted out an emotional plea.

"Please...p-p-please don't hurt me...I won't be any bother...in fact you won't know I'm here!" To the chief weasel the pig projected a pitiful looking creature, one without backbone or strength of character and he began to wonder what to do with him. Lost in thought for a few moments his deliberations led him nowhere, and it was not until Gritch voiced his concerns that a decision was made.

"Belius, we can't waste any time, after all the boars might still be after us, and it's only a matter of time before someone in this country spots us and the alarm goes off."

Belius looked at his deputy and with some reluctance nodded in agreement, for although he disliked decisions from within his ranks he was shrewd enough to recognise any words of wisdom.

Pulling the stolen treasure map from his trouser pocket he ran his sharp claws across it while peering up and glancing at his surroundings to estimate his position.

"On the right track?" asked Gritch.

His leader turned towards him and shook his head, for the map was quite vague and just showed one route to get to the coast, when in fact there were paths and tracks leading in all directions.

"Come ere and take a look, see if we can't work it out between us" he uttered.

Monty was feeling uneasy about his situation, and his seated position with his glum face resting on his front trotters said it all.

As he stared down at the ground his feeling of hopelessness was forgotten for just a moment as he became lost in the world of ants that were scurrying around the trunk of a nearby tree. This didn't last long though, as a sudden and unexpected attack of loneliness came over him such that he had never felt. Mind you he wasn't one for making friends, after all he had no use for them; not until now that is. It then dawned on him that although he had felt reluctant to go to Hamilton's tea party earlier that day, he wished he was there now; eating sandwiches and apple pie, and perhaps even enjoying himself.

"Oh what a mess," he thought to himself.

Monty had never really known any hardship, after all he was taken into the bank and trained as a clerk from a tender age by his father, and after his sad passing became bank manager when only a young adult. However pigs are well known for stubbornness and single mindedness, and Monty had oodles of both.

And being used to running the bank he had developed a good range of decision making skills that enabled him to work out the most prudent financial decisions.

Thinking of his current precarious position, he began to lean on these abilities and toy with some possible scenarios, but he always came back to the same one; it was tenuous, but at least positive.

"Maybe I'll be missed by Hamilton and she'll send a search party...perhaps that dog was looking for me?" he pondered excitedly.

At last he was beginning to feel more upbeat about things, but it was a fleeting feeling of optimism and soon dampened by what he thought was more likely.

"Why would they come looking for me, after all they don't really know me, and probably don't even like me?"

A sensation of despair overcame him and he released the deepest sigh you had ever heard. But then an unexpected, yet welcome voice filtered through the air and began to lift him from his moment of pessimism; it was a voice from his past and one he knew so very well.

"Never give up my son, never give up, and you will be surprised at what you can achieve."

Looking upwards, he studied the grey clouds, patches of blue sky, and slowly drifting wispy clouds, while savouring that familiar phrase. Monty knew at once these were words he would hear from his father when he was a young clerk and things were getting on top of him. Although buried deep in his subconscious, their warmth and encouragement began to rally his spirits once again.

Meanwhile Belius and Gritch had spent a few minutes examining the map, during which time they had disagreed on several occasions over which route to take, but Belius finally had the last word and Gritch was forced to agree with him; even though he didn't.

"Right you lot follow me, and get a move on!" ordered Belius.

"And if Mr Piggy is uncooperative you know what to do, don't you," he added in a gruff tone, looking towards Hubble and Ruevic.

The chief weasel then set off at a brisk pace through the orchard towards the cliffs and Smugglers Cove, with Gritch, Yabek and Ugg in line behind, and after a sharp dig in the ribs from Hubble and Ruevic, Monty rose from the ground and reluctantly followed.

After walking for about a minute Monty's face lit up as he saw his beloved umbrella leaning against a tree just off the track.

"Oh that's where I left you," he announced excitedly.

Feeling a mixture of joy and relief, and keen
to grasp the brolly in his trotters once again
he took a few steps towards it, but upon
his deviation from the column his ears were
unexpectedly filled with a piercing cry from
Hubble.

"Where you goin!"

"J-just to get my umbrella," replied Monty
nervously.

"Leave it!"

"But it's my lovely umbrella," replied the pig still
walking towards his brolly.

"Leave it I say!" snarled Hubble, as he gave
Monty a sharp scratch across the leg.

"Ow!" screamed the pig reeling from the
stinging pain.

Reaching out for the umbrella, Hubble gleefully
snatched it away from Monty, but his moment
of triumph soon transformed in to outrage
as he accidently caught the locking fastener
causing the umbrella to spring fully open in to
his face.

"Blasted thing," he shouted as it caught his
cheek, and then in temper he threw it to the
ground.

"My umbrella, my lovely umbrella, how dare you!"
For a fleeting moment Monty had found the
courage to show his anger, but the weasel's
aggressive expression and snarling sharp teeth
weakened his resolve.

His rage now quashed he felt bitterly
disappointed with himself for not standing up
to the weasel; for in that moment of fight or
flight he had chosen the easy option.

"Well there are too many for me anyway," he
uttered under his breath, making an excuse for
backing down.

This calamity had attracted Belius, who
instantly stopped in his tracks and turned
around.

"What's goin on now!" he screamed at the top of
his voice.

"It's the pig, he wants his umbrella bless him!"
uttered Hubble sarcastically.

The shouting weasels had disturbed a nearby
rookery and as the birds took to flight their
noisy cries momentarily attracted everyone. In
contrast to the others who paid little attention
to the fleeing rooks, Monty found the process
of their chaotic getaway very engaging and
looked on in amazement at how they avoided
contact with one other even during this display
of erratic and unchoreographed flying. He
began to feel there was a hidden significance
in the birds' behaviour, and believed this
demonstration of the impossible was a sign that
even when things look glum, there can still be a
way forward. Remembering his father's words,
he realised more than ever he must not give up

on his pursuit of freedom, and that an attitude of hope was better than no hope at all. And even though it was going against the probable, he began to focus on the possibility of rescue by Hamilton and her friends.

"Supposing someone does come looking for me, how can I help them find me?" he thought his mind racing for an answer.

Fortunately little time was wasted on searching for a solution as it came in a flash.

"Clues that's it...I'll leave clues," he pondered triumphantly.

Knowing he could at last do something positive made him feel much more upbeat, and with a secretive smile he planned to leave clue number one.

Seeing the pig's behaviour as nothing more than interfering with his progress to find the treasure, Belius reluctantly headed back towards him wearing a bitterly disgruntled expression. Upon reaching him, he stretched up as tall as he could and stared straight in to the pig's eyes with a look devoid of emotion; it was cold, intense and hostile, and created an extremely uncomfortable feeling in the pig

"I only want my brolly," pleaded Monty.

"Well you can't ave it," growled Belius.

Monty felt a little tearful, for the umbrella had belonged to his father and meant a lot to him.

"Alright...I'll leave it here then."

"Make sure he does Hubble," snapped Belius as he turned and stomped off towards the front of the column.

The pig carefully picked up his precious brolly, closed it up back up, shook off the dust, and then proceeded to lay it back down again.

"You're a strange one, you are," uttered Hubble with a puzzled expression.

Not wanting to get left behind by Belius, let alone suffer any of his wrath for doing so, Ruevic turned on the pig.

"Come on you've wasted enough time!" he shouted furiously.

Monty averted his eyes from the angry looking weasel, took a final glance at his beloved umbrella, before obediently trotting off to follow the others.

The pig's actions may have seemed strange to Hubble who thought him over possessive of his umbrella, but what he and Ruevic failed to notice was the direction in which it was pointing; for this was the pig's first step in his plan to leave clues.

As Montagu followed his captors, he noticed that with the exception of Belius and Gritch all the others carried rucksacks, and tied to them with thick stranded string was either a shovel, or pick axe.

He studied the implements for a moment before contorting his face in to a questioning expression.

"What can they want with those?" he wondered.

Back at the front of the column a sly grin crept across the face of the leader; as something had suddenly come to mind, and he wanted to share it.

"You know Gritch, that idea of Ruevic's may not have been so silly after all."

"What ya mean, robbing the pig's bank?"

"Yep"

"But what you said before made sense. I mean we'd be asking for trouble if we went in to Zanimos Town." replied Gritch, a quizzical expression forming on his face.

A look of smugness came over the chief weasel and he curled back his lips to reveal his pointed yellow stained teeth.

"Not if we go at night," he chuckled.

A sudden look of delight filled Gritch's face.

"Of course at night, now that's a great idea!"

Belius nodded his head excitedly. "Yeah, so once we've got the treasure we can go to Zanimos Town, and mister piggy can let us in his lovely bank."

"Yeah...it's like an extra bonus init!" laughed Gritch.

The two looked at one another and broke in to uncontrolled laughter, which after a time transformed into giggling and hissing that lasted for some time after.

Belius realised he must have made a number of wrong decisions when faced with more than one path to follow, as their journey to Smugglers Cove seemed to be taking forever. He was reluctantly about to swallow his pride and ask Monty if he knew the way, but was saved from this embarrassing situation as the saltiness of the sea air, and the coastal breeze confirmed they were headed in the right direction. Monty had fleeting ideas of running off. Oh how he'd love to escape, but with Hubble close behind and Ruevic regularly turning around and eying him up, he knew he wouldn't get far. And besides he didn't like the look of Ruevic's sharp sword, which the weasel was using to slice off apples from branches hanging close to the ground.

As the group progressed through the orchard, Monty began to feel the soft fertile soil transform in to a hard chalk base indicating they would soon reach the top of the cliffs. But just before reaching the end of the orchard, a faint crying sound could be heard high up above; and it was quickly growing in volume.

Turning and peering towards the sky everyone caught a glimpse of a large bird flying rapidly in their direction. The weasels looked particularly concerned, but to Monty there was no reason to be worried; it was after all just a bird.

"Ha ha ha, ha ha, ha ha ha!" cried the bird as it soared above them.

The bird, a seagull was flying in a westerly direction, and it looked as though it might just fly over them and continue out to sea, but prior to reaching them it rolled over and dived vertically, picking up terrific speed as it did. For a moment it appeared to be travelling too fast to stop before it hit the trees, but this bird was an expert flyer, and with a fluttering of its large wings quickly reduced speed and began to hover above the canopy of the orchard.

It seemed to be very interested in the proximity of where the weasels had seized Monty and it continued to circle around and around as if searching for something, or someone.

"Get down get down!" ushered Belius, and the weasels immediately dropped to the ground.

"What's up?" questioned a bewildered Yabek. Belius and Gritch looked at one another in amazement at the question before turning towards Yabek and shaking their heads.

"For goodness sake, look at the bird will ya?!" snapped Belius.

"See it flying in circles do ya" added Gritch sarcastically.

Yabek watched the gull for a moment. He was captivated by the beauty and grace in its movement, the way it turned, and banked and the magical way it hovered motionless in the wind; and then it struck him

"It's looking for the pig?!" he uttered excitedly under his breath.

"Could be, and if it is, it mustn't see us," replied Belius looking up at the bird through a gap in the trees.

His face took on a worried expression as he knew the importance of not being spotted by a local animal, as this could indeed ruin their plan to steal the treasure. Pointing a sharp claw at Yabek he uttered a stern command.

"Now listen, tell the others to get behind a tree and keep out of sight, got it?!"

Yabek crawled backwards and whispered his leader's orders to the others and everyone complied, finding the nearest tree and keeping out of sight; but Monty and Hubble were too far away to hear the instruction.

Belius and his second in command Gritch found shelter behind the unusually large trunk of a pear tree that was a loner amongst the apples.

But after a few moments curiosity got the better of them, and they peered around trunk of the tree searching through the gaps in the trees in the hope of catching a glimpse of the bird.

Yet as soon as they sighted the gull they promptly darted behind the tree and sat back to back. Then ever so slowly they turned and looked at one another, each having a feeling of bewilderment, for the gull wasn't the only animal they had seen.

After a mutual look of consternation they popped their heads around the tree once again to double check what they thought they had seen, only to find their worst thoughts were confirmed. It was unforgivable, unbelievable, and what's more maddening for both of them as they caught sight of a lone weasel lying on his back sound asleep without a care in the world. And to make things even worse Monty was standing next to him and making no attempt to hide from the inquisitive gull.

Belius was furious and without thinking about whether the gull might hear him he shouted out in an angry tone.

"Why that stupid Hubble!"

Belius' face became distorted and reddened with anger, it appeared that any minute he might explode, but the distraction of the crying gull overhead, made him realise the importance of being undetected, and helped by a huge sigh of exasperation, his simmering temper soon abated,

"Wake him Gritch, and get that pig out of sight too," he ordered under his breath.

"Will do."

Gritch sped past Ugg and motioned Yabek to follow him.

"Get up ya lazy good for nothing," growled Gritch as he planted a firm kick to Hubble's buttocks.

"Ow, ow!" complained the weasel in response to the sudden and unpleasant interruption to his slumber.

"Shush...shush," continued Gritch and Hubble nodded in compliance.

"Get that pig outta sight too," instructed Gritch as a yawning Hubble got to his feet.

"Help him," snapped Gritch, and Yabek grabbed Hubble by the shoulder and dragged him forward.

"Hey," complained Hubble shrugging off Yabek's grip.

"Well wake up sleepy head!" shouted Yabek

Monty hadn't felt the need to hide, as he was sure the bird was no threat to him, and just like Yabek he had enjoyed watching it.

He had always been puzzled at how birds
seemingly disobey gravity and have the ability
to undertake such wonderful aerobatics.

"Oh to be a bird...how wonderful," he thought.
It was a pleasant moment of escapology from
his predicament, but it was only momentary, as
his captors would not permit his daydreaming to
continue.

"Ah!" he cried, as he felt the sharpened points
of cold steel against his throat, and Yabek and
Hubble sniggered as they held their swords
firmly against him.

"Right Piggy get down behind that tree," hissed
Yabek.

"Now!" added Hubble growling under his breath.
The two weasels walked Monty backwards until
the three of them were behind a large tree and
then Yabek brought the flattened part of this
blade onto Monty's back.

"Ouch," cried Monty.

"Get down Mr Piggy," was the gravelly voiced
order.

Monty slumped to the ground and lay quiet.
He felt saddened that his brief respite had
been so harshly and abruptly interrupted; but
seeing the bird did bring a glimmer of hope that
someone was looking for him.

The bird spent some moments circling before
dropping to the ground and disappearing, during

which time the weasels feeling a little safer began to pop their heads from behind the trees and search for it. They looked to the sky and back into the orchard but could see no sign of it. Suddenly the air was filled with loud shrieking cries, as the gull rose up above the trees and headed eastwards, and flying speedily off it quickly diminished in size until finally disappearing.

Feeling certain that the bird was no longer a threat, Belius waved a foot in the air and called for the others to join him.

"Phew, that was close," uttered Gritch with a sigh of relief.

Belius grinned complacently, "I think we got away with it, I don't think it saw us."

"Right you lot gather round!" he ordered, shouting at the others.

He paused for a moment waiting for everyone to close up, before slowly and deliberately peering directly into their eyes, instilling fear where he could; as he liked to lead by terror.

Then in a low gravelly tone he continued.

"Now listen up, we're here to get the treasure, not to baby sit Mr Pig," he growled, pointing a sharp claw towards Monty.

"And if he's going to prove a nuisance we gotta do him in, get it."

"A yawning Hubble nodded in agreement.

"With ya boss," uttered Ruevic.

"Got it!" yelled Yabek, raising his sword.

Ugg turned and stared at the pig. "Me too," he sniggered, taunting him.

He didn't bother to ask Gritch, as he knew he could rely on his second in command.

Monty didn't like what he heard one bit, and was unable to quell the trembling feeling rising in his stomach, nor subdue his troubled expression.

Belius spotted terror in the pig's eyes and felt very satisfied, as he loved nothing more than imbuing others with fear.

"Right let's get on our way," he began, nodding to Gritch.

However, Belius was a clever if not devious creature, and realised that you cannot get loyalty by bullying alone, and so before moving off, he uttered a few rallying words.

"Just remember us weasels are brave, strong in battle and experts in stealth. So let's use these weasel ways to get hold of the treasure, take it home and celebrate, alright?!"

"Alright!" shouted the other weasels in chorus.

Belius then set off with his gang close behind. His tempo was quick, and Ugg who wore a puzzled expression had to take on a burst of speed to catch up with Yabek, with whom he had a question.

"Yabek, what does stealth mean?" he asked in a quizzical tone.

He had barely uttered these words when he clumsily trod on a large piece of dead wood producing a loud cracking noise.

"Being quiet," replied Yabek.

"And not making a noise!" shouted Gritch turning around with a scowling expression.

"Uh huh," responded a vacant looking Ugg before falling back in to line behind Yabek.

They were soon out of the orchard, and after reaching the edge of the cliffs Belius led them southwards along the rough and bumpy chalk path. He was pleased to reach this as they would leave no footprints in the chalk, which may mean any pursuers might go in the opposite direction; but unfortunately the path wasn't too kind to their feet, and some of the others did start to complain a little. Hubble and Ruevic were keen to vent their discomfort on to Monty with sharp jabs from their swords, and took great satisfaction in poking and prodding their prisoner; and his complaining yelps made them do it all the more. In frustration and anger Monty grabbed at a button on his waist coat, and as it was hanging by a single threat it came off very easily. He was about to throw it away

in temper when suddenly the idea for his next
clue came to him, and so he held on to it.
He wasn't initially happy at the prospect of
spoiling his splendid waistcoat, but if it would
help to bring a speedy end to his uncomfortable
situation, he was willing to do it.
So trying not to attract attention he began
to tug away at the remaining five buttons; he
twisted and pulled and yanked, and one by one
they came off. There was however one which
was determined not to leave the waistcoat;
still in total he had managed to free five
shiny silver buttons each with the letters M F
ornately engraved on them. Monty was bright
and intelligent, qualities one would expect from
a bank manager, and he realised that even the
lethargic Hubble must not catch him purposely
dropping his buttons, or his plan would be foiled.
"But how to distract him?" he thought.
And then it came to him.
He felt anxious at first, but his yearning to
escape drove him to pluck up his courage. He
decided he needed to get Hubble closer to
him, and so quickly came to a halt, causing the
sluggish weasel to bump into him.
"Oi watch what you're doin!" snapped Hubble.
"Um s-s-sorry, but somethings just crossed my
mind."

"What is it?" asked Hubble, with a screwed up look of disinterest.

"Just wondered why you weasels don't like birds?" he asked with a squeaky tone.

"What ya mean by that?" snarled Hubble.

"Well we had to hide from that gull didn't we?"

"Yeah but that was cuz he might ave been looking for us."

"What like that one over there?" pointed Monty out to sea.

The weasel looked alarmed and peered out to sea wondering if it was the bird from the woods following them. Engrossed in searching the sky he didn't see Monty step to the side of him and toss his buttons back along the chalk path as far as he could.

"What are you doin," shouted Ruevic as he noticed Hubble staring out to sea.

"Looking for a bird."

"I saw a large gull a short distance from the cliffs," uttered Monty.

"Be quiet piggy!" bellowed Ruevic.

"Sorry," replied the pig subserviently.

"There's nothing there Hubble!" cried Ruevic staring out to sea.

Hubble looked disappointed, "I think you're right."

"So where's this bird then eh Mr Piggy!?" questioned Ruevic sternly.

"Er...it must have dived below the cliffs," blurted Monty, momentarily lost for words. Ruevic feeling a little sceptical of the explanation fixed his eyes menacingly on Monty causing his stomach to flutter once again, as he remembered what Belius had said about doing him in.

"Think you're clever don't you mister piggy," cackled Ruevic, as only a weasel could.

"Clever, what do you mean?"

"There wasn't no bird...you just made it up, didn't you?"

"B-b-ut why would I do that?" replied Monty shying away.

The weasel shook his head. "I don't know," he uttered, in a gravelly voice toned with aggression.

It was an awkward moment when Monty wondered if the weasel might even strike him, but a timely interruption diverted his attention, and Monty breathed a sigh of relief.

"Come on, we gotta catch up with the chief or we'll be for it!" shouted Hubble vigorously.

"Go on get to it then," ordered Ruevic giving Monty a formidable stare.

Initially Monty was hugely relieved that the threat was over, however as he began trotting off to catch up with Belius and Gritch his tummy began to feel more settled, and his old characteristics of arrogance and conceit quickly returned; after all he had cleverly outwitted the two weasels, and left yet another clue. "Not too shabby, not too shabby" he gloated complacently.

Hamilton was seated in her favourite soft cushioned armchair with her back propped up by a floral cushion, but even this most comfortable situation couldn't provide a pleasant distraction from her concern over Monty; and she was fretting. Horace seated opposite was delicately sipping tea from one of Hamilton's fine bone china cups. His tea tasted lovely, as it always did when Hamilton made it, however the look of worry on her face was marring his enjoyment. "Come on old girl, chin up, I'm certain things will be alright, they usually are you know," he uttered in a philosophical tone.
"Do you really think so?" she replied pessimistically.
"Look here," continued Horace putting his cup and saucer down.
"I'm certain if anyone can find Monty, Rufus can."
The mention of Rufus seemed to strike a positive chord with Hamilton.
"Oh I do so hope you're right," she uttered with a momentary smile.

"Why you know I am, there's something very special about him, and I'm certain he won't let us down."

A warm and friendly smile ran across the hare's face.

"Now come on, drink your tea and cheer up...and that's an order," he continued in a kindly tone.

Hamilton's face beamed.

"Oh how glad I am to have you as a friend."

Then suddenly and without warning there were three loud thumps as the brass knocker struck the plate on the front door.

"Hamilton, Horace, its Rufus open up!"

Hamilton quickly scampered in to the hall and unlocked the door.

"Any news?!" she questioned in earnest as she opened it.

Rufus was about to respond but on noticing her attention had been diverted remained quiet; for after all he didn't wish to spoil her surprise.

For an instance she stood perfectly still, her vacant and wide eyed expression doubting reality, but having taken things in, her heart skipped a beat and her senses were flooded with joy and delight.

Unable to control her excitement any longer she produced the most wonderful beaming smile, and darted past Rufus, along her garden path, straight in to the arms of an old friend.

"Oh Charlie, it's so wonderful to see you!" she exclaimed excitedly.

"And you too!" replied Charlie, gently lifting Hamilton off her paws.

Recognising more familiar faces her heart began to pound with excitement, but unable to control her euphoric emotions tears of joy slowly trickled down her cheeks. For like Charlie's they were faces of her past, not forgotten, but kept as memories, and to be in their presence once again was so unbelievable she wanted to pinch herself.

"Captain Tonga!" she yelled, as loud as hamsters can.

"Hello Hamilton," smiled the strong Tonga.

"And don't forget me?!" called out Sergeant Kolo.

"Oh how could I," she smiled.

"It's so lovely to see you all, she continued as she exchanged friendly smiles with Buna and Wicklop.

And then someone she had known from a youngster caught her attention, and she looked towards him with great affection.

"Why its little Tunashi, and all grown up too." The young boar initially looked a trifle embarrassed, but his mutual affection for the hamster made him forget his shyness, and show his true feelings.

"Oh it's so good to see you Hamilton, we really miss you at the tea house, don't we father?" Kolo smiled. "Yes we do."

Hamilton blushed.

"Well that's very kind of you, but I'm sure Sasha's looking after things well enough?"

"Yes he is, you couldn't have sold your tea house to anyone better than Sasha...he's doing a wonderful job." Uttered Tonga,

"And Bloomsberry, how's she?" asked the hamster waving her paws animatedly.

"She's just fine," replied the captain.

"As dependable as always," added Charlie.

A satisfied smile crept across her face as she felt so pleased all was well with her old tea house, but then something crossed her mind which caused her to start to playing with her whiskers, as her kind often do when mulling things over.

Charlie recognised this behaviour.

"Something bothering you?"

"W-well I was just wondering...what brings you all here?"

Tonga produced a low growl.

"It's those dreaded weasels, they've stolen my treasure map," he uttered still rubbing his head, even though the lump was barely detectable.

"And we're going to make sure they don't get it!" added Charlie firmly.

Hamilton had been told all about the great cat and her legendary treasure by Horace, who loved to tell stories, but presently gems and jewels held no importance to her; all that mattered was finding Monty. She was still quite beside herself with worry and looked towards her old friend with a desperately imploring expression.

"Will you help us to find Monty; it appears the weasels have kidnapped him?"

The collie gently patted her on the side of the shoulder and smiled.

"If the weasels have him, we'll find him."

Hamilton felt reassured by her old friend's words and a faint feeling of hope began to outweigh her sinking despondency.

Rufus remained silent while old friendships were renewed, but having never lost track of the urgency in pursuing the weasels, tactfully began to break up the reunion.

"Ahem ahem," he coughed, and everyone looked towards him.

"It's time to move, and move quickly."

His voice was firm and clear, and as he turned around to lead the way forward, he gave the hamster a reassuring smile.

"Now don't worry yourself Hamilton, we'll find Monty."

Captain Arcadius Tonga

Chapter 9

Underground

Having trekked along the top of the tall cliffs for some distance, Belius was relieved to see wooden guard rails signifying they had reached the path down to the beach. The strong breeze from Auricious Bay made it difficult for him to consult his map, and on several occasions Gritch had stood behind him acting as wind break, while he checked their progress; but at last they had found this important landmark in their journey.

"Right Lads down here!" he shouted.

"Getting nearer then?" asked Gritch.

"Yep," was the curt reply.

The path, not much more than a narrow ledge, meandered downwards along the face of the chalk cliffs, finally reaching the beach, where a narrow strip of golden sand followed the contours of the cliffs around the otherwise pebbled shoreline of Smugglers Cove.

Yabek and Ugg both gasped as they peered down at the long drop to the beach below; still they found some relief in the wooden railings on the outside edge of the path. Monty hadn't trodden this path since he was a piglet, when his small size enabled him to keep close to the cliff wall and avoid the frightening view over the edge. Now having a bulkier frame, this was no longer possible, and after a few steps he accidently nudged the railings causing them to momentary tremble and wobble, which scared the life out of him; and even startled some of the weasels.

"Whoa better take it easy!" he uttered holding his chest.

Not wishing to show the weasels he was frightened he quickly pulled himself together, and continued along the path much more carefully, allowing his pounding heart to gradually calm down.

Like most young animals of Zanimos he had travelled along this walkway to reach Smugglers Cove in search of the legendary treasure of Catsumo; and just like those before him he had come away with nothing. Although he remembered little of his jaunts in to the many caves of Smugglers Cove, the one remaining memory was the engraving of a giant cat at the end of a deep tunnel.

Unlike any of the other carvings found in the caves, the outline was three dimensional with a luminous sinister glow that wavered in brightness and colour. The cat was sat on its haunches, two front paws with sharpened claws were stretching out in front, and its mouth was wide open declaring a set of dangerous teeth. But the most frightening and memorable aspect, was a mysteriously sinister aura that infused the impression with life.

He shuddered at the mere thought of going back in to that cave, he was not keen on the idea one bit, and the feeling of goose pimples running down his back made him less inclined to go there once more.

Like all young Zamosians he had been told the story of Catsumo, the giant black cat who led an army of cut throat pirates and mercenaries, and how coming to Zanimos was her great undoing. For although she possessed dark and evil magical powers, these were no match for the wizard Mortuleez and his wife Julianna.

Legend has it that her defeated army was forced to set sail from Zanimos leaving her behind to be pursued by Mortuleez deep into the caves of Smugglers Cove, where she had hidden her treasure.

History tells of a long drawn out magnificent battle of good versus evil, but as to the outcome no one really knows the truth.

Some believe Catsumo met her death at the hands of the mighty Mortuleez, while other give credence to the tale of a dark demonic power spiriting her away; but whichever occurred her body was never found.

Although these frightening reflections had proved unpleasant, they had at least kept his mind off his weariness, but alas his strength was now beginning to fade, and tiredness was taking over.

He was after all just used to pottering about in his bank, doing clerical work and talking with customers; hardly what one would call energetic activities. He had actually felt fatigued well before the weasels captured him; as the repeated work of climbing the ladder, picking apples, and putting them in his basket, had proved very tiring. Strangely enough the shock of being kidnapped and the threat of being killed had given him renewed vigour which helped to keep him going, but that couldn't last forever and with his energy fading, each step he took became more tortuous.

Belius was now some twenty yards along the beach from the bottom of the path with his number two Gritch by his side, when he paused

and turned around to check the progress of the others. Ugg and Yabek were not too far behind and were keeping up a reasonable pace; but where were Ruevic, Hubble and the pig?
Staring back up the cliff path he saw how slowly the three of them were moving and saw red, his face looked like thunder and he screamed over to Hubble at the top of his voice.
"Get that pig moving, you're lagging behind!"
Belius shook his head and glanced at Gritch in disbelief, before looking back towards Ruevic and waving his foot frantically.
"Get that pig up to speed, and if he doesn't move kill him, do you hear, kill him!"
Ruevic had not long stepped on to beach, but in response to his leaders outburst he hurried back toward the cliff path as fast as he could, slipping on the loose sand as he did so.
The admonishment from Belius had also propelled Hubble in to action and he immediately pulled his sword from its scabbard and gave the pig a sharp jab in the back.
"Ow, ow!" cried the Monty reeling from this discomfort.
Hubble drew back his sword in preparation for another thrust, but this was not needed, for Monty's fear of further discomfort drove him to fight through his weariness and pick up pace in to a gentle trot. But as he was about to step

on to the small area of wooden decking and begin to descend the two steps to the beach, the sight of another pointed sword held by Ruevic caused him to miss his footing and trip forwards.

Ruevic's reaction was fast and he leaped out of the way of the flying pig who soared past him. For Monty it was one of these slow motion moments, flying though the air felt magical, but this was soon spoiled by the discomfort of hitting the wooden railing, and then even worse was his impact on the sharp sand as it rubbed his snout raw and filled his nostrils. He remained motionless for a moment and even Ruevic and Hubble thought he was no more. But then he pulled himself out of the sand, got to his trotters and began shaking himself to rid the sand from his body, spraying the two weasels in the process.

"Oh my poor snout," he uttered, feeling a stinging pain.

Ruevic laughed.

"Serves you right for lagging behind."

"So hurry up!" shouted Hubble who was about to jab him once again. Monty gave his snout a quick rub before stepping out of range of the flailing sword of Hubble. But as he did so a strange floating sensation suddenly came over him, his vision clouded and he felt disconnected from his surroundings. Things had finally come to a head for Monty, as the strain of a forced march, cruel bullying, and death threats had totally sapped his mental and physical being; and he had no more to give.

"Can't we rest for a moment?" he pleaded.

"Ah like a nice rest would ya," said Ruevic sarcastically.

"Ah bless, the poor little piggy's all tuckered out," he continued turning towards Hubble with a grin, which soon transformed into a look of vexation when he saw his fellow weasel open mouthed and yawing.

"Don't you ever stop!" he snapped.

"Stop what?" replied Hubble mid way through a yawn.

Ruevic's face contorted.

"Your wretched yawning!"

"But I'm tired Ruevic, I'm really tired...I think I need to sit down for a moment."

The words had barely left his mouth when he collapsed in a heap on the sand and started to snore noisily. Monty also laid himself down on the sand but more sedately, and feeling so utterly fed up and exhausted, he couldn't even care less if he was prodded or poked or even done away with.

Devoid of all energy he immediately fell in to
the deepest slumber, producing rasping snores
which even eclipsed those of Hubble's.

Ruevic looked on in disbelief.

"You've asked for it you have," he said shaking
his head.

Knowing that Belius would be angered by the
behaviour of Hubble and Monty, and wishing to
avoid trouble himself, he called out to his chief
at the top of his voice.

"Belius...Belius...Belius!"

Looking across the beach towards the cries
of Ruevic, the chief weasel's eyes were
immediately on stalks as he observed Hubble
and Monty lying down on the sand, seemingly
fast asleep.

His anger wound up inside, he was not merely
annoyed; he was infuriated, and tugging on
Gritch's shoulder to follow him, he ran back
across the sand towards Ruevic and the others.

"Come on you two!" he shouted as he reached
Yabek and Ugg who turned around and
begrudgingly followed.

"Oh what now?" whispered Yabek to himself,
but his question was soon answered when he
caught sight of the two dozing animals.

"You two are gonna catch it," he uttered,
shaking his head.

As Belius and the others reached Ruevic he held his front feet out in a perplexed gesture, trying to appease his leader.

"What can I do Belius, what can I do, they're sound asleep?!"

Fortunately for Ruevic, Belius was more interested in the slumbering twosome, and immediately vented his rage on the weasel by administering a sharp kick to his side.

"Hey stop that!" complained the weasel drowsily.

"Stop that, I'll give you stop that!" screamed Belius, and planted an even harder kick to Hubble's rump.

"Ow!" screamed Hubble, opening his eyes to behold the angry countenance of his leader.

"You...why I bother, I don't know! You're useless.

Now get outta my sight!" Growled Belius

Slowly rising to his feet, Hubble nervously moved away from Belius and stood behind Ruevic. But he needn't have worried about any further mal treatment from his chief, as his attention was now focused completely on Monty. Strangely enough, even the noisy complaints of Hubble had not roused the pig who was still sound asleep and filling the air with an outrageously droning grumble, occasionally broken by a gasping sharp intake of breath. The lead weasel looked upon the sleeping pig with disgust before drawing his sword, and raising it above his head in readiness to strike. He had reached the end of his tether, and wondered if keeping Monty alive just to rob a bank was worth jeopardising his quest to get the treasure. The sword was ready to do its deed, but before Belius had decided whether or not to use it, fate intervened in the guise of a large sand fly.

Deciding to land on the pig's snout, the fly crawled around aimlessly for a few moments before disappearing inside his nose.

Now Monty like any other pig has very sensitive nasal passages, and the fly's movement soon created such overwhelming itching that his body's natural response created the most explosive and sonorous sneeze. It was in fact so loud that all the weasels covered their ears to avoid the awful din, and it surprised Belius so much he released the grip on his sword which dropped towards Monty.

"Ouch!" exclaimed the pig feeling the impact of the pommel on his head.

Slowly and unsteadily getting to his trotters, he started searching his throbbing head for any signs of injury.

"Oh! Oh! I'm bleeding!" he cried, finding a small cut with a spot of blood on it.

"Bleedin, you're a bleedin nuisance that's what!" shouted Belius, unaware that he had made a little quip.

"Ruevic and Hubble thought it funny and began to laugh.

"Quiet you two!" snapped Belius, and the recipients cowered nervously.

Belius quickly picked up his sword before staring at Monty, who peered down at him with a feeling of great trepidation.

"You're causing us weasels a lot a trouble, and we can't put up with this can we lads!?" cried the leader looking around at his subordinates.

"No!" shouted the others obediently.

The sharp sword of Belius was pressing against the throat of the pig, who was beginning to strain his neck upwards to reduce the pressure.

"L-l-look Belius...I-m-m sorry but I'm so tired, so very tired. If only I could have a little rest I'm sure I wouldn't be a burden."

Belius curled his lips and growled under his breath.

"Give me one reason, one reason why I don't kill ya now?"

Monty's mind raced for an answer, his heart beat quickened, inducing a fearful sensation that overcame his whole body, making it feel like it would shake apart; and then just in the nick of time it came to him.

"L-l-listen, suppose there's no treasure. N-n-n-early everyone in Zanimos has searched for it at one time or another, yet no one's ever found it."

Belius adopted an inscrutable expression, and Monty knew he had to convince him, or it could be his end.

"W-w-well supposing you don't find any. I can let you into the bank, and you can take all the money."

He looked pleadingly in to the soulless and harsh eyes of the weasel, but there was no response.

"Theres some jewellery too," he blurted, in desperate hope that this may save him. But the lack of change in the weasel's hardened composure only served to increase his already booming heart rate. Dizziness followed, clouding his thoughts and filling his body with a numbness that drew him away from reality; he was now a spectator not a player.

Belius had thought hard about the pig's offer, and his idea made sense, for if there was no treasure at least they could rob the bank and go home with something.

"So where's the key to the bank then Piggy?" he growled under his breath.

The pig's eyes flickered, as he slowly began to process the question, but his failure to respond

immediately irritated Belius; who was in a hurry
for an answer.

"Where's the key, did you ere me, I said
where's the key!" he screamed; his harsh and
booming words instantly jolting the pig from his
stupor.

"I-i-t's in my house," stuttered Monty, slowly
returning to his senses.

Belius stared dispassionately at Monty for
what seemed like an eternity, his eyes never
faltering, and it was only after a cruel grin
crept across his face that he finally spoke.

"Okay Mr Piggy, we'll have a little rest here for
a while, but once we're on our way again you're
gonna stay at the front with Gritch and me, got
it!"

"Yes...thank you," replied Monty, a look of
gratitude on his face.

Feeling a huge sense of relief, he took a series
of deep breaths, bringing about a gradual
welcomed calmness which slowly displaced these
uninvited and distressing emotions. He certainly
didn't relish experiencing them again and quickly
realised he must endeavour to curry favour with
Belius - even though he despised him greatly
- for to cause further irritation to the weasel
could possibly be fatal.

"Stay with him you two idiots," uttered the leader glaring at Ruevic and Hubble who bowed submissively in response.

The weasels soon split up in to their little cliques of Belius and Gritch, who moved well away from the others and began to chat quietly. Yabek and Ugg who walked to the edge of the sea and tossed pebbles into the foaming water, and Ruevic who lay down next to Hubble and Monty.

Hubble as usual found falling asleep very natural; Monty on the other hand was tossing and turning in frustration. Feeling absolutely dead beat with nothing more to give he desperately wanted sleep, yet was unable to relax enough to drop off, and Hubble's noisy breathing was an aggravating distraction. Turning his attention seawards his mind drifted away from his struggle to sleep as he became captivated by the breaking waves and the deep blue water of Auricious bay. Feeling the breeze on his face he began to picture himself on a small boat, rowing out to sea away from the weasels – it was a wonderful thought. But Monty was no fool and realised he was being lured in to fantasy by the distant horizon where vision ends and anything seems possible. Reluctantly back to reality again, he began to gaze closer at the coast line where he became transfixed by the incoming tide. He watched with great interest as curling, tumbling crests of waves broke into a swash forcing pebbles further up the shore line, only to see the ebbing tide drag them out to sea a moment later.

Yabek and Ugg seemed happy in their escape from their duties and were trying to splash each other by throwing pebbles in to the nearby surf. For a fleeting moment Monty wanted to join in and so dragged himself up on to his trotters and walked slowly across the sandy strip towards the pebble line. However, as he reached the stony beach the truth of his predicament returned, and he released a deep despondent sigh realising what a fool he was to think he could play games with his dangerously unpredictable captors.

Lost in his misery once again, Monty began to stare at a solitary white pebble lying on the sand, and this lonely pebble prompted him to remember his training as a young bank clerk. Why this thought of years gone by suddenly returned was quite strange, and he looked at the lonesome pebble with a most quizzical expression. Without thinking he began to pick up random pebbles and lay them on the sand, and as taught by his father laid down nine pebbles in a shape of a diamond, as this was a standard method for counting bronze and silver coins.

To explain briefly; the currencies of Zanimos and Unger are made up of bronze, silver and gold coins, where nine bronze equal one silver, and nine silver one gold - only gold coins are counted in tens, which might sound strange, but that's how it works.

Anyway, Monty's recollections of those good old times with his father initially filled him with sadness, as he recognised they could never be experienced again. But after a deep and drawn out sigh, rationale returned, he told himself that was life, nothing could be changed; and that after all he was so fortunate to have such wonderful memories.

After a few moments of gazing down upon the unevenly shaped, but smooth stones forming four straight sides of equal length, he began moving them around so as to produce different patterns. For a while it felt therapeutic and he started to relax, forgetting all his worries, but this calmness didn't last as he became annoyed with himself for wasting time playing around with silly old pebbles, and in a fit of petulance knocked them around with his trotters.

It was his frustration of feeling helpless that made him do it, and anyway it felt good too.

Fed up with scattering them on the sand he

started to hurl them up in the air, and then a strange thing caught his eye as he tossed one exceptionally high. He watched in amazement, as for a fleeting moment the stone appeared to remain stationary, as if just floating in the air, but attraction to the ground soon took control again, and it plunged rapidly downwards until a sharp crunching indicated its collision with another pebble. Monty continued to watch as it bounced off the one it had hit, and awkwardly rolled a short distance before finally coming to a halt. For an instant he was spellbound, disbelieving his vision, yet here it was, another idea for a clue; and it was jumping straight out at him.

The clue would be in the shape he could create with the pebbles, and although not quite there yet, he excitedly adjusted their position, until it was done.

A huge smile then broke out across his face. "What a clever pig I am, a most clever pig indeed," he whispered, with a smug look on his face.

Belius and Glitch had been talking at some length about the possibility of being followed, and they both wondered if that was the case how long would it take a search party to catch them.

This lead Belius to look back across the sand to the bottom of the cliff path, shaking his head at the sight of all the imprints they had made.

"These tracks worry me Glitch." He said sounding very concerned.

Glitch sighed, "And they'll be tracks in the orchard too."

Belius nodded, "True enough, though we shouldn't have left any on the chalk so that might send em the wrong way."

"But these ones ere will make it easy to follow."

"We gotta hide em Gritch...but how?"

Gritch screwed up his beady eyes, studied the tracks in the sand, glanced out to sea and then began to peer southwards where something caught his attention. In the distance three large odd shaped chalk stacks were lying in a straight line from the shore out into the cove; and as he studied their position an idea instantly struck him.

"Chief let's have a butchers at your map?" he asked excitedly.

Belius quickly obliged, and within moments they were studying the area where the treasure was shown, and both sets of eyes fell upon three tiny dots next to which were sketched two words – 'Serpent's End'.

"I got it!" exclaimed Gritch.

Belius looked intrigued. "Go on?" he grunted.
"My old dad was always telling me that if you're being chased the best place to hide your tracks is in water."

Gritch paused and a grin ran across his face.
"And we got plenty a that," he continued pointing at the sea.

Belius's face was a picture as it turned into a glow of happiness.

"You know Gritch you're not as silly as ya look. In fact you're pretty smart."

For a moment Gritch bathed in the glory of his great idea, but Belius wasn't entirely happy that he hadn't thought of this himself.

"But not clever enough to be chief," he hissed under his breath.

"N-no, of course not," replied Gritch subserviently.

Belius quickly ran over to the bottom of the cliff pathway where he picked up two fragments of wood that were part of the railing Monty had broken off when he fell over.

"Ugg, Yabek stop playin with those blasted pebbles and come ere!" he shouted.

The two weasels looked at each other disappointedly; they were having fun, which is something they seldom did in Belius' company. But knowing they dare not ignore their chief they threw their last pebbles in to the surf and obediently trotted towards him.

"Here you two grab these," called Belius as he threw a piece of railing towards each of them. The one aimed towards Yabek landed safety by his feet, but his friend was not quite so lucky.

"Ow!" cried Ugg as the sharp piece of wood hit his leg.

"Oh give over!" yelled Belius dispassionately. "Now you two listen and listen good," he continued.

"The rest of us are going to walk in to the sea, and you two are going to follow behind and drag those sticks across our foot prints, got it?

"Why?" asked Ugg looking baffled.

"To hide our tracks stupid," uttered Yabek.

Ugg thought for an instant and then his face glowed excitely.

"Ahh I get it, it's in case we're being followed innit?"

Their chief not known for his patience scowled at Ugg.

"Just get over by the cliff path and work back to the sea."

"That's not too ard is it?" he added, harshly staring at them both.

"N-no chief," replied Yabek grabbing Ugg and dragging him off.

Reaching Gritch, Belius shook his head in disbelief.

"You know Gritch I sometimes wonder why I keep that lazy Hubble, and idiotic Ugg in my gang," he sighed.

Gritch laughed.

"Right everyone let's all go for a lovely paddle!" shouted Belius, before leading Gritch in to the warm waters of Smugglers Cove.

After some aggressive shaking from Ruevic a complaining Hubble eventually got to his feet; and then it was pick on Monty time.

"Come on Piggy that includes you," ordered Ruevic waving his sword in the air.

Monty slowly and carefully got to his trotters keeping his pattern of pebbles behind him.

He was worried about stepping away from the stones as they might easily be seen, but fortunately for him they were not.

Meanwhile Belius was bellowing out his orders to Ugg and Yabek who were hastily doing their best to disrupt all visible tracks, while making their way towards the pebble beach.

"Hurry up you two, and don't miss a single print!" he yelled at the top of his voice.

As the old scratched and battered brass telescope was fully extended the viewer followed the crests and troughs of waves as

they broke upon the pebble shore line, where
he beheld a small band of animals dragging their
damp bodies out of the sea.

"Take her in lads, we can get much closer!"
commanded the holder of the telescope, and
Estee, Sango and Quarto, the three rats on the
rudder, responded accordingly.

Very shortly the Lady Bamboozler was as close
to land as her captain dare take her for fear of
running aground.

"Drop anchor!" shouted Sileenus.

After a moments silence there were loud
splashes immediately followed by the sonorous
clattering of the steel chains as the ship's
anchors made their way towards the seabed.
The ship drifted slightly for a moment before
the anchors bit in to the sandy bottom and
securely held her against the tide. The fox
satisfied that his ship was held firm turned to
his two coxswains to give his next order.

"Spika, Tufta! a shot off the port side...and
without a ball if you please.

"Yes sir!" they shouted in unison and summoned
up a group of rats from below deck to prepare
a cannon for firing. Having been trained by the
Nordeamium navy, the rats proficiently rammed
gunpowder into the barrel, lit a long wooden
fuse and held it against the touch hole.

Kaboom! exploded the cannon with a deafening roar and the rats cowered and covered their ears.

Training his telescope on the beach Sileenus was pleased to see the cannon fire had the desired effect, as Belius and his group turned seawards and began frantically waving and cheering.

"And what's this then, looks like they have a prisoner?" uttered the fox in an alarmed tone of voice as he caught sight of two weasels brandishing their swords towards a pig to hurry him along.

Taking a sharp intake of breath Sileenus slowly shook his head, a look of exasperation covered his face, for their quest to find the treasure relied on stealth and secrecy, and forcing a Zamosian to tag along may be sheer folly.

"I do hope you've not scuppered our plans Belius," he sighed deeply.

Sileenus continued to watch the band of animals until the last one disappeared into a cave before lowering his telescope and giving his next instructions.

"Spika, Tufta, each of you take a row boat, and wait on the beach for Belius and his gang."

"Aye aye," replied the two rats respectively.

Belius felt much happier now he knew his
exit from Zanimos was assured, for it had
seemed a long time since he and his pack had
landed earlier that day on the golden sands of
Auricious Bay.

And as he had watched the wooden dinghy
- that had dropped them off - being swiftly
rowed back to Lady Bamboozler, he was
overcome with a great sense of isolation, for he
knew too well the only way he could leave this
country was by sea. However he found great
comfort in the fact that Sileenus would have to
return to collect them if he wanted his share
of the treasure; and he felt certain the fox's
greed would ensure he did.

After waving animatedly towards Lady
Bamboozler he shouted back at the others to
quicken their pace and led them into one of
three cave entrances which all connected to
the same enormous cavern. While waiting for
the others to assemble he took stock of the
flotsam and jetsam that the tides had washed
ashore. There were many old wooden planks
and beams; probably from ships that had been
lost in battle or storm, and there were several
broken barrels with rusted hoops once used
to store rum, brandy, or some other alcohol.
There was also an old leather boot, a piece
of rigging, a broken and rusted cutlass, and a

couple of green glassed bottles half buried in the sand, and an upturned wooden rowing boat with part of its hull wripped open; but much to the disappointment of Belius there was nothing of value.

However his hopes of finding treasure quickly rose as he spotted a large wooden chest taking central position in the cave and he wasted no time in approaching it. The chest was sunken down to its lid which was barely hanging on by two corroded hinges, and looked like it had been there for decades. The metal lock had been levered off and could be seen laying in the sand, but alas any valuable contents had long since gone only to be replaced by sand, pebbles sea water and kelp, and a large crab who had made its home there.

"Gritch, candles!" ordered the leader towards his second in command, who in turn nodded towards Yabek.

Yabek knew exactly what to do next and turned around to allow Gritch to undo a pocket in the side of his rucksack and after a few moments of fumbling he pulled out half a dozen candles and a crushed box of matches.

Candles lit, Belius led his band of weasels along a narrow tunnel, with Monty being the only one without a light to guide him. Further and further they trudged, and as the tunnel gradually inclined they had to work harder to maintain their pace. Daylight quickly diminished making them totally reliant on their candles to illuminate the dark and twisting subterranean passage that seemed to be rapidly becoming more cramped. On several occasions Belius was faced with choice between different branches and each time he would refer to his map before making his decision; and on every occasion Gritch could sense that his leader was worried he had chosen incorrectly.

Ahead they heard the faint sound of dripping water, and very shortly they began to feel dampness under foot, the water wasn't deep at all, but it made the chalk a little treacherous to walk on, as one of them found out.

"W-w-hoa!" screamed Ugg, trying earnestly to maintain balance.

The others found great amusement in his predicament and were too busy enjoying themselves sniggering and giggling to come to his rescue. It was a funny sight though, for his feet now with a mind of their own were sliding in all directions, and failing miserably to achieve purchase on the floor; and his frantically waving arms made him look like a bird struggling to take off. But it didn't last long as once his legs had shot out from beneath him there was only one way it could end.

"Ow, ow!" he cried as his head thumped against the chalk floor.

The onlookers had no sympathy for the hapless weasel, they found the incident simply hilarious, and began to laugh uncontrollably; so much so that many were doubled up in pain from being unable to stop, and holding on to their tummies wasn't much help either.

"Unbelievable Ugg, you're the first weasel to fly," laughed Ruevic uncontrollably.

"Yeah, and he crashed on his first flight," added Yabek in stitches of laughter.

"Alright alright, that's enough!" yelled Belius a twinkle in his eye, as he had also found some amusement in Ugg's mishap.

"You two help him up," he commanded glaring at Ruevic and Yabek.

"And you can shut up too," he snarled, looking at Hubble who was still shaking with laughter.

"Belius turned towards his number two.

"You know the last thing I need is a group of blithering idiots."

Gritch chuckled.

Once Ugg was helped back on to his feet Belius steered the group slowly and cautiously along the slippery wet chalk surface, and after a short while reached a point where the tunnel opened up on either side forming a small cave.

Water was slowly seeping through various cracks in the roof and in several areas misshapen formations of icicles were hanging from the ceiling, as if waiting and ready to fall. On the cave floor in some areas were mineral deposits growing upwards towards the ceiling, and in some cases the stalagmites and stalactites had crystallized in to a single structure to join ceiling to floor.

Having walked further along the cave they all welcomed the arrival of the dry chalk path once again; although this positive was offset by the coldness they began to feel as they got deeper in the tunnel. After another fifteen minutes of trudging along the tunnel at a reasonable sort of pace, Belius began to hear a sinister howling noise further ahead of them. It wasn't something he could identify, and the fact that it made the hair on his neck bristle was enough to fill him with a slight trace of trepidation. Nevertheless the seasoned warrior gritted his teeth and continued onwards, albeit at a slower and more cautious pace. But all the same he wanted to ensure the others were nearby if trouble was ahead.

"Close up everyone!" he growled, and the echoing patter of scurrying feet from behind signalled his weasels had instantly obeyed.

"What's up?" asked Gritch sensing something was bothering his chief.

"Hear that noise?

"That sort of crying you mean?"

"Yeah that's it, and I don't much like it either."

"Don't worry I'm behind you."

"I aint worried, just be prepared that's all," snapped Belius, putting on his typical air of bravado.

Reaching the end of the tunnel he drew a deep breath before carefully stepping in to a large cave, where to his great relief the cause of the eerie sound was merely the blustery sea breeze rushing through a small opening and whooshing around the chalk walls. The opening which was some two feet in diameter provided some additional illumination, however the cave remained quite dank and creepy and candles were still essential. A quick glance through the hole in the wall revealed a drop of about fifty feet to the gently rolling waves of Auricious Bay, and as Sileenus' ship could not be seen Belius realised the cave must be on the other side of the headland to Smugglers Cove. Turning around to peer back in to the darkness of the cave, he was for a moment captivated by the flickering candles held by the other weasels as they cast dancing shadows on to the dark chalk walls. And in this time of relative peace a sudden realisation of success began to slowly overwhelm him.

"Have I actually found the place where the treasure's hidden? "Could it really be here?" he pondered to himself excitedly.

Belius now felt a great sense of triumph, and with visions full of sparkling treasure, he started to run around the edge of the cave holding up his candle to the grimy white walls in the hope of finding what he was searching for. There was the odd bit of scribble now and again, probably made by young Zamosians who had explored before, but this was not important to him and he continued around the cave until without warning he stopped dead and took a sharp intake of breath.

"Look, look!" shouted Belius turning to his weasels, a broad self satisfied grin across his face.

The weasels looked on in surprise, and curiosity at what their eyes beheld; but for Monty the sight of that long remembered drawing was one of sheer dread.

"What now?" asked Gritch.

"This is it lads, time for picks and shovels," responded a happy looking Belius.

Gritch sidled up to his boss, with a slight puzzled expression.

"So this is it...this is the hidden entrance?" he asked.

"Yeah," replied his leader, leaning his head back and laughing.

"We just gotta knock through this wall with the cat on it, and we've found the treasure," he continued, pointing at the sketch of Catsumo. Gritch frowned.

"So that's why you spoke with that slimy Nomah in the pub?"

Belius nodded, a look of complacency about him, before clapping his front feet noisily together.

"Right lads, let's get to it, and quickly!" he commanded.

Within moments four rucksacks were on the ground and Ugg and Yabek proceeded towards the carving of Catsumo holding pickaxes, while Ruevic and Hubble followed behind with shovels. A cruel grin ran across Belius' face.

"Wait, wait a minute!" he shouted excitedly.

"Let Mr Piggy ave a go, after all a big piggy like him will knock through in no time!"

Monty was surprised - or shocked might be a better description?

"Me do that...oh no, oh no not me," he pleaded. After all, he had never done any manual work, and the thought of using a pick axe was very demeaning to him.

"What's a matter piggy not used to ard work,"
uttered Gritch with a tormenting grin.

"Never eld a pickaxe have ya then," added
Ruevic sarcastically.

Monty felt awkward, it was a difficult situation
for him as he had never held any sort of tool in
his life, but that didn't make any difference to
Belius who snatched the pickaxe from Ugg and
thrust it up towards the pig's face.

"Ere grab this and get on with it!" he bellowed.

Monty took hold of the axe which being made
for a weasel was a little small for him, and just
stood motionless and frozen to the spot.

"What's up now piggy!" shouted Belius.

W-w-well I'm not sure how to use it?"

"Gritch!" shouted Belius at the top of his voice
and his second in command obediently stepped
forward.

A look of disbelief appeared on Belius' face.

"Show Mr Piggy how to use this ere implement
will ya?" he uttered brusquely.

Gritch grabbed the axe from the pig's trotter,
moved towards the wall, and without a moment
wasted swung it back over his shoulder before
pulling it down over his head and driving the
chiselled head into the chalk; producing a loud
thud that echoed around the cave and back
along the tunnel. He repeated this several times

before walking back to Monty and thrusting the axe in his trotter.

"There you go piggy, easy innit," he grinned. Monty looked at Belius and moved closer to the wall, he stood square on and stared the deadly cat straight in her face and then with a blundering attempt he swung and drove the axe into the chalk face.

As pieces of the wall broke off and flew in all directions the weasels took several steps further away from the pig to avoid being hit by the flying debris. But prompted by the expression of shock and discomfort on Monty's face - caused by shock waves from the axe impacting on the wall running along his trotters – the weasels broke down in to hysterical cackles of laughter; still he had broken off a large chunk of chalk which seemed to please Belius.

Walking up next to the pig, the chief weasel bared his familiar sharp yellow teeth and hissed.

"At last Mr Piggy you've found something you can do."

"Ha ha ha!" he sniggered, promoting further laughter from the others.

Monty had perceived Belius' cutting and sarcastic remarks to be indignant and irritable

and they triggered the rebellious trait in his
character.

"I'll show em what I can do alright," he uttered
under his breath wanting to prove his worth.
Drawing back the axe he studied the evil face
of Catsumo, and although she was but an outline
cut in to the chalk he hesitated for a moment
as a little fear crept into him; for her eyes
seemed piercing and threatening, as if saying,
"you dare".

He concentrated hard, took a deep breath
and sighted what he thought would be the
position of her heart if she were alive, and then
summing up all his being struck the pick straight
into her. The sharpened point of the pick hit
the target and made a small cut in the chalk
but that was all; and feeling very disappointed
with himself Monty slumped his shoulders
and looked dejectedly at the ground. Then
they started with their smirks, hisses, and
sniggers, for weasels love nothing more than
having fun at another's expense; and Monty's
pathetic attempt at using the pickaxe had given
them something else to laugh at. But amid the
teasing and sarcasm the weasels were dishing
out at the pig, a popping sound began; softly at
first but quickly rising to a level that caused
everyone to feel a strange pain in their ears;
and then it happened....

From the point at which Monty struck the wall, cracks began to slowly creep outwards before running haphazardly at great speed in all directions emitting a bright incandescent light. So brilliant was the illumination that everyone covered their eyes leaving only their sense of hearing to detect alarmingly loud cracks reminiscent of lightening. All the animals felt in fear of their life as they could only stand still and hope this horrendous din would abate. But their hopes were ill founded as the cracking transformed in to a thunderous boom that rocked the cave so violently it felt as though they were on a ship in a storm rolling from side to side; and it was as much as they could do to remain standing. Then to make matters worse, a howling swirling tornado appeared from out of nowhere and began to race around the cave wrapping itself around the animals, trying to pull them off their feet. Everyone became petrified as they uselessly struggled against this faceless superior force, but just as they had accepted their fate, a strong vacuum dragged the cyclone in to a void in the centre of the cave as the malevolent force exhausted its power.

The first to uncover his eyes was Belius but he could not see in the darkness now the candles had been blown out.

"Get me some light!" he shouted, and after some moments of searching, a candle was found and lit.

"Give it here!" barked Belius snatching it from Yabek.

Holding it high the flickering flame cut through the darkness of the cave, and Belius' eyes dilated in astonishment at what he beheld.

"Look lads, look lads the walls gone!" he shouted excitedly.

A cloud of mist hung in the air like a curtain, but it was plain to see that the wall with Catsumo's engraving had disappeared.

"What magic is this?" asked Gritch in a confused tone.

"I'll tell you what this is, it's the magic of the giant cat, that's what," replied his leader.

Gritch laughed, "Maybe you're right, but where's the treasure then?"

"Ave some patience," snarled Belius.

All the others including Monty had moved closer to Belius and Gritch, and like them were straining their eyes to get the first glimpse of what was in the secret chamber; but the mist was reluctant to clear.

Belius had had enough of waiting and began to walk through the cloudy haze.

"Come on then!" he shouted, as he disappeared from view; and the others quickly followed him.

Once through the thickest of the mist they became lost for words at what they had discovered. You know the sort of things you witness, maybe only a few times in your life that are so amazing you are struck still with an open mouth, a drawn breath and time seems to stand still; well this was such a moment for these animals. Belius was completely dumbstruck; all he could do was remain silent and absorb his observations; and it was no different for the others either. And so six weasels and one pig stood motionless and speechless, for they had achieved what countless others had failed to do; they had found Catsumo's secret hoard of treasure.

In the cave were seven large wooden chests, three were closed and looked inert and uninteresting. But the other four with their lids open wide, were overflowing with jewels of every kind, and their lively twinkling and sparkling gave them a sense of animation that set the onlookers pulses on fire. Red rubies as big as an ostrich's egg, huge oval sapphires of the deepest blue, silver necklaces, diamonds, golden sceptres and crowns of kings and queens, were all there to shiver the senses. Rings of platinum, gold and silver, lie scattered on the ground close to the chests, as though insignificant and worthless, while strewn around the cave were pearl necklaces, jewelled bracelets, silver candelabrum, and many more valuable trinkets; it was indeed a veritable treasure trove.

Belius and Gritch traded glances.

"We're rich, we're rich!!" yelled Belius grabbing his lieutenant by his shoulders and dragging him into a dance. The other weasels looked on as Beilus and Gritch pranced around the cave in the most blundering fashion with no regards for timing or grace, but that didn't matter to the other weasels as they cheered and clapped as loudly as they could.

All this frolicking around in circles was causing Belius and Gritch to become a little giddy and it was only a matter of time before they would collapse in a heap; but thankfully the onlookers prevented this from occurring.

"Hooray for Belius, hooray for Belius!" they cheered, and their leader feeling so pleased with himself broke off the dance and nodded to his weasels in acknowledgment of their appreciation.

But the compliments kept on coming, and so revelling in this over exuberant adulation Belius quickly forgot about the urgency of the situation - but his level headed number two did not.

"Boss," shouted Gritch.

"What is it? Can't you see I'm enjoying myself," snapped Belius.

"I'm sorry chief, but don't you think we should get the treasure on board Lady Bamboozler as soon as possible."

Belius growled under his breath, his gaze towards his lieutenant was less than friendly, he didn't like being told what to do, and felt it a challenge to his leadership; but on the other hand he realised Gritch was right.

"Alright Gritch, alright," he grunted.

"Right then Lads," he began, turning to the others. "Load up your packs and take everything you can."

"We can't take everything, you know that?" uttered Gritch.

Belius growled under his breath.

"We'll take what we can now, and come back for the rest with Sileenus and his crew...okay?"

"Spose so, but what if Tonga's on our trail, or we've been spotted by the locals, isn't it best to get out with what we can?"

Belius took a short intake of breath though his yellow teeth, his patience with Gritch was beginning to wane. But Belius wasn't stupid, although he wouldn't tolerate any challenge to his decisions or his leadership - for which he would fight to the death - he realised that

Gritch was without doubt the most useful
member of his gang, and to lose him would be
sheer folly. And so being cleverly devious he
thought it best to play him along.

"Gritch, Gritch, you disappoint me," he hissed
softly.

"You'll never make it to be a great leader unless
you take risks...and after we've travelled all this
way, why leave some treasure for someone else,
when for a tiny gamble we can take it all."

Belius moved closer to Gritch and spoke more
softly.

"And the more for me, the more for you my old
friend.

Now help the others load up will ya?"

Gritch looked at his leader and smiled, he wasn't
completely gullible, but he was like any other
weasel - very greedy.

"Alright chief," he replied courteously.

Brodney

Chapter 10
In Pursuit

Once Rufus had subtly broken up the heart warming reunion of Hamilton and her old friends he had pressed his motley group hard to reach Delicious Orchard as soon as possible, and they had only travelled a short way when Rufus sighted a distant bird coming towards them. Although flying against the wind, the bird soared up and dived down and banked left and right in a zig zag fashion to make headway against the strong gusty breeze, and he was so skilled at doing this that Rufus was soon able to identify the gull as Albert.

Rufus didn't let up when the Albert reached him and continued to maintain a quick pace, even though there was the odd complaint from some of the others such as:

"I wish he'd slow down!"

"I'm pooped!"

"Can't we have a short rest?!"

All of which had no effect.

Albert glided around in an arc and settled at a height just a few feet above the malamute, and although the wind was now in his favour he still had to work hard to keep pace with Rufus.

"Find anything?" asked Rufus.

"I saw something, saw something!" screeched the gull.

"Well what was it?"

"An animal on its back, on its back asleep."

The malamutes face look quizzical.

"And what else can you tell me?" he asked, leaping so high over a mound that Albert had to frantically gain height to avoid contact with his head.

"It ran off...ran off and disappeared it did," replied Albert getting his breath back.

The malamute peered upwards and sighed.

"Can you at least describe it?" he pleaded.

Albert blinked his eyes.

"Brown it was, smaller than a hare, with beady eyes."

"Ah ha...definitely winchow," uttered a satisfied Rufus under his breath.

Albert fell silent for a moment rocking his head from side to side and making strange humming noises, for there was something else that irritated him; he'd seen their sort before - but where?

"There's something else, isn't there?!" shouted Rufus sensing that Albert knew more.

But the gull remained deep in thought and continued to hum. In fact its intermittent humming was rather like listening to a dripping tap where one hopes it will stop; but it never does.

It was beginning to get on some of the animals' nerves now, and in particular some of the boars.

"Oh shut up!" shouted Buna.

"Yeah, shut –" began Wicklop, but he was sharply cut off by Albert's high pitched screeching, which was enough to silence anyone.

"Ha ha, ha ha, ha ha!" cried the gull excitedly banking from side to side.

"Come on Albert tell me?!" cried Rufus hoping for some useful information.

"I've seen that kind before, seen em before I have!" he cried.

"But where and when?"

"Yesterday, I saw em yesterday, on a ship they were."

Albert's statement had confirmed Rufus' thoughts about the weasels coming by sea, which of course meant the ship would be waiting for them nearby.

Peering up at the gull he had one more question to ask, and it was most important, for he wanted to know their strength.

"One last question Albert. How many of these creatures did you see on the ship?"

"Only two, only saw two, and they looked ill... proper ill they did."

"Didn't you see any other creatures Albert?" The gull began rocking his head and humming again, which much to everyone's relief didn't last too long.

"Yes yes," I did," replied Albert with an irritating whine.

Rufus looked up and shook his head a little in frustration, as it was sometimes very difficult to get a complete answer from the gull.

"So what were they?" he urged.

"Rats, there were three large rats."

Rufus found this to be interesting, as he had heard that over the years large numbers of Nordeamian rats had deserted from the service of the Emporer Porturios', and there was some talk that they had headed east to Moorsher or perhaps Arven.

Knowing that rats or corvats, as was their old name in North of the World, tended to congregate in a group called a mischief, Rufus had no choice but to assume that there were many more than just the three Albert had spotted; the problem was how many?

He'd also have liked to have known how many winchow there were, but Albert hadn't helped at all with this either; still he thought they may find out more about their numbers from the footprints in the orchard.

"Hurry your pace lads!" he cried as he increased his speed making a larger gap between him and the young Har Vesta - who had until then been keeping up with the sprightly malamute.

He didn't run fast enough to lose his followers but just enough for them to run faster than they thought they believed possible and their commitment to stay within sight of him soon paid off as the great malamute came to a halt soon after entering Delicious Orchard.

There was much huffing and puffing; especially from the boars and Barnaby as they were not build for speed; and even Charlie had to take some deep breaths too.

"I'm not the dog I used to be," he uttered between breaths.

"You did very well...very well my friend," smiled Papachuan, himself feeling just a tad out of breath.

Within moments everyone closed up to Rufus and followed his every move, it seemed there was great purpose in everything he did, and the onlookers fascinated by his actions, watched him intently.

Firstly he approached a ladder that lie on the ground, lifted the top of it and pulled a tiny

piece of material from it. He then picked up
the odd apple and plum that lay nearby and
after a quick survey discarded them. And finally
he seemed to wander around in circles lightly
touching the ground in some places, and talking
to himself. That last act made some of them
more curious, but not the experienced warriors
amongst them.

"How many do you think Rufus?" asked Tonga.

"Five or six winchow, and one set of pig's
trotters," replied the malamute.

"No match for us then," uttered Har Vesta
confidently.

The words from the Labrador were nothing
less than Rufus would have expected from a
youngster eager for his first taste of battle,
and smiling inwardly he remembered way back
when he was in a similar situation; desperate to
prove his worth and valour. However, he knew
too well the mistakes that could be made in
war, and being overconfident was one of the
greatest; besides it was important for the
others to be aware that the weasels may have
confederates out at sea. And so with a warm
and friendly countenance he addressed the
young Labrador.

"Never underestimate an enemy Har Vesta,
especially one as treacherous as the winchow,"
he uttered solemnly.

"I'll remember that," replied the young Labrador, fully understanding the wisdom of the malamutes words.

"And besides," continued Rufus now addressing everyone, "I'm convinced there is a ship close by waiting to collect them, which may mean they have reinforcements...so we must keep alert."

"That don't put me off!" grunted Brodney.

"Nor me," added Papachuan.

"I'm going to get that Belius no matter what!" growled Tonga kicking a basket so hard it fell over, scattering green apples in all directions.

Rufus smiled.

"Then let's get after them!" he yelled, suddenly launching forward and racing off further into the woods.

"Oh not again!" complained Charlie.

"Come on you can do it," uttered Har Vesta trying to spur him on.

Thankfully for Charlie the next run didn't last too long because all the others ahead of him soon came to a halt again.

"What is it, why are you stopping again?" asked Tonga.

"Behold," replied Rufus pointing towards something lying on the ground.

Tonga, Kolo and Barnaby trotted over to where the malamute had gestured and came across something that they had not seen at first.

"Why it's an umbrella...does it belong to your missing friend?" asked Tonga.

A quick grin crossed Rufus's face.

"I have a feeling it does." he replied.

"What do you think Papachuan?" asked Rufus, nodding at the Labrador to come and take a look.

The town mayor obliged, and quickly appeared at the malamute's side, where he caught sight of the umbrella.

"Well it's red, and I know Monty has a red brolly," uttered Papachuan in a slightly sombre tone.

Rufus smiled. "Do you know what?" he uttered.

"What?" asked Papachuan shrugging his shoulders.

"I believe our Monty is trying to help us to find him."

The Labrador looked at the malamute with a doubtful expression, as all he saw was a brolly just lying on the ground; but Rufus could see the significance.

"Look at the umbrella, why it's not been thrown down or dropped indiscriminately. It's been laid down to ensure we follow the right trail."

"And it's directing us to that one," continued Rufus, pointing to one of several paths leading through the orchard. The malamute trotted off towards the path indicated by the umbrella and as he reached it stopped to make further analysis.

Walking around in circles he studied the sandy path closely for a short while, before bending low and inhaling the air, his enhanced senses picking up the residual trail of the winchow and pig confirming this was indeed the way they should go.

"Come on my friends," he beckoned. "This is the way we must go".

Rufus kept up a good pace, and never missed a footing as he guided the group along a meandering path that was at times only single file in width, as it cut through the heart of the dense orchard of fruit trees that was Delicious Orchard. Throughout all this Rufus was feeling a little hampered by the much slower animals behind him, but even with his special powers he realised that they would be very important allies should the enemy have large numbers and so every so often he had to reign in his speed to allow then to close up. On one such occasion he actually drew to a halt because he could see his friends drifting further behind and didn't want to lose them. He had barely stopped when a distant boom made his ears prick up, but the disruptive explosion quickly faded, for the strong easterly breeze carried it away as quickly as it had come.

However it was long enough for Rufus to identify it.

"Canon fire, a signal from a ship I bet...and not too far away by the sound of it," he uttered to himself.

Turning around and seeing his friends were almost upon him he immediately accelerated away.

"Come on slow coaches!" he shouted, a slight playfulness in his voice.

It wasn't too much longer before the crisp salty air reached everyone's nostrils and it became evident to all that they were close to the coast. Feeling assured they were gaining on the weasels, Rufus slowed down to allow the group to close up; a move that was well received by the less speedy.

Gradually the sandy track became chalkier and out from the trees they emerged to face the conflicting winds from the east and the strong sea breeze that circulated around the Smugglers Cove.

The path ran in either direction around the cliff tops, but unlike the sand where the tracks were occasionally visible, the hard white limestone path gave no evidence of which way Rufus and his friends should go. The malamute stopped and waited until everyone had caught up and gathered around him, and then he looked towards Captain Tonga.

"Can you remember anything on the map that may help us Tonga...you know directions, landmarks, that sort of thing?"

"I'm pretty sure the treasure was in Smugglers Cove-"

"Aye it was that, and in some sort of a cave too!" interrupted Charlie.

Tonga scratched his head.

"There was some writing on the map...in the old language, but we couldn't understand it could we Charlie?"

"No...but if you hadn't lost it Tonga, I bet old Boo San could have translated it."

"Oh dear," thought Charlie feeling terrible, for he belatedly realised he shouldn't have said that and began to wish the ground would open up and swallow him.

Tonga felt angry, after all it wasn't his fault he'd lost the map; he was bashed on the head and mugged.

"That's right I lost it on purpose!" he said loudly and sarcastically, his outburst causing the collie to drop his head in embarrassment.

"Sorry Tonga, I didn't mean it," replied Charlie, a genuine tone of repentance in his voice.

Rufus shook his head in surprise at this unnecessary and petty behaviour, and quickly vented his exasperation.

"This is not helping is it!" he exclaimed firmly, glancing between Tonga and Charlie, who both looked equally embarrassed.

The boar gazed toward his old friend, "Sorry Charlie," he uttered with a deep sigh.

The collie smiled warmly. "That's alright...I understand your anger, and I didn't mean it to sound the way it did."

"Friends again?" asked the Malamute, and Charlie and Tonga both nodded.

"Good, so let's get back to the facts," continued Rufus.

"Now we know the treasure is in Smugglers Cove, and most likely in a cave, so what we need to do now is to find which one?"

An excited young Har Vesta was quick to respond.

"Well, this is Smugglers Cove so it can't be far away."

Rufus turned at smiled at the young Labrador.

"So which way to the cave then?" he questioned expectantly.

For a moment the buoyant expression of Har Vesta gave hope of a forthcoming answer, but within moments a look of consternation took over as he realised he had no idea in which direction they should go.

"Sorry Rufus, I don't know," he uttered despondently, inciting a look of disappointment on the malamute's face.

But Rufus forever an optimist turned to the young Labrador's Uncle hoping he would know the answer.

"Have you any idea Papachuan?"

Papachuan frowned.

"Trouble is they're all around the cove Rufus. You can go south or curve around to the north, but whichever way you choose you'll find caves," replied the Labrador shrugging his shoulders.

"I'll tell ya what...I went in all these caves when I were a young badger and I never found no treasure," grunted Brodney in a negative tone.

"True enough, I think most Zamosians have been in the caves.

I've been in all of them myself, even the one with that awful sketch of Catsumo, and found absolutely nothing either," added Papachuan shaking his head.

"It's all Zamosian folklore and no truth in it." muttered the badger dismissively.

"Well whether it's folklore or not, I'm going to get that Belius. You see if I don't," remarked Tonga angrily.

Everyone expected a response from the malamute, the clever malamute, but he was conspicuous by his absence, and for a moment the others wondered where he was; it was as if he had disappeared. But they needn't have been concerned for as the dazzling evening sun slowly slid out from behind the grey cumulus clouds, his brilliant silhouette was cast across the top of the cliffs for all to see.

For a moment it looked as though he was the source of the light, he was the sun, a ray of hope, an aura of magic. He stood silent, unmoving and relaxed, focusing all of his extraordinary senses to detect the slightest residual evidence of the winchow. Staring out towards the distant horizon to gather his thoughts, he closed his eyes and inhaled the fresh sea air, and all the while the blustering wind buffeted his coarse hair. He could discern a slight trace of winchow, they had been here alright - but which way did they go?

Tonga eager to continue the chase and not to waste any more time impatiently called out to the malamute.

"Rufus! -"

"Let him think captain, let him think...he'll know what to do," interrupted Barnaby in a reassuring tone, and Tonga reluctantly nodded in compliance.

The malamute considered the options. It was a fifty, fifty choice, go north or south, or split into two groups; those were the choices he had, but neither was ideal. He wasn't particularly interested in whether any treasure existed or not; but he was concerned about Monty. And if they divided their force to go in either direction, they may not have insufficient animals to successfully beat the weasels; especially as they may have reinforcements from a nearby ship.

It was a dilemma, but Rufus being Rufus wasn't an animal of indecision; he was clever and resourceful.

"I've got it!" he began, wheeling around to face the others.

"I will head south with Albert, and the rest of you go north."

But his words ignited an argument and that promptly turned into disarray, as raised voices began to argue.

"Now wait a minute!" uttered Tonga in a complaining tone.

"That's sheer folly!" exclaimed Papachuan.

"You can't go on your own Rufus," pleaded Charlie.

"What if you meet the weasels?!" questioned Kolo.

Barnaby shook his head. "I know you can look after yourself, but is it really a good idea?!" And so it went on, arguments and "I know better" opinions were heatedly exchanged, and for a few moments it didn't look like there would a resolution – that is until Rufus spoke. "That's enough!" he commanded forcefully, and everyone began to calm down and stop what they were saying, or were about to say. "Now listen. I can run faster than any of you, and Albert can fly like the wind, so we will head southwards as fast as we can, and should we find the enemy I will send Albert back to you." He paused and smiled. "And if we find nothing we will know the weasels have gone north and so we will return at speed to aid you in battle. There was an initial look of doubt in most, but as Rufus looked towards each of them in turn, his warm and friendly eyes imparted a pleasant soothing sensation that brought an inner calm, and no matter what they had thought before, they immediately agreed with his decision. Having no more arguing to do, a few "good lucks", were exchanged between Rufus and the others before he and Albert set off southwards.

Papachuan then turned to Tonga and smiled. "North it is Captain," he uttered.

Tonga nodded in agreement before shouting.
"Let's go lads!"
As they began to trek northwards some
of them would occasionally look over their
shoulders to watch the malamute, as they were
in awe of the speed in which he left them; but
then something unexpected happened.
"Captain Captain!" bellowed Tunashi.
But Tonga intent on catching up with his
enemies as quickly as possible did not reply,
instead he turned and nodded at his sergeant to
respond.
"What is son?"
"Its Rufus...he's stopped?" replied a bewildered
Tunashi pointing back along the path.
These words were quick to have effect as both
Tonga and Kolo instantly stopped, spun around
and stared southwards. Feeling perplexed at
seeing the shape of the stationary malamute in
the distant they gave one another a mutual look
of consternation.

When Rufus had parted company with the
others, he had raced off southwards along the
chalk path at great speed, but in focusing on
reaching the weasels as soon as possible he had
forgot at what speed he was travelling and had
begun to leave the gull behind. Like Tonga, he
was determined to catch the weasels, but unlike

the boar he was not seeking revenge; he wanted to save Monty's life. Realising the gull should stay near to him he began to reduce his pace to allow it to close up. As he decreased his speed, he felt the warmth of the bright sun as it crept slowly out from behind the cloudy curtain once again, and the dim path began to take on a much brighter hue as the dull white chalk kissed by the sun's rays began to brighten and glisten. But something else had been brought to life by the radiance from above which quickly caught the malamute's attention, for just ahead some inanimate objects sparkled and twinkled as the sun swept over them.

Drawing up to these gleaming objects Rufus quickly scooped one up, and from his first glance was immediately taken aback by what he saw. Scanning around nearby Rufus easily located the other four silver buttons the pig had cast away; and then it came to him.

"Well I never, you clever old pig," he chuckled.

"What is it, what is it?" cried Albert.

"A clue...Monty's left another clue!" he said excitedly.

He was about to ask Albert to fly off and tell the others when his senses were alert by a rumbling sound that vibrated though the very substrate of the chalk. Although faint at first it was gradually increasing in severity and so

turning towards the din he was relieved to see
it was the other group coming towards him with
Har Vesta out in front barking excitedly.
The young Labrador was the first to reach
Rufus and was keen to know why he had
stopped.
"What is it, what is?!" he questioned.
Rufus opened a large paw and showed the
Labrador his find, but the Har Vesta didn't see
their significance.
"Buttons?" he queried looking puzzled.
"Found something Rufus?" asked a slightly
breathless Tonga as he arrived on the scene.
"Buttons...he's found buttons," shrugged Har
Vesta.
Tonga like Har Vesta looked a little perplexed,
but Papachuan was soon on hand and knew the
importance of Rufus' find.
"Why they're Monty's...from his waistcoat!" he
exclaimed.
"Rufus smiled. "Yes they're his alright they have
his initials on them."
"Do you suspect foul play," asked Papachuan
sounding very concerned.
"I don't suppose he's having an easy time, for
winchow can be cruel and nasty creatures, but
I think he's alive, and what's more I believe this
is yet another clue he's left for us."

"Then there's hope?" asked Papachuan, concern in his voice.

The malamute put a paw on the town mayor's shoulder.

He hadn't really known Papachuan very long, but they had built up a firm friendship, and even though neither of them was overly keen on the pig, they were both caring animals and wanted nothing more than to find him alive and well.

"Yes there's hope my friend," nodded Rufus, a reassuring smile across his face; and the mayors mood lifted.

"Okay everyone let's go!" shouted Rufus in a positive tone.

Heading southwards with the others behind him, he now felt more confident that they would find Monty, but being well aware of the impulsive and temperamental nature of the winchow he hoped nothing terrible would befall him before they did.

The malamute led the group quickly along the undulating chalk path, and then on to the narrow ledge with its old wooden railings that took them down the side of the cliff, but just before they reached the beach Rufus suddenly came to an abrupt halt and waved at everyone to stop behind him.

"Wait there," he uttered, and carefully stepped from the chalk ledge on to the wooden decking, and then on to the beach. He noticed some disturbance in the sand which appeared to have been partially covered up, and there were also a couple of broken pieces of wood that he matched up with missing sections of handrail. "Looks like someone came a cropper here," he uttered under his breath. Looking closer he could see that something had been dragged back and forth over the sand forming a scrapped area a few yards wide that went onwards towards the sea.

"Hmm," he uttered intrigued by this.

"Alright everyone you can continue down!" he shouted and slowly the others walked down the path and on to the beach.

Rufus didn't wait for the others but hurried off towards the sea following the marks in the sand all the way till they reached the large pebbles. He then stood still and gazed at the incoming tide and the rolling waves, and listened to their roar and crash as they fell upon the beach, he knew winchow were responsible for the marks in the sand, and he knew why; trouble was they had done their job well.

The others looked on in silence, hoping the malamute could pick up the trail of the weasels.

"Do you think we've lost them Uncle Chuan," asked Har Vesta sounding a little downbeat. But his uncle was absorbed in watching Rufus. "Har Vesta gently nudged him.

"What?" responded Papachuan, sounding rather irritated.

"Do you think we've lost them?"

His uncle sighed. "I hope not."

Hearing this downbeat reply, Barnaby who was nearby felt he could at least try to cheer them up; after all he had been on many adventures with Rufus, and had absolute faith in his old friend.

"Now listen, you two," he began in a positive tone.

"I've seen Rufus do some incredible things, simply incredible, and if anyone can track down these vermin, it's him."

Okay?" he added with a smile, and the immediate appearance of happier expressions confirmed he had successfully roused their spirits.

Rufus began to slowly scan along the shoreline, firstly southwards and then to the north.

It looked hopeless as there was nothing to indicate which way they had gone. He was about to suggest splitting the group up once again when an interesting group of pebbles laid out in the sand a few feet away caught his attention.

"Look," he shouted, trotting off towards them.
"What have you found!?" yelled Tonga walking
after him.
"Is it something important!?" shouted Barnaby
feeling confident that his old friend had found
another clue.
"Come on all of you and take a look, it's amazing,
quite amazing!"
Shortly everyone had joined Rufus, and blinking
in the sunlight that was still peeping out
defiantly from the clouds again, every animal
had a smile on their face; it was after all as
Rufus had said quite amazing.
"Incredible!" shouted Papachuan.
"So clever," added his nephew.

Although the tide had begun to brush against
the pebbles, and would soon drag them into the
water erasing any trace of them, fortunately
it had not yet done so, and the unmistakable
pattern was still visible.
"Why, the stones form the shape of an arrow!"
exclaimed Charlie.
"That's right, and it's pointing southwards,
replied Rufus.
Tonga shook his head and smiled.
"This friend of yours Monty, he's certainly a
clever and resourceful pig," he uttered smiling
towards Papachuan.

"Oh he's clever alright...and sometimes far too clever for his own good," replied the town mayor with a hint of sarcasm.

"Ha ha, ha ha," chuckled Brodney who could see the funny side of it.

"Hmm," grunted Tonga. He hadn't met Monty but he understood what Papachuan meant, for it reminded him of Fosfero, who was always trying to be clever; especially in front of King Rosfarl and Queen Rosia.

"Well whatever we think of him, he's certainly shown how inventive he is," uttered Rufus looking at Papachuan.

The Labrador chuckled to himself, for he had to concede that Monty was indeed a brainy fellow.

"True enough," he said with a smile.

Tunashi being young and inexperienced, especially in tracking animals, scratched his head feeling a little baffled.

If this marker is true, why aren't there any tracks in the sand?" he asked, glancing towards his captain.

"Hmm, good question?" replied Tonga searching for an answer.

"I think I have it," began Rufus.

"You see this sand has been dragged around by the Weasels, and they did it to –"

"Cover their tracks!" blurted Tonga impulsively.

"That's right Tonga, and they've used these bits of wood," replied Rufus picking up a piece of broken railing.

"Trouble is, in doing this they've made it obvious they've gone into the sea," he added, tossing the wood into the surf.

"Into the sea?" questioned Har Vesta.

"Yes, to hide which way they went."

"Why those clever so-and-sos!" exclaimed Papachuan.

"Good job Monty left that clue then," added Brodney.

"Yes, if he hadn't we'd probably had to split up again," replied Rufus.

"But my guess is they won't have come back on to the sand until they got past those rocks," he added pointing southwards towards to where a clump of chalk rocks was lying just off shore.

The rocks formed three haunting shapes starting a short distance from the shore line and running straight out in to the cove for some ninety feet. The shape of each was individual yet inextricable from the others; as if they shared a common bond and purpose. The stone nearest the beach rose out from the shallow depths of the blue sea and climbed almost vertically before forming what could be perceived as a giant skull. Behind this crown was the highest point of the three rocks at just over twenty feet tall resembling a sail of a ship, a large fin; or perhaps two enormous wings clenched tightly together? The portion furthest out to sea was serpentine in appearance and formed a huge arch through which the never resting and undulating tides crashed against sides of its milky white rock. Rufus had seen their type before, for off the north coast of his country were three similar formations and he knew only too well the stories surrounding them.

Brodney grinned.

"Them there rocks are known as Serpents Rest," he uttered solemnly, as if there was something important about them.

"Interesting, where I come from such things are known as Dragon's End," replied Rufus.

"Huh?" grunted the badger in surprise, scratching his head.

And he wasn't the only interested party either.

"Really, can you tell us more?" questioned Har Vesta animatedly.

"Oh please do Rufus?" added a pleading Papachuan.

A fleeting smile crossed the malamute's face before he became more serious, his mind drifting back to a bygone era when the very existence of worldly rule was forever being

challenged. Of the cruel and vicious rise to
power of sea dragons, and how they reigned
supreme crushing every challenge, until finally
meeting defeat and death from the emerging
powers of alchemy. And here, as in North of
the Word was a rare monument to their kind,
once a giant ferocious beast, now merely a
lifeless entity, frozen in chalk for eternity by a
sorcerer's hand. Being an avid storyteller, Rufus
was sorely tempted to begin an enthusiastic
account of the defeat of sea dragons by his
forefathers - but common sense prevailed.
"Another time my friends, right now we must
make haste, for I truly believe we will soon
catch our quarry."
Now come on!" he shouted and took off
southwards towards Serpents Rest.
The others followed as quickly as they could,
but after only a short while the difficulty
of walking, let alone running on the powdery
granules began to tell.
"Phew this is ard goin!" complained Brodney.
"You're not kidding," replied Tonga breathing
heavily.
"Best to slow a little, and walk at a fast
pace, it's no good trying to run on this stuff,"
suggested Papachuan.

"You tell him that?!" uttered Charlie looking
towards Rufus who covered ground on the sand
so easily.

"That's unbelievable!" exclaimed Har Vesta
looking on with incredulity at the way the
malamute trotted effortlessly across the
beach, neither slipping nor sliding; the sand
proving no difficulty for him whatsoever.
Papachuan smiled, "Hmm...he's full of surprises
is Rufus."

A frenzied cackling and laughter reverberated
along the walls of the dark and empty tunnel
until it reached the chamber of stalagmites
and stalactites where it was finally dampened
and deadened. The sound originated from
a cave at the far end of the tunnel and the
generators of this excitement were none other
than Belius and his gang, for the riches they
beheld were a king's ransom, and they were
celebrating their find with riotus screaming
and shouting. Wandering slowly around the cave
Monty's greed got the better of him too, and
he couldn't help but pick up the odd sapphire or
diamond ring and pop it into a trouser pocket;
and who was to stop him, for the weasels were
so focused on racing around collecting their own
booty, they completely ignored him.

"I'm the king, the king!" exclaimed Ruevic holding a bejewelled crown on his head and making a majestic stance.

"All hail the king," uttered Yabek sarcastically, and did a mock bow before dissolving in to laughter.

Hubble wasn't really watching the others; he was more interested in securing the loot in his back pack, and was busy tightening the strap on it.

"Oh no you don't sleepy, you got plenty of room left in that pack," yelled Belius.

But it's heavy," complained Hubble struggling to lift his half full backpack.

"Then drag it! And that's the same for all of ya. Fill your bags and drag em...got it!" shouted Belius, his words echoing around the cave.

"What about us chief, we aint got no bags, and my pockets are full up?" asked Gritch.

"You and I can drag a chest apiece."

Gritch nodded and was about to turn away, when an unexpected brain wave brought a twinkle to his eye.

"I've got an idea!"

Belius looked curious, "What?"

"Why not get the pig to help, I bet he can drag at least two chests...maybe more."

"That's just what I thought...see to it," growled Belius through his sharp yellowed teeth. In

fact he had thought of no such thing, and
for a moment began to be concerned about
these clever ideas from his number two; ideas
which he felt as leader should have been his.
Watching Gritch walk over towards Monty,
Belius hissed through his teeth like an old
locomotive releasing steam.
"I'll ave to watch you very carefully."

Gritch found some old rope in the cave, and
after tying one end to two chests, he made
a noose at the other end to fit over the pig's
head and under his forearms. Treasure loaded,
the weasels began the arduous task of dragging
their plunder back along the tunnel towards the
beach.
Yabek, Ugg, Hubble and Ruevic had their
rucksacks full to the brim, and were dragging
them along behind them, while Belius and Gritch
were each hauling a heavy chest. Meanwhile
feeling downtrodden and looking rather sulky,
Monty's indignance at having to haul two chests
was occasionally and unpleasantly diverted by
the rope, as it rubbed across the top of his
neck.
It wasn't an easy task for anyone and
complaints showered around the caves.
"Come on-n!" yelled Yabek at his pack's
reluctance to slide over a small rock.

"Phew this is ard," complained Ruevic.

Hubble looked across and raised his eyebrows, "You're telling me."

Even their leader found things tough as his chest got stuck between two stalagmites.

"Come on blast ya!" he shouted, kicking away at the base of one of the mineral columns which made a loud crack as it broke off allowing him to tug the chest onwards.

"Ah ha!" he shouted exuberantly.

More complaints followed but slowly and surely they progressed further towards the mouth of the cave, and at long last a glimmer of light could now be seen in the distance.

It was early evening now with only about three hours before darkness, the grey clouds were still trying to subdue the sun as they had been doing all day, but an orange glow of defiance was beginning to brighten up the day once more. Unsurprisingly Rufus reached the large rock formation before the others, but didn't go beyond as he felt sure that someone was on the other side and didn't want to give away the advantage of surprise. After asking Albert to fly up and take a look, he trotted in to the sea, and once out of his depth began swimming towards the nearest rock. Reaching the front edge of the rock he began to tread water, and while doing so used his telepathic link to speak with Albert.

"What can you see Albert"?

"I see two rats, two big rats."

"No one else?"

"Just two rats!" replied the gull with an ear piercing shriek so loud that Rufus could hear it without telepathy.

"Shush," uttered Rufus.

"Sorry, "came a whispered reply.

Rufus shook his head and smiled, "Alright, now just stay there and keep quiet okay?"

"Yeah okay, okay."

Albert hovered around for a moment playing in the breeze before settling down on top of the rock, where he studied every move of the two unfriendly looking rats.

The great malamute looked up at the tall white chalk rock before hauling himself out of the warm sea and resting on a small ledge. Shaking his course fur coat vigorously to remove the remnants of the salt water, he glanced up towards the peak of the rock before turning around and catching sight of Har Vesta and the others approaching. Acknowledging Rufus' signal to stop, the young Labrador came to a halt, and waited for the rest of the group to catch up. As the group stood together awaiting further instruction, there was a common feeling of frustration amongst them, however this quickly transformed in to awe as they were treated to more extraordinary talents from Rufus as he began his climb up the steep and rugged chalk face.

He made it look so simple and easy, and everyone was aghast at how quickly he proceeded up such a steep gradient without falter or slip. It was truly a sight to behold; for none of them had seen such dexterity and adroitness, and never imagined such a large dog would be endowed with these abilities. Yes, he had immensely strong legs to propel him, and sharp claws to provide incredible grip, but it was the way he defied gravity that impressed. Having reached the rock's summit, he cautiously crept across to the far side, careful not to make a sound, before dropping down to his stomach and peeking down below. Sure enough, as Albert had said there were two corvats, but not only that, there was a trail of foot prints leading from the edge of the pebbles across the sand to the cliffs where they disappeared in to a cave.

Rufus was always willing to give credit where it was due and he felt a little admiration for the clever way the winchow had taken advantage of the sea and Serpents End to cover their route.

For a moment a studious expression appeared
on his face, as he remembered how expert
they were at using ploys and deception, and
how their cunning was second to none. But on
thinking about how clever Monty had been in
leaving those valuable clues behind, a smile of
contentment crossed his face.
"Good old Monty,"he chuckled.

The two rats had each rowed a wooden dinghy
out from Lady Bamboozler, and as instructed by
Sileenus turned them around to face their bows
seaward, so they could launch as soon as Belius
and his gang arrived.
Spika was leaning against the stern of his
dinghy while Tufta was oddly enough paddling in
the warm sea nearby.
"Ope them weasels aint gonna be much longer,"
muttered Spika.
"Weasels...I hate em, and I don't like bein a
lackey to em either," replied Tufta in a gravelly
tone.
"Me neever, and if you ask me that Belius is far
too full of imself."
"Yeah, but he don't alf look mean though."
"That don't mean nothfink, you look at Captain
Sileenus, he looks like a real gent...but I tell ya
he's lethal with his sword."

Tufta laughed. "Aint he got some posh cousin in Unger...who runs a tea house?"

"Yeah I fink he has...now can you imagine our captain serving tea and cakes," chuckled Spika. Tufta found his friends remark very funny and began to visualise Sileenus dressed in a pinafore, which caused him to break into a titter of laughter, and shake uncontrollably.

"Ha ha ha, ha ha ha, ha ha ha ha, not likely." Tufta's uncontrollable bodily behaviour immediately drew Spika into involuntary fits of laughter, and the two of them became so engrossed in this merriment they lost all sight of their surroundings; that is until an eloquent tongue jolted their senses.

"Hello there...having fun are we?"

Alarmed by this vocal interruption they instantly stopped their hysterical giggling and looked towards the speaker.

"Err, err... who are you?" spluttered Spika in awe of the giant dog.

Rufus smiled. "I am Rufus, Rufus O'Malley."

"And what ya want then?" asked Tufta, nervously looking under his frowning eyebrows.

"I'm afraid to say I'm here to send you back to that ship," replied the malamute, pointing his nose out to sea to where Lady Bamboozler was anchored.

A cruel smile appeared on Spika's face.

"Na, I don't think so," he snarled.

The rats looked at each other, they had been asked to wait for the weasels, and even though they disliked them, they were very loyal to their captain. And so exchanging a fleeting false grin - a sort of do or die expression one would do before battle - they turned to Rufus and drew their short pointed swords.

"Ahhhhhh!" they cried in unison, as they launched themselves towards their formidable opponent. But unfortunately for them, the tide began to lap against the beach that very moment slowing them down considerably and Rufus couldn't help but chuckle as they stumbled and splashed awkwardly towards him. Although the rats felt a little apprehensive in attacking such a large adversary, the fact that he didn't appear to be armed spurred them on. There was now only a few feet of pebbles to cross before they reached Rufus, and as the stones grinded under foot they felt very confident that their weapons would give them the upper hand. Almost upon him now and ready to strike, their confidence was high and seemed unshakeable, but the remarkable appearance of a large and lethal sword in Rufus' possession brought alarm to their faces and foreboding within.

But even though they were sailors and not soldiers, and had only received training in the rudiments of sword craft, their innate courage and aggression, made the rats very dangerous opponents; and ones who would fight to the death.

"Come on!" screamed Spika

"I'm with ya!" yelled Tufta.

They approached the giant dog head on, slashing their swords from side to side and swishing their tails as rats do when angry.

Their movements of body and swords were haphazard, which in some ways made it more awkward to defend against; but the malamute's quick thinking and rapid movement was always going to give him a huge advantage. Quickly getting into a swing now, he parried each lunge and strike and was soon able to anticipate their every move. The smaller narrow pointed swords of rats made a ringing noise as they struck Rufus' solid blade, and no matter how hard or fast they wielded their weapons Rufus blocked their every move.

Deciding to go on the attack Rufus leapt forward, and applying a rapid close cut spin, his sword encircled Spika's weapon and dragged it from the rat's grasp, driving it so high in to the air it disappeared from sight. Spika foolishly made a grab for Rufus' sword and received a sharp nick to his foot for trying.

"Ow!" he yelped.

The malamute shook his head. "That was silly" he uttered, stepping back and blocking a strike from Tufta, who was desperately trying to break the malamute's defence.

As he checked and deflected the rather ungainly swiping and thrusting techniques from Tufta, Rufus kept an eye on Spika who was peering up at his rapidly descending sword, which he realised must not return to its owner. And so quickly rising up on one of his muscular back legs he leapt forward and kicked Tufta straight in the chest, which not only caused the rat to wince and release his sword, but propelled him across the pebbles and in to the sea, where he lay coughing and spluttering. Without a moment lost Rufus blew a short sharp stream of cold air towards the descending sword of Spika, who was willing it to fall quicker so that he could continue his fight against the malamute.

It was almost in reach now, and looked like it would fall ideally for him to grab, but his body was suddenly enveloped by a strange blue vapour so cold it sent shivers down his spine. And once the sword entered this frigid mist it suddenly crystallised, broke into pieces of ice,

before defrosting in to tiny droplets of water
that fell on to the pebbles; leaving only a brief
trace of dampness that rapidly evaporated.

"Oh my gawd!" he yelled in disbelief.

But he had hardly any time to digest what he
had witnessed before he felt a series of sharp
smacks on his rump.

"Ow, ow!" he cried, turning to face the pointed
sword that had struck him.

"Guess ya got me," he grinned passively.

"I think so...now if you don't mind," replied
Rufus, ushering the rat towards one of the
dinghies.

A dazed Tufta still spluttering from having
swallowed too much sea water scratched his
head and staggered to his feet just in time
to meet his friend and the sword bearing
malamute who stood behind him.

"Alright Spika?" he coughed.

"Spose so," replied his friend glaring evilly at
Rufus.

"Right you two into the boat," directed Rufus.

But Spika was defiant. "Why should we," he
snarled.

Rufus growled and pressed his razor sharp
sword against the rat's throat.

"Because my verminous corvat," he began,
staring deeply into the rat's eyes.

"It's not just swords I can make disappear."

Spika recalled what the giant dog had done to his sword, and as he realised the dog must have supernatural powers, a nervous throbbing sensation filled his tummy.

"Alright, alright," he replied under his breath, trying not to show his fear.

"Come on mate let's go," uttered Spika to his friend, but as Tufta began to walk towards the other dinghy; he felt something brush rapidly across his shoulder before coming to a halt against the side of his throat. It was cold, metallic and its blade so sharp he dare not move a muscle for fear of being cut.

"Just take one...just one," commanded the malamute.

"Okay, okay," uttered Tufta, feeling extremely relieved when the sword left his throat.

The two rats feeling just a little miserable after their defeat traipsed across the pebbles towards one of the dinghies and launched it in to the surf, while Rufus quickly trotted around and picked up the rats' swords. Then holding them both in one paw, and without any apparent consideration or thought for where they might go, he aimlessly lobbed them over towards the two rats, who were at that time struggling to push their dinghy over the pebbles.

As the swords few rapidly in the air, they began to spin around each other, making a cyclic

whirling sound as they performed perfect
somersaults. The two rats were just beginning
to win their fight to float the dinghy when the
sound of the approaching swords caught their
attention.

"Get down!" shouted Tufta, and the two of
them immediately ducked their heads in a vain
attempt to avoid injury.

Fortunately for them the two swords struck
wood and not flesh, producing a simultaneous
thud as they did so, followed shortly after
by reverberating ringing as the weapons now
impaled on the inside of the bow persisted to
tremble for a few moments longer.

The rats both let out deep sighs of relief; but
they needn't have worried for the swords were
perfectly aimed to fly above them, and their
guidance secured by a little magic.

After leaping into the dingy, the rats sat next
to each other on the hard wooden board in
the middle of the boat, before securing their
oars in the rowlocks, and beginning to paddle.
It was very slow going at first, as the tide was
against them, and they struggled to make way.
But an inexplicable breeze arrived from out of
nowhere and gave them a big enough push to
overcome the tidal current and send them on
their way towards Lady Bamboozler.

Rufus smiled to himself, he didn't like to use his

magic unless it was really necessary, as in the case of Spika's sword, but helping the corvats on their way did after all serve a purpose. However he was certain they would return, and in bigger numbers, so he knew it was essential to set up some sort of defence against them. "Albert, get the others will you!" he called telepathically, and the gull lifted off from the top of the white rock, banked around in a semi circle before heading northwards.

There were lots of excitable questions when the rest of the group caught up with him, but Rufus didn't want to go into much detail about his fight with the rats. He was more concerned about reinforcements from the Lady Bamboozler; and wanting to engage Belius, and rescue Monty before they could arrive, he set about following the winchow's tracks.

"Follow me...it won't be long now!" he called back as he trotted off ahead.

"He never stops does he?" uttered Papachuan shaking his head.

Barnaby chuckled. "You can say that again."

"Come on Uncle Chuan," Try to keep up," laughed his nephew as he galloped off after Rufus.

Barnaby and Papachuan exchanged smiles.

"Wish I had his energy," voiced the Labrador exhaling quickly.

The Giant brown dog chuckled. "I just wish I could run faster."

Tracing the winchow tracks to the cave entrance in the cliffs, Rufus soon found himself inside a vast cavern where he sat on his haunches to take in his surroundings. Casting his eyes around the huge vastness of the place, he followed the cloudy chalk walls to the far corner where he could just make out the entrance to a narrow tunnel leading in land; but it was the areas that daylight could not reach that interested him the most. For he realised they could take advantage of their shadows, using them as places to hide in before making a surprise attack on their opponents.

As the rest of the party approached, Rufus motioned them to form up in a line and remain silent; and within moments five animals stood on either side of him frozen like lifeless statues; their darting eyes giving away the anticipation they all felt.

After a few moments silence they all peered towards Rufus whom they could see was in deep concentration. His eyes were closed now and it was his senses of hearing, smell and even vibration that he was harnessing.

A little chatter from Har Vesta and Tunashi distracted him.

"Quiet, I must have silence," he snapped.
The two youngsters finding themselves at the
centre of disapproving glares promptly stared
at the floor and fell mute.
Returning to his deep concentration Rufus
slowed his breathing to a virtual stop and as
his senses of vibration and sound came to the
fore; he shut everything else away. For a while
there was nothing, all was quiet, but gradually
he picked up faint noises emanating from the
tunnel in the far corner of the cave. Initially
he could not interpret them but little by little
he found some clarity in what he heard. The
sound of gruff complaints, joking, elation, and
huffing and puffing all reached him, and the
gravelly cackling voices confirmed it was the
winchow. The scrapping and bumping noises,
heavy breathing and frustrated cries, indicated
to Rufus that they were dragging heavy items
which could only mean they had found the
treasure?
"Good, with any luck they'll be tuckered out
when they reach us," he chuckled, slowly
opening his eyes.
Seeing the malamute come out of his trance like
state and being unable to contain himself any
longer Tonga quickly questioned him.
"Anything?" he asked eagerly.

"Yes it's them alright. They're back in the tunnel away, but they're moving quite quickly considering they're dragging the treasure...so let's get ready."

There was instant excitement felt by all at the mention of treasure.

"So they'll drop it right in our laps," uttered an excited Papachuan.

"Looks like it," smiled Rufus.

"Now, what do you think of the battleground?" he continued, glancing at Papachuan and Tonga with a serious demeanour.

"Well there's plenty of room to fight in, and the dark areas might be useful," replied Papachuan.

The darkness appealed to Tonga too.

"Yes we can hide there, and then pounce on those horrible creatures," he uttered in an optimistic tone.

"Exactly," agreed Rufus nodding towards the boar.

Tonga knew what the malamute expected and ushered his commands.

"Sergeant Kolo, Wicklop, Yabek take up positions over there," he ordered, pointing to where the walls of the cave were hidden in blackness. There was no reply, only action as the three boars did as they were told and were soon out of sight, hiding in the dark shadows.

"But what about me?" pleaded Tunashi feeling he was being left out.

Tonga searched his mind for a moment; it was the young boar's first battle, and he felt he ought to shield him, but by the same token his concern for the youngster must not distract him from his duties as this might be dangerous to him and the others.

For a moment he felt hesitant in making a decision, but happily for him there came a welcome interruption.

"Might I suggest he and Har Vesta wait on the beach," suggested Rufus.

Tonga looked puzzled.

"Why the beach Rufus?"

"To fend off any reinforcements from that ship in the harbour."

As the captain began to understand the malamute's plan his face lit up.

"Of course, he's an expert archer," he gushed.

"And so I understand is Har Vesta," replied Rufus, feasting his eyes on Papachuan whose face lit up with pride.

"That's quite right he is."

"Off you go then," uttered Tonga to Tunashi.

"And you too...and be careful Vesta," instructed the mayor to his nephew, a tinge of worry about him.

Rufus turned towards the collie with a winsome expression.

"And to make sure they you don't get in to trouble would you go with them?"

"I'm not frightened to fight," said Charlie, an air of boldness about him.

Rufus looked him in the eyes and smiled, he was certain the collie was brave, but not being a trained fighter could prove a hindrance to the others, who may risk their lives to protect him.

"No one's saying you are, it's just well...I'd rather you look after the two youngsters," he said softly.

The collie smiled. "Well I suppose someone has to keep them in order."

"That's the ticket," replied Rufus.

"Good luck Charlie, "uttered Tonga.

"And you," called back the collie, trotting off after the other two.

Rufus felt relieved he had successfully got the least battle hardened animals out of the cavern, for he felt certain it was here that a vicious battle would occur. Nonetheless the three of them may be called upon to defend the beach, but at least the sea would give the young archers time to do their duty, and possibly even keep Charlie from any conflict; and any way he wouldn't leave them to face the enemy alone.

"I'll be out in a moment," Rufus called out after them.

"Not staying here for the battle?" queried Tonga looking a little worried.

To allay the captains concerns Rufus placed a giant paw on this shoulder.

"Don't you worry, whenever you need me I'll be there," he uttered in a calming tone.

"But I should think there will be enough of you to take on the winchow - don't you?" he continued.

Tonga smiled, "Oh yes," he replied, an air of confidence about him.

"What about us?" questioned Barnaby, who with Papachuan was anxious to prepare for the melee.

"Yeah and me," grunted Brodney.

Pointing to the two dogs he gave a quick instruction.

"You two make for the cover of darkness and prepare for battle."

"Okay," whispered Papachuan and Barnaby in unison as they crossed the cave to join the boars.

"And take care of yourselves," called Rufus after them.

His two friends gave him a momentary smile before vanishing in to the darkness, but there was no hiding from Rufus as his enhanced senses allowed him to detect both their presence and the boars.

Looking towards Brodney he gave him his orders.

"You are to stay here with Tonga, while I go and attract the winchow into our little trap...okay?"

"Alright," replied the badger gruffly.

It was a momentous scene for certain, three brave animals poised in patience and silence for battle, their shadows cast across the spacious empty cavern, it was the peace before the storm.

Rufus nodded to Brodney and Tonga, and walked forward to take centre stage, where he would wait for their enemy: his gait was elegant and his paws silent on the loose sand. Everything seemed calm and tranquil, the only distraction being the subtle howling sea breeze entering the cavern. But this relative calm was not to last for much longer as a large herring gull abruptly entered the cave and began excitedly flying around; in and out of the dark shadows it flew, disappearing and then reappearing – he was having fun.

He'd been in this cavern many times before and was always bewitched by the wonderful reverberation of his cries cycling around it.

"Albert's here! Albert's here!" he cried, and Rufus glared upwards hoping that his disapproving face would calm him down; but frustratingly he was unnoticed. Albert as always being fascinated by the echoing of his voice began to cry and shriek incessantly.

"Ha-ha-ha-ah, ha-ha-ha-ha!" he cried, banking ever closer to the walls for the best effect. But the worst was yet to come as the vast emptiness of the cavern with its dome like ceiling was such an effective amplifier that the din was transformed into an unbearable ear splitting scream.

"Shush shush!" shouted Rufus angrily, as he waved at Albert to come down.

Rufus peered over his shoulder towards Tonga, a look of frustration upon his face, which was immediately reciprocated by the boar. They both knew the importance of surprise and its advantage, but Albert had probably shattered this plan.

The herring gull surprised by the sternness of the malamute compliantly rolled over and dived towards him, and with just a few feet to go opened his large white wings, glided for an instant, and then touched his pink webbed feet gently down on to the sand.

"Albert what was that all about?!" asked Rufus harshly.

Albert thinking about how to reply moved his head from side to side and looked awkward and uncomfortable.

"Just having fun, having fun," he uttered.

Rufus realised the innocence in Albert's larking about, but now was not the time for playing; it was a time to prepare for battle.

"Well your fun might have cost us the advantage of surprise.

You do realise that!" glared the malamute.

The gull knowing he had done wrong bowed his head down and peered at the sandy ground trying to hide from the embarrassment he felt. Then slowly he began to alternately lift each foot and sway his body from side to side; he always did this when brooding or sulking. He felt so angry with himself now, for only a few moments ago it was all so different; he had felt rather pleased with himself for doing a good job for Rufus, but now he'd let him down.

Initially enraged by the behaviour of the gull, Rufus began to calm down for he could see contrition on the birds face, and not wishing to keep his morale down knew encouragement was the best way forward.

"Come on Albert there's important work for you to do," he uttered energetically

The enthusiastic voice of Rufus made him quickly raise his head, and looking into the malamute's large forgiving eyes, his spirits lifted, and his embarrassment disappeared.

"Albert sorry, Albert sorry...Albert really really sorry."

Rufus leant downwards towards the gull, with a look of cordiality.

"I know Albert but you won't do it again will you?"

His confidence reignited by the malamute, the gull smiled and shook his head.

"Hope we aint got far to go," complained Hubble, pausing for a rest from dragging his heavy pack.

He had found it a difficult task, pulling the heavy load, while at the same time struggling to hold up a candle to show the way; and he desperately needed to take a breather. The trouble was he hadn't picked a good place to stop, for this was the narrowest part of the tunnel with only room for a single file.

"Come on mate, you're in the way," grumbled Yabek slowing to a halt. Reuvic who was bringing up the rear was also displeased that he had to stop.

"Get a move on Yabek!" he cried, not realising that Hubble was the culprit.

"It's sleepy's fault not mine!" snapped Yabek loudly.

Yabeks voice echoed along the chalk walls of the narrow passageway and quickly reached the ears of their leader, who was a little way ahead, followed by Gritch, Monty and Ugg.

Growling under his breath he instantly stopped in his tracks.

"Hold it there pig," he yelled, and Monty very gratefully stopped hauling the two heavy chests and collapsed into a heap on the ground. Belius raised his candle to look back along the tunnel and could just about catch a glimpse of the shadowy outline of a stationary weasel.

"What's going on!" he hollered at the top of his voice.

"N-n-nothing," replied Hubble immediately staggering forwards.

Another growl came from the leader.

"Well hurry up, you're lagging behind," he screamed at the top of his voice.

Hubble swallowed nervously. "Y-y-yes, coming chief!"

As Hubble began to build up a little extra speed in an attempt to catch up with the leading party, the other two just couldn't help but tease him.

"Now whatever you do, don't fall asleep on the job," uttered Yabek sarcastically.

"Don't say that we'll be trapped down here until he wakes up," joked Ruevic, and the two of them began to chuckle.

Hubble wasn't amused. "Ha ha, ha ha, very funny," he snapped.

Belius held his candle up to illuminate the resting pig.

"Come on Piggy, up we get," he sneered, and Monty struggled to his trotters. He was feeling so very exhausted now, and wished he was in the bank performing his easily undertaken clerical duties. It had been over half the day since his capture, and in that time he had experienced bullying, teasing, and threats.

His emotions had gone from hope to despair, swinging from one to the other like a pendulum, and he was beginning to wonder how much more of this he could take?

His mind drifted back to earlier in the day before his kidnap, and he visualised the warm and friendly face of Hamilton, inviting him to tea. He remembered how resistant he had been to her invitation, which now seemed so foolish, as he would give anything to taste her freshly baked apple pie topped with cream.

His face began to contort with bliss as he imagined placing a large spoonful in his mouth.

"Ummm yummy," he whispered to himself.

But nothing lasts forever, and this delightful and welcome illusion was abruptly destroyed by a mysterious and eerie sound reverberating along the tunnel. The ghostly sound made everyone's ears prick up and they instantly stood still; a frosty chill running through their bodies. However, much to everyone's great relief, the dreadful din was short lived, and as nerves began to settle down, Belius was soon barking his orders again.

"Come on you lot, get a move on!" he shouted, and amidst grumbles and complaints, the burden of hard labour returned, as chests and packs were once again hauled along the tunnel.

The noise had intrigued Belius and Gritch, who both had ideas as to the cause, but Gritch was the first to speak.

"What do you reckon of that noise?" he asked.

"Not sure...a bird maybe?"

"Yeah, that's what I thought."

"Then nothing to worry about," replied Belius confidently.

Gritch drew an intake of breath.

"I'm not so sure chief?"

"What ya talking about?" replied Belius with a questioning look.

"Well just supposing, it's that bird from the orchard, and it's looking for us?"

The chief weasel's eyes darted everywhere, as he began mulling over the seriousness of what Gritch had said.

"Could it be, could it possibly be the same bird, and if so were there other creatures with it... searching for the pig maybe?" he contemplated. Feeling greatly annoyed with himself for not considering this possibility was one thing, but admitting it to Gritch was another – especially as he was in command.

"That was at the back of my mind too," he uttered through clenched teeth.

Gritch smiled and turned away, he wasn't convinced.

The return journey along the tunnel seemed a great deal longer when having to drag a load behind and a despairing Monty was struggling along the best way he could; and it was only fear of abuse by the weasels that drove him on. Although complaints were rife amongst the ranks of the weasels, strangely enough it was their intently greedy temperament that actually helped them overcome the mentally arduous trek.

Gradually making progress, it wasn't too long before they were almost back to the beginning of the tunnel.

"Right you lot, when we get in that big cave I want full alertness do you hear, full alertness!" called Belius back into the tunnel.

"Might be an ambush!" added Gritch.

"So be ready for anything," continued Belius wanting to get in the last word.

Obedient replies followed and the group proceeded on their journey, with whispered questions floating between the other weasels at the back of the group, which soon began to annoy Belius.

"Shut up, shut up!" he screamed - and they did.

Engraved in ancient runic symbols are the words
HONOUR TRUTH JUSTICE PROTECTOR
NORTH OF THE WORLD

Chapter 11
Bitter Engagement

The sun had eventually beaten the clouds in to submission and won the day, however evening was now approaching and it was beginning to lose its strength as it fell towards the distant horizon. A gentle breeze stoked the curly hair of Charlie's coat as he stood on the beach next to Har Vesta and Tunashi - who had with him his bow and quiver of arrows. The three of them were glaring out to sea where a schooner lie anchored some half a mile away from shore. Above it a large gull could be seen banking and gliding and generally flying around in circles; it was as if it were keeping an eye on the movement below.

Being concerned about the threat of additional support from Lady Bamboozler Rufus had directed Albert to watch over the ship and report back to him immediately if any troops began to disembark.

Down on the wooden deck below Albert could see two rats animatedly talking to a very dapper fox dressed in crimson breeches and waistcoat who appeared to be their commanding officer. After hearing their frantic report the fox promptly began to walk back and forth screaming at the top of his voice.

"On deck, on deck lads and make it snappy!" Within moments the deck was covered with a mass of noisy dark brown rats scurrying about in what looked like a disorganised state, but very quickly, neat lines were formed, tails tucked in, and a state of attention was adopted, as they listened to instructions from the well groomed fox.

Wanting to hear what was being said; Albert reeled over and gently fell like a leaf from a tree. From side to side he went, gracefully and gradually losing height until he came to rest on the top of the foremast. However the fox's orders had been brief and Albert was too late to overhear them, for he had barely settled on the mast when the large party quickly split up and disappeared below deck. There was quiet for a moment or two, and then the bustling returned as rats flooded back on deck, now clad in armour, and holding swords and shields. Four dinghies were made ready, twelve rats climbed in to each of them, and in a matter of minutes they were lowered on to the sea.

 Albert had seen enough, he immediately launched himself from the mast and headed inwards towards land, and realising the importance of his mission he put maximum effort into every stroke of his wings.

"I must warn Rufus, must warn Rufus!" he cried.

The scene was all set for battle, with Rufus taking centre stage. Sitting on his haunches adjacent to the central cave entrance, he could feel the day's fading sun bring warmness to his body, while the moderate breeze ran across his fur. Some thirty feet behind stood captain Tonga and Brodney, each ready to do their duty and run forward to aid the malamute, while hidden in the dark shadows were the rest of the group poised and ready to leap out on the unsuspecting weasels. Rufus' enhanced senses had detected the movement of the weasels trudging along the tunnel for some time, but the reverberation of awkward shuffling, and heavy breathing was now heard by the others too. The boar and badger glanced at one another; both of them beginning to feel the tension rising inside, as the blood began to course through their veins. For Captain Tonga who was a battled hardened veteran this was a feeling he knew well and accepted it as part of the precursor to a battle, but Brodney who had only limited battle experience fighting for the Zamosian militia, found these blistering emotions irritable; for he hated waiting and was always impatient to fight. The malamute with his extraordinary faculties became conscious of their unsettled feelings and knew only too well that the onus was on him as leader to keep their spirits up.

"Calm my friends, all will be well," he whispered under his breath, and the words permeated through air with a spiritual current that brought a sensation of tranquillity, soothing of the mind, relaxation to the body, and composure to Brodney and Tonga.

Belius was grateful to see the light ahead get brighter as it had been a real struggle dragging the heavy chest along the uneven chalk surface of the tunnel, and he was beginning to get very tired. Pausing for an instant he turned and eyed up his second in command.

"Gritch pass the word...get ready."

Gritch nodded and looked back along the tunnel.

"Ugg, tell the others to get ready," he uttered under his breath.

"Ready for what?" replied Ugg.

Gritch shook his head. "For an ambush stupid got it?" his candle illuminating the weasel's vacant expression.

Ugg turned around to call out to the others. "Get ready for an ambush!" he shouted, his words so loud they resonated along the tunnel like a ricocheting bullet.

"For gawd sake be quiet," hissed Gritch angrily.

"That's done it," snapped Belius.

"Yeah, if anyone's waiting for us they'll know we're coming now that's for sure," added Gritch, frustration showing in his voice.

The word ambush immediately struck a chord with Monty and lightened the weight on his mind, for the physical exhaustion of hauling heavy chests along the tunnel had made him lose any thought of rescue, but at last he felt a rising sense of optimism.

Daylight was rapidly increasing visibility and the uneven greyish white chalk surfaces of their surroundings could be at last be seen without the use of candles, indicating the end of the tunnel was near.

"We'll stop just before the entrance to the cave and have a quick breather," uttered Belius. Gritch nodded, he was relieved to hear his leader's suggestion of a rest, as he realised the importance of getting their wind back if they were to engage in battle.

"But what about him?" questioned Gritch pointing towards Monty.

Belius glared at the pig and chewed on his bottom lip considering his options.

"He can stay behind, looks worn out anyway," he snarled.

Gritch sniggered. "Yeah he does, poor ole piggy." Belius gave the instruction and they all stopped short of the end of the tunnel, put their packs and chests together in a heap and gathered around him.

"Now listen up you lot, I don't know if anyone is out there in the cave but we gotta be prepared. So when I give the order, follow me, swords drawn and look sharp."

His eyes narrowed and the corners of his mouth turned up as he eyed up his gang of weasels, pausing to scrutinise each one before looking at the next. He knew they would all fight, for their overwhelming averice would drive them on; even if their loyalty to him might fail.

"Everyone ready," he uttered under his breath.

"Yes," was the unanimous reply.

"Then follow me, and be quiet," he whispered as he waved his sword forward and continued towards the opening of the tunnel.

Try as they may to tread quietly they could not approach Rufus unheard and he listened

intently, picking up every step they made until
he could see a lone winchow appear.

As he exited the tunnel Belius' eyes were on
stalks as he gazed upon the ghostly silhouette
of a giant wolf, cast across the floor of the
cave by the sun's beams.

"Wait!" he commanded.

Nervously proceeding forward alone, he
regained some composure when he realised the
spooky apparition was merely a dog; however
the sheer size of the beast made him quickly
motion the others weasels to join him.

"Close up," he ushered.

Rufus sat quietly watching their every move,
and counted their numbers; but where was
Monty?

"Perhaps he's back in the tunnel?" he thought,
keeping his eyes on the approaching winchow.
The leader was of particular interest, and
prompted Rufus to remember a painting that
hung in a corridor of his father's castle. It was
a very old oil painting, with the gilt worn off the
wooden frame in most places. And just like many
of the battle themed paintings in the castle, it
had fascinated him since he was a young pup.
This particular canvas depicted a scene of
battle with the winchow, where just like
the soldiers in the painting the one leading
the group towards him wore a metal helmet

and chainmail; and had an equally aggressive
expression to boot.

Instructed by Belius the winchow came to a halt
some twenty feet from Rufus, and raising their
swords high, looked paused to attack. Belius
moved a few steps forward before stopping,
his dark soulless eyes squinted and bored in to
those of the malamute.

This was the weasel way of out psyching your
opponent, by trying to instil fear and doubt into
them; but much to Belius' dismay the controlled
expression of the dog did not falter. Deciding
to take the initiative, he slowly crept towards
Rufus, and as he did so he became aware that
his heart was fluttering. It was an undesired
emotion, and one he seldom experienced; but
he had never faced an opponent who looked as
formidable as this one. He had heard tales of
the great malamutes who lived in North of the
World, and how many years ago they forced his
kind to move southwards with no country to call
their own, and he despised them for it.

Stopping some ten feet away from the
malamute his breathing quickening and his
heart began to pound as he took on the true
dimensions of the dog that towered above him.
Determined not to show fear, he puffed out his
body to make him look larger, and glared at the
malamute, trying to exude an air of boldness.

"What's a giant dog from the north doing here?"
he growled.

"I'm helping some friends," was the emotionless
reply.

The weasel tittered. "Really?"

Sensing sarcasm the malamute fleetingly smiled.

"Yes, they're back there," he smiled looking
over his shoulder.

"You two!" growled Belius, spotting Tonga and
Brodney in the distance, before returning his
glance back to Rufus.

"I see you know them," smiled Rufus, and Belius
raised his lips to display his sharp yellow teeth.
The malamute put a paw to his mouth.

"Now um...Belius isn't it,"

The weasel stuck his neck forward. "Yeah," was
the heavily growled response.

"Oh that is good, good that I've got your name
right, after all no one likes to be called by the
wrong name do they?"

Rufus was being a little naughty and teasing
Belius, and his mocking tone soon did the trick
of annoying him, for the weasels' expression
became very hostile. Rufus as usual was
completely calm, and he felt very confident
that his tormenting would soon anger the weasel
enough for him to charge; for he knew only
too well that an angry fighter loses control
and focus. Time seemed to stand still for a

while, as the two combatants remained utterly motionless, and silent, each eyeing up the other and preparing for action. It was a strange sight to see; the lithe body of the weasel dressed in armour, standing opposite the immense muscular dog. Could this be another David and Goliath moment perhaps?

But Rufus was never one to underestimate an opponent, and knew only too well how tricky the winchow could be in a fight. They could move exceptionally rapidy, and could dance around their adversary, teasing them with sharp strikes to the body, frustrating and tiring them, until they had insufficient energy to fight; and then it was all over.

After a short silence the malamute rolled his eyes and the spoke; a cheekiness in his tone.

"It appears you have something that belongs to Captain Tonga... some treasure I believe?"

"Try and take it," snapped the weasel.

Rufus grinned. "I believe you've also kidnapped Montagu Frazzelbach...hmm?"

"You can ave mister piggy once we're at sea, but not the treasure, that's coming with us," snarled Belius.

Unbeknown to all, this exchange of words was also being witnessed by a large red brown coloured crab who was peeping over the top of a nearby broken wooden chest. His sleep interrupted, he had climbed to the edge of the chest, his stalk like eyes excitedly following every move of the antagonists.

"Oh this is thrilling" he uttered clicking his pincers.

He already felt an affinity with the malamute and watched with great interest as the dog gazed down at the sandy floor of the cave for a moment, before lifting his head to lock eyes with Belius once more. Although Rufus would never shy away from a fight, he was always concerned for his soldiers, and although it was inevitable injury or death would befall some of them, he felt great sorrow every time this occurred. He knew from experience his friend Barnaby could look after himself in battle, and he could count of the tough boar soldiers to hold their own. Brodney and Papachuan having fought in the Zamosian militia had lived through fighting, but what about the partially trained Har Vesta, the inexperienced Tunashi, and dear old Charlie.

Realising he had a duty to avoid conflict if at all possible; he began harnessing his mystical powers in an attempt to enchant the weasel. Intensifying his concentration, he urged his powerful sense of morality to penetrate the very soul of Belius, instilling him with emotions of goodness, kindness and charity.

The weasel was spellbound for a few moments, his head spinning with uncharacteristically positive sentiments bombarding his soul. For a short while he was losing his mind to new values he had never experienced before, and the malamute could sense the weasel was in turmoil. But it didn't take long before Belius' natural malevolent psyche began to fight back and repel the unwelcome sentiments; the inside of his head becoming a battle ground for good versus evil. But with Belius' long years of underhand devilment, the weasel was too far down the path of wickedness to capitulate.

"Get out, get out!" he screamed, shaking his head violently as if to rid his mind of these abhorrent ideals.

His head clearing he looked up at Rufus and snarled.

"What are you, some sort of wizard?"

An innocent expression appeared on the malamute's face as he shrugged his shoulders.

"Sort of," he replied slowly.

Belius screwed up his face and clenched his yellow teeth.

"Well whatever you are I don't like ya, and I don't trust ya.

"No get outta my way!" he growled at the top of his voice.

Rufus remained still and unaffected; however his mind was rapidly sifting through two trains of thought. On one side he felt disappointed in his failure to change the heart of the weasel, but at least now he knew for certain Belius personified the worst kind of animal; and he realised the only course of action left was to fight.

"Trust...you speak of trust," he growled, turning on Belius.

"Your kind can never be trusted, that is why you were driven from my land. You lie and cheat and pick on the weak and vulnerable. But today winchow you have made a grave mistake."

The malamute's words hit their mark and the weasel's face reddened and contorted, and his guttural snarl increased until he exploded.

"You're nothing but a stupid big puppy, now outta my way," he screamed.

The weasel lunged forward confident of striking his opponent but was completely taken aback by the unexpected appearance of a sparkling silver sword that parried his move. But it wasn't just the speed of the malamute's block that astounded him, for the dog instantly moved behind him and gave him an ignominious smack on his back side with the flat of his sword which drove him forward several feet.

"Oi!" shouted the weasel, feeling annoyed and a little embarrassed.

Turning around to seek revenge he was aghast to see his adversary had disappeared.

"Ha ha coward!" he laughed victoriously.

The moment Belius moved on the offensive, Rufus had picked up a sub conscious message from Albert – it was rather frenzied and agitated.

"They're coming, they're coming Rufus!" the bird had shrieked and the malamute knowing the importance of the message reacted instantly, and within moments stood beside Charlie on the beach. Now don't be fooled into thinking that Rufus could simply disappear from one place and instantaneously reappear in another, as if to travel through space and time; for this is not the case at all. He was merely utilising one of his special powers which enabled him to cover short distances at incredible speeds, a feat which often caused great astonishment to the onlooker.

Charlie, standing behind Tunashi and Har Vesta, was the first to see the sudden appearance of Rufus, and he was so flabbergasted his heart began to pound heavily.

"Oh my goodness," he uttered, clasping a paw to his chest.

Rufus smiled. "Take it easy Charlie, it's just one of my little tricks that's all," he replied, gently tapping the collie's shoulder.

Charlie feeling a little more relieved gave a deep sigh of relief."

Overhearing the malamute's voice the other two animals turned around, their faces beaming with joy, both taking great comfort from his presence.

"Rufus!" exclaimed Tunashi excitedly.

"Are we glad to see you," added Har Vesta pointing a wavering paw seawards, where four dinghies could be seen coming towards them.

"I see we have some company," replied the malamute with a composed tone of voice.

"Yes we have," responded Har Vesta excitedly.

"But what are they Rufus?" asked Tunashi, unable to clearly see what the boats held.

Charlie put a paw to his mouth. "I bet whatever they are they're friends of Belius."

"Most probably," responded Rufus coolly.

All four of them stared out at the incoming boats but it was only the malamute with his superior sight who could make out who was on board.

Watching the wooden dinghies rising up and down on the surf, his worst thoughts were quickly confirmed, for each dinghy was crammed full with corvats. Their black soulless eyes, pointed noses, and sharp incisors making them look very intimidating indeed. But even so, he had to afford himself a little smile as he saw them blink their eyes each time the boats crashed on to a wave spraying their bodies with salt water. There were four rats working hard on the oars of each boat, driving them on at maximum speed towards the beach. Every rat wore an iron helmet, and apart from those on the oars, held a short sword and round shield which had a sharp pointed boss in the centre. An order was given and the rats seated on the outside of the boats began to place their shields on the edge to form a protective cover enveloping the boat; rather like the Vikings did thousands of years ago on their longships in the world of men. Rufus spotted Albert flying well ahead of the dinghies; he was making good headway and would soon reach the beach.

"Well it's as I thought, there are corvats on board," said Rufus with a deep heart.

The others looked puzzled.

"Corvats, what are they?" asked Charlie.

"You probably know them as rats," replied Rufus.

"I know them all right. Don't get many in Unger but the ones I've seen looked decidedly dangerous," replied the collie.

The word rat made Har Vesta harp back to his
school days.

"I've heard stories about them; they tried to
invade Zanimos years ago."

"Aye and Unger too," added Charlie.

Rufus turned towards Tunashi, his expression
serious, his tone of voice solemn.

"Its time to show us how good you are with that
bow, young boar."

Tunashi smiled. "I won't let you down, you'll see,"
he replied confidently.

Taking an arrow from his quiver and placing it
against the bow, Tunashi located the string in
the nock of the arrow and pointed the bow up
towards the sky, before drawing the string
backwards as far as his strength would allow.
His eyes looked towards the leading boat
and his mind calculated the angle at which to
release the arrow, and once satisfied his aim
was on target he let the arrow loose. All looked
on and eagerly followed the arrow as it flew
rapidly in an upward trajectory, before losing
thrust and falling downwards in curved angle of
descent. Tunashi in particular looked pleased
with himself, for the arrow was on target and
falling directly into the densely packed group of
rats; right where he had aimed it. He was about
to cry out in triumph, but success was briskly
whipped away, for rats have most excellent

hearing, and once they heard the whistling sound of the arrow they quickly grouped together, and raised their shields overhead to form a protective umbrella.

"No, no!" he shouted as the arrow struck a shield and bounced off into the waves.

"Quickly try another...no try several in quick succession," commanded Rufus, who was angry that the arrow had not met its target. Tunashi responded immediately and launched three arrows in rapid sequence, which was a sight to behold.

The four of them watched the arrows whizz through the air, each of them hoping that at least one would find its mark; but it was to no avail; for the shields held and the arrows were deflected away and disappeared in to the sea. The look on Tunashi's face said it all, for he felt so dejected by his failure to break through the defensive wall of the rats.

"Wish I had a bow," uttered Har Vesta.

"Think you could do better!" snapped Tunashi staring him in the face. The Labrador was initially taken aback by the sharpness of the boar, but being young and feisty he wasn't going to put up with being spoken to like that.

"Well maybe I could," he growled walking towards the boar.

For a moment it looked like there might be an issue between them, but Rufus put paid to that. "Hold it you two, the battle is with the rats not each another!" he snarled, stepping between them.

Peering into their eyes the calming effect of the malamute was instantaneous, as both animals realised their foolishness

"Sorry," began Tunashi looking toward Har Vesta.

"Me too," replied the Labrador with a gentle smile.

"Shall I try some more Rufus," asked the young boar.

"No don't waste your arrows. What we need is a two pronged attack.

"If only I had a bow," uttered Har Vesta kicking some pebbles in frustration.

Rufus rolled his eyes. "Hmm...now let me see." Har Vesta wasn't sure what the malamute meant but like the others he was intrigued to watch him slowly walk off along the beach, occasionally stopping to drag at the pebbles with his massive paws and then bend down and inhale deeply.

As its name suggests Smugglers Cove had at one time been a haven for pirates and unscrupulous mariners. And during those years the beach had been the home of wreckage and debris washed up on the shore from sea battles, storms or just items thrown overboard as waste. But over time pebbles had been washed up on the beach and covered them over, hiding their existence from the naked eye. As Rufus progressed further away from the others he succeeded in digging up all sorts of items that were hidden under the pebbles. Most of these he discarded but several items he studied for an instant before throwing together in a heap.

The first to be kept was a length of sturdy rope, next came a broom handle and then after some frantic digging where he drove pebbles and sand in all directions he finally pulled out a large conch shell of iridescent colours that glimmered as soon as the fading sun struck its surface. He smiled as he studied the large shell for he hadn't hoped to be so fortunate enough to find this particular item.

"Marvellous, simply marvellous," he said excitedly.

But within a moment his smile was replaced with a look of frustration.

"Oh dear, there's one ingredient missing," he muttered slowly shaking his head.

Sitting down on his haunches he began tapping a hind leg on the pebbles. For a hair or rabbit this was used as a warning to its friends that danger is about, but to Rufus this was one of the many things he sometimes did when deep in thought.

But the princely malamute was never one to give up and began to stare intently at the pebbles, moving his head from side to side as if to scan the shingle area by area. The others looked on with great interest and quickly became totally engrossed in what he was doing; so much so that they forgot all about the threat of the incoming rats and even the echoes of angry voices and clanging of weapons that emanated from the nearby cave fell on deaf ears. Rufus's expression soon softened into a beaming joyous smile, and after taking a half dozen steps or so forward he began scrabbling at the nearby pebbles with such ferocity that he soon dug down to reveal his find.

"Got you...you'll do nicely!" he cried exuberantly.

"What is it, what have you found?!" shouted Charlie.

"Come and see for yourselves."

The other three animals enthusiastically rushed across to take a look, but their optimistic excitement was positively dampened when their bemused expressions beheld a large pile of dried up greyish white bones.

"What on earth are they?" quizzed Tunashi.

Charlie smiled. "They're some sort of fish bones aren't they?"

"That's right, cuttlefish bones," acknowledged the malamute.

"Thought so, I've got some in my shop. Some pieces are just like those, but others have been carved into jewellery. Mind you no one wants to buy em," replied the collie shaking his head.
"But what are you going to do with them?" asked Har Vesta.
"You'll see, now each of you grab as many as you can and follow me," instructed Rufus taking the large conch shell in his paws.
After walking a short distance Rufus placed the shell on the pebbles next to the other items he had dug up, and as the others reached him he asked them to do the same with the fish bones.
"That's it, that's it, put them down here next to the other things," he commanded in a gentle tone.
"Right then, stand back stand back," he continued and the others moved further away looking on with deeply puzzled expressions.
Grouped together, the old broomstick, length of frayed rope, conch shell, and pile of cuttlefish bones looked a very strange mix indeed; but Rufus had been very particular in choosing these items. Standing over them he closed his eyes, bent down and drew a deep breath. The others were glued to his every move and were excitedly anticipating something wonderful to occur, but the arrival of Albert soon changed their mood.

His wings beating he was squawking
uncontrollably.

"They're coming they're coming, soon be here!"
Rufus broke off from his concentration and
looked up at the gull.

"Albert calm down, all will be well. Now just
settle down and give me some peace for I have
important work to do."

"Albert do, albert do," he replied and spotting
his friend Har Vesta he set down gently on the
pebbles next to him.

"Good to see you, good to see you!" he cried
excitedly.

The malamute frowned in frustration for he
needed quiet.

"Shush!" he hissed brusquely.

And if this wasn't enough to quieten the bird
the evil glares of the others certainly was.

"No let me begin again," pronounced Rufus
slowly.

Assuming a crouched position, he drew a deep
breath once again, and after holding it for a
moment he began exhaling a murky white mist
that gradually encircled, and then completely
covered the articles on the stones.

"Oh my!" uttered Charlie under his breath,
feeling in awe of this mystical phenomenon.

Tunashi softly nudged Har Vesta.

"What's he doing?"

The Labrador shook his head. "Let's just watch and see...and be quiet," he whispered.

The four bystanders studied the malamute intently as he swept a paw back and forth over the mist, whilst subtly reciting an ancient chant that had no meaning whatsoever to them. And then after taking several relaxing deep breaths, he slowly opened his eyes.

"Now for the exciting bit," he gushed, with an expectant expression.

For a moment or two, and much to the others disappointment nothing happened, but then the magic took control and they became riveted to the spot.

Firstly faint pulsating lights of red and yellow began to slowly appear deep within the mist, and as they gained in luminance and size they began to accelerate around the inside of the hazy cloud, darting haphazardly in all directions. With this coloured display came the addition of some eerie whirring and howling, as if something was alive and moving within the mist – which was very disconcerting to the audience.

Albert in particular wasn't comfortable with this bizarre and chilling display, and so to avoid it, he tucked his head under a wing. But his fear was soon outweighed by his curiosity, and he began to afford himself a little peep now and then so as not to miss anything. The noise kept

on increasing until it reached such a crescendo
that all ears except Rufus' were covered. Then
a vivid white flash occurred, the mist vanished,
and all was strangely still and peaceful.
"Well what do you think?" asked the malamute
proudly.
The gasps of incredulity and marvel said it
all, for it was truly an unbelievable feat, and
the others were left in no doubt that Rufus
possessed the most incredible powers.
The malamute bent down and picked up one of
his new creations which he presented to the
Har Vesta.
"Your bow," he uttered.
"I can't believe it, I truly can't," responded the
Labrador slowly and hesitantly taking the bow
from the malamute.
"Thank you, thank you," he continued studying
the beautifully crafted long bow, hardly able to
believe that a few moments ago this was just an
old stumpy broom handle and a piece of rope.
Rufus grinned. "Haven't finished yet, you'll need
this," he replied holding out a beautiful rainbow
pattered quiver complete with a bright red
strap. As the Labrador took hold of it he was
equally staggered to observe it was completely
full of arrows, and so after putting the quiver
over his shoulder he enthusiastically pulled one
out.

"These look strange, feel strange too?" he questioned, examining the dull white coloured arrow with its absolutely smooth and polished surfaces.

"My goodness," added the boar with a quizzical expression.

For unlike a traditional arrow there was no steel point, wooden shaft or feathers and it appeared to be made of only one material, and although it was beautifully crafted, one could also sense it had a deadly purpose about it.

Rufus looked at Har Vesta and smiled.

"Don't worry yourself my young friend, for these arrows will always go where you want them to," he said confidently.

Har Vesta shrugged his shoulders.

"But what are they made from?"

"The arrows are made from those old cuttlefish bones...oh and the quiver is from the conch."

"Amazing absolutely amazing," replied Har Vesta placing the arrow back in the quiver.

Charlie was standing quietly still and slowly shaking his head.

"You know I've heard some incredible stories from animals who visit my shop, but I have never experienced anything like this."

"Well let's not tell too many others eh...let this be our little secret," whispered Rufus.

The instant that Rufus had disappeared to help the others on the beach, Belius had called his troops to battle.

"Come on lads follow me!" he shouted, beginning to run towards Tonga and Brodney.

With the exception of Gritch the remaining weasels screamed at the top of their voices and ran forwards following the path of their leader. Gritch was as keen as the others to get in to the fray, but his suspicion of something hiding in the darkened areas of the cave compelled him to walk cautiously forward. As he did so his eyes nervously darted back and forth in search of an unseen enemy; and his fears were soon proven. For dark shapes with glittering weapons sprang from the obscurity of darkness and charged forward.

"Look out look out!" he yelled at the top of his voice.

Within moments utter chaos prevailed with many animals rushing around the cave and striking out blindly at anything that moved; but it wasn't long before order was established and individual duals began to take place.

As Tonga watched Belius getting closer an uncontrollable rage began to burn inside him, and screaming at the top of his voice he stormed forward to meet him. The swords of the two enemies whooshed in the air before producing a loud clang as steel met steel. Tonga's rapier sword gave him a length advantage over the weasel's shorter blade, and his military training ensured his techniques were precise and well judged; but this was not enough to keep Belius at bay, for he was very experienced in combat and his naturally aggressive nature made him a fierce opponent. The boar would thrust his body forward and lunge to the one side and then the other of the weasel, who would block when he could, or use the weasel dancing skill to avoid the blow. It was going to be a long drawn out brawl, where possibly the fittest would be the victor, rather that the most skilled.

Sleepy Hubble had managed to rouse himself sufficiently to join the melee and spying a scruffily dressed badger whom he recognised from the tea house in Unger, dashed forward with sword at the ready. Unfortunately for him Brodney was in no mood for any long drawn out exchanges, so without any hesitation drew his two pistols.

"Bang-g!" went one off the pistols smoke gushing from its barrel.

"Aah!" screamed Hubble as the shot brushed across the edge of his shoulder causing him to spin around and fall to the ground.

He remained still and quiet, his injury feeling like a hot iron had rubbed across his skin; he was feeling traumatised, in great discomfort, and for a few moments lost sight of all of his surroundings.

The swords of Ruevic and Buna produced a resounding ringing as their rapidly exchanged blows almost played a constant tune, and each combatant barely took a breath between before executing another move. Ruevic was focused on defeating the boar as quickly as possible, and he may well have had the slight upper hand for he began to drive Buna back towards the wall of the cave. But the distraction of Hubble's cry and sight of his falling to the ground made him lose concentration, and Buna punished him for this with a sharp nick to the arm.

"Blast you!" yelled Ruevic angrily lashing out with his sword.

Knowing the weasel would want revenge Buna stood ready for a vicious attack, but much to his great surprise, instead of resuming his fight, Reuvic raced off towards Brodney.

"I'll deal with you later!" he shouted back at Buna.

"I'm not going anywhere!"

Ruevic was not listening; he was on a mission to get even with Brodney for hurting his friend

Hubble, and although he often teased him, underneath it all he held him in great affection. Although some distance away from the badger, he had the distinct advantage of surprise, as Brodney had his back to him.

Buna seeing what was about to occur wasted no time in kicking off with his trotters in pursuit of the weasel with all the speed he could muster. Ruevic was almost upon the badger and already felt a sense of triumph as he raised his sword above his head ready to strike. Realising he would not be able to intercept the weasel, Buna put paid to his stealthy approach by beginning to shout as loud as he could.

"Brodney Brodney look out behind you!" Responding immediately, the badger turned and glared at the aggressive and enraged weasel who was quickly bearing down on him, and without a moment's hesitation trained his gun towards him. The mere sight of the gun directed towards him compelled the weasel to come an abrupt halt, and staring apprehensively into the barrel he deliberated his next move.

"Stop don't do it Ruevic!" appealed Hubble contorting his face in pain as he began to gain consciousness.

Glancing towards his injured friend, Ruevic saw the discomfort the weapon could inflict, and at this range he realised it might just end his life - and it was quite obvious that the steely eyed badger wouldn't hesitate to use it. With no choice but surrender, the aggressive expression of Yabek slowly faded into submission as he reluctantly dropped his sword to the ground.

"Over there," grunted Brodney, pointing to where Hubble was lying, "And sit next to him." Ruevic begrudgingly did as the badger ordered, however he made no attempt at hiding his contempt for him, and began to snarl and glare at Brodney on his way to join Hubble; his expression only becoming more congenial once he reached his friend.

"Okay mate?" he asked, as he sat down.

Hubble gave a fleeting grin.

"It really hurts, but at least I'm alive."

"Yeah, thank goodness for small mercies eh," chuckled Ruevic, gently tapping his friend on his good shoulder.

"Oh very funny, very funny," replied Hubble. The two friends smiled at each other both feeling relieved they had not perished in this battle, and for a moment they forgot all about the other struggles going on around them - until a loud cry of frustration grabbed their attention.

"Argh!" screamed Kolo, as he was once again thwarted by the quick witted Gritch.

The boar having made no progress in his battle with the weasel was now beginning to show his frustration, after failing once again to break through his opponents defence. His once fluid and economical movement was becoming more haphazard as desperation and exasperation took control. The boar had continually thrust his rapier towards the face of Gritch, who consistently replied with a perfect parry followed by a fast lunge forward with his short sword. And so it went on, the boar moving on the attack and forcing the weasel to retreat a few steps, before Gritch counter attacked and forced Kolo back to his starting point. The whole process was becoming very repetitious now, but it only needed one mistake and the conflict could be lost. And it certainly didn't help either of them when their concentration was interrupted by the battling Ugg and Wicklop who were now beginning to encroach on their battle ground.

Wicklop had Ugg on the back foot and was forcing him ever closer to Gritch, who was now decidedly fed up with this interference. For an instant it looked like the two weasels would collide, but Gritch had other ideas and aimed a perfectly planted kick to the buttocks of Ugg which propelled along the sandy floor in a series of gambols until he collapsed in a heap.

"Hey what's that for," shouted Ugg shaking his head and getting to his feet.

"Do your fighting over there and stay outta my way" shouted Gritch angrily, before unexpectedly lunging forward and catching Kolo off guard.

"Come on boar, do you worst!" he hollered.

Ugg barely had time to get his breath back before Wicklop was upon him, driving his wooden shafted glaive in continuous movements that resembled a figure of eight. His technique was so fluid and rhythmic that it had the effect of mesmerising the weasel, which was exactly what the boar wanted. And then leaping forwards he thrust the glaive as far forward as his arms would permit and Ugg released a loud scream as the sharp blade pierced his chest.

"Aah! wailed Ugg.

"Give up?" taunted the boar.

Though he was not the brightest of weasels, and was certainly not adept with the sword, the one attribute Ugg possessed in abundance was bravery.

"Never never!" he yelled defiantly, slicing his sword erratically in all directions.

In another area of the cavern, the air was filled with gasps, gulps and sighs of relief, emanating from a large brown dog who nervously following every conflicting move between Yabek and

Papachuan. Holding his sword and standing
at the ready in case things took a turn for
the worse for his new friend, Barnaby's eyes
moved rapidly as he studied every move of
the gladiators, cringing each time he thought
the boar had broken the Labrador's defence.
Papachuan was initially thrilled to have an
excuse to use the longsword which had been in
his family for generations, and went into battle
with an air of expectation. He was relieved
to find he had lost none of the fencing skills
he had honed as a youngster, and thoroughly
enjoyed the initial engagement when he easily
parried the boar's crude challenges, and counter
attacked with great skill. But after wielding the
weighty weapon for several minutes he was now
beginning to tire, and his ability to use his skills
to outclass the weasel were gradually waning.
Yabek could sense the tiredness and rushed
forward, raising his sword in preparation to
deliver an overhead blow, but even though he
was tiring, Papachuan still had the advantage of
size and strength and managed to successfully
parry the blow, forcing the weasel to back off
once more.
"Phew!" uttered Barnaby.
But his sigh of relieve was short lived as the
boar continued with this attack. Without
missing a beat the Yabek immediately raised

his sword over his shoulder and leaping forward made a downward diagonal stroke feeling confident he would reach the dog's flank. Papachuan had practiced his response to such a move many times before, and even though he felt tired, he was thankful that the counter move required little effort to undertake. Adroitly taking a side step to avoid his enemy's sword, he promptly followed through with a perfectly executed strike to the boar's hind leg. The astonished expression of Yabek was promptly followed by a painful grimace as he felt the burning sensation on his leg, and fell to the ground in pain.

"Yes!" yelled Barnaby excitedly.

Within seconds Papachuan held his sword against the neck of Yabek and applied a little pressure to discourage further resistance from the boar.

"Drop it!" he ordered.

Feeling the uncomfortable coldness of the sharpened steel against his skin Yabek let his weapon fall to the sand.

Slowly peering up at Papachuan, his face contorted in pain, his eyes full of anger, Yabek's immediate thoughts centred on retrieving his sword, the moment the Labrador gave him a chance. But this plan was soon dashed as

Barnaby trotted forward and collected his weapon.

"Well done, well done old boy."

"Less of the old," replied a smiling Papachuan catching his breath.

He was thrilled to be the victor, but also extremely relieved the fight was over, for he knew too well that his fitness had been fading and shortly his energy would have been spent; and that might have been his end. This wasn't a sign of his age, for he was still in his prime, it was the heavy commitment of sedentary work in his role as town mayor that curtailed any chance of physical exercise. But as he looked down on the grisly and dangerous looking weasel, he made a promise to himself there and then that this would change.

"Come on let's go, over there," gestured the Labrador pointing his sword towards Brodney who stood guard over the other captive weasels.

The four dark wooden dinghies stood out in sharp contrast to the vivid crimson backdrop of the horizon, and while Rufus had been doing his magic they had covered a considerable distance and were fast approaching the shore. On seeing they were now significantly closer; the malamute swiftly led the others to a point directly facing the oncoming boats, and motioned the archers to take up their positions.

"Ready lads?" he asked, looking at the two youngsters.

"Yes," replied Tunashi and Har Vesta in accord.

"Now Tunashi when I give the word, fire a volley of four arrows directly at the centre of the leading boat, and you Har Vesta, your target is the bow."

Har Vesta looked confused. "The bow, why the bow," he queried.

Rufus smiled. "You'll see, now nock your arrows." The two of them prepared their arrows and stood ready.

Then the malamute did a very strange thing indeed, he stepped over towards Har Vesta and producing a grin like a naughty young puppy, scratched the point of his arrow with his giant paw; and as he did so he caught a glimpse of Charlie peering at him with a puzzled look.

"More magic?" asked the collie, which made the other two glare at the malamute with excited expressions, hoping the answer would be yes.

"Maybe," he replied grinning cheekily, creating an air of enthusiastic anticipation.

Stepping back behind the archers Rufus gave the instructions they were eagerly awaiting.

"Okay lads, take aim...draw...fire!"

The strings of each bow twanged simultaneously and were followed by a quiet whoosh as the arrows were set free, and Tunashi, Har Vesta, and Charlie looked on in hope that two pronged attack would this time bring success. They followed as best they could the rapid flight of the arrows, and looked on as the rats reacted as before and deflected all Tunashi's arrows in to sea. But this time was different, for there was a second archer aiming at another target and as the rats held their shields up to stop the first salvo they had left the front of the boat totally unprotected from the second.

There was a subtle thud as the arrow struck the bow before rooting itself firmly in the darkened wood. The rats gave a loud cheer and began to laugh hysterically and wave teasingly at the animals on the beach, and once again a look of disappointment appeared on the boars face.

"Oh not again-"

"Wait, just wait," uttered Rufus, a sense of optimism in his voice.

Tunashi returned his gaze to the dinghy, desperately hoping something remarkable might occur, and surprisingly enough it did. Captivated and entranced by the slow materialisation, he became rooted to the spot; as did Har Vesta and Charlie.

To begin with, it merely resembled the igniting of a match, as a tiny blue and yellow flame flickered from the arrowhead embedded in the bow of the dinghy. But this was no ordinary flame, and appeared to have a life of its own, for after dancing on the spot for a moment or two it leapt on to the top of the wooden bow, where it flared out in all directions. Rapidly growing in height and intensity, the flames transformed in to a raging inferno, before finally exploding into a monstrous fire ball that began to completely engulf the dinghy.

The rats' laughter instantly ceased, and discarding their shields, helmets and swords, they jostled with one another to evacuate the blazing boat. Finding safety in the gentle undulating waves, the rodents began to paddle seawards towards the haven of Lady Bamboozler. And within moments of their departure, amid hissing and bubbling, the dinghy began to sink beneath the surface until the last flickering flame was extinguished by the salty water; and then it was gone.

"Hooray!" shouted Tunashi as he turned towards the malamute.

"Amazing Rufus, I didn't expect that," he continued.

"Nor did I," added Har Vesta.

"You never cease to amaze us Rufus," uttered Charlie shaking his head in disbelief.

"It wasn't really me, it was these great young archers," replied the malamute modestly.

"Oh, and by the way there's another three boats to sink you know?" he continued, glancing at Tunashi and Har Vesta.

The two youngsters faces lit up as they were looking forward to a repeat of their success, but as they turned around to seek out their next target, their spirits were instantly lowered as a feeling of disappointment filled their hearts.

"Oh no!" exclaimed Tunashi.

"I was so hoping to sink another boat," complained Har Vesta.

But Charlie felt very different." Hooray, hooray!" he shouted.

The three remaining dinghies had turned around and were being rowed out to sea as fast as they could, for having seen the fate of the first, none of the other rats wanted to risk continuing and so turned about for the open sea.

"Come on lads." uttered Rufus in an uplifting tone.

But it had no affect as their heads were held low.

"Look, you've done your job and stopped them... and no one was killed either," he continued.

"You should be proud," added Charlie.

"I supposed so," replied Har Vesta shrugging his shoulders.

"But Rufus, isn't war about killing?" questioned Tunashi.

The malamute slowly rolled his eyes and deliberated for a moment.

"Tunashi, war is an evil and ugly undertaking, and if death can be avoided it should, for life is sacred and should only be taken as a last resort."

"But my father –"

"Your father is a soldier, and to most soldiers killing is part of their being." Pausing briefly, he looked closely at Tunashi, his emotions of kindness and clemency penetrating the very soul of the young boar.

"Listen," he continued in a solemn tone. "I have fought many battles, and have slain a great number of creatures, but I can say with the fullest heart that I have always acted honourably, and every time I killed, I did so because my enemy would give me no quarter...do you understand?"

Tunashi nodded. "I've never thought of it like that, but now you've explained it, I'll try to remember this when I go in to battle."

"Good, now let's see how the fight in the cave is progressing."

The youngsters' expressions erupted in to
happy excitement as they realised there might
be another chance to get involved with the
fighting, for they had forgotten all about the
battle in the cave. And so with cheery faces
and playful nudging, they set off towards the
battleground, their outwardly confident veneers
of joy hiding an unsettled mix of uneasiness,
and adventure, they each felt churning inside.
However, before they had got very far Rufus
called out after the young Labrador.
"Har Vesta...a moment if you please!"
"Why of course," replied the Labrador feeling
curious as to what the malamute wanted.
"I hope I haven't done anything wrong," he
thought, a sense of guilt welling up inside him.
"What is it," he asked in a subdued tone, as he
reached the malamute.
Sensing the young dog's concern Rufus smiled.
"You've nothing to worry about Har Vesta,
you've done a marvellous job, but I'm afraid it's
time to leave your bow, and quiver behind."
A look of disappointment crossed the
Labrador's face.
"Oh dear, that's such a shame; I feel I could
conquer anything with them."
Rufus raised his eyebrows, "Yes that's often
the case with enchanted weaponry."

"Is there no way I can keep them," pleaded Har Vesta.

Rufus slowly shook his head. "I'm afraid not... they've done their job."

Har Vesta reluctantly offered the bow and quiver to Rufus.

"Just lay them down there," requested Rufus softly.

"But wont someone steal them?" queried Har Vesta, gently placing them on the pebbles as if they were made of the most delicate china.

A broad smile opened up on Rufus's face.

"No, there's no chance of that."

Now, let us join the fight!" called Rufus, rushing off across the sand. As usual the others found it difficult, if not impossible to keep up with him, but even at their slower rate it didn't take long before they could hear the sounds of combatant's cries and clanging of weapons. Nearing the cave entrance Rufus slowed down to let the others catch up, and as the young ones reached him he studied their fresh and innocent expressions, eluding excitement and bravery. The last thing he wanted was for them to be hurt, but he realised they would at sometime probably have to experience battle; and he consoled himself with the thought that at least he would be on hand to help them out if necessary. He could sense their anxiety and uncertainty, but outweighing this was strength of heart, and a great commitment to acquit themselves.

"Young brothers in arms indeed," he thought. "Right you two, it's time to win your spurs...now in to battle, and be careful," orderd Rufus, a sense of paternal concern in his voice. Filled with the sudden rush of adrenalin, Tunashi and Har Vesta briefly exchanged smiles with the malamute before charging forward with gritted teeth.

"What about me, I want to help too?" questioned the collie, feeling slightly dejected. A brief smile shot across the face of the malamute.

"Then follow me Charlie. I'm certain I can find something for you to do," he replied, walking off towards the melee.

The malamute's words lifted the collie from despondency, for here he was, walking next to this giant and unique animal, on a day to treasure and remember, feeling absolute confidence that the omnipotent Rufus would ensure they win the battle.

The tide was gradually coming closer to the bow and quiver that lie abandoned on the pebbles, and it was only a matter of time before the incoming tide would draw them out into deep water. The bow would of course float, and in time and if good fortune permitted it perhaps find a new owner to use it, or if not it might be smashed to pieces on a treacherous reef. The fate of the quiver and its beautifully crafted arrows would almost certainly be sinking into oblivion never to be seen again. But magic can sometimes be very fickle and not always be trusted to last forever; which in this case Rufus was well aware of. And the appearance of a dense milky mist hissing out from the ends of the bow and from the mouth of the quiver was just what he would have expected to see; as was the ghoulish waling and whining, beginning as little more than an eerie whisper, before rapidly increasing in volume to an agonising shrill. Having enveloped the bow and quiver, the mist remained over them for a few moments before it was promptly drawn into an invisible portal and vanished. The enchantment returning from whence it was summoned had abandoned its beautiful creations, and left behind a heavily cracked and split stumpy old broomstick, a badly frayed length of rope, a drab looking conch shell full of fractures, and a heap of charred ebony fish bones; in fact there condition was even worse than before. You see, magic comes at a cost, and even innate cast away objects have to pay the toll for a short lived transformation into something remarkable; sad though this may appear.

Upon entering the cave Rufus was pleased to find that three weasels had been defeated and were held under guard, but his feelings of hope were stifled as he studied Tonga and Kolo struggling with fierce opponents who looked to have the upper hand.

The expressions of Har Vesta and Tunashi on the other hand were of wonder and delight for they had never witnessed weapons being used in anger.

"Wow look at that!" gasped Tunashi, as Wicklop demonstrated his excellent skill with the glaive and drove Ugg backwards.

"He's bound to beat him soon!" responded the Har Vesta excitedly.

"Isn't it marvellous?" continued the young boar totally absorbed in the savage combat.

"But unlike the youngsters Charlie found it all very alarming.

"I wouldn't call it Marvellous," he said shaking his head.

"Especially if you are Tonga or Kolo," he added, pointing at each of them in turn.

"Oh no, no!" cried Tunashi seeing his father being dangerously outclassed.

It was not Gritch's ability with the sword that gave him the advantage, but his expertise in the deadly weasel dance, where he could twist and bend, and spin around like a ballet dancer evading every attack that Kolo attempted. And now the frequency of his successful jabs to the boar's body had begun to frustrate kolo and leave him with a series of stinging wounds. His anger mounting, Kolo made a series of powerful thrusts to the head of the weasel hoping that his extra size and weight would win the day. But the defensive move of Gritch was poetry in motion as he spun around like a spinning top, sliced his sword across the trotter of Kolo causing him to cry out and drop his weapon, then skipping forwards he forced his sword into the throat of the boar.

It was all too much for Tunashi to bear and he buried his head in his trotters hoping, against hope that his father would survive.

But unbeknown to the young boar, Rufus had made contingency plans for the boars defeat, and had gestured to Barnaby to take up a position close to the fight of Gritch and Kolo. So with his eyes tightly closed Tunashi was unable to observe the giant dog charging forward towards the boar.

"Argh!" screamed Gritch as he was tossed in the air like a rag doll. Up and up he went reaching about seven feet high, before gravity took over and he dropped like a stone landing on the sand with a soft thud. Kolo was dumbstruck and stood motionless just staring at the congenial looking Newfoundland.

"He's out for the count!" shouted Barnaby proudly looking over towards Rufus.

"Great work!" replied the malamute with a big smile, as he turned towards young Tunashi.

"You can open your eyes now, it's all over," he said in a soft tone.

Tunash's face gleamed with joy and happiness, and wiping his tears from his eyes he received a welcoming smile from his father.

"Thank goodness," he uttered drawing a deep breath of relief.

A friendly paw wrapped around his shoulder.

"There's no more need to worry now," came the soft voice of Charlie.

Meanwhile Ugg was struggling to keep the lethal glaive of Wicklop from inflicting further injuries, for his chest wound although not fatal was causing him much discomfort, and the loss of blood was now sapping his energy.

"The end's near for you weasel," taunted Wicklop.

"Not before yours!" replied Ugg struggling for breath.

The boar smiled confidently before launching a ferocious onslaught that forced the weasel to drum up all his remaining energy to avoid defeat. Yet despite feeling extremely fatigued, Ugg was determined to continue the fight, and so after drawing in a deep breath of fresh air, and feeling slightly revived, he began lashing out crazily; hoping against hope that one blow would strike home against the boar. But Ugg's attack was driven by desperation not skill, and his sword was soon trapped by the barbed hook of Wicklop's glaive, and as the boar swung his weapon to the left the exhausted Ugg had little choice but to be dragged in a semi circle and thrown to the ground.

His weapon wrestled from his grip, Ugg lay helpless and breathless, waiting for his end, and seeing the boar draw back his weapon he prepared to meet his maker.

Wicklop bared his teeth and showing no mercy drove his glaive towards his trembling victim, but as he extended his thrust to administer the fateful blow his weapon hit neither bone nor sinew, but solid steel.

A loud reverberating clang followed and the impact produced a vibration that ran along the length of his arms causing a shaking sensation that created temporary paralysis. As his feeling came back to him, Wicklop was disturbed to find he was no longer in possession of his favoured glaive, and so without hesitation drew out his short sword. Determined to destroy his defenceless victim he raised it above his head ready to strike.

"Shall I stop you again!" shouted the malamute. A look of surprise and consternation appeared on the face of the boar who stood fast, yet remained poised to take the life of the defenseless weasel.

"Do you rob me of my prize," snarled Wicklop. Rufus glared at the boar.

"Your prize is victory, isn't that enough," he growled.

The malamute looked deeply into the eyes of the boar and after a short period of inner conflict Wicklop's expression began to slowly soften.

"I suppose your right, but would he have been so generous?"

Rufus took a deep breath, while searching for the right words, and then he remembered those of a revered teacher.

"In war we should use a code of conduct that is never influenced by evil; or to kill for killings sake...remember that well."

Being a battle hardened warrior Wicklop had never even considered surrender as an option, and had always slain his opponents. Yet

after hearing these solemn words a feeling
of contrition flowed though his veins, making
him think that in future he must try to act
according to the malamute's principles, and only
kill as a last resort.

"I will try Rufus, I will," he uttered reverently.

CHapter 12

Victory

The defeated weasels were sitting together
with an ill tempered looking badger holding two
loaded pistols standing over them, and more
fire power was added when Buna arrived holding
the musket he had lost in the early stage of
battle. To ensure security of the prisoners,
Barnaby and Papachuan were also on hand, so
any thoughts of escape by the weasels would
have been sheer folly. Anyway the captives
were more concerned with the only remaining
duel, and were sitting up to attention, glued to
the conflict, gasping at every strike and parry,
as the battle between their leader and Tonga
looked near to conclusion.
Tiredness of the two combatants was all too
evident as their encounters were now quite
brief, with more time being spent getting their
breath back than fighting. Each engagement
consisted of wild and untimely sword strikes,

with barely enough vigour from either animal to propel their weapons effectively.

There was a moment when it looked like the two warriors, bent over and breathless would at last give up their arms, but as they exchanged glances their expressions of mutual hatred rekindled a fire inside them and conflict resumed. Staggering forwards their swords awkwardly clashed together causing a haunting resonation that filtered around the walls of the cave. Snarling and growling followed from both sides, and the futility showed as swords locked together they leant forwards, each relying on the other to remain standing. Most of the onlookers found this feeble exhibition agonising to watch, and Rufus in particular wanted this hopeless struggle to end. For no victory would alter the fact that the weasels had been defeated, and their inept and clumsy behaviour might bring about unnecessary injuries or death; either of which Rufus would prefer to a void. Considering he had no option but to intervene the malamute stepped forward.

"That's enough you two, it's foolish to continue!" Belius fell back from Tonga and drawing sharp breaths stared menacingly at the malamute.

"As long as my heart is beating I fight," he snarled.

Rufus shook his head.

"Then you're a fool, for all is lost."

"Let me finish him!" yelled Tonga barely able to stand.

"You will both stop now," screamed Rufus, so loudly that the reverberation around the cavern made all the animals wince.

But even before the echo had subsided two antagonists had their weapons torn from their grasps and driven across the sand far out of reach by the unbelievable skill of the malamute. The two looked on in awe as Rufus proceeded to demonstrate an incredible display of sword craft, manipulating his gleaming silver knightly sword at immense speed and agility, the like of which they had never seen before.

"Now then, do we see sense?" he uttered, and the two animals reluctantly nodded in agreement.

Staring at Belius he nodded in the direction of the other weasels.

"Now join your soldiers."

Belius gave a brief protesting snarl, which was pure bravado at this stage for although he did so want to defeat Tonga underneath it all he was relieved the fighting had ended, for he felt completely exhausted. Breathing deeply and walking with a clumsy gait he made his way across the sandy floor towards to his fellow captives, where upon he dropped to the ground.

"You alright Belius?" asked a concerned Gritch.
But Belius did not want any sympathy, he
was more interested in apportioning blame
to his troops for losing the battle, and more
importantly the treasure; and seeing them
huddled together quietly and subdued, made his
blood boil.

"You lot make me sick," he hissed, causing the
others to look at one another with dismay, for
each thought he had given his best.

He was about to carry on with this angry
onslaught but was overcome by uncontrollable
and violent coughing.

"Careful now chief," uttered Gritch slapping his
boss on the back several times.

"Alright alright!" that's enough sputtered
Belius, glaring at his number two, and doubting
if his concern was genuine.

"What about me?" moaned Ugg holding his
chest.

"What's up with you?" snapped Belius.

"I'm bleeding, look," replied Ugg pointing to his
seeping chest wound.

Belius tossed his head back unbothered by
Ugg's injury.

"Oh diddums," he retorted.

"And my shoulder's in agony," whimpered
Hubble, still feeling the discomfort that
Brodney's gun has inflicted.

Belius shook his head from side to side unmoved by the hurt felt by his two soldiers.

"You're a bunch of softies you two, no wonder we lost," he growled, staring at each of them with an evil expression.

Gritch felt differently, he really wanted to help the wounded, and was in two minds as to call for assistance, but was concerned if he did it would irritate his chief; fortunately the conversation was overheard by another.

"Barnaby over here," called the malamute, as he approached the sedentary weasels.

"What is it Rufus?" asked Barnaby, as he reached his friend.

"We have some injuries to tend."

"Yes they look a little nasty......should have brought my rucksack have some podilla in it."

Rufus smiled. "Good job I brought some then," he replied, producing a paw full of large bright red leaves well known for their healing properties in North of the World.

"Mine?"

"No I always keep some on me, just in case."

Barnaby smiled and shook his head, as this was no great surprise to him. For unbeknown to the others Rufus wore an invisible and weightless backpack created by ancient and powerful sages who gave it the ability to store an unlimited number of items without adding any load whatsoever.

Taking the leaves from his friend, Barnaby was relieved to feel a familiar gentle pulsing, for lack of this would mean the leaves were devoid of healing properties.

"Okay you, you're first," he continued staring at Ugg.

"Oh leave him, he'll be alright," interrupted Belius brusquely.

Appalled by this callous attitude Rufus immediately turned on the weasel hurling anger towards him.

"Be quiet winchow!" he retorted.

There was a brief exchange of glances but the penetrating and resolute glare from the malamute made the weasel quickly avert his eyes.

"Winchow indeed," he muttered under his breath.

Rufus didn't like bullies like Belius and was always pleased to put one in his place. So feeling a little self satisfied, he afforded himself a little smile before walking off to leave Barnaby nursing the injured.

"Oh and don't forget our side will you?" he called back.

"Course not, I'll check them over as soon as I finish here."

With the podilla leaf pressed against his chest
Ugg felt its therapeutic power begin to work,
as a soothing warmness began to penetrate his
body, bringing great comfort and relief.
After only a short while Barnaby removed the
leaf, and amazingly the bleeding had stopped,
and the wound was now clean and sterile.
As the leaf was dropped on the sand its colour
dulled from bright red to faint brown, and
omitting a slight rustling sound, its power now
spent, both ends curled up and it died.
"There you are," said Barnaby softly, and Ugg's
thanks came in a gentle nod.
Next he attended to Hubble's injury, and then
to the little cut that Ruevic had sustained.

Tonga meanwhile had been helped along by
Papachuan to join the other boars, who were all
smiles when he arrived, and Charlie in particular
was thrilled to see him.
"Thank goodness you're safe."
The boar breathed deeply, "It was a close
thing."
"Now let me sit for a moment," he continued,
and the Labrador gently lay him down on the
sand.
Peering up at his soldiers he ran his eyes across
each and every one of them counting their
number and a great feeling of comfort and

gladness filled his body when he found no one was missing.

"Well done lads," he gasped, his chest heaving heavily.

"Take it easy captain; they'll be plenty of time for talking later," uttered Buna.

Celebrations followed as Tunashi met his father, who for once forgot all about formalities of sergeant and trooper and gave his son a large hug, even though the gash on his trotter caused him to grimace as he did so. There was more embracing as Papachuan met Har Vesta, and the two Labradors began to get carried away and dance around in circles laughing and smiling.

And then without warning excited cries rang out around the cave and everyone turned towards Albert.

Look, look over there!" he shrieked, flying off towards the far side of the cave where a tired and weary looking pig was struggling to drag two heavy wooden chests behind him.

"Its Monty, it's Monty!" cried Papachuan, before excitedly trotting off towards him.

"Oh no you don't!" grunted Brodney staring at the weasels as they got to their feet.

The weasels looked disgruntled and moaned and groaned in protest, but with the Badger's guns brought to bear, complaining was all they could do.

Rufus was the first to reach Monty, and immediately untied the rope from around his neck, and tossed it to the ground.

"Look!" uttered Monty huffing and puffing, as he threw open each chest in turn.

"And there's more!" he declared rapturously pointing back into the tunnel.

"Oh my word," sighed Rufus in disbelief, transfixed by the contents of the chests.

Within moments the others had reached Monty, but they were so utterly mesmerised by the valuable contents of the chests, they completely ignored him.

"Incredible," uttered Tonga turning to Charlie.

"And to think I had my doubts," replied the collie with a beaming expression.

"Simply marvellous," gushed Papachuan.

There were 'oohs' and 'aahs' from the others, and then silence as everyone absorbed the enormity of the amazing sight they beheld.

Rufus was the only one aware that in all the excitement Monty's deliverance had not been recognised, let alone rejoiced, and could see the deep look of disappointment on the pig's face.

So clearing his voice he spoke loudly and deliberately, purposefully bringing this important oversight to attention of everyone present.

"Well anyway, I'm thrilled you're okay Monty!" he uttered in a matter of fact tone, stepping forward and giving the pig a friendly tap on the shoulder.

The others realising their ignorance, released a series of apologetic gasps, before becoming shamefully silent, leaving the whistling sea breeze gently swirling around the cave as the dominant sound – but this didn't last long.

"I'm pleased, I'm pleased too," squawked Albert who took off and hovered over head.

Instantly the cave was alive with voices once again, and the Zamosians in particular feeling guilty over their ignorance of Monty, at once rallied around to shower him with love and affection. The boars were also keen to join in the happy moment, and after introductions they too added words of relief and joy that he was found. This was the most significant day in Monty's life to date, for at last he felt part of something and no longer alone, and revelled in the attention he received; this was indeed a very different Monty to one that got up this morning.

Rufus felt delighted that Monty was at last being acknowledged and given the treatment he so deserved; and the pig's glowing and cheery face filled him with great contentment.

Silently trotting off into the cave, Rufus studied the backpacks and chests that the weasels had left behind, and then peering in to the dark depth of the tunnel he raced off into the blackness.

Using his exceptional burst of speed together with his uncanny senses he detected the path taken by Monty and the weasels, and soon reached the cave where the treasure had been found.

He immediately caught sight of three wooden chests, each with steel bands and a padlocked lid. The wood still looked in good condition relative to the corrosion of the metal parts, but tugging on one of the locks it still held firm. Stepping over a pick axe that had been discarded by the weasels, he produced his broad double edged sword, and gripping it behind the gold guard he raised it above his head and stood still and silent in meditation. Although the cave was pitch black the pure silver of the sword sparkled and radiated through the darkness, and for an instant the ancient words written along the side of the long blade blinked and twinkled. Rufus drew the sword downwards at a speed too fast for the eye to see towards the padlock, and as it

hit the lock's shackle there was a fiery glow
of white light followed by sounds of metal
hitting the ground and the cave wall, as the
lock exploded into tiny fragments. He repeated
this action on the remaining chests and then
throwing open the three lids he stood in wonder
at this momentous vision.

His face was a picture, for it was not often that
he was lost for words, or amazed at anything he
saw; but this was different. He was no stranger
to jewels and valuables, for as a youngster his
father would take in to the castle vaults and
show him precious heirlooms, such as orbs,
sceptres, crowns, and jewellery that had been
in his family for generations; but that amounted
to nothing compared to the treasure in these
three chests, let alone the other chests and
backpacks the weasels had attempted to steal.
Peering around the cave he spotted the odd
piece of treasure left on the ground that the
weasels failed to collect and so he walked
around for a moment picking up everything he
could find.

Then something shimmering caught the corner
of his eye and walking over to the one of the
wooden chests he bent down and carefully
dragged out a beautiful gold necklace from
beneath it. He studied the thick links of the
chain and could feel with a slight tug that

it was immensely strong, and being gold it
was obviously very valuable, but it was the
significance of the trinket attached to it that
Rufus found much more important.

Substantial in thickness, the diamond shape
golden pendant had jewels of every type set
close to the outer edge, and etched deeply
within this border of flickering gems were
five oddly shaped inscriptions that Rufus
found vaguely familiar. Concentrating on these
symbols he thought back to his schooling in
ancient wizardry and tried to recount if he had
been shown such writings, but as he did so an
icy coldness brushed against his thick coarse
fur.

He had felt this many times before, and knew
instantly there was a presence of an unnatural
malevolence which he must either destroy or
evict immediately, to avoid a drawn out struggle
between his power of goodness and the faceless
demon.

Not frightened or unduly alarmed, Rufus
produced a roar of lionesque proportions
before spiralling around in a complete circle,
and breathing out a fierce yellow mist that he
fanned around in all directions. As the mist
permeated the air, there were horrendous
screams of pain and torment as his goodness
struck the very soul of this frigid and heartless

devil. Utilising his wizardly power, he was able to break through the shield of invisibility revealing a translucent yet unrecognisable shadowy being – the source of the evil. Then without hesitation he directed the mist to spiral around it in ever decreasing circles. Faster and faster he drove it, and tighter and tighter the circles became, until amid desperate pleas of harrowing squealing and waling, the wicked entity was drawn in to a vacuum of oblivion and vanished.

Feeling relieved and pleased to have driven off the vile manifestation, he gently squeezed the necklace in his paw feeling quite certain it was connected to the evil he had expelled. And although it no longer possessing the power it once had, the spectre's intense desire to avenge was extremely palpable.

"I wonder what the old Sages at home would make of this?" he pondered.

"I'd better keep it safe," he added, a momentary expression of solemnity crossing his face.

And with a twist of his paw it was gone.

After slamming the lids closed, he began to quickly drag two of the chests back along the tunnel, and as he did so a resounding sound of excitement and laughter began to increase the further he progressed. Moments later he was able to detect deep breathing and shuffling, and soon after a number of shapes appeared just ahead of him casting faint shadows along the tunnel. He could easily make out from the large shadow that one of them was Barnaby, and in no time at all he could see he was accompanied by Charlie, Har Vesta, Papachuan, and some boars.

Oh what commotion there was, as the happy and cheerful animals noisily laughed and joked as they dragged the chests and packs left by Monty and the weasels, back along the tunnel. Rufus being at times a little mischievious thought it would be great fun to catch up and surprise them with a ghostly howl, or a spooky cry, but as they were nearing the entrance to the cavern they soon disappeared from sight putting paid to his naughty idea.

"Right so we've got four chests and four bags of treasure so far," uttered Barnaby totalling up the booty they had grouped together.

"Yes and there's still more chests back in the cave," added Monty.

Papachuan shook his head still unable to take it all in.

"More, I can't believe -"

"Here's another two for you!" shouted a familiar voice.

"Rufus!" exclaimed Papachuan.

After watching the malamute haul the chests across the sand for a moment, Har Vesta turned towards his Uncle.

"Makes it look so easy doesn't he?" he uttered, shaking his head in astonishment at how effortlessly Rufus pulled the chests along.

"He's a strong one, that's for sure," replied his uncle.

Charlie in particular was feeling very excitedly about the amount of treasure they had found, for this was more than in his wildest dreams, and so unable to contain his emotions any longer shouted out at the top of his voice.

"Tonga we're rich, we're rich!" and the words reverberated around the cavern; a strange eeriness in their meaning.

In response to his friend's excited outburst the boar's face beamed with delight, for underneath his calm exterior, he too was greatly impressed by the magnitude of their find. But Charlie's declaration troubled Har Vesta who reacted immediately and gave his uncle a gentle nudge.

"Uncle Chuan surely it's not all their treasure?"

"No it's not Vesta!" said Papachuan loudly and firmly, provoking angry expressions from two Ungerians.

"Now hold on, you were in search of your friend and we were after the treasure!" snapped Charlie completely out of character.

"And now we both have what we want, there's no need to argue," added Tonga, firmly and emphatically.

Sadly it was the age old sin of greed that was clouding Tonga and Charlie's judgment, and the anger the boar felt towards the weasels for stealing his map, and breaking the Tonga jug certainly didn't help.

"Well you're both forgetting one thing," uttered Papachuan firmly.

"And what's that," questioned Charlie, his voice rising in pitch.

"The treasure was found here in Zanimos!" asserted the Labrador firmly.

The boar and collie looked awkwardly at each other, for the thought of sharing the treasure had never entered their minds.

Seeing things might get a bit heated Belius took the opportunity to stir things up.

"Would ya look at that, they're fallin out over the treasure!" he cackled loudly, and the other weasels joined in giggling and sniggering.

"You can't trust those boars you know," yelled Gritch trying to agitate things further.

"Na you can never trust em!" added Ruevic
shaking his head, and joining in just for the
sake of it.

"Shut up the lot a ya!" yelled Brodney waving his
pistols in the air.

Gritch trying to play it clever, thought if he
could provoke things further, perhaps even
cause a fight, the weasels might escape.

"Don't waste your guns on us badger, might need
em for the boars," he uttered, a cunning look
upon his face.

For one moment Brodney was in a quandary;
he realised that guarding the weasels was
essential, but at the same time he couldn't let
his friends down if there was a fight with the
Ungerians. And so repositioning himself to cover
the weasels, and watch any possible escalation
with the boars, he stood prepared to act, guns
at the ready. Fortunately Rufus wasn't fooled
by the weasel's ploy to cause trouble, and
quickly intervened.

"That's enough you foolish creatures," he
enunciated, stepping between Tonga and
Papachuan.

"Brodney, concentrate on the winchow, and Buna
go help him!" he commanded loudly.

So strong and direct was the command that
Buna didn't even look towards his captain

for agreement, but followed the malamute's instruction immediately.

"Now calm down, and don't be so stupid for haven't we won the day," continued Rufus appealing for calm.

Tonga and Charlie looked and one another and felt terrible, each realising that avarice had driven their unforgivable behaviour.

"Please forgive me Papachuan," begged Charlie his head bent low in shame.

The Labrador smiled. "Why of course Charlie."

"And I'm sorry too...friends?" said Tonga extending his trotter.

Friends," replied Papachuan, smiling warmly.

With paw and trotter shaken there was a great feeling of calm and relief all around, with the exception of Belius and Gritch whose shared disappointment showed on their faces.

Rufus thought it best he mediated an agreement and so beckoned Charlie, Tonga and Papachuan to come and sit down with him.

"Firstly I will act as intermediary is that acceptable," he stated, in such an unyielding tone they had no option but to agree.

Then after looking at each in turn, he began.

"Right, well it's really quite simple, the treasure will be shared equally between Unger and Zanimos," he stated firmly.

"Alright Papachuan?"

The Labrador smiled, "Yes of course Rufus."
"Alright Charlie...Tonga?"
The two of them looked at each other, before nodding in agreement, each realising this was indeed the fairest way.
"So, three chests each and split the seventh between us then," uttered Charlie eagerly.
"Sounds fair to me," responded Papachuan, with a joyous expression.
But then a thought suddenly occurred to Rufus, the idea sounded good to him, however he immediately realised it would seem distasteful to the others.
"Ahem," he began, clearing his throat. "I would suggest we give the odd chest to the weasels."
And just as he had expected, protestations were forthcoming.
"What!" complained Tonga, his face full of incredulity?
"Surely not?!" protested Charlie.
Papachuan on the other hand was filled with curiosity.
"Why should we do that Rufus?" he asked softly.
"Let's just say there's plenty to go around, and if they hadn't found the secret to unlocking the whereabouts of the treasure, there would be none for any of you. So I say let them have a little."

Papachuan shook his head disbelief at the malamute's decision

"You're far too gracious Rufus."

Tonga felt very disgruntled by the idea of sharing treasure with the weasels, for it was the last thing on his mind, but nevertheless he begrudgingly capitulated

"Well I suppose you know what you're doing Rufus, but I have to say I don't like it," he uttered shaking his head in disapproval.

The malamute raised his eyebrows for there was good reasoning behind his decision.

"There's more to it than that, look out there," he pointed, to where Lady Bamboozler cast a sleek silhouette against the fading glow of sunlight.

"It's getting dark now, too late to go home for us, we need food and sustenance to help us through the night, and I'm sure the captain of that ship will willingly provide this for a little bit of treasure."

"And how will we do that?" asked Charlie.

"Oh that's easy. Albert will take a piece of jewellery out to the captain, with a message from me that the weasels will be set lose and given a chest full of treasure, if a boat full of supplies is sent out to us."

"Tonga let out a gasp of relief, his faith in Rufus restored.

"What a great idea!" he exclaimed, feeling much better about the whole thing.

Papachuan grinned.

"I thought there might be method in your madness Rufus," he chuckled, patting him on the shoulder.

Feeling greatly relieved that all parties were pleased with his plan, Rufus afforded himself a broad smile.

"It's wonderful when things work out," he thought to himself

Albert was quickly despatched to Lady Bamboozler carrying a small tiara laden with jewels, and a hastily handwritten note in his large beak. On board Lady Bamboozler things had now settled down to normal, after the disorder and confusion created by the returning rats frantically clambering aboard after their retreat from the deadly archers. They were now huddled together below deck wrapped in blankets, and had been going at the rum over enthusiastically, which was making them rather obnoxious. Although initially enjoying friendly banter the excessive drinking had brought to the fore their pugnacious temperament, and they had now started shoving, pushing, and arguing just for the sake of it; which is typical of Nordeamian rats when they become drunk.

They were getting louder and more aggressive and their noisy behaviour was beginning to cause great annoyance to the animals on the main deck.

"Close the hatch Tufta, there's a good chap," ordered Sileenus, and the rat quickly slid the wooden door across the opening deadening the din from below.

"I suppose you would like to join them?" questioned the captain.

The rat smiled. "Well could I?"

"No, not yet, let's wait until there's something really worth celebrating shall we."

"Now Tufta, tell me more about this giant dog?"

"Well as I said skipper-"

"Captain, captain!"

"What is it?" responded Sileenus, a tone of exasperation in his voice as he turned towards Spika.

"There's a bird coming towards us!" came the enthusiastic reply.

"Oh really," replied Sileenus, snubbing the rats's observation.

Spika who was on watch had spotted the bird through Sileenus' telescope and continued to watch it approach the ship, and once he set eyes on what it was carrying he felt compelled to call his captain.

"Sir take a look, you'll be surprised at what it's got!"

The fox sighed. "Very well then, give me the scope."

After a moment of adjusting the focus, a large grin replaced the nonchalant expression on Sileenus' face.

"Amazing, absolutely amazing, bird's got some sort of crown in its mouth," he uttered, turning towards Spika with a look of incredulity on his face.

Spika felt pleased with himself. "See told ya."

The fox continued to watch the bird until it was so close that the telescope was redundant, and then followed it with his naked eyes as it overflew Lady Bamboozler before setting down a few feet away on the wooden deck. Sileenus captivated by the jewel encrusted tiara quickly sprang forward and made a grab for the gull, who immediately released the contents of his mouth, and taking advantage of a strong gust of wind managed to evade capture. The fox slowly walked forward and picked up the small crown and began to closely examine it, completely disregarding the piece of paper that lie next to it on the deck. He moved the petite gold tiara around in front of his face inspecting every inch of it, and was particularly interested in the band of encrusted precious stones which gleamed and sparkled even in the fading light. "What do you think lads!" exclaimed the fox, grinning from ear to ear.

"Bet it's worth a bit!" said Spika his eyes on stalks.

"Reckon so," agreed Tufta.

A puzzled expression appeared on Sileenus' face as he wondered why the bird should bring him this piece of treasure, and so he began to search above for him.

"Hey you there!" he shouted spotting Albert in the rigging, but the bird remained stationary, and just stared back at him.

"Look I won't hurt you...just want to talk that's all," he implored.

Albert dropped from the rigging and catching the wind in his wings glided downwards and began fly around in a circle just off the port side of the ship; and more importantly to him out of reach of the fox.

"Why did you bring this?!" shouted Sileenus waving the tiara.

"Read the note, read the note!" cried the bird.

Sileenus frowned. "Note, what note?!"

"Look on deck, on deck!"

Scratching his head the fox began to scan the area for any sign of the note. He was indeed very eager to read its contents, but his immediate lack of success in locating it promptly turned his curiosity to exasperation, and so he called upon the rats for help.

"Give me a hand you two?" he ordered, and Spika and Tufta began to scurry around and assist in the search.

"Hey what's that!?" laughed Spika pointing to Tufta's foot where the corner of a white piece of paper could be seen.

"Tufta hopped on one leg and giving the paper a sharp tug unstuck it from his foot.

"This anyfink?" he asked, offering his captain a neatly folded sheet of paper.

Sileenus carefully unfolded the paper and his eyes widened as he was greeted by the most beautifully executed writing; it was clearly legible yet very artistic, and every letter was embellished with a flourish.

"My my," he uttered, sounding impressed.

But as he read onwards the real beauty for him was not the calligraphy but the actual content, and once he had finished reading it a satisfied smug crept across his face.

Being of a mercenary nature he wasn't really bothered about the safety of Belius and the weasels, but if exchanging them for some of his valuable food and drink meant getting hold of more treasure, then that was a price worth paying.

"And this Rufus, he will keep his word?" asked
Sileenus, shouting up to Albert.
"He will, he will," nodded the gull.
"Okay, consider it done."
The words had barely left the fox's mouth,
when Albert banked into the wind and
gracefully glided around towards the shore.
A moment later the fox displaying a joyous
expression turned around and addressed the
two rats.
"Spika, Tufta, I've got a little job for you."

"Any sign of Albert yet?" asked Papachuan
peering out to sea.
"No, but I'm sure he won't be long," replied
Rufus sounding confident.
The sound of something being dragged across
the sand began to filter through the whistle
of the sea breeze and very shortly Barnaby
arrived with one of the wooden treasure chests.
"Here you are," he uttered releasing the chest.
"Thank you," replied the malamute
acknowledging receipt of the chest with a nod
and a smile.
"Hope your plan works Rufus, I'm starving,
"proclaimed Barnaby rubbing his stomach.
"Me too," uttered Papachuan.

"Have faith my friends, for I'm certain a pirate won't turn down the chance of getting hold of treasure so easily."

"That's true enough," replied the Labrador nodding his head.

"By the way Barnaby, how's the fire coming along?" enquired Rufus, turning towards his old friend.

"Everything's prepared. We've chopped up that old boat and piled up the pieces into a fair sized heap. Should give off lots of heat once it gets going."

Papachuan felt relieved about this, "Good, we'll be glad of that when it gets colder."

Rufus' psychic connection with Albert enabled him to hear the birds satisfied squawking, and so using his telepathy he began communications.

"Did everything go as planned?" he asked.

"All good, all good, captain agreed!"

Rufus felt pleased.

"Well done Albert...by the way I can see you now."

"Can't see you."

"Don't worry you soon will, I'm on the beach with Barnaby and Papachuan."

Rufus peered seawards beyond the outline of Lady Bamboozler to where the sun was slowly slipping below the horizon, leaving a fiery orange glow, which engulfed the grey cumulous clouds.

"Soon be dark," he declared.

The Newfoundland sighed, "Yeah, and still no sign of our goodies."

"Be patient, they'll arrive, you'll see," replied Rufus in an upbeat tone.

While Papachuan and Barnaby exchanged views about pirates and the question of their trustworthiness, Rufus stood still and quiet, while he probed the grey evening light with his highly developed sight. It was but a small white speck in the distance at first, but the increase in its brightness indicated it was slowly moving towards the shore.

The malamute uttered a loud sigh of relief that drew the attention of the other two, who promptly stopped their chatter.

"Rufus what is it?" asked Barnaby.

A huge smile appeared on the malamute's face as he turned towards his old friend.

"It's coming, the boat's coming."

Papachuan squinted his eyes.

"Are you sure?" he asked, unable to locate it.

"Just keep looking out to sea, and in time you'll notice a white light," replied Rufus.

"I can see a white bird," laughed the Labrador.

Rufus shook his head and tittered.

"No not Albert, look beyond him."

It took a short while before the inferior eyesight of Barnaby and Papachuan were able to detect the white light, but once they did they were all smiles.

"Yes I see it," cried Barnaby excitedly.

"It's gradually getting near too," added a delighted Papachuan.

Slowly but surely the light drew nearer and nearer, until a small wooden boat could be identified. It was being rowed by two large aggressive looking rats and hanging off the bow and swinging gently from side to side was a copper lantern emitting a white incandescent light.

"Right Barnaby, get all the others out here including the winchow," ordered Rufus, a sound of urgency in his voice.

"Will do," replied the Newfoundland as he trotted back towards the cave.

As the wooden dinghy gradually approached the shore the remainder of the animals rushed out of the cave and prepared for its arrival. Brodney together with Buna, Kolo and Wicklop stood guard over the weasels whose spirits began to lift as they clapped eyes on the small craft just off the coast.

The heavy load of cargo and the ebbing tide made progress of the boat very slow, and feeling somewhat frustrated by this Rufus ordered Barnaby, Monty, Tonga and Papachuan to wade out and help bring her ashore. And after some splashing, sploshing and submerging by some, the four of them gained control of the wooden craft and steered it successfully ashore, where the keel groaned and complained as it ran aground on the rough pebbles.

"Okay let's unload her," shouted Rufus as he began to paddle in the sea.

The sight of the giant malamute made the two rats instantly feel uneasy, and they hastily made their way to the stern of the dinghy to keep away from him; although when their eyes momentarily met his they put on a brave face of belligerence. With the exception of the weasels and their guards, everyone joined in and helped unload the cargo, and after some ten minutes or so the boat had been emptied and its load taken into the cave and laid down in an organised pile next to the treasure.

"All done Rufus," smiled Tonga.

"Thank you. Barnaby can you put the chest in the boat?"

"Of course," replied the Newfoundland always pleased to help.

"I'll give you a hand," offered Tonga.

"Thanks."

One part of the bargain being made good was the chest being put on board, and the other was release of the weasels; and so after a nod from Rufus, Brodney ordered them out to sea.

The winchow began to enter the surf one by one, but for some strange reason Gritch turned away from the sea and stepped towards the malamute. Kolo reacting quickly, drew a sword and held it across the weasel's chest arresting his movement.

"That way," he grunted nodding towards the wooden dinghy, but Gritch ignored him, stood his ground, and gazed at Rufus with such an enquiring expression that it triggered his curiosity.

"You wish to talk winchow?"

"Yeah."

"Let him pass sergeant, let him pass."

Kolo unsure if it was safe to release Gritch responded slightly hesitantly, but a after a smile and nod from the malamute he stepped out of the weasel's path.

As he walked slowly forwards Gritch looked the malamute up and down. He had never seen a giant dog from North of the World before today, but was mightily impressed by his large stature and obvious strength.

"Thought I knew all about your kind, from the stories I was told as a young kit," he began, almost in a whisper.

"And what did they tell you?"

Gritch began to chew on his lower lip.

"That you were cruel, harsh and wicked, and you drove us from the north out of pure hatred."

Pausing for a moment he looked the malamute squarely in the eyes.

"But you're not like that, there's someink mysterious about you, and even a power that's unnatural, but you are good...I can feel good."

The malamute looked solemnly at Gritch.

"Don't' believe all the stories you are told, for it was your ancestors who sort to control North of the World, and it was only out of defence of the realm that they were driven southwards."

Rufus paused for a moment before adopting an instructive approach; something like a professor or teacher might use. His tone was serious, but heartfelt, for he detected a tiny trait of goodness in the weasel.

"Do yourself a great service Gritch and seek another path. For following Belius will bring you nothing but misery."

"I'll bear that in mind," replied Gritch in a gravelly tone.

Belius had watched this conversation with great interest, and glared at Gritch as he climbed aboard the dinghy.

"What did he have to say for himself?"

"Told me you are a wrong un Belius, and tried to send me on the road to salvation," grinned Gritch pretending to be unaffected by his conversation; but infact Rufus's words had struck a chord which had caused him to contemplate a new future – and one without Belius.

"Who needs salvation when fools like him let us free with a chest of treasure," chuckled Belius.

"Right shove off!" shouted Barnaby, and together with Tonga, Monty and Papachuan, he pushed with all this might to propel the dinghy out to sea. There was an initial bit of struggling over the crashing surf, but slowly the boat began to disappear into the darkness, for the sun had retired for the day and night had taken over its shift. But the blackness wasn't having complete ownership of this night, for a series of lanterns were lit on board Lady Bamboozler, and as the oil soaked wicks began to burn, white lights flickered in to life from stern to bow.

The fire had been lit several minutes ago and was already providing illumination and heat inside the cave making the vast soulless cavern a friendlier place. There had been much excitement as the cargo supplied by Sileenus was quickly opened, and once inspected there was certainly no disappointment or complaints.

Barnaby being a bit of a gourmet decided
to take over as chef, and had taken great
pride in preparing a fish stew that was gently
bubbling away in an iron cauldron on the fire.
Papachuan had assisted in the preparation and
had made a mental note of all the ingredients
so he could duplicate the dish in future. The
main constituent was the fresh sea bass which
was skinned, filleted and chopped in to square
chunks, after which Barnaby added tomatoes,
carrots, celery, leeks, garlic, and oil.
As he stirred the mixture, a hot aromatic
vapour permeated the air and tantalised all
the animals, as they breathed in and savoured
the lovely odour. Much to the joy of the boars,
Sileenus had supplied a large barrel of beer,
and some wooded jugs to go with it, and they
were guzzling the brew like there was no
tomorrow. Brodney had also consumed copious
amounts of beer, which seemed to soften
his normal brusque manner, and give him an
altogether more agreeable countenance.
"Hey this is some of that Arven grog aint it?"
he uttered.
"That's right it is," replied Buna spilling beer
down his neck.
"Oops, silly me I need a top up," he added,
giggling to himself.

"You've had this before then Brodney?" asked Wicklop.

"Oh yeah, they sometimes have it at the Rosfarl Inn."

"That's right they do," responded Buna with uncontrollable hiccups.

"Hey need a bit of help with that mate?" giggled Wicklop.

But before Buna could respond his friend gave him a hard slap on the back causing him to emit a huge burp.

"Better?" asked Wicklop.

"Better," replied Buna, and then everyone began to laugh.

"You know," began Brodney a slight slurring of his speech, "We need to make a toast.

"Great idea, great idea!" yelled Kolo rocking back and forth, under the influence of the strong brew.

"I propose a toast to Rufus," shouted young Tunashi.

"Hear hear!" shouted Har Vesta, and after some excited whooping and hollering, they all stood up and toasted the malamute.

With a broad gentle smile on his face Rufus raised his wooden jug in the air and looked at each and every one of the animals.

"Thank you, thank you, but there is someone who perhaps deserves recognition far more than

I, for without his bravery and quick thinking we may not have been victorious today."

The partying animals surprised by this statement were immediately quiet, leaving only the sounds of a crackling fire, a gentle howl of the wind, and the burbling stew to fill the cavern.

They looked on in silence at Rufus, jugs of ale poised in mid air, their faces impatient to hear whom it was he wanted to honour; and after a short pause he spoke.

"I give you Montagu Frazzelbach," roared the malamute and after a moment's hesitation, all the others looked towards the pig and heartedly cheered. And after refilling their jugs and gulping down their beer, repeated the toast with even more rumpus enthusiasm.

"Montagu Frazzelbach," they all screamed at the top of their voices.

This rousing recognition took Monty by complete surprise and his embarrassment showed as his cheeks became as bright red as a tomato. But once he had got over the initial shock of the enthusiastic ovation, a wonderful feeling of happiness crept over him, and for the first time in his life a sense of pride pulsated through his body; which to him was thus far the most wonderful emotion he had ever felt.

The malamute gave him a subtle nod as if to say well done, and the two animals smiled at one another. Rufus was so pleased Monty was alive and well, and Monty so glad that a wonderful animal like him had cared enough to come to his rescue.

After placing his jug on the sand Rufus trotted silently out of the cavern across the wide strip of sand until he reached the pebbles, where he sat on his haunches and took in the salty air. The malamute closed his eyes and listening to crashing waves, he breathed gently and steadily, contemplating what had occurred that day. Although he could tolerate extremes of hot or cold weather equally, being from North of the World where the winters were extremely cold he found some comfort from the gentle cool breeze as it ruffled his thick coat. There was stillness and calm in the air, similar to one might experience after a fierce storm, which for Rufus reflected the atmosphere of tranquillity after the brutal battle with the weasels. Slowly opening his eyes he detected a row of white lights moving away in the distance. They were heading in a northerly direction indicating that Lady Bamboozler had turned one hundred and eighty degrees and was probably sailing back to whence she came. As he watched the lanterns of the schooner gradually fade in to the distance an amusing grin appeared crept across his face.

"I wonder what fun and games they will have on board arguing over the treasure," he chuckled to himself.

After a further few moments of reflection on the day's events, his peaceful solitude was interrupted by some friendly voices.

"Alright if we join you?" said one.

If we're not intruding?" added another.

Glancing over his shoulder Rufus saw Barnaby and Papachuan approaching him.

"Glad of your company," he called out to them.

"Lovely evening," uttered Papachuan peering up towards the myriad of sparkling stars that disobediently penetrated the black veil of night.

"It is that. It's the perfect end to a most gruelling day," replied Rufus.

"Yes, a battle won, a friend found and oodles of lovely treasure for our country," uttered Papachuan smiling contentedly.

"And no one killed," added Barnaby solemnly.

The malamute nodded, "Thankfully not."

"Rufus?" began Papachuan speaking slowly, "Do you think it would be alright if I have some treasure to pay for the repair of the town hall roof?"

The remark brought a broad smile to the malamute, who responded slowly and deliberately.

"Being a stranger to your country it's not for me to say. But I do believe the fairest thing is for everyone in Zanimos to benefit from this extraordinary find. And as the town hall is an important place for Zamosians to meet, I would imagine they would much prefer to do so in the dry...wouldn't you agree?"

"That I would," replied a happy Papachuan. But then very slowly the Labrador's smiling countenance changed to a perplexed looking expression, as something had begun to bother him.

"You know what I find strange?" he began.

"What's that?" asked Rufus.

"Well, I am so utterly amazed that the stories and rumours we were told as youngsters are actually true...that Catsumo's treasure was really there all the time. But what I don't understand is why it wasn't found before. I mean I went in that cave loads of times as a young pup, and never found a single trace of any treasure. The only thing I found was that dreadful carving, which never failed to send shivers down my spine."

Rufus not being one to accept the inexplicable thought back to the feeling of latent heat he had experienced as he entered the cave. His eyes motionless, he stared straight ahead as he searched for an explanation, and within moments his genius identified a possible solution.

"I think I've got it!" he uttered excitedly.

"The answer?" queried the Labrador.

Rufus smiled.

"Yes, I believe I have. That wall you've mentioned Papachuan, the one with the carving of Catsumo, well it wasn't a real wall at all."

The Labrador shook his head in disagreement.

"But I've seen it."

"I'm quite certain you have. But it's not there anymore."

Papachuan looked bewildered.

"What do you mean not there?!"

"It's gone, vanished."

The Labrador shook his head yet again.

"But how can that be?"

Always having faith in his old friend's knowledge and understanding of the paranormal, Barnaby was certain that he could provide the answer to this mystery, and was excited to hear it.

"Do tell us Rufus?" he beckoned.

"Yes please do?" added Papachuan sounding a little sceptical.

"Okay," began Rufus with a broad smile, looking deeply into the eyes of his two friends.

"It is most likely that wall was some form of magical creation, made to hide the treasure, and that either by pure luck or because they had found out how to do so, the winchow destroyed it."

A bewildered expression appeared on the Labrador's face.

"Just think, Catsumo's treasure was there all the time, right under our noses," he uttered, a tone of astonishment in his voice.

"And I'm so glad she's not alive to reclaim it," he added, releasing a large sigh of relief.

As he absorbed the words of the Labrador, Rufus' expression took on a more serious demeanour.

"I hope you're right Papachuan, for I found this in the cave," he announced, producing the necklace he had discovered,

A disturbed look appeared on the Labrador.

"That looks familiar, there was one just like it on the carving, it was around the neck of that evil cat."

"I had a feeling it might belong to her," replied Rufus.

Looking more closely at the ancient runes, he managed to recognise a couple of the engraved hieroglyphic squiggles, and he felt certain his interpretation was correct. And as he looked up from the pendant the others could clearly see a look of graveness about his demeanour.

"What is?" queried Papachuan.

Barnaby could also detect something had disturbed the malamute.

"It's something in those symbols isn't it?"

Rufus Nodded.

"Is it significant Rufus?" asked Barnaby softly.

"Well," he began, solemnly, "I only have a brief knowledge of these particular ancient runes, as they are a corruption of those used by my forefathers. But I believe this pendant is a symbol of loyalty and subservience to a great power, and an evil one at that. It possibly forms some sort of covenant between a living creature and the spirit world, offering the creature incredible powers in exchange for their loyalty and ultimate sacrifice of their life."

"A bit extreme isn't it, I mean giving up one's life!" exclaimed Papachuan.

"To sane and good animals like us yes, for we value life and want nothing more than to live. But for some, living simply isn't enough and they will swear allegiance to any master, no matter how dark and demonic to achieve their own evil goals."

Papachuan looked a little reassured, "I am so relieved that's she's dead. I know it sounds harsh but all the stories about her were simply horrid."

"It was the wizards that once lived here that destroyed her wasn't it?" asked Rufus.

Papachuan smiled, "Yes that's right, Mortuleez and his wife, the white witch Julianna...but that was hundreds of years ago."

"You don't think she could ever come back do you Rufus?" asked Papachuan, feeling a little nervous about the response he might get. The malamute deliberated for a moment, tapping his paw delicately against the pebbles as he did so.

"As to that I'm not certain Papachuan," he began," but I've seen many extraordinary things attributed to magic and the supernatural, and have learnt to accept that nothing is impossible."

The Labrador looked a little glum, "Oh dear."

"So what shall we do with this necklace?" asked Barnaby, sounding a trifle agitated.

The malamute breathing deeply began to speak in earnest.

"We must lock it away and keep it safe, and never allow it to fall in the possession of wicked and evil creatures; for should it do so a new era of darkness may be unleashed, bringing death, horror and sadness."

"Where will you take it Rufus?" asked Papachuan.

"I must take it home, to North of the World."
The Labrador looked a little puzzled, "Why
there?"

"Because it will be safe in my father's...I mean
the king's palace, where the wise old sages may
be able to neutralise the pendant and render it
impotent."

Rufus uncharacteristically averted his eyes and
stared at the pebbles, hoping that Papachuan
hadn't understood the slip up about his father
being king. But it was all in vain, for the
expression of captivation on Papachuan's face
showed he had interpreted the verbal blunder,
and with a look of wonder and astonishment, he
quickly looked at Barnaby for confirmation.

The Newfoundland shook his head and smiled at
the Labrador.

"You might as well tell him Rufus," he uttered
softly.

The great malamute looked at Barnaby and
raised his eyebrows conceding that he must
do so, and as he slowly stood up on to all four
paws he gave his fur a perfectly groomed look
by a quick shake of his body, before standing
tall and proud, and adopting a most noble
expression.

"Well my friend you had better do the
honours?" he asked in a dignified tone, glancing
at Barnaby.

"Ahem," began Barnaby clearing his throat.

"Your highness," he began, bowing to the malamute.

"Wait a moment there's something missing!" exclaimed Rufus and with his customary magical adroitness he revealed a solid gold coronet which he immediately placed firmly on his head. Papachuan looked very impressed.

"My you look so-"

"Royal?" interrupted Rufus.

And the three of them broke in to chuckles.

"Now prey begin," uttered Rufus in a slightly playful tone.

The Newfoundland cleared his throat once again, keeping an eye on Rufus in preparation of another intervention but a friendly wink assured him this would not happen.

"Your highness," he began, in a louder and more polished voice than before.

"May I introduce The Lord Mayor of Zanimos, Papachuan," to which Rufus responded with an over emphasized bow, and a broad grin, that brought a momentary smirk to Barnaby.

"And my Lord Mayor, may I introduce his Royal Highness, Prince Rufus, Thadgrum, O'Malley, son of Odana, King of North of the World, and the five realms within it.

The Labrador stood open mouthed, trying to take in the enormity of it all, and then his face filled up with the most magnificent smile.

"My goodness how wonderful, why this is simply marvellous Rufus, I mean your highness," he uttered.

Barnaby began to giggle, "Now you must bow, my Lord Mayor."

"Bow...oh of course," replied Papachuan bending his head slowly and deliberately. But as he raised his head Rufus couldn't help but notice his look of uncertainty.

"What is my friend?" he asked with smile.

"You're not teasing are you; I mean you really are a prince?"

Rufus smiled "Yes, yes I am."

Barnaby put a giant paw on the Labrador's shoulder.

"Don't let our tomfoolery deceive you, for he takes his royal duties very seriously, don't you Rufus?"

Rufus nodded, "Yes I do. I just thought a little levity might save embarrassment all round, that's all."

"Well it was a bit of a shock," sighed Papachuan. "Would it be alright to tell the other Zamosians that you are a prince of North of the World?" he continued enthusiastically.

"No please don't do that," protested Rufus.

"But Rufus, I mean your highness, why not?"

"Because being a royal can attract all sorts of unwanted attention, so please keep it our little secret...at least for the time being that is."

Papachuan looked very disappointed.

"I suppose so, your highness."

"It's Rufus, remember just plain old Rufus."

"Unless he's on duty and then you bow and scrape to him," laughed Barnaby.

Rufus lent this head back and tittered, "Ha ha ha...you know that's not true Barnaby."

"Course I do my friend, for just like your father you are a most modest animal, and one who would never take advantage of their aristocratic position...unlike someone I could mention."

"Let's not mention my uncle, for it will dull the edge of our celebrations," replied the malamute seriously.

Barnaby raised his eyebrows and nodded.

"And now my friends," began Rufus in an upbeat tone, "tonight we must party, for tomorrow I begin my journey home."

"Shall I come too?" asked Barnaby with a hopeful expression.

"That would be perfect my old friend, but on this occasion I must use all my speed to get this symbol of evil under lock and key as quickly

as possible, and I fear you would only slow me down."
The Newfoundland tutted and looked disheartened, but deep down he understood the importance of haste in this matter and knew he could never keep up with the immensely fast malamute.
"You're quite right of course Rufus," he replied, nodding reluctantly in agreement.
"But you'll be back, won't you?" uttered Papachuan with an imploring expression.
Rufus stepped forward and looked into Papachuan's eyes with kindness and fondness.
"Of course I will. For Zanimos has a very special place in my heart, as do you Papachuan."
The Labrador beamed with happiness, as he felt very touched by Rufus' affection.
"And besides, I couldn't leave my old friend here to get into trouble could I?" added Rufus with a chuckle, patting the Newfoundland affectionately on the back.
Barnaby giggled, "As if I would."
"Now my friends feast your eyes on the beautiful heavens!" uttered the malamute at the top of his voice.

As the three companions peered up towards the celestial darkness, an unexpected bright glow appeared from nowhere and raced across the night sky directly over head. It dashed across the heavens at an incredible rate leaving a trail of thin white streaks that quickly dispersed. Fanning out in all directions these sparkling rays sliced through the blackness of space, demonstrating that wherever darkness reigned, light could always penetrate, bringing optimism and hope. The display looked to be finished as the brightness of the meteor began to fade, but then without warning a mighty explosion occurred, producing a momentary brilliant blinding light; and then as quickly as it came the shooting star was gone.............

LOOK OUT FOR
RUFUS IN HIS NEXT ADVENTURE
'CATSUMO'S WRATH'